# NOT GOOD NEIGHBORS

# ~~NEIGHBORS~~ NOT GOOD NEIGHBORS

VIOLET LUMANI

AMARA

Entangled Publishing, LLC
644 Shrewsbury Commons Ave., STE 181
Shrewsbury, PA 17361
rights@entangledpublishing.com

Amara is an imprint of Entangled Publishing, LLC.

Visit our website at www.entangledpublishing.com.

Edited by Rebecca Heyman
Cover original illustration and design by Elizabeth Turner Stokes
Cover image by ksuview/Shutterstock
Edge design by Elizabeth Turner Stokes
Edge images by judyjump/Shutterstock,
Ihor Biliavskyi/Shutterstock, and souga.biz/Shutterstock
Interior design by Britt Marczak

Paperback ISBN 978-1-68281-667-7
Ebook ISBN 978-1-68281-678-3

Manufactured in the United States of America
First Edition June 2026

10 9 8 7 6 5 4 3 2 1

*To the Lodi Public Library. I'm sorry for smuggling out romance novels as a teenager—I would have checked them out, but I didn't want my mom to catch me. I always snuck them back in when I was done. You made this book possible. Lift the ban?*

*Not Good Neighbors* is a laugh-out-loud, forced-proximity, enemies-to-lovers romcom with an HEA. However, the story includes elements that might not be suitable for all readers. Parental narcissism/gaslighting, financial stress, strong language, alcohol consumption/hangovers, and explicit consensual sex are shown on-page. Parental abandonment/estrangement, cheating/infidelity, and divorce are mentioned. Readers who may be sensitive to these elements, please take note.

# Author's Note

*Not Good Neighbors* features a diverse cast of characters, including Gence Delpi, the superintendent of Penny and Jack's building. Like me, Gence is Albanian. His personality and dialect are a loving amalgamation of various men in my family, who I imagine would have a lot to say about the *gomarë* causing trouble on the fifth floor. I am honored and delighted to include my heritage in these pages. You'll find a glossary of Gence's favorite Albanian words and catchphrases at the end of this book. Thank you for reading.

# 1

My mom raised me to be super independent, which is why I dutifully fill her in on the details of my Saturday like a field reporter.

"And then I ran out to buy some cheese at this really cute little place that opened up not far from—" I say.

"How close is it to Times Square?" Mom interjects. "I saw on AOL News a hot dog vendor got robbed there!"

A laugh snorts out of me before I can stop it, though my shoulders hitch, bracing for what is sure to be another barrage of well-intentioned safety advice. I adore my mom, and her concern is born of caring, but no crime statistics will ever shake her certainty that New York is a cesspool her precious daughter is ill-equipped to handle.

"Mom, I promise you, no one who lives in New York City willingly goes to Times Square on a Saturday. And besides, that area is very safe." I palm my mug of steaming chamomile tea tighter, the heat biting into my palm. "Scariest thing there is the price tourists will pay for a pic with knock-off Elmo."

"Stone Harbor is safer, just saying," she sniffs.

"Didn't you just tell me Mr. Marino was arrested yesterday?"

"Oh, Penny, you know he likes his whiskey. He was a little rowdy. It happens," Mom says.

"He stole someone's dog! And resisted arrest. And then pulled down his—"

"It wasn't as bad as all that!"

I flick my gaze skyward, asking the divine for patience. It was definitely "as bad as all that" five minutes ago, when Mom shared the latest hot gossip from my sleepy beachside hometown. "Okay. It wasn't as bad as all that. Make sure you take your pills."

"I took them already. Are you talking to me on those ear things? I told you to only use speaker phone. The radiation—" Mom starts.

I set my scalding cup down, pull out my earbud, and flick it onto a table with a sigh. "Sorry. You're on speaker now."

"Good. Now don't think I missed that bit before the cheese. Tell me why you were working on a Saturday. We talked about this."

"I know..." I stand, filled with a sudden rush of restless energy. I fluff the navy blue pillows on my couch and drift to the tall windows that look out on a row of brownstones freckled with air conditioner window units. "Rochelle needed some slides for a conversation with a sales leader."

In the dying light of another summer day, I peek at my fire escape Eden, which makes up for being totally illegal by adding some much-needed greenery to the otherwise cement-colored landscape. My botanical babies look ready for a night of beauty sleep. I lovingly pull closed the glorious, gauzy curtains that set me back a week's pay.

"So you needed to work on a Saturday"—Mom's voice fills the room—"because Rochelle's arms are broken and she can't do it herself?"

"No, she's my manager. It's an assignment," I say, gaze bouncing around my apartment for more to do. A moment later, with my telescoping duster in hand, I demolish an errant cobweb dangling from the crown molding overhead. Can't blame a spider for having great taste in New York real estate, but these high ceilings are all mine.

"If I've said it once, Penelope, I've said it a thousand times: they don't pay you to work on the weekends. Or much at all, for that matter."

She makes a disappointed noise and my stomach tenses—Pavlov's daughter, reacting to a familiar bell. I settle cross-legged in front of the Carrara marble divot in the wall where there was once a working fireplace. Now the divot floor is covered in pools of hardened wax from the pricey coconut-scented candles I'm addicted to. I take up the little bowl and scraper tool I left there earlier.

"I mean… I could've done it Monday, but I figured I'd knock it out." Proving Mom's point about my salary, I peel chunks of wax off the floor and toss them in the bowl, which I'll set over a pot of simmering water later. Why pay for an obscenely expensive candle twice, when you can destroy your manicure rescuing the melted wax and painstakingly repour it into a Mason jar later? The heavenly smell reminds me why I risk my super's wrath to light candles in the fireplace at all.

"Milk gallons keep longer than your relationships, Penelope! You need to worry less about your job and more about finding someone. I don't want you to end up like me, alone and without resources. Maryellen's son Brian asked about you the other day, you know? I ran into him at the grocery store. He's a realtor now."

I wince, reducing the volume on my phone, hoping that last diatribe wasn't loud enough for my neighbor—my nemesis—to hear. Jack usually announces his arrival by banging on our shared wall or vacuuming nonstop, but hell's waiting room is quiet for now.

"I have resources. I have a job, remember?"

Mom continues on, ignoring my gainful employment and pivoting hard into advice for finding the right man. "I was with Monica the other day at the garden center. She said her little Sarah ended up with a guy who's downright homely, but he's got a great personality and is completely family-minded."

I pause my increasingly aggressive scraping, realizing I've left dark streaks on the marble. "That's nice," I say, picturing my mother and my old high school friend's mom discussing Sarah's husband. Poor guy.

"Look what happened when your father left us," Mom says, and my throat tightens. I don't need to be reminded of the days we had a negative balance in the checking account, the times before we got back on our feet when we didn't have enough to even buy bread. I jerk to a stand, bringing my bowl and scraper back to the kitchen.

"...so I told her," Mom continues, oblivious to the mental rabbit hole I'm in danger of falling down, "if you ask me, those societies with arranged marriages have the right idea. You need to look at the family. The bank account. The whole package. Leave the emotion out of it. Forget about looks unless he's got money enough to pay you out when it all ends. If your father had at least had any money... No, forget looks. You need to tell your boss you—"

Her advice is interrupted by the roaring drone of Jack's vacuum, so loud and close it might as well be hoovering my ear canal.

"What is that? Is that your neighbor again?" Mom shouts.

I was tapping out a jittery staccato against the counter, but now I curl my fingers into a little rage ball. If junk mail wished on a star and became a real boy, I'd know exactly where to find him. I storm over to bang my fist on the living room wall, which only draws the sound closer. It becomes louder and more aggressive, as if someone is vacuuming right against the wall on purpose.

Because *of course* Jack's vacuuming against the wall on purpose.

The only thing separating me from my neighbor's enormous head is a few inches of prewar plaster. And maybe some wood? I don't know, I'm not a contractor. Though I'm sure that not even a twelve-inch-thick steel panel would be enough of a buffer for my peace. Jack vacuums to irritate me.

Because he hates me as much as I hate him.

Which is a lot.

"Yes, he sucks," I shout over the din. Her response is lost in the drone and thump of a vacuum butting up against a baseboard. "I can't hear you! I've gotta deal with this. And I'll talk to my boss. Okay? Love you. Call you tomorrow." I end the call and pound on the wall again.

My phone vibrates, Mom texting:

I love you. You can always move back here, you know. Then you wouldn't have to deal with that nonsense.

The place just under my ribs tightens. I don't want to move. I've had six years of rental bliss in this apartment—six years of space to be myself and make my own decisions. All that changed ten months ago, when the demon moved in next door.

"I'm not going anywhere," I announce to no one. I stormily return to my little bowl of wax and set it up on the stove in a water bath. It's not long before the apartment is enveloped in the soothing scent of coconut.

After pouring the wax into a jar and standing up a wick, I migrate over to my built-in bookcases to dust. They're overflowing with my favorite romance novels and a never-ending collection of to-be-reads, organized by steaminess rating. I run the duster over the spines, pausing to glance at the back cover of one I don't remember reading. Instantly, I get sucked into the jacket copy. My jaw relaxes. My hands unclench. I deserve a break. Start a new release or lean into the tried and true? As if that's a real question.

Book in hand, I return to my sofa and almost unconsciously bang my fist on the wall again. Jack doesn't have the square footage to warrant that much fucking vacuuming. I should know, since our apartments are mirror images of each other.

The vacuum falls blessedly silent, leaving only the muffled murmurs of Jack's TV.

"Dick," I mutter, eyeing my long-forgotten chamomile tea with regret. Tugging my softest throw blanket over my lap and snuggling into my couch, I can feel tension leaking out of my body like an exorcised spirit when I open Karin Shelby's *The Pirate Duke's Pleasure*.

*Bethany advanced on the Pirate Duke, her temper sparking. "I am not interested in softening you," she gritted out. "I rather like you...hard."*

*Her words were a direct hit, landing with a cannon's force. Ronan pulled in a bracing breath, willing his heart to slow and his manhood's ache to subside.*

*The robe slipped off Bethany's shoulders, and the moonlight through the cabin's porthole illuminated his Venus. Tantalizing, succulent...and just as out of reach as a goddess of old for such as him.*

*"The man you knew is dead! Charles Hawthorne, Duke of Merrow, is no more," he snapped.*

*Her cobalt eyes flashed like a tempest-tossed sea. Her hand moved down her ribs, grazing lower until it reached the juncture of her thighs.*

*"Bethany—" he said, her name emerging somewhere between warning and prayer. Ronan turned his back, forcing himself to reject her and their past. "You know you are a—"*

"Waste of a goddamn meat suit!" Jack shouts. "Throw a strike!"

I clench my jaw, set my novel down, and bang my fist on the wall again, so hard that my hand aches. There's an immediate bang back.

My temples throb. I just want to read my smut in peace. I've had the TV on mute, mostly just to make the place feel less solitary, but now I turn the volume way up and watch as Ray Liotta and Lorraine Bracco verbally assault each other in *Goodfellas*. How far does this TV volume go? Let's find out, fucker.

Jack bangs on the wall, but I can barely hear it over the movie. I smile. The images on the screen are replaced with my own fantasy of marching to Jack's door and smooshing my hand into his face when he answers, startling away that ever-present smug expression. I'd grab for his vacuum, pull it into the hall, and launch it over the stair railing.

Jack's gray eyes would darken like storm clouds. He'd grab my arm and turn me toward him. I'd crow, victorious, hearing the smash of the thing landing in the lobby. His breathing would be labored. My chest would heave, the tips of my nipples brushing the front of his shirt with each breath. His pupils would overtake his irises, and those eyes would settle on my mouth. He'd pull me closer, wrapping muscled arms around—

A loud knock interrupts, startling me out of my awful thoughts.

Ew. *Ew*. I kick the novel next to me off the sofa—hard.

*The Pirate Duke's Pleasure* and Jack Fucking Craig have no business mingling in my rotten brain. Mom could probably tell me the exact day and time of my last date—I certainly don't care enough to keep track—but *clearly* it's been too long.

The knock sounds again, more insistent. I'd almost forgotten that that's what stopped the porn train from leaving the station in the first place. I stand, run a hand down my face, and open my door.

Gence Delpi, a sixty-three-year-old family man with kind eyes, silver hair, and a craggy face dominated by his bulbous nose, stands in the hall. He gusts out an exhale, as if disappointed in me, and looks past my shoulder at the TV. I understand immediately.

Goddamn Jack.

"*Hajde bre*, Penny. Please. Please. *Boll tash.* You know it's quiet hours now. Why the TV need to be on so loud?"

I dip my chin, shamefaced, and return to the sofa to retrieve the remote like a toddler forced to confront their crayon art on the wall. I mute the TV and return to the door.

"Let me guess: the nightmare in 5B complained?" I ask loudly, masking my regret at putting out our poor, long-suffering superintendent under a thick layer of Jack-directed anger. "I—ah—I left you a little something, Gence. Did you see it?"

I've been bribing Gence with batches of homemade cookies every week for the past few months, in the hopes of getting him to do something about soundproofing or give Jack the boot. Fingers crossed all those snickerdoodles and lemon shortbreads have made the latter option irresistible.

Gence sighs loudly, ignoring my question. "Everyone in this building gets along. Nice! Nice people, everyone. You two, oil and water. If you hate him, why don't you move already? Huh?

I have real estate business on the side. I can help you, *t'hangert dreqi*."

My jaw sets. *You can help me by catapulting Jack into the street.* "This apartment is everything to me. I'm not leaving. He can move," I fume. "Or maybe you can do something about soundproofing the walls? I can't hear the people in 4A, and they can't hear me. It's just between my apartment and *his*." I make "his" sound like the vilest of four-letter words. Gence's mouth, surrounded by rough salt-and-pepper stubble, firms ominously.

Gence escaped awful conditions in Kosovo, then braved war and hunger and poverty to come to this country with his family. He deserves better than having to put up with two childishly idiotic Americans. He's sick of us, and if I tell him that today's dust-up started over some vacuuming—that *that's* the reason he had to hike up four flights of stairs at 7:30 PM—he might grab me by the back of my shirt and toss me out a window. I wouldn't blame him, either, honestly.

I sigh. "I'm sorry you had to come up here. He was vacuuming and... It won't happen again. And you can always just call instead, if—"

"*Dreq o dreq*." He harrumphs and turns on his heel, mumbling something else in Albanian. I follow him into the hall and call out, "*Natën e mirë, Gence!*", wishing him good night in an Albanian accent I'm almost proud of. I mentally high-five the elephant mascot from my language-learning app. Gence lumbers down the creaking, dark stairs without a backward glance.

The door to apartment 5B opens. Jack steps out, hands on his hips, to watch Gence's retreat. He's a tall drink of cyanide, standing barefoot in his olive-green sweats and dark-blue T-shirt.

His head, I begrudgingly admit to myself, is not huge. It's a normal size, and topped with dark-brown hair, currently mussed.

On days like today, Jack reminds me of Han Solo without the charm, slightly disheveled and with an arrogant swagger that tells you he's convinced of his own appeal. But there is no appeal. Or if there is, I'm immune. Physical beauty is negated by an ugly soul every day of the week on my calendar. Mom's advice to take a cue from Sarah and find myself a homely boy to settle down with floats through my mind, and I nearly laugh out loud.

Jack cocks his disgustingly average-size melon to slant me a casual glare before I can spring back into my apartment. I brace for impact.

"Was he able to fix your TV?" he asks, his deep voice tinged with faux concern. He turns to face me more fully, taking in my veg wear—threadbare short-shorts covered entirely by a long Rolling Stones concert tee—with raised eyebrows.

"Great job, forcing an old man up all those stairs for your nonsense."

"That old man could bench-press four of you, you know," he says.

"Is that what you do with women? Bench-press them? Be still my heart."

His eyes light up with a look that usually precedes what he *thinks* will be a return zinger, but then they dip to the hem of my shirt. There's a mocking edge to the speculative look, and Jack most certainly means it to be insulting, but…

The back of my neck prickles. I'm never reading a romance novel again. Goddamn *Pirate Duke*. It's given my body ideas that my brain finds revolting.

The silence lasts a beat. Two.

"Oh, suck it," I spit out.

"Sure. If you beg," Jack says immediately. He leans against his doorjamb, one leg crossed in front of the other. "Gence was already in my apartment trying to fix a plumbing thing when you started blaring your TV."

"Sure he was," I scoff. "You call him for everything."

"No more than you."

I narrow my eyes, noticing his shirt. *I knew it.* "You took my clothes out of the washer," I grit out. "I had to pay for two cycles to get rid of that mildew smell. And I *know* it was you because I can *clearly* see certain articles from that wash load on your"—I glare at his chest, then quickly avert my eyes—"person."

"Sorry, having trouble hearing you. Someone was clanking pots and pans during my playoff game last night. Still got some ringing in my ears," he says, reaching up to tug on his earlobe.

"Do you vacuum at all hours because you're such a dirtbag?"

"D'you know you talk in your sleep? And moan."

I go rigid with shock, then cross my arms protectively against my middle and gawk at him, my mouth open like a carp's.

His glance dips again to my legs, and he smiles—not the snide smiles he's lobbed like cannonballs across the hallway at me from time to time, but a *real* smile. The first I've gotten from him since the week he moved in. It's boyish and blinding and causes dimples to bracket his mouth in what would be a distressingly appealing way if he wasn't a demon. He backs into his doorway.

"'Be still my heart'? 'Suck it'? A guy starts to wonder if it's all just a sloppy attempt at seduction." He cackles in a manner reserved for hellspawn. "G'night, 5A."

"I do not moan—"

His door closes with a passive-aggressive *snick*.

My face is hot, lit by an internal Easy-Bake Oven of hate and mortification. My bedroom and his, like our respective living rooms, butt up against each other. I have been known to talk in my sleep, but I've *never*… Oh, he knows exactly how to push my buttons.

I slam my door, willing the sound to reverberate into his apartment as loudly as possible. The show of temper feels like the official loss of a skirmish, no less so when a retaliatory bang sounds on the living room wall.

I snort, but my phone vibrates in my hand, forcing a momentary ceasefire.

**Margie:**

Meet me at La Smith.

I have news.

Might as well call in sick now for Monday.

It's only Saturday, and I text back to tell her so.

**Margie:**

I know. Make the call. See you in ten.

I chuckle and head to my bedroom to change and throw on some makeup, supremely pleased with this well-timed excuse to beat a strategic retreat.

# 2

Fifteen minutes later, Margie sweeps into La Smith, our favorite corner gastropub, and joins me at the bar. She is effortlessly polished, elevating jeans, heels, and a simple top to haute couture. The proof that God has favorites is clear in her pixyish black curls and the high, gold-dusted cheekbones setting off her light-brown skin.

I grimace and swipe a hand over my copper bun. We're like Lady and the Tramp. The Princess and the Frog. The hot French female chef from *Ratatouille* and the fucking rat. I share as much as we greet each other with an air kiss.

"Stop. You're gorgeous. Plus I just rolled out of bed," she says.

"Was the bed in *Vogue*?" I hand her a glass of wine, which she downs in a few impressive gulps before signaling to the bartender for another.

I frown, looking her over from her amber eyes to the tips of her Louboutins. A review once called Margie "a talent-to-watch who will be known for her nuanced and emotional performances," but she saves all those nuances for the screen. For her friends, she always wears the same inscrutable smirk, so I can't tell whether she's been nominated for an Emmy or just watched an illegally parked Honda get sideswiped by a garbage truck.

"Prepare yourself," she finally says. "You're about to be murdered. By my news. Deceased." Her deadpan monotone is in full effect as she punctuates her words with an airy wave that might be a loose sign of the cross. She accepts the fresh glass of wine from the bartender with a nod and takes a sip.

Concern and excitement ripple through me. Trust the actress to play this for maximum drama. "Okay?" I grab for my glass and lean against the bar.

Margie takes a deep breath. "Series regular," she murmurs.

My hand flies to my mouth. "Shut your face." I set my glass down. "Margie!"

"Sorry. I don't know who this 'Margie' is. I'm Leslie Linkletter, Esquire, now."

I fling my arms around her, jumping up and down. She embraces me with one hand and downs the rest of her wine with the other. "This is amazing!" I shout, breathless with joy.

She inclines her head regally, but her brown eyes glow with excitement. Margie has had a handful of scene-stealing guest appearances in the last year on a legal thriller called *Glass and Carter.* And apparently she made enough of an impression for the show to want her on full-time—something she's hoped for but wasn't sure would actually happen.

I spy Avery at the entrance, ducking his way into the bar as only the very tall do. The only right angle in our little friendship triangle, he looks, as always, like Regé-Jean Page disguised as a librarian. "What happened? What's going on?" he asks, approaching us. I cheer and pull him forward.

Margie musses his tidy hair and wrinkles her nose. "Series regular."

He laughs and grabs her up in a hug, twirling her around with a whoop. "Tell me everything! Also, I can't believe you told

Penny before me."

Margie smiles at his grumble. "Next time try and get here when I say we're meeting."

"You gave me a twenty-minute heads-up, and luckily I happened to be a few blocks away, grabbing a bite. If I'd been home—"

"You'd have been even later, I know. Tsk."

"I live on the East Side! You're lucky you see me *ever*!" He shakes his head and gratefully accepts the stupid-expensive gin concoction I've ordered him.

"You guys celebrating something?" a husky voice observes from behind us. "Or fighting? I can't tell."

Lara Smith—La Smith's namesake—has paused her four-star-general patrol of the perimeter of her restaurant, eyes narrowing in amused assessment. She's a woman of few words, but a single quirk of her eyebrow is as effective as an hour-long interrogation.

"Margie's going to be a regular on *Glass and Carter*!" I crow.

La grins and enfolds Margie in a tight embrace. She is pale and petite, barely reaching Margie's shoulders, but she pulls her in with the force of someone twice her size before turning to the busboy at a nearby high-top table. "Hey, Greg, tell Joe to stop flirting with the new waitress and get back behind the bar. I need a round of drinks for these guys. On the house." To Margie, she says, "I'm not surprised, you know. You're incredible on that show."

Margie stills. "You watch the show?"

La winks and passes a hand over her thick brown hair, clubbed back by a colorful bandana. "Only for you."

"Well, now you've gone and complimented me, which means you have to join us for the toast." Margie laughs.

La complies, and that one glass of wine becomes a bottle of champagne, which in turn becomes many, many rounds of complimentary drinks, since La sticks with our little party all night.

I'm lifting my wine to my lips, pondering the fact that tomorrow is going to bring a monstrous hangover, when La is called to the kitchen. Avery orders a water from the bartender and hands it to me, plucking the wineglass from my hand.

"You look wiped. Everything okay?" he asks, peering down at me.

He still looks shockingly sober, his green eyes bright with concern behind his black-framed glasses. Kind, sturdy Avery. Like a redwood tree. I shuffle, a little unsteady on my feet already, and reach up to tap him gently on the nose. "Boop."

He laughs and swats at me. "Seriously."

I sigh and fill him in on my neighbor drama between sips of water. Margie leans back against the counter, still laughing at La's parting remark, and catches part of my tale. It's a familiar complaint of mine that now has her rolling her eyes.

"Just move in with me already. I'm sick of hearing about this guy. I've got the second bedroom."

"It's a closet, not a bedroom, but I appreciate it. You know how hard I worked for that apartment—I *love* my place. Love the way I've made it mine. The crown molding. The fireplace!" I proclaim my apartment's virtues with the drunken gusto of a founding father declaring his love of country.

"Fireplace is fake," Margie points out.

"I light my coconut candles in there. Technically a fire. And the windows! So tall!" Margie opens her mouth to shit on my sundae, so I rush to add, "Yes! I know, sometimes during the winter the heat is out of control, and I need to throw those windows open to prevent myself from roasting like a chicken. But whatever its *alleged* flaws, that building—that apartment—is my sanctuary. It's a goddamn warm hug of a place. Nearly perfect. Or was, until that jackass moved in next door and kicked off this whole war of attrition," I finish glumly.

"That soliloquy was practically Shakespearean," Margie says.

"There's always Jersey. Your mom still pressing for you to move back?" Avery asks.

The pulse in my jaw jumps. "I mean, I'm her best friend. Of course she wants me closer."

Margie changes the subject, sick unto death of my apartment woes, and fills us in on her discussion with the showrunner. She pulls a stapled stack of paper from her purse and hands it to me. "The script that'll intro my storyline for the season. Run lines with me?"

"Why don't you ever ask me?" Avery asks, furrowing his brow.

I brighten and grin. "She doesn't ask you because you're not the *actor* I am." I toss an imaginary scarf over my shoulder.

"Drunk Penny is my favorite Penny," Margie says.

"Not mine." Avery looks at the ceiling like a dad whose kid missed curfew.

Margie points out the character bits I'm to read and frowns when I bust out an overly deep, cartoonish voice. Whenever she asks me to run lines, this sort of behavior is par for the course, but alcohol has given my idiocy muscles. Consummate professional that she is, she rolls with it.

"Linkletter, I've got a bone to pick with you," I say, channeling Marvin Gaye.

Avery barks out a laugh.

"Mr. Kelvin! How did you get in— Shelly!" Margie exclaims.

"I'm so sorry, Leslie. He slipped by me and—" I squeak in a dog-whistle decibel.

"It's fine. He won't be staying."

"Do you know how much that little maneuver of yours has cost me? If you think I'm going to spend one red cent on those…" I growl and trail off.

"Those…what, exactly? Tenants? People? I recommend you choose your next words very carefully."

The script says that Mr. Kelvin "blusters." So I bluster. Margie rolls her eyes at my award-worthy performance. "I know people. If you think—"

"I won't get into what I think." She sniffs derisively. "But here's what I know: you're a slumlord. And now that the defects at 54 Baxter have been laid bare, you have no choice but to bring that building up to code. I priced it out, you know. Structural issue… *Yikes.* At least a million. And you're on the hook for all of it. *That's* what I know."

"Wait, is that—" I clear the Marvin from my throat and try again. "Is that real?"

"What?"

"What you just said. Defect uncovered, old building being forced up to code." My sluggish mind whirs, a bicycle with its chain off the track. "It's real? The landlord has to fix it, even if the building is old?" The thread of excitement in my voice is bright and clear, even to those around us.

"I hate to tell you how TV works and ruin the magic, but Pen… I'm not a real lawyer." Margie laughs at the expression on my face, puckered and sour.

"But…if it's real, it could solve all my neighbor drama."

"Come to set. There's a legal consultant who works on the

scripts. We can ask her. And if it's true..." Margie's lips curve slightly, but the sparkle in her eyes is pure mischief.

Avery escorts us to my building not long after, making sure we get into my lobby before hailing a cab to take himself home. Margie and I stumble up to my apartment. Even tipsy, I'm incredulous she isn't even remotely winded after climbing five flights in stilettos.

"I get why you love your apartment. Schlepping all your shit up these stairs," Margie drawls. "Who needs an elevator?"

"Burglar deterrent," I pant, reaching the landing. "Plus my ass has never looked better."

Margie snorts in response.

"You sleeping over?" I whisper, fitting my key into the lock.

"No, I need to give Cashmere her insulin," she says in a voice designed to tell the cheap seats about her cat's diabetes.

I shush her.

"Give me my nightcap, and I'll be on my way, shusher."

She sails by me and into the kitchen, picking up the bottle of wine on the counter.

"Twist cap? Savage," she says, setting it back down and pulling my Brita from the fridge. She pours herself a glass of water and kicks her legs out like an old-timey chorus girl, sending first one shoe flying and then the other—right into the far wall with a thud. I wince.

The pounding on the wall of the living room follows almost immediately. He must've been on his sofa.

"Oh, what a pain in the ass," Margie says.

"Told you," I whisper.

"You two are still doing that wall-banging thing?" she whispers back. Tipsy as she is, she still picks up on my cues. "I can't wait for you to come to set and ask Genevieve on Monday.

If that law is real, we're fixing this"—she waves a hand toward the wall—"for good."

My kitchen is narrow. I gesture for Margie to move over before draining the last of the water into a fresh glass. The room tilts one way, and my stomach tilts the other. This much activity is too much for me, evidently. "Margie, you're the worst. I haven't been this drunk since my twenty-second birthday." I grab hold of the counter to stop the spins.

Margie cracks out a laugh. "You always blame me. But I didn't funnel wine and vodka down your gullet by the glassful tonight. And your old college pals Goldschläger and Jägermeister did it to you back then."

I moan and plug my ears. "Never mention those two beverages to me ever again."

"And by the way, *ingrate*," Margie continues, "for your twenty-second, Avery and I threw you a *very* nice surprise party."

We both grin. "'Drink specials? All of our drinks are special!'" we recite at the same time, mimicking the bartender's proclamation from the birthday party in question.

Another bang from next door.

Margie narrows her eyes and marches over to the wall. She kneels on the sofa, her mouth right up against the plaster. "Instead of bickering with your hot neighbor, Pen, you could be sinking your teeth into that ass of his."

I stumble in my haste to make it to the sofa, alarm pouring out of my every cell. I wave my hands in Margie's face and mouth "Oh my God" and "Stop" and a whole lot of other four-letter words.

Margie's smile just widens. "I mean clearly there's some sexual tension that needs working—"

My hand is over her mouth. I feel her tongue against my hand. Skeeved, I rear back. "Ew, you licked me," I hiss.

"Bet you wish it was the hot… Okay, okay!" Margie laughs as I smack her with a pillow.

We settle on the sofa next to each other, and I hold on to her arm for dear life, the spins starting in earnest. To the wall, I loudly state, "I wouldn't get with that d-bag if you paid me."

"Didn't know you were selling your services," comes Jack's immediate response. His voice is muffled by the wall but still too loud and clear for a man who's currently sitting in an entirely separate apartment.

Margie laughs. At my glare, she holds up a hand. "I know we hate him, but that was funny."

# 3

I push my mouse around, a tired cat playing with prey out of habit, and wish my headache away. Margie was right: it's day two of my hangover, and I should've called in sick. It didn't help that Jack cooked something yesterday that made the hall smell like a cow died in his apartment, and then played LMFAO's "Party Rock Anthem" full blast, on repeat, starting at an ungodly hour. I can almost admire his style—he's suffering to make me suffer, which takes a lot of commitment. But hearing the lyrics "Every day I'm shufflin'" thirty thousand times in the space of forty-eight hours buries my admiration under the animal urge to take a machete to his head. Or to my own.

"It absolutely makes sense," I hear my boss, Rochelle, say. She sounds close. I'd peek above my beige cubicle to see where she is, but sudden movements shake up my innards and worsen the jackhammering in my skull, which in turn worsens my nausea. At the thought, the necessity for the bathroom overtakes every other item in Penelope's Hierarchy of Needs.

My phone vibrates against my desk, a rhythm that mirrors the throbbing behind my left eye. Call from Mom. I almost answer despite my pain, but my brain is now liquid, and it just sloshed out of place. I text instead, asking if we can chat after work.

I stand on newborn colt's legs and start when I see Rochelle and another VP about to pass my cube.

"Oh, hi, Penny," Rochelle says. "Sam, this is Penelope Huff. She's on my team."

The man, in his expensive navy suit, his silver hair slicked back over bare patches of shiny scalp, smiles at me. I clamp my lips tight, turning up the corners as much as I dare, and Rochelle continues with the introductions. "This is Sam Greenfield. He heads up—"

"Marketing for North America. Right. Nice to meet you, Mr. Greenfield." I shake his hand, desperate to be away.

He inclines his head, his grip firm. "Call me Sam."

"Sam's actually about to be promoted to global vice president—hush-hush until the announcement. But I'll be filling you in on a project that came up just as soon as I walk Sam out. Pretty exciting. We're going to be building a new global marketing framework with the other regions. It'll transform how we go to market, harness economies of scale…" Rochelle smiles brightly. "I mean, we need to keep the lights on until implementation, but this is going to be a fun problem to solve."

That last bit lands like a tart cherry, bright and jarring. I swallow with difficulty. In Rochelle-speak, "fun problem to solve" loosely translates to "Lots of work. You're in for a world of hurt," and "lights on until implementation" means "This is your new night job."

I race to the bathroom the second they continue on and beat Rochelle back to my desk by only a few seconds.

She glides over, professional and poised in her brandy-colored pencil skirt and cream silk top. I don't know what time she wakes up each day, but her tan skin always glows with good health, and her makeup is expertly applied. Her dark brown, auburn-highlighted curls are forever perfect, too, and she owes her enviable physique to what she calls "pre-workday workouts." Nothing short of not sleeping would have me out of bed early enough to work out *and* make myself that exquisite by eight thirty in the morning.

Rochelle looks me over curiously but doesn't comment on my appearance. Instead, she begins to read me in on the project, and the more she tells me, the more I recognize that I was right.

"And since you're my superstar, you're going to lead the charge for me," she finishes.

My throat tightens. "Superstar" means I do what she asks with very little pushback. I am a driven doormat, desperate to maintain a steady paycheck. I don't want to lead any charges. I want my apartment. I want my comforter and my Rolling Stones tee. "That sounds great," I hear myself say. But then I hesitate and pray to the Patron Saint of Spineless Bitches. "It doesn't… It won't come with additional pay, will it?" I fold my arms around my torso, a self-hug.

It's a question I try not to ask too often, rounding up the nerve maybe once a year. Rochelle's face twists into a maybe-so, maybe-no kind of expression. She's a good manager. Kind. Recognizes my value. But she hasn't been able to get me a salary increase in three years. I brace myself for the answer I usually get, and when it lands, it barely stings. "You know how corporate is about that stuff, but with this project… Maybe we can try and make the case for it."

Rochelle-speak for "fat chance."

In all the years Margie's been acting, I've visited her on set only a handful of times. And every time I'm blown away all over again by the amount of controlled chaos that goes into filming. Grips, makeup artists, camera people, and boom operators fill the shadows that surround the brilliantly lit set, tons of effort being put into creating something to keep me entertained on lonely Saturday nights.

And speaking of lonely nights… Lucas Webb, the actor playing one of the main characters on *Glass and Carter*, storms onto the scene to confront Margie's character, and I find myself blushing. He is a bronzed god, from the top of his buzz-cut tawny hair to the tips of his brown dress shoes. I will forever connect that impossibly handsome man with the night after a nasty Valentine's Day breakup when I binge-watched a series he used to star in, inhaled an entire box of Ferrero Rocher, and tried to use him for fantasy fodder. The evening ended with me falling asleep to his period gangster drama, surrounded by an embarrassment of gold-foil wrappers and snotty tissues, my romantic plans foiled by dead batteries.

Those were the days. Yeah, I was a disaster, but at least I was a disaster with privacy. The day after that debacle, I lay in bed listening to a particularly cheesy sad song on repeat for hours. No one pounded on the walls. No one even came to check if I was alive. It was glorious. My last neighbor, Mrs. Vasquez, was hard of hearing and quiet as the dead.

In all fairness, she did actually die in 5B, but it took a few days to realize it because, again, *so quiet*.

My phone vibrates. Mom. I smooth my hair reflexively before I answer, even though she's not here to see how rough I look.

"Sorry, I was about to call, but—"

"Hi lovey, you're invited to Katie Singer's baby shower next month. I told her mother you're going to come!" she says.

My stomach heaves a half-hearted flop and my head throbs. *No choice. Best to just agree and get it over with.* "I—I don't really know them that well," I murmur, conscientious of staying quiet on an active set.

"Of course you do. Katie is a sweetheart. You have to come."

A tug of guilt prevents me from arguing the point. "Okay, send me the date, and I'll see if I can make it work?" I whisper. "Did you get the flowers by the way? Tracking said they were delivered."

"Yes, chrysanthemums this month. Very nice. But save your money, Penny. I don't need gifts. And why are you whispering?"

"Sorry, I'm visiting Margie. Quiet on set. Can I call you later?"

"Call me when you get home so I know you're safe. Love you."

I approach the craft services table, searching for something to settle my stomach, just as Margie's scene wraps. It only took two takes for the actors to nail it. She looks lit from within as she steps behind the camera to talk to the director, and I am so puffed up with pride and happiness for her that it overtakes my hangover. She catches my eye just as she's waylaid by some of the crew and holds up a finger. I nod, grinning.

"Episode Ten, we're going to need a boardroom. But a stately one. Acres of mahogany. Windows with a view. Gilt-framed oil paintings of long-dead white guys on the wall," a man at the craft services table says to a woman next to him. He nods a polite hello as I move beside them. "Jim's thinking an old-money, board-of-trustees type of space."

"Sounds like my office," I say, reaching for a water bottle.

"Where do you work?" the man asks. The woman next to him pulls out her phone and awaits my answer.

"Uh. Evadon Tech?" I say. "Been around forever. Near the Flatiron."

Margie, who has broken away from her admirers, appears just as they're offering their thanks and clearing out.

"You were amazing," I say, giving her a hug.

"Beautiful work," a woman agrees from nearby, smiling at Margie.

"Thank you," Margie says. "Felt good." The woman enters our orbit, examining the craft services table, and Margie says, "Genevieve, this is my best friend, Penny. Penny, this is Genevieve Duro. She's one of the legal consultants on the show and my fashion inspiration every day."

Genevieve shakes my hand and chuckles. She's an older woman but with unlined skin pulled taut by her high, tight, steel-colored ponytail. Her diaphanous dress makes her look like she's about to go swanning about the deck of a cruise ship in the 1960s.

"Nice to meet you, Penny. Is this the one you said needed legal advice?"

"Yep," Margie says.

I give her a blank look and treat Margie to the same. I literally have no idea what she's talking about. Margie rolls her hand slowly in a spit-it-out gesture.

"I don't—"

"You can't handle your liquor. We talked about this," Margie interjects. To Genevieve, she says, "Penny has a shitty neighbor. Script we're filming today, the scene with the landlord having to make updates to his old building. Is any of that true?"

Genevieve starts nodding halfway into Margie's question. For all that she's dressed for leisure, she seems the sort who moves at a fast pace. "Yes. New law passed last year. How old is your building?"

I shoot Margie an exasperated look and say, "Prewar. Probably 1910s?"

"The walls are so thin she can hear everything her neighbor is doing. It's like he's squatting on her coffee table," Margie offers.

"Hm. Prewar buildings are usually pretty decent in terms of soundproofing, since it's all concrete and plaster. Your apartment and your neighbor's may have been a single unit originally. It's not Sheetrock, the wall?"

I shake my head, though I'm not entirely sure.

"Hmm, so here's what I'd recommend." She pauses. "Off the record. I am not your lawyer; you are not my client." She picks up a small plate and begins grazing at the table, adding raw veggies and a dollop of dressing as she waits for me to nod my understanding. "There should be an 'accident' that somehow opens up a hole on your side of the wall in question. You were moving furniture or something, and bumped the wall, and oops, there we go. Just enough for the city inspector to see what's going on in there. The city can't force these grandfathered-in buildings to bring things up to code *unless* a defect is made apparent. That hole is how you make that happen for your apartment. If a defect *is* made apparent, not only does the landlord have to address it, your security deposit can't get tapped for the original damage." She smiles and pops a small cherry tomato into her mouth.

I gnaw at my lip. This is dumb. There is no way I will do any of this. And yet... "Would it even help, though? With my problem, I mean. Like, do they have to do any soundproofing or—"

She waves a hand. "They'd have to make it so that the wall between your apartment and your neighbor's is the same as what goes up in new apartments in the city. Anything they do will improve your situation. I'd bet if the noise is as bad as you say, that wall was either illegally put up, or it was put up so long ago it's bound to be problematic. So the building fixes it, and—"

She shrugs. "Good fences make good neighbors."

"There you go, Pen. You're welcome. Problem solved," Margie says.

"Who has a problem?" Lucas Webb walks up to the table, and despite the fact that I've never been the fangirl type, I find myself flushing a deep crimson. He is even more dazzling in person, close up, than he is on TV. His sexy buzz cut is the perfect minimalist frame for that face of his, all jutting cheekbones and symmetrical beauty, and his costly blue suit hugs his sculpted body. He's shorter than I realized, about my height at 5' 6" or so. But *God* is he delicious.

"Lucas, this is my best friend, Penny. Penny, meet Lucas. Penny had a legal question, and Gen was kind enough to help out." Margie catches my eye, and I see her repress a smile.

Lucas tilts his head and reaches out a hand.

I put mine in his, but he doesn't shake it, just holds. And I thank every deity on the planet that I got a manicure on my lunch break today. His eyes, the color of warm tropical waters, are appraising. "Legal advice? Everything okay, I hope. Divorce?"

I shake my head vigorously. "I'm not married." I've evidently been inhabited by the spirit of Marilyn Monroe. I clear my throat. And because I babble like a lunatic when nervous, I add, "It's for a murder. Actually. The advice."

Lucas Webb's lips, slightly pouty when he's rocking his Resting Hot Face, stretch into a smile, and he releases my hand. I feel the loss keenly. "Oh, no. Who'd you eliminate?"

"No one. It hasn't happened yet. It's premeditated. I'm premeditating it now."

He laughs, and someone calls his name. He nods in acknowledgment, and his mouth twists when he looks back at me. "It was very nice meeting you, Penny."

The specter of Marilyn wheezes out a response, my brain functioning on autopilot.

Genevieve makes her goodbyes, and I find my eyes straying to Lucas, not hearing whatever Margie just said until she's standing shoulder to shoulder with me, stabbing at me with her salad fork. "Earth to Penny. My God, you're in bad shape today. Is the murder-victim-to-be your neighbor or me?"

"Both," I say, huffing out a laugh. "My head is killing me."

"Need to build back your tolerance."

"And by the way, why would you tell Lucas fucking Webb I had a legal question? I didn't know what to say without sounding ridiculous."

"So instead of telling the truth, you yammered like my grandma dipping into the cooking sherry," Margie says drily. She smiles fully at my disgruntled look.

"Dead meat, Marjorie."

Across the space, someone wheels a camera by, and Lucas is once again visible, laughing with the director. I gush out a sigh.

Margie follows my gaze and points with her fork. "He's very into redheads. If I get you that for Christmas, do I get a stay of execution?"

I purposely turn away, like someone regretfully waving away the dessert menu.

"My friend…uh, Calvin…stopped by this morning. And he noticed the hole I'd accidentally put in the wall when I was moving my…"

"Hammer?" Jack raises a brow from my doorway. He's back from a run this morning, his dark hair damp from the shower. He's dressed in an über-casual dark jeans and green T-shirt combo. The shirt brings out the malevolent spark in his eyes. "Some accident. That thing's got a three-foot diameter."

I glare at him and turn back to Calvin, the man the city sent to check out the hole after I called about it. Except I don't want Gence to know I called the city—thus, my "friend" Calvin was born. My eyes dart to Gence and away. He is standing next to Calvin and glowering at me. I feel a trickle of sweat roll down the small of my back. He knows. I'm not a good liar. I shouldn't have let Margie talk me into doing this, Jack hatred or no.

No. I can't blame Margie. I'm an adult. And I have never been susceptible to peer pressure. Except when Margie convinced me to do shots until I was guaranteed a three-day hangover this past weekend. Or when she goaded me into taking a hammer to my wall last night to "fix the situation so you can shut up about your neighbor already." She's a bad influence. I should have listened to Avery. Bad, bad Margie. Dumb, dumb Penny.

"Anyway, so Calvin was visiting, and—"

"How do you guys know each other?" Jack asks.

"We—"

"Not you," Jack adds, pointedly looking past me at Calvin. "Him."

"High school," Calvin says, looking desperately uncomfortable that I've asked him to lie.

I swallow my groan. Calvin looks eighty years old if he's a day. And Jack looks like he's trying desperately not to laugh. The nosy douche wandered over when Gence started flipping out about the hole.

"Oh. Were you a senior when she was a freshman, then?"

I march over to Jack, giving him my meanest glare. I ignore his scruffy, dimpled smile and grit out, "He was my teacher, actually. We had a torrid affair that culminated when I turned eighteen and he was finally able to ravage me on his desk."

I slam the door in his face before he can respond, then return to the grandfatherly pair in my living room. They're both awkwardly averting their gazes, staring at the wooden beams and the back of Jack's wall through the enormous hole I've put in mine "by accident."

Heat climbs up my neck. *Nice work, dumbass.* "Ah…Gence, that last part was a joke."

"*Eh, lopë kosit. S'ka marre hiç,*" Gence mutters.

Calvin fills Gence in on exactly what Genevieve told me, and Gence shakes his head, as if denying all the work that'll be required of him to bring the wall up to code.

I feel a twinge of conscience and resolve to give him a bigger holiday gift than usual this year.

But then Calvin drops a bombshell: Genevieve was right, and this wall was put up illegally. Which means that the building owner either needs to take it down and make it into a single apartment again, or he needs to legalize the unauthorized work and put up a new wall to code.

"Either way, the defect needs to be remedied. Sixty days, no extensions," Calvin says.

As they're leaving, I see Gence eyeing me and Calvin doubtfully, probably picking up on our less-than-familiar demeanor. Or at least I think that's the look he's giving me.

"Bye, Calvin! So good seeing you again. Say hi to the family for me," I say, an octave this side of suspicious. I hold my hand up to Calvin for a high five, which he slowly reaches up to deliver. But in the split second he hesitates, I decide to go in for a hug instead. The result is an awkward hug-handclasp combo that makes it look as if we're about to launch into a hallway waltz.

Fantastic. I've accosted a city official all because I couldn't remember how normal human friends say goodbye.

I realize too late that Jack is lazing on the threshold to his apartment, lapping it all up. When Gence and Calvin have descended out of sight, I wheel on him, bracing for the onslaught.

"May I have this dance?"

I roll my eyes.

"No? Okay. Need help cleaning up the plaster instead?" He's smirking, the right side of his lips quirked, his eyes more than a little amused.

"Not from you," I snap, trying to preempt whatever insult he's cooking up.

"Maybe we should call your good buddy Calvin back. He can help, since you guys are so tight."

I sniff and cross my arms. "He's the best."

Jack shakes his head and leans against his doorframe. "Destruction of property, compulsive lying… What levels won't she stoop to? What won't this girl do, folks?"

"You. This *woman* won't do you. I'm pretty sure Dante wrote about it as one of the circles of hell."

He grins and straightens, taking a few steps toward me until we're a breath from each other. I force myself to stand my ground and look up at him. His gray eyes twinkle like plummeting pieces of a defunct space shuttle. He should smell like sulfur. Instead, he smells woodsy. Like Pine-Sol. Or the air freshener from a cab I puked in once when I had the flu. It makes me want to gag. No human man should smell like air freshener. It's disgusting.

"You bring up sex with me an awful lot for someone who claims not to want it. Your subconscious speaking?"

"I bring it up in the *negative*. Scary but not surprising that I say 'no' and you hear 'yes.'"

"The neighbor doth protest too much, methinks. Maybe I'll open up a hole on my side of the wall, too," he muses, a finger tapping his mouth as he stares up at the hall ceiling. "We can pass each other secret clubhouse messages through it. Or you can pass me love letters."

My eyes flare wide with alarm, and I fall back a step. There is now only a very thin coating of plaster and some wooden slats separating his apartment from mine. "You wouldn't dare."

He shrugs noncommittally. "You don't know me very well, 5A."

After he closes his door, he starts to whistle.

Today was supposed to be a good day. I woke up well rested, since my new noise-canceling headphones managed to drown out DJ Dickhead's latest idea of a funny song to play on repeat: Extreme's "Hole Hearted." The new Evadon global marketing framework launch call went reasonably well. We've gathered, Avengers-style, a solid virtual team to make it happen, and though I'm only a senior manager, people seemed receptive to me leading the project. I got my hair done yesterday post-hole-inspection, a fresh trim and golden highlights to break up the copper. And I'm wearing the skirt that makes my ass look like it's been raised on a steady diet of StairMaster and squats.

This isn't how this day was supposed to end. I sit down hard on the sofa and stare.

*I really like his barstools.*

The thought floats through my mind because my brain is protecting me from the shock of what my eyes are really seeing: the three-foot hole in my wall now goes *straight through to Jack Craig's apartment.*

Jack is dressed in a baby-blue dress shirt and dark pants, just back from work, and is standing on his side of the hole, arms akimbo, lips pursed tight.

No, not the hole. This thing is monstrous, catastrophic, game-changing. It's The Hole now.

"Gence. What the fuck, man," Jack snaps.

Gence peers through The Hole at Jack. "Sorry, I have an *accident*. Now I am trying to make sure everything is to *code*." He slants me a sidelong look.

"This isn't happening," I murmur.

Jack's nose scrunches up like a subway rat's, and the space between his eyebrows furrows into a mean-looking eleven. He looks stupid when he's livid, like someone beaned Indiana Jones with a shovel.

"Oh, it's happening, 5A. You and I have taken the next step in our relationship and moved in together thanks to your antics." He runs a hand through his thick hair.

The image of Jack moving in with a woman floats through

my mind. Poor pretend woman.

I swallow hard and turn my best imploring expression on Gence, calling on the goodwill I've earned with dozens of cookies. "There has to be some way to fix this. Can you board it up for the time being? We can't live like this."

"No, I can't. Plaster here and… No, no. Need to bring it to code, Penny." He shrugs. "I'll work on it more tomorrow."

"But what are we supposed to do tonight?"

Gence mimes chewing. "You have maybe some bubble gum and a sheet, *kastravec*?" He laughs at my horrified expression and pulls his tool belt higher over his paunch. I plant my face in my hands and my elbows on my knees and hear Jack take over, proposing a few solutions, none of which Gence thinks feasible. I let their sharp words circle around me. I thought I had no privacy before. But now?

"Tomorrow, I come and take the rest of this wall down, *t'kap kolera*. It's drywall so easy job. If lath and plaster, then it would take longer time. I do the framing, drywall one side, mudding. Then you have privacy. Next day, inspector come, I put drywall up other side, mud there, sand here. Bam boom, boom bam, three or four days, brand-new wall. *A morre veshë*? Just no walking around the living room in your underwears, heh? For one day, *shtazë t'egra*."

"I need to go to sleep," I announce. "*Please*, Gence. Tomorrow you'll fix it?"

"Of course. For you two, Gence work all day."

"The hole didn't look this big in the pic you sent me yesterday," Margie says, staring at the now six-foot hole in the center of the wall between my apartment and Jack's.

Avery shakes his head. "I'm going to have to institute a crisis intake form so I know what the hell I'm rushing over straight from work to deal with from now on."

"Because it *wasn't* this big yesterday," I snap at Margie. "Where the fuck is Gence? He isn't answering his phone." I dial him again on speaker, and a ringing sound fills the silence. I hang up.

Margie levels a look at me. "Maybe he's pissed. This is a lot of work. I told you this was a bad idea."

"No. You didn't. You introduced me to a lawyer who told me to do this, and then you cheerleaded every step of the way."

"Oh, yeah. I guess I just *thought* it was a bad idea." Margie's lip-twitch explodes into a proper grin at my glare.

My shoulders sag. *You did this to yourself.* "I made it all worse. I'm such an idiot." I rub my temples and begin pacing.

"Stop," Avery says. "It'll get fixed."

"And cheer up," Margie adds. "At least he's nice-looking. What if you lived next door to a Gorbachev and had to see *that* in his boxers?"

"Why Gorbachev?" I ask wearily, rubbing at my eyes.

"He took down the Berlin Wall. I guess I thought it was fitting." Margie shrugs and crunches on carrot sticks I didn't know I had.

"I'd be Gorby in this scenario," I mutter.

"I need to get out of here," Avery says. "Got to go shower."

"Not showering once after work won't unleash a plague on New York," Margie says, mocking Avery's daily ritual after finishing work in the lab.

Avery hefts himself up from my plush sofa with effort. "Incidentally, a woman is being treated for the plague right now at Beth Israel Hospital. There's an average of about seven cases in the country each—"

"Why are you standing? Are you giving a lecture? Or leaving? What is this?" Margie demands.

"You're a plague." Avery chuckles and kisses her forehead before hugging me, interrupting my pacing. "I'm headed home to shower, eat, and pretend I'm not best friends with people whose problems include holes in their walls *that they put there*."

The door closes behind him, and Margie turns to me. "I love that stick-in-the-mud. So, this distracted me from what I wanted to tell you, but we're filming in your office next week."

"Oh, no kidding?" I say, trying my best to show interest. "I think I'm the one who gave your location scout the idea when I visited you. Boardroom scene?"

Margie nods and crunches slowly on a carrot. "Lucas asked about you."

"Yeah, okay. Sure he did."

"Whatever, Gorton's Fisherman. Believe it or not. He said you reminded him of Sophie Turner." She sets her plate down. "I told him you're not down to mess around."

"If you ordered her from SHEIN, maybe. And good—I'm not. I'm done with dead ends."

Margie makes a skeptical sound in the back of her throat and pulls out her phone. "New phone. Give me your wifi pass—" She chuckles.

"What's so funny?"

"Your wifi network name is..."

"'Penny for your thoughts.' And?"

"Guessing this one is your neighbor's?"

She holds up her phone. I grab it out of her hand. Right under my network name is one that reads, "Dollar to go away?"

I shake my head and set Margie up on my network. "That's

some of his weaker work."

"You two are a mess."

"I'm serious. Last month he put globs of Vaseline on my doorknob. Or lube. It was so fucking gross. And then he denied it when I confronted him and said maybe I'm just naturally greasy."

The memory teases me out of my funk for just a moment. "So I told Mrs. Russo down in 2B, who is the sweetest lady and the most religious person I've ever met, that I hear him through the walls worshipping Satan. Maybe sacrificing chickens. She was horrified. She's taken it upon herself to save him, I think. I've heard her in there trying to pray over him a few times."

Margie accepts her phone. "Just another day at the zoo." She abruptly shifts and kneels on the sofa to peek her head into Jack's apartment.

"Get down! If he comes home and sees you…"

Margie pops her head back in. "Maybe he has better snacks. I'm gonna snoop." She extends one long leg through the hole. The rest of her follows before I can do more than gawk.

*"Margie!"* I scramble after her and dangle a leg through The Hole, mimicking her move. But my legs aren't long enough to reach the sofa on the other side, and I end up falling through in a heap, sending plaster all over Jack's sofa in my wake. "Margie!"

She opens his fridge, and the massive laminated Poison Control card anchored to the door by a magnet gives me pause. Margie's already on the move, closing the fridge and then opening and closing all his cabinets willy-nilly. I catch a glimpse of a fire extinguisher under his sink before she shuts the cabinet. She finds chips in a cupboard and smiles, reaching in to grab a handful and then handing the bag to me.

I toss the bag back into his cupboard and run after her. She's now in his bathroom.

"Margie, I'm going to kill you. This is breaking and entering."

"Technically this is just entering. Gence did the breaking." She polishes off her chips and dusts off her hands before inspecting the contents of Jack's medicine cabinet. It is shockingly well stocked. Is that…a pulse oximeter? And a blood pressure cuff?

"You said you wanted snacks! What are you looking for?"

"The right pills can be snacks, Penelope," Margie drawls. "But mostly I'm looking for evidence of STIs. Incontinence. Erectile dysfunction. Anything interesting. Maybe Viagra?"

"Why? You're not going to—" I don't finish the thought. The image of Jack smiling affectionately at Margie, her pulling off his snug tee, running a hand up his chest, him cupping her face tenderly… I swallow a grimace.

"Not me, girl. He's *your* snack. All that passion and anger? And now you two hot tamales have no wall to contain your libidos? It's my job as your best friend to make sure your ticket to Bonetown ensures a safe ride."

She clicks her tongue. "He must get migraines. My mom takes these." Margie rattles a bottle of pills. Then she pulls out her phone to look up the label for one of the tubes of cream. "This one is for an allergic reaction. Thought maybe he had a fungus. Okay, I think he's clean. You're clear to do the no-pants dance."

"I need a new best friend."

"You love me too much."

Margie leaves me to close the mirror, and I catch my expression. My hair is honey at sunset, tousled from my couch dive. My blue eyes are extra vivid. My cheeks are pink, flushed with…fear? Excitement? I'm not going to lie, the adrenaline makes me look pretty damn good. Maybe marketing isn't for me… Cat burglar. That'll make Mom proud. I pluck a piece of plaster off my head and toss it into Jack's wastebasket. Then I hear a crash.

I rush to the bedroom in time to see Margie on her hands and knees, picking up coins. "Knocked over that little bowl of quarters."

"Margie! What the fuck?" I'm on my hands and knees next to her, gathering them up as quickly as I can. When we've collected what I hope is all of them, I look around. His room is neat: white walls, bed made. Masculine, but not in a spartan, bachelor way. There's some character here. Beige curtains streaked with razor-thin vertical blue lines. A surrealist painting of… Is that Citi Field? Pictures on the walls of people who look to be his parents, another of a dog, one of Jack shaking hands with an older man while they both hold up an award. Another of him and a tall woman, side by side, captured mid-laugh. Margie looks at it over my shoulder.

"He has a girlfriend?"

My chest twinges. A memory leaps into the fray, desperate to be tagged in by my consciousness. "They broke up, I think. Right after he moved in." I turn away, my dislike for Jack crowding out what little tolerance for him I've built up. I'm glad for the reminder.

"He's pining," Margie says. "That's sad." At my expression, she tilts her head, curious. "Why don't you like him, anyway? There had to be something that kicked all of this off. You don't just instantly hate someone."

"I told you why." I reach under his bed for a renegade quarter.

"Nope."

I sigh and sit back on my haunches. "When he moved in, I ran into him in the hall. He was carrying a sofa in, helping the movers. I— I mean objectively, if you overlook his awful personality, his shitty tree-candle smell… I mean, he could be considered okay-looking in some circles."

"Young Harrison Ford," Margie says. "Continue."

"Yeah. Fine. If you squint and then take some shrooms. Whatever. He made a comment—something funny. Funny-adjacent. I don't know. I laughed. We didn't even exchange names, but it felt like… Anyway, I had to run because I was meeting you downtown for that thing? The day Chris got food poisoning and you had the extra ticket?"

"Ugh, Chris." Margie is briefly distracted by the mention of her ex.

I haul in a breath and release it, trying to control the disdain and anger that course through me at the memory. "When I got home, I was coming up the stairs and this woman…*that* woman," I say, gesturing to the photo, "came running out of his apartment in hysterics. I stopped her and asked if everything was okay and she… She said, 'No. I'm not okay. Cheating asshole. I thought he loved me,' or something along those lines. And then she bolted."

"Oh, Pen." Margie is well aware of the nerve that episode would have touched. She's heard about my cheating father more than once, from me *and* my mom. I'm sure some people can rebound from being cheated on, but not us. It was the cloud that hung over our house my entire life, the thing that tainted almost every memory from my childhood.

*Why?* Mom's anguished face as she stared down at me drifts through my mind. *Why did I say anything to him? Why didn't I leave well enough alone?*

"So, the next morning, when I ran into him in the hall, he was all smarmy, as if a woman he clearly cheated on hadn't fled his apartment the night before. Like he didn't hurt someone in that way. And he had the audacity to *ask me out*." I wrinkle my nose.

"So I borrowed your line from *Geneva Convention*."

Margie covers her face with both hands, but I hear the laugh in her voice. "You told him you'd rather slather honey on your belly and hug a beehive than go out with him? That is, like, the worst line in the worst B-movie I've ever done."

"It was all I could think of in the moment. I gave him the deep freeze after that."

Margie stands and sets the bowl on the dresser. "He's still got that picture, Pen. Maybe he regrets—"

"They don't change. Ever."

Margie opens her mouth to say something, but we hear a sound that makes the blood freeze in my veins: keys.

"Go!" I whisper.

We race out of his bedroom and back to the sofa. Margie climbs over quickly, and I dive-bomb after her, landing in a sprawling heap on my floor after bouncing off my sofa, just as the door on Jack's side opens.

My pulse thunders. For a moment, there is silence. Margie doesn't make a sound. I hold my breath. Jack doesn't move right away. Then many things seem to happen at once. The door slams, and Jack appears in The Hole like an Emerald City guard from *The Wizard of Oz*.

"Can I help you?" I force myself to release my breath in a controlled hiss, and glance up with what I hope is casual disinterest.

"What are you doing on the floor?" His voice is suspicious. He looks at Margie, maybe thinking this stranger is more likely to tell the truth. But actors are capable of poker faces. I'm the weak link. His gaze swings back to me.

"Yoga." As he watches, I raise my hands, pretending my undignified sprawl is somehow an intentional and very Zen pose.

His lips purse. “That’s yoga? Maybe you need an instructor.”

“You’re ruining my flow. Go away.”

Jack looks back at his apartment, then into mine again. “Why is this thing now double the fucking size?”

“That’s what she said.” I slap my hands over my mouth. Nervous babbling is a curse.

Margie issues a strangled sound, but she remains completely blank-faced.

Jack’s brows gather, his stormy eyes narrowing with focus.

“Maybe you can call Gence. He won’t answer when I try him. Tell him to get up here and plug my hole. This hole.” *Oh God.*

The strangled sound comes from Margie again. Jack looks back and forth between us, his hands on his hips, and disappears out of The Hole. I stand slowly, then duck to observe him inspecting his apartment. He suspects something.

I turn to whisper that to Margie, only to find her shoulders shaking, her face pouring her amusement into my blue throw pillow. “Your fault,” I whisper instead, which just makes her laugh harder.

I’m almost grateful when I hear Jack’s vacuum going.

# 5

I knock on Gence's door, but there's no response. My chin drops. He's not making this bribery business easy. I sigh and hang the bag containing a Tupperware of peanut butter hi-hat cookies from the knob.

Trudging down the hall to the lobby, I pause to let one of the tenants from 3B pass. He's carrying a trifold project board as big as his elementary school–aged daughter next to him. By the looks of it, the project has something to do with fashion.

"I don't think you used enough glitter, Olivia," I joke, smiling at the little girl. 3B rolls his eyes and laughs.

"She's kidding," he says to his daughter. To me he adds, with a hint of desperation, "This stuff gets everywhere. *Everywhere*."

My skin prickles like a sunburn. Jack is making his way down the stairs, gussied up for work. 3B and that poster board are blocking my exit. I'm trapped. Jack reaches the lobby before I can make my escape. I open my mouth to speak, close it.

"Hey look, it's the human wrecking ball," he says.

"At least I just wreck walls, not vibes. You're a walking rain cloud." I scowl up at him. The faint funk that always hangs in the air here from the nail salon next door is extra funkified, mixed as it is with his piney air-freshener smell.

"Oh good," Gence's voice rings out. "You are both here."

Jack and I straighten guiltily.

"Gence, when are you going to sort out the wall?" Jack asks. "What's taking so long?"

"*Mos ma çaj bythën*. You have questions, I know. I will answer. The owner of your apartments, Mr. MacManus, is very upset. He says he will not renew your leases. He ask me to knock down wall, *t'raftë pika*, so he can sell as one apartment to one of you."

"What?" I cry out at the same time Jack shouts, "Sell?"

The edges around my vision blur. This isn't real. I can't lose my place. "Gence, I will talk to Mr. MacManus," I say.

"No. *Mos pjek pordhë në tepsi*," Gence says.

"He told you not to bake a fart in a pan. That can't be right?" Jack says. He holds up his phone, the translation written on the screen, clear as day.

"Oh, you know things, *hajvan*?" Gence says.

"Why are you mad at me? She's the one who put the hole in the wall!"

"I know things too. I know *everything*." Gence glowers at Jack.

"I met Mr. MacManus once, a couple of years ago. I've got his number. There's no way he can kick me out! I love my apartment!" I insist. I fumble with my purse, pulling out my cell.

"No, no!" Gence's eyes shift, taking in Mrs. Russo's descent into the lobby. The old woman shuffles past us to the mailboxes, pausing to clutch the cross hanging from her neck and give Jack a disapproving glance.

Gence's voice is softer when he says, "No need to bother Mr. MacManus. He did say maybe he sell the apartments separately. But only if *you* fix the wall and do anything else that is needed.

You remove wall, you get permits, you can split the work, cost, to put up wall maybe with each other if you both want to buy. If you do all of that and make official bank-approved offer to buy before city deadline, you get apartments. If not, Mr. MacManus sells as one apartment. Full price. And we know how fast condos go here, *a din*?"

"What's—" I lick my lips. "What's the price?"

Gence cites a number that freezes my insides. "For the entire floor?" I ask hopefully.

"Each."

I force a smile. "Oh. Okay. Great!"

Gence walks on down the hall to his apartment. I stare after him.

"Nice going," Jack murmurs.

"What? I don't know where you can get live chickens," I say, loud enough that Mrs. Russo hears. She moves with purpose in Jack's direction.

My heart beats against my chest like a demented caged bird. I could own my apartment. My baby would be mine. Permanently. I hurry to the door.

My own patch of city—*if* I can somehow, miraculously, come up with the money and build that wall in less than sixty days.

The walk is marked by an emotional yo-yo within me. It crashes violently when I think of the cost of buying and buoyantly jerks back up when I think about my place being my forever home.

An hour later, while I'm on what has easily become the most painful conference call of each day, I multitask and fill out a mortgage pre-approval application. Anthony, a colleague of mine from our European region, drones on and on.

Application submitted, I sit back in my chair and smile.

"And so, perhaps we can regroup on this second agenda item," Anthony says, finally arriving at his point. I've dubbed him "The Professor" in my mind, since he loves to pontificate and poke holes in others' work while never volunteering to do anything himself. Academia in the corporate world at its finest.

"Actually, Anthony, if we can just review this one piece—"

"No, Penelope, I must insist. Moving on to agenda item three..."

I open my mouth and shut it, my shoulders slumping.

"You know what? I don't need you after all, Jolly Green. I did it all by myself," I say to Avery, adjusting my earbuds and balancing on the ladder I borrowed from Gence. I push the sticky Command hook firmly against the plaster wall, about a foot above and to the left of the giant hole in the wall.

"I don't understand. One night of drinking to excess and you've devolved to College Penny. Why didn't you just put a Taylor Swift poster over the hole?" he says.

I step down and survey my work. The hook looks even enough with the one to the right of The Hole. My call waiting beeps, but I send my mother to voicemail. "I blame Margie."

"You always do. Adulting is hard."

"I called you for freakishly tall person help, not character assassination," I tell him. I exhale in a mighty puff and grab the end of the sheet I bought to serve as my new wall tapestry. It features a delicate blue and white and yellow pattern of trees and birds and was the least like a college wall hanging I could find. I climb again and jam my earbuds more firmly into my ears.

"Well, you potato, you called the wrong friend if you didn't want to be judged about your wall-hole problems."

"I wasn't complaining. And The Hole is being temporarily handled as we speak." I tie off one end of the sheet and hop off the ladder, grabbing the other. "But, you know, I sure would like to have the wall fixed permanently. It's probably not safe to have it open to an apartment where a weirdo lives..."

Avery is silent.

"That's my super-slick way of asking you to help me take down this wall and rebuild it? Please? Pretty please?"

"Hi, Dr. Vaughn. Sorry to interrupt," I hear a husky female voice say on Avery's side of the conversation.

"Dr. Cassidy, hi. I didn't know you were back."

"There's a matter I need to discuss with you. I'm—"

"Excuse me for one second," Avery says. "Penny, I've got to—"

Jack's door opens, and a woman follows him in.

"Gotta go." I don't wait for his response, instead hanging up on him and ducking behind the sheet to avoid detection. I hear him offer the woman something to drink, and she accepts a glass of water with a smile. She's pretty, in a garish kind of way. Long black hair, big gazongas, and tight black pants. Nothing like the ex-girlfriend I met. Whatever. He doesn't have a type beyond "willing," I guess.

I crouch down again, just in time to hear her ask about The Hole.

Jack sighs. "My next door neighbor is a little...eccentric. She attacked it with a hammer and opened up a can of worms. I'm sorting it out. It'll be fixed in the next few weeks." He adds the last bit in a rush, probably desperate to have her come back.

I hear them walking around the apartment, with Jack pointing out its architectural features, the ones I'm obsessed with in my own. I'm surprised the bonehead knows them, to be honest. And that woman *definitely* doesn't look like a history buff.

I mentally slap myself. *What the hell are you doing?* I'm always preaching the gospel of Women-Need-To-Stop-Tearing-Each-Other-Down. I don't make catty, shitty comments about other women. I should be rescuing this stranger, not comparing my bra size to hers and finding myself lacking.

I rub at my eyes wearily and hear my moment of opportunity present itself.

"Sorry, I need to call my sister," Jack says. "Her cat just died. The thing always made me itch, but she's— That's her calling. Excuse me a second."

I wait until I hear the click of his bedroom door.

"Hey! Hey! Psssst!" I lift the sheet and lean through The Hole, waving my arms wildly.

The woman yelps, spilling the water she was just sipping down her front. She looks anxiously to the door—the one Jack disappeared through—then approaches The Hole slowly. "Can I help you?"

"No! You can help yourself. By getting out. You don't know what kind of hurt you're in for with—"

She backs up a few steps and gulps, audibly. "Hurt? What do you mean?"

"I'm trying to warn you. The last woman I saw here was destroyed. Broken."

"Oh. Okay." The woman abandons her glass on the counter and retreats toward the front door, backing away with purpose.

I lean farther through The Hole, and she fumbles with the knob. She seems nervous, which she absolutely should be if she was this close to making the biggest mistake of her life. "Uh. Thanks for letting me know. I'm going now. Goodbye." She opens the door and bolts through it.

I race to intercept her in the hallway. She screeches when she sees me and grabs for the stair rail. "You'll thank me later!" I crow triumphantly as she hurries away.

# 6

The air in my area of the office smells of pungent boiled eggs and thick floral perfume, courtesy of my elderly colleague and cubicle neighbor, Donna. Though I've strategically placed plants along the ledge that divides our spaces to block unwanted conversation, nothing can be done about the odors. I rest my elbows on my desk and press at my temples, my headset digging into my ears as the voices on the conference call hum on around me. God help me.

I need a distraction or I'm going to gag. No one is talking to me or about a part of the project I own. *Seize the moment, brain. Check out and shift gears.* I click over to my personal email and lean forward eagerly when I spot a message from my bank.

*Please, please, please.*

It's just impressions of words, but they set my eyes to watering.

*Regret to inform…salary is insufficient…would need to meet this minimum threshold…would still require mortgage insurance…*

"If I may interject…?" Anthony cuts off a soft-spoken woman from APAC, and I slam at the mute button on my phone before I groan.

There's a pause, and then, "I'm sorry. Did you say something, Penelope?" Anthony asks. I'm not on video, but to my horror,

Zoom has illuminated my name like a Rockefeller Center Christmas Tree. My audio is still on.

I straighten. "Ah, no, sorry. Just stretching. I did want to make sure that we get to the other items—"

"And we will. However, I must object to the definitions as set out in slide five. If someone could..." The Professor lectures some more, a roadblock to all progress.

A little while later, I knock on Rochelle's door. She waves me in and lifts a brow when I nervously close the door behind me.

"Hey, Rochelle... Something has come up, and... Remember how we talked about a raise?" I force myself to sound confident, authoritative. "I think I've proven myself even before this whole project, and I've never said anything about putting in the occasional night or weekend, but now it's an every night kind of thing. This stuff is intense, and some of the personalities are... tough."

She frowns.

"And I'm totally *not* complaining. We'll get there. It's just... I want to buy my apartment, and I need the extra income to qualify—"

"Penny, I'm going to cut you off there. An off-cycle raise is going to be tough, but if you get this framework hammered out—at least the first iteration that we can present to leadership—I'll have the ammo I need to try and make it happen. Your target timeline for the proposed framework is when?"

I swallow. I've got seven-and-a-half weeks to have a shot at buying my place at a price I can just about *reach* to afford. "Not the *final* framework, right? Just the first stab at the framework?" At her nod, I say, "Another month?" Which is actually doable, if Anthony can shut his yap long enough to let anything get worked out.

"Okay, so let's revisit this then. Sound good?"

My stomach sinks. I want to say no. I want to slam my hands on her desk and say that I more than deserve one based on past performance alone, and the new responsibilities I've taken on—which, by the way, are above and beyond my job description—shouldn't be the thing that tips the scales. But I don't. "Thanks, Rochelle. I'll get back at it then. Do you want your door open or closed?" I give her a small smile and walk away before my mask falls.

The rest of the day is an uphill slog, and by the time I insert my key into the building's front door, I feel as if every person I passed on the sidewalk on the way to and from work hitched a ride on my back. Each step jars my aching joints, and I nearly weep when I finally step into my apartment.

The dam to the reservoir I've built up fails. I look around my apartment and remember sitting in the middle of the empty living room floor the day I moved in. At the time, I couldn't afford new furniture, but piece by piece, I filled this space with the proof of my hard work and independence. It might look like a white sofa, bookshelves, and gauzy curtains to someone else, but to me, this apartment—*this* one—adds up to freedom. It adds up to me.

I toe off one shoe and then the other and step onto my area rug. My apartment pulls me in, hugging me tight.

This is my home. I *need* that raise. I *need* this global project to take off, and I *need* roadblocks to move so I can get that raise. I suck in a deep breath through my nose and release it slowly through my mouth. My home is my happy place, and I'm not going to worry about losing it until I have to. I'll figure out a way.

With that, I announce, for emphasis and not because I'm unhinged, "The day's stresses are over!"

The insistent knock at my back disabuses me of that notion

immediately.

I open the door to a towering, angry, fresh-from-work Jack. "What the hell did you do?" he growls.

"What?" I back up a step.

His face—handsome, if you're concussed—changes from enraged to a slightly constipated consternation. "Why are you crying?"

"It's none of your business." I raise my chin and, to my horror, my eyes well once more. *Don't cry in front of the enemy.*

"Hey! What..." Jack runs a hand through his dark hair and takes a step toward me. He reaches out.

I rear back. "What are you doing?"

He lets his arm drop, and he snaps, "Clearly, I'm comforting you."

I laugh out loud. The thought of Jack comforting anyone, me especially, is so outlandishly stupid, I can't help myself. "And you're really good at it, I see. But I don't need you to comfort me. Also, don't vampires have to be invited in?" I look pointedly down at his feet, standing just inside my door.

Jack's nostrils flare like a bull seeing red. "There she is, all piss and vinegar. Fine. No comfort. How about you tell me why you scared the shit out of my appraiser instead?"

I gape at him dumbly. I have no idea how to wrap my head around those words.

He leans forward so that his face is directly in front of mine. His warm breath smells of mint. For a second, my only thoughts revolve around the blue flecks in his silver eyes. Around letting him hold me. Resting my head against his chest. And maybe sinking my teeth into his shoulder.

The radiating heat of his body invites me close, pulls me in, not unlike the feeling I get from my apartment. My pulse beats a rapid staccato against my throat, a reaction wholly related to his closeness. This is...unexpected. And invigorating? Hot? Why are none of these adjectives negative?

"If you think the way you're going to get rid of me is by scaring away the bank people, think again."

"Appraiser?" I repeat, latching onto the last word I registered. I step back again. He follows and shuts the door behind him.

"Yes. My *appraiser.* Who disappeared from my apartment yesterday. Who wouldn't answer my calls until about an hour ago, when she told me some loon appeared in the hole in the wall, threatened her life, lunged *into* the hole toward her, and when she ran out, the 'dangerous hole lady'—her words *and* mine—*chased* her down the stairs."

His words snap me out of my daze. "Excuse me? You're talking about that woman you were putting the moves on—?"

He takes a step closer to me, and I force myself not to step back. I can feel his body heat, hot as a building radiator in winter. "I wasn't putting the moves on her. She was here to *appraise my apartment*. For my *mortgage*. And you scared her half to death before she could do her job."

He must observe the dawning horror on my face because he crosses his arms and purses his lips, the picture of irritated manhood.

I hold up a hand. "Okay, so... Yes, yeah... That's not what happened at all? I mean. Some of it did, but not like how she said. I leaned through The Hole to *warn* her, not threaten her. And I ran to the hall to finish my thought because she bolted before I could—"

"Warn her about *what*?"

*"You!"*

"What about me?" he roars, any semblance of patience gone.

"Is this what I have to worry about if I bring people over?"

"Only until The Hole is patched. But yes, I will chase away every woman you think you've scored." I raise my chin a fraction, breathing heavily now.

He stares at me, incredulous. And then he surprises me by tipping his head back and laughing. A full-throated laugh.

I frown, watching the smile transform his features as the rumbling in his chest continues. My shoulders melt away from my ears. The tension, the fight in me, is draining away, replaced by confusion. "*What* is so funny?"

"I knew it," he mutters.

Before I can ask what he's talking about, he reaches up and brushes his thumb across my cheek, wiping away a lingering tear. His expression is inscrutable.

"Tell me to stop, and I will," he says.

My mouth opens, the rest of me paralyzed by shock. And then he moves, curling an arm around me, his other hand sliding under my hair to the back of my neck.

Every nerve ending in my body stands at attention. Synapses, long dormant, fire. Misfire. I can't breathe. Every inch of me is pressed against his hard body. My chest is heaving. I'm ready for battle. His lips are close, so close. His eyes are intense, darker than I've ever seen them. He's closing them. He's going to…

"What are you doing?" I choke out.

He pauses and opens his eyes. Then he whispers, "The jealousy is a little nutty, but—"

I plant my hands against his very firm chest—which I do not think about at all, thank you very much—and push as hard as I can. "What the hell are you talking about?"

He stumbles back, his lips tipped into an irritatingly self-assured smirk. Meanwhile, I am a quaking mess. "I suspected, sure, but confirmation is good. I'm not a huge fan of over-the-top jealousy—it screams trust issues. The warning-other-women-away thing and the crying are a *little*..." He trails off, correctly reading the gathering storm clouds in my eyes.

"I. Am. Not. Jealous," I grit out.

He straightens and slants me a look. "You literally scared away a woman you thought I was hooking up with."

"Away *from you*. Because you're a cheating asshole. Not because I was jealous, you creep!"

His facial expression is almost comical. It's like his dick's sudden realization that he isn't getting any is warring with the story he just told himself. He wipes a hand down his face.

"Cheating? I've never cheated in my life."

"I met the girl in the picture. Your ex."

"The girl in the picture—"

"The picture on the wall of your bedroom!"

His face contorts in confusion. "The only pictures of women on my wall are of my family. Are you talking about my sister? And how the hell do you know what picture I have there?"

"Sister." He said "sister"! The word ricochets around my brain as I gawk at Jack.

"Well?" he asks, crossing his arms.

My mind shuffles cards like an Atlantic City casino dealer, struggling to reconcile everything I've ever thought about Jack with this new revelation. My eyes keep flitting to his and then skittering off, images, impressions, preconceived notions falling away, like a time traveler's photo album after they've set the past to rights.

"I—" I've got nothing. "Why would you try to kiss me? You don't even like me!" I sputter out, not sure whether I'm saying it for him to deny, or to remind him of that fact, or just to change the subject.

He doesn't deny it. Instead, he presses his thumb and index finger into his closed eyes. "Listen, you're a pretty girl. Abrasive, argumentative for no reason, but okay to look at. I figured I could close my eyes and think of England. But you're right. This was a lapse in judgment."

The comments sting, and there's extra venom in my retort as a result. "I would *never* get with you. I don't hate myself enough for that to ever happen."

"You don't hate yourself enough?" he jeers, and plants his hands on his hips. "Because you're not at all damaged, right? How long do your relationships typically last? Blink and you miss them? Milk keeps longer than guys last around you, right?"

My breath seizes in my lungs, my mind reeling. Mom's words coming out of Jack's mouth. He heard that, and possibly—definitely—more.

"You're a dick," I whisper.

He laughs. "How do you know? You told your friend a couple months back that you haven't seen one in two years."

I suck in a shuddering breath. It's one thing to be semi-aware of a seam deep within yourself, a self-sabotaging wound you've slapped a Band-Aid on despite suspecting it requires stitches. But it's another for someone who already doesn't like you to discover that seam and hold a mirror up to it. To have the ability to poke a finger in it whenever they want to win an argument.

I am bad with guys. I know this. It's been a running joke between me and Margie forever because she's the same, but in a different way. But it's not a joke, really. I actively look for little deal-breakers that conveniently move the goalposts of what I'm looking for beyond the reach of whoever I'm seeing. I preemptively break up with guys because of my dad. His betrayal of Mom and me has trickled down through the cracks in my defenses and polluted the well of who I am. So I've avoided getting involved with anyone for the last two years, because it's better than suffering breakup after breakup.

"Get out of my apartment. *Now.*" I'm shaking.

He stalks up to me, his quicksilver eyes churning with anger and a whole host of other emotions I can't read.

I stand my ground, bracing myself for his next verbal lash, or God forbid, a kiss.

But Jack stalks past me, steps onto my sofa, flips the sheet up, and disappears through The Hole.

Like a goddamn gremlin.

# 7

I wave Margie into my apartment. "It took you forever!"

She gives me a dead-eyed look. "You had me battle crack-of-dawn, rush-hour train traffic to bring my child here for nefarious purposes. You're lucky I'm here at all. Is Jack home?"

I shake my head. "He left for the gym twenty minutes ago. We have to hurry. Cashmere ready for showtime?"

Margie holds up her carrier. Cashmere, two years old, small, with gorgeous amber eyes and white fur interrupted by the occasional patch of light gray, peers out at me from within. She's an extraordinarily sweet-tempered cat, surprising given that Margie found her with BB pellets lodged in her side courtesy of some evil humans. But she's healed, and she's purring loudly as Margie pulls her from her carrier.

"Let's do this," Margie says, tucking her cat under her arm and climbing through The Hole.

When we're both in, she pulls a toy from her back pocket and sets Cashmere onto Jack's sofa.

"Make her run back and forth," I say eagerly. "Really get those kitty juices on that Belgian linen."

Margie complies, waving the toy back and forth. "I'm a professional actor. On a prime-time show. And right now I'm making my cat rub her ass on my best friend's neighbor's sofa."

"I appreciate you!"

Margie raises an eyebrow.

The cat leaps from the sofa, inspecting different corners of the room before lounging on the living room rug. Margie picks her up and heads for Jack's bedroom. There, Cashmere has a good deal of fun with Jack's coverlet and pillows. Margie even pulls back the white comforter so that Cashmere can explore Jack's sheets. I laugh at the cat's antics, running my hand over her head and scratching her belly.

"You said the sister's cat made him itch? If that boy has an allergy, we'll know," Margie says.

"He's an asshole, but I trust him to know what makes him itch."

Margie picks up Cashmere, crooning to her and scratching behind her ears before heading to the bathroom. She proceeds to run her cat's rear over Jack's toilet seat for good measure.

"You're a good friend."

"I know."

"You think Avery would help us bury a body?"

Margie snorts. "If either one of us killed someone, he'd narc us out so hard."

"I don't know. He roughed up that guy who dumped a beer on your head senior year. He's not *all* goody-goody."

"Avery is my bestie, but I'm not blind to who he is," she says as we climb back into my apartment. "He's predicable, dependable, and so straitlaced it's a miracle he can breathe. Like he's wearing a moral girdle."

My cell alarm goes off—too late for Margie to leave now. "I can't risk you running into him. Cashmere needs an alibi. Hang out for a bit? You can help me brainstorm how to save money for my mortgage." I gesture toward my open laptop, where I've outlined my monthly expenditures.

She picks up my computer and lounges on my sofa, gently petting Cashmere as I fix my face for work. "Monthly flowers to Mom are in your 'can't cut' column?"

I tip my chin up a fraction. It's not a little bit of money, but I'm grateful to Mom. She sacrificed so much for me when Dad took off. "She misses me. I think she likes knowing I'm thinking of her." Margie sets the laptop down with a shrug, silent judgment in her raised eyebrows. I return my gaze to my mirror, blending my foundation a little too vigorously.

"Since when do you play violin?" Margie finally drawls, nodding toward the instrument case on my kitchen counter.

I grin into my tabletop makeup mirror. "I don't. It's for Jack. I just put on my noise cancellers and run the stick thingy over the strings a bunch while I'm watching *Jeopardy!* with closed captioning. I found it on a curb."

"Oh, okay. That's sane." She reaches into her bag and pulls out a script. "Here. Are you done? We're running lines as a thank-you to me."

I help Margie rehearse until Jack returns home. When she's confident she can leave without running into him, she collects Cashmere and departs, a smirk playing about her lips.

I leave for work just after her. And it isn't long before I realize that watching Margie rub her cat's ass on a toilet seat is probably going to end up being the highlight of my day.

Besides the usual work fuckery, my big global campaign conference call runs on past its end time as The Professor proposes ludicrous hypothetical after hypothetical.

"One central coordinator from each region sounds good *in theory*. However, what would happen should one be, say, hit by a bus? And in a perfect world, your schedule for translation and localization would be feasible. But it hinges on Marci. What if Marci goes on maternity leave?"

"I'm not pregnant." Marci looks alarmed as she leans toward her camera.

"Not *now*, but—"

"I'm sorry, Anthony, we're going to need to wrap—" I say into my headset mic.

"And last, I'm sure you're aware, Penelope, but the software you propose everyone use across the globe still needs to go through strenuous security vetting."

I freeze, fumbling with the papers on my desk. "I proposed that software because we've already launched pilots with it in every country."

"Perhaps you should add that to the agenda for next week. I think if we pull at that thread now, the whole sweater might come undone," Anthony says.

I end the call and close out the online mortgage prequalification calculator on my browser. I've pinpointed the exact raise amount I need, and if I can get even a modest one, I can buy my apartment. It'll wipe out most of my savings, which scares the shit out of me, but it's doable. With Anthony on this team, that dream is slipping further and further away.

I trudge home, stopping only to buy myself an emotional-support crêpe filled with chocolate and topped with whipped cream. It's gone before I reach my front door, and so is the napkin I must've dropped en route. Once I'm inside, I quickly realize just how tricky opening my mailbox one-handed will be. Looking around for a newspaper or some other makeshift napkin, I finally wipe my messy fingers down Jack's mailbox, leaving chocolate streaked down the front. I hope he thinks it's dog poop.

My amused satisfaction is cut short when Jack himself enters a few beats later. I open my mailbox and act casual, except for a single weird, darting glance we exchange. I try not to think about his hands on me, try not to wonder if he's thinking about it, too, and instead chuck my mail into my bag and lock up quickly. Jack eyes the brown stains on his mailbox before apparently deciding against opening it.

I begin the five-flight climb and hear Jack just behind me. I stop, waving him past. He stops, too, holding onto the banister. He has a strange look on his face, almost guilty—but he would have to have a conscience for that.

"Ladies first."

"Just don't stare at my ass."

I continue the climb, thinking about Jack's arm wrapped around me, pulling me against him. It was one thing when *Pirate Duke* put ideas into my head and I thought they were entirely one-sided. Gross and confusing and disconnected from reality, but one-sided. But now, with an almost-kiss…

We reach the landing, and there's a faint sheen of perspiration on Jack's face, though I've never seen him break a sweat on the stairs before. Maybe he's sick? Is it the kitty juices? He doesn't appear to be itchy, and he would've left for work shortly after me. I rush to my door and try to ignore the prickle of conscience the thought brings.

"Can I talk to you a sec?" he asks.

I jam my key into the lock. "What?"

"I wanted to say… I misread the situation last night, and I didn't have a right to put my hands on you without your explicit consent, and…"

I'm having a hard time following the thread of this convo. Is he *apologizing* to me? And saying things like "no right" and "consent"? No wonder he looks ill. I gape at him.

Jack runs a hand through his hair and then loosens his tie, unbuttoning the top of his blue dress shirt. I'm briefly distracted by the reveal of that patch of skin. "I'm sorry," he says.

"Okay," I say, bewilderment and suspicion at war with each other. I turn to close my door on him, guilt over this morning's feline antics growing.

He reaches out a hand, stilling the motion. "And?" he says.

"And… What? Thank you?"

"And don't you have anything to apologize for?"

"No?"

He grits his teeth and spits out, "Yelena?"

*What the hell?* "My name is Penelope," I say, slowly. My eyes search his face for signs of real illness.

Jack bends his head, and when he finally speaks, it's with insultingly exaggerated patience. "I'm talking about the appraiser. Her name is Yelena."

"Oh. That." I bite the inside of my cheek. "Okay, fine. I— I'm sorry. I didn't know she was there to appraise the place, and…" Oh, fuck it. This war with him is exhausting. At least if we can return to a Cold War, I won't feel so disoriented all the time. I need to conserve my energy to focus on my project at work. "And even if she wasn't there for that, I should've minded my business. Happy?"

He rubs at the back of his neck and nods. "I wasn't blameless in that whole thing, either, I guess," he mutters. "I just remembered telling her my neighbor was eccentric. She must have thought I was underselling it when you launched yourself through the hole."

I glare, but there's no real heat in it, and a smile tugs at his mouth. "Kiss and make up?"

"Ugh. The worst."

"Hey, you're the one who tried to move in with me." At my blank look, he continues, "The hole?"

"Whatever. Speaking of, you're definitely planning on buying your place?" *Please say no. Please say no.*

"Yes."

My shoulders slump. Damn it. "Okay, well then, do you—" I grit my teeth. "Do you want to help me put up a new wall?"

"Nope."

"Why?" I cry. "That's the only way we can keep our places!"

"Not exactly. I want your place, too, and I talked to Gence about it. I plan on knocking down the wall entirely and making it one big apartment. Just like it used to be before they put up that piss-poor wall."

"You want *my place*?" I shout, as appalled as if he's demanded my firstborn. "Like hell you'll get my apartment."

"Maybe. But regardless, I won't help you patch up a wall I would need to take down anyway if I were to get your apartment. Waste of time and money. I'll help you take it down, though."

I give him my stormiest, hall-hath-no-fury-like-a-woman-whose-apartment-is-threatened look, and slam my door in his face as hard as I can.

Forget Cold War. I'm going nuclear.

Avery surveys The Hole, his green eyes squinting in concentration. I hold the tape measure out to him and he accepts, whipping the yellow metal tape out in a blur and then fumbling with it when it bends and catches on my rug.

"Not the first time that's happened," Margie says. "According to Krista."

Avery mutters something under his breath about the pressure of exams and big mouths. He's still friends with every ex he's ever had, so he's no doubt debating whether or not to bring up this breach of trust the next time he connects with his former girlfriend from grad school.

He sorts out the measuring tape and threads it out carefully so that it sits along the length of the wall with The Hole. He squats and peers at the number, and then we wait as he presses the button to coil it noisily back into its holster. It takes an absurdly long time.

I give him an expectant look as he straightens.

"Shit, I forgot the number," he says. "We should write it down."

"How are you so hopeless with home improvement but so brilliant at work?" Margie asks. "And why are you measuring something that needs to be taken down?"

Avery glares. "Why are you so good at crying on command but laugh like you're burning down a house full of orphans?"

Margie scrunches her nose. "My laugh almost won me a daytime Emmy for *Alcott Landing*."

"Almost."

Margie laughs out loud, and Avery chuckles.

"You guys, stop," I moan. "I need someone who knows construction. What am I going to do? That monster wants Mary Sue."

"Who's Mary Sue?" Avery asks.

"Her apartment. Because it is perfect and without flaws," Margie responds.

"Hire someone? I told you, Pen. I'm not handy. My super had to hang up all the photos in my apartment. I'll help take the wall down, but putting it back up again is going to require a pro."

"Everyone keeps offering to take it down, but no one can put it up. And I can't afford to hire someone. I can't even afford to buy my place. No—before you start, I'm not taking money from you. Why couldn't I just be friends with a contractor?" I cry, flopping down on the couch and throwing an arm over my eyes.

"Meaningful years-long friendships, heartfelt talks, being there for one another, and it's all down the drain because we can't swing a hammer," Margie muses.

"I meant in addition to you both."

"Nice save," Avery says.

"I think La has some construction experience. She was involved in the reno at her restaurant. We can ask her." Margie pulls out her phone and types a text.

"You have her number?"

Margie shrugs. "Yeah, we're friends—friendly."

We don't have to wait very long for an answer. Margie's phone pings right away. "She's in. Buhhh... *Stop.* Don't get too excited. She says we've got to handle the demolition ourselves—"

"Which is fine because you guys can help me demo it," I interject excitedly.

"Yeah, but she also won't be able to rebuild the wall entirely since she's got the restaurant to take care of. *But*, once we're done with the demo, she can swing by, get us started on the build, show us the ropes, and check in every once in a while to make sure it's going okay. I'm sure we can manage this thing," Margie says, waving an arm at my wall with the giant cyclops eye in the middle.

"I love you." I launch myself at Margie, pelting her with kisses.

Avery nods, pursing his lips. "Looks like you're all sorted, so—"

"You're still helping with demolition."

He sighs. "Can I pay someone to stand in for me instead of providing the free labor myself?"

I hear Jack's door open, and my joy at besting that dildo knows no bounds. I poke my head through The Hole. Jack is shrugging off his dress shirt. He cocks a dark eyebrow, staring at me, as he drops it onto the back of a chair. This isn't Victorian England. I'm not distracted by the flash of tanned skin above the neck of his undershirt. I'm simply confirming that there are no signs of a cat allergy yet.

"Hiya, roomie! Welcome home." My gloating floats over to him like a noxious yellow cloud.

"These two are a disaster," Margie says to Avery. I shoot her a quelling look.

"Heads-up that construction is underway. I've assembled my crew, and we're measuring and stuff before starting demolition."

"Your crew," he deadpans. He approaches The Hole, smelling of piney evil, and glances through. "Why are you measuring the wall before you take it down?"

"See?" Margie says.

Avery snorts.

"Because we need to know how much material to buy for the rebuild. That's why." In my head, the answer sounds like it could be correct. I, myself, didn't question why Avery was measuring, and we have recorded exactly zero metrics, but Jack doesn't need to know that.

Avery nods at Jack. "Hi. I'm Avery," he says. "This is Margie."

Margie salutes.

"Jack."

"A face to go with the bathroom," Margie murmurs, drawing Jack's sharp eyes.

I'm going to murder her.

"Nice to meet you both. I've heard so much about you." He waggles his eyebrows at me, and I'm immediately overcome by fury at the reminder of his eavesdropping. Guess what keeps longer than my relationships, Jack? My grudges.

I push at the sheet I've draped over my sofa so that it once again covers The Hole…and Jack's gargoyle dimples.

# 8

Happy hour at La Smith's is always a crush of swaying bodies, bass, and laughter. Today is no exception. After successfully navigating the crowd, I nod a greeting at La's bartender and plop myself on the chair across from Margie. She wordlessly hands me her drink, and I dutifully take a pull on the straw.

"Why isn't breaking shit a faster process?" I moan. "Everything aches. Everything, all day today at work. And I work out!"

Margie tosses me a look.

"Sometimes. I work out sometimes. But based on what we accomplished last night, my muscles shouldn't be hanging out in painful little knot gangs like this. We didn't even put a dent in the wall demo."

"Hmmm hmmm." Margie bites the inside of her cheek and nods. "I was surprised at how slow it was going."

"Maybe it would've gone faster if you didn't spend all your time taunting me about Jack and playing a construction helper on TV," I grumble. Margie swung exactly zero hammers, though she put on and took off a pair of safety goggles multiple times.

"I have a new show!" She gestures to her body with a sweep of her arm. "I can't risk messing up my moneymaker. I'm there more for moral support. And I'll carry debris downstairs for you.

Also, not for nothing, I got you La's promise to help rebuild after you take the wall down."

I grunt. I don't want her risking her job, and getting La to help *was* a coup. But my head is throbbing. If there is ever wind in my sails, Jack has to act as a hidden reef. Last night, after Margie and Avery went home, Jack started playing "What Was I Made For." And then never stopped. Even a song I love loses its charm after the eight hundredth repetition. Paired with my achy body, it made for a particularly trying day at work today, which makes for a cranky Penny now.

"Okay. Sorry. I appreciate you."

"You're so moody."

My phone vibrates in my back pocket, and I pull it out. Mom. My shoulders tighten. I missed talking to her yesterday. "Give me a sec to take this, Margie?" I steel myself and press the button.

"Hi, Mom."

"No call from you yesterday?"

"Sorry. It's been wild. I've been working a ton." *And destroying my wall, weaponizing cat's asses, and forcing myself to maybe get evicted.*

"You work too hard, Penny! You need to find a better job. They're not treating you right there."

"You're right. I do work too much," I say, in my most soothing tone. "It's just I'm trying to buy my apartment, and—" At her indrawn breath, my heart slams into my throat. *Shit, shit, shit.* Eyes wide, I mute myself and switch to speaker at Margie's questioning look. "I'm so fucked," I moan, seizing the napkin in front of me and shredding it.

"Buy? You're not buying there. If you want to buy something, come home and buy! Cathy Santini died about three weeks back—you remember her? She was the one who used to hand out the whole candy bars you liked so much on Halloween. Over on Greenly Street? Heart attack, right in her kitchen. And her house is on the market now. Come back and buy that! It's perfect for you. Or come back and stay with me and buy when you finally find a boy to settle down with. The city is just filthy, sweetheart."

My breath catches. *You can't hack it there*, is what she leaves unsaid. Why do I feel guilty for working, for wanting to make a decision for myself? I like my life here. I just need her to be okay with it. Her approval is sunlight, and I'm a desperate houseplant turning my face to catch her rays. I ball up my shredded napkin and squeeze it tightly in my fist.

Margie's lips twist. "The dead lady's ghost *is* an awesome selling point," she says.

I unmute the phone. "Right. I'm not sure I want to move back, Mom." I close my eyes, bracing for impact.

"When you find a guy—"

"Not even then."

"Of course you will."

I breathe in and out, almost dizzy. I don't want this to spiral more than it has. "Maybe, yeah. I'll think it over. But listen, Mom, I'm having drinks with Margie. Did I tell you she's a series regular? So amazing. I'm thrilled for her. I've got to run, but I'll call you later and fill you in."

"Alright, Penny. Love you. I'll ask about pricing on the Santini house," she says.

"Thank you. Bye, Mom. Love you."

I hang up and slump in the chair.

"You okay?" Margie asks.

I massage my jaw, trying to unstick the tension there. I wouldn't have slipped and told Mom if it wasn't for Jack and his nighttime antics. "No." I move my fingers up to my temples and mutter, "Billie Eilish is a treasure. She shouldn't be used as a weapon of war."

Margie gives me a puzzled look, but in an effort to lighten the mood, she launches into a set story about a recent A-list guest star whose shifting hairline kept ruining the continuity of scenes. I'm chuckling by the time La joins us at the table.

"Hey Pen, I talked to my contact in the permit office. I've pulled what you need. Stop by the bar tomorrow and I'll give you the paperwork," she says, offering to do something I forgot I even needed.

"You're an angel and I'm in your debt," I say, so grateful that I don't even mind when Margie shares a greatest-hits version of my war with Jack with her.

Hearing all our antics laid out like that makes me feel and sound very juvenile. Is it so wrong to just want to enjoy my apartment in peace? I was adult-ish before Jack barreled into my world like a juiced-up bull. I fold my arms across my chest and harrumph, but watching them both laugh, La guffawing and leaning against Margie for support, I find my own lips twitching in amusement.

"How did it go with the cat allergy stuff?" Margie asks before sharing the details of our Cashmere caper for La. I grin and lean back in my chair, cradling my wine.

"I don't know. After you left, I worked on the wall a bit and then cleaned up and showered before I turned in. I didn't spy on him because I guarantee it would've been written all over my face."

"And can I ask: what could he have done to inspire cat warfare?" La asks.

"He insulted me. I— I insulted him, too, but it was a mess with him trying to kiss me—"

Margie's eyebrows launch up. I left that part out when I asked her and Cashmere over. "And then I found out he didn't cheat; it was his sister I saw leaving his apartment. But he threw some stuff he heard through the wall in my face. Said some very mean things like a real scumbag. Scum. Bag."

"I thought Margie was the dramatic one, and you were so go-with-the-flow," La says.

Margie pulls a mock-severe look.

I *was* go-with-the-flow. Until Jack.

The walk home with Margie is a quiet one, with both of us lost in our own thoughts. And then Margie glances at me.

"Think we're due for story time. That's a pretty major detail you left out about the kiss."

I blanch. I avoided telling Margie or Avery, partly because I didn't want to give them ammo to tease me with, but mainly because I didn't want to think about that moment too much myself. *Pirate Duke* is scorching, bless Karin Shelby's heart and pen, but that book and Jack's clumsy advance have burrowed together into my hippocampus and procreated, birthing some truly *awful* thoughts.

Yes, I admit it. He's handsome if you're extremely near-sighted. *Have some self-respect, lady! He insulted you!*

"He's the worst," is all I volunteer. "It was nothing. I just want to forget he exists."

"Maybe tonight he'll be too busy itching to pay attention to you," she muses before hugging me goodbye and continuing on to her apartment.

The thought brings me joy. I carry that joy with me on the walk home, images of Jack loading his shit into the back of a moving van prancing through my mind. Sad little garbage bags filled with his piney-scented wardrobe, those barstools I like so much…

My daydream morphs as I practically skip to my apartment: Jack handing his keys over to Gence. Me closing our building's front door on him with a smile.

Once inside, I fill my watering can at the sink and envision my neighbors cheering as I triumphantly hold my mortgage papers aloft, my beautiful apartment mine forever. I imagine Gence high-fiving me as I enter the lobby, happy to see me now that my nemesis is gone. I grin like mad—until I notice my beautiful fire-escape garden.

The air leaves my lungs in a quiet gasp. I gently set the watering can down onto the floor next to me and force my mouth closed. My fire escape looks like the bottom of a bird exhibit at the zoo. Everything—literally everything—on my black fire escape is white. Or gray.

It's covered in bird shit, is what I'm saying.

How does this happen? I open the window and lean out, looking up, eyes squinted in case I'm surprised by the biker gang of birds responsible. There's nothing there. I inspect my plants. Feathers all over, enough that they compete with the bird crap for pole position. Some of my seedlings have been uprooted entirely.

And…seeds?

I pick one out of the dirt in the pot closest to me, analyzing it like Detective Poirot. It's a small yellow millet seed. And beside it is a cracked sunflower seed.

My lips firm. Jack fucking Craig. This was no accident. Jack knows what I did. And now I know he knows. And he's going to know that I know.

I march to my kitchen, retrieve what I need, and stride toward The Hole. And then I'm through, rushing toward the radiator over by his windows. I kneel and reach into the tin, pulling out a scoop of tuna and smearing it onto the back of the radiator. I repeat until the can is empty and then move to the second one. And then I look out the window at the blindingly beautiful blue sky and wonder how my life has landed me at this new low.

Jack returns later, when I'm working at the wall, and pokes his head in on me.

"Hey!" he calls out. His skin is patchy and red. His eyes are puffy and bloodshot. For a second, I worry that I didn't think things through. What if he'd gone into anaphylaxis? I just assumed it was a minor cat allergy since his own sister had a cat, but… I didn't want to *kill* him. Not even maim him. I just want him to move away. A spark of remorse lights up the dark side of my mind, illuminating things about myself I'd rather not think about.

No. Black and white is the only filter for this situation. Jack = bad. Penny = good.

"What?" I ask, returning my attention to the wall.

"I'm ready to start taking this thing down if you're game for the help. Though… You're making so much progress with your *crew.*"

He surveys the pathetic patchy damage I've done to my side of wall with an evil twinkle in his red eyes, and I mentally take back what I said about maiming.

"Okay."

"You can be reasonable? Who knew?" He gathers up my wall covering and drapes it over the sofa so that The Hole is exposed, then fetches some tools wrapped in a cloth and a few rolled-up blankets from his bedroom before returning. I accept them and he steps through, grabbing my broom and waving me away as he sweeps up the debris. "First thing is setting a tarp or blankets down, or you're going to destroy my future floors. Not to mention that it helps keep the dust to a minimum. Surprised your crew didn't tell you that."

"My crew is made up of a scientist and an actor, so."

He moves my sofa and stuff out of the way and takes the blankets from me. "We're going to try and rip this side of the wall down, and then we'll stab through the lath." He reads my expression correctly. "That's this wooden slatting."

"I *know*. Avery told me."

Avery did not tell me.

"All of the walls between apartments on this side of the building probably started as quarter walls that divided two rooms in the same apartment. You can tell because they used different building materials. They drywalled over lath and plaster closer to the front door, and over here in the middle of the room it's mainly Sheetrock. Which is why you were able to punch that hole in the wall so easily and kickstart this entire fiasco."

I yawn and barely reach up a hand to stifle it. "I don't need a history lesson. I just want to tear this wall down, rebuild it to code with extra noise-muffling properties—"

"Not helping you with that second part."

"And then carry on with my life. Find a guy who is the opposite of you in every way, you know, in that he doesn't make me want to vom-gag. And then I'll get married, have babies, and with my soundproofed walls, it'll be like you never existed."

"Thanks for the play-by-play. It'll come in handy for the biography I'm writing about you: *Moaning into the Void: The Penelope Huff Story*."

"Cool. It can be the companion piece for the self-help book I wrote about your life, *Repulsing Women: The Jack Craig Handbook*. I've already sold the movie rights, too." I wave my hand so he can picture it in lights.

A glance in the mirror by my door confirms that I look just like I did when I sneaked into his apartment: cheeks flushed, eyes bright. And it's not just my appearance that's impacted. It's like my senses are heightened; the colors on my wall hanging are more vibrant, the fire truck siren outside is louder. He hands me a scraper-like tool, handle first. I grip it, but he doesn't let go, instead staring into my eyes with a smolder that is part annoyance, part *something.*

I swallow.

Sparring with Jack sets my pulse racing. With rage, obviously. Nothing more. I yank the tool away from him.

He lifts an eyebrow and then scoops up a second tool before aggressively stabbing one edge of it through the wall.

I follow his lead.

We work side by side, me in my yoga pants and a tank top, him in joggers and a faded green T-shirt. At one point, I try to squeeze past him but fail to calculate for the sofa at his back. My breath hitches at the slide of my thigh against his, the heat of his chest against mine. Stuck between Jack's body and the wall, I freeze and tip my chin up, my startled eyes meeting his inscrutable ones. He sets a steadying hand on my hip. I'm enveloped in the crisp, woodsy scent of pine forests and something decidedly Jack. The intense urge to press my nose against his chest and inhale is mortifying.

*You do not like him. Not physically. Not his personality. Not anything. He might not be a cheater, but he's still a dick. And he doesn't smell like a pine forest. He smells like cab air freshener.*

"Hands off me." The bite in my tone is jarring even to my own ears.

"Reflex. There is literally nothing I want less than my hands on you."

"Super! We finally agree on something." My voice is chipper, but I want to swing my stabby tool at his head.

He grits his teeth as I press on past him. "Next time, go around the sofa," he says, his voice strained.

I clamp my jaw shut and continue chipping away at the never-ending debris coming out of this wall. I catch him watching me one or two times after that, though I'm not sure if he's dissatisfied with my demo technique or if he's noticed these yoga pants are the most flattering I own. After his proclamation, it's probably not the latter.

The light beyond my curtains dims, and the streetlights come out to play, sending our shadows dancing across my apartment floor. I glance at the time on my phone and yawn reflexively when I see the hour. It's contagious, and Jack struggles to contain his own as he hands me a bag for our debris. It's a good two hours of bending and grunting before everything is cleaned up.

And then Jack walks through The Hole—no more climbing, since he managed to rip out the wall in that area all the way to the floor—to get his vacuum. I watch him methodically attack every corner where dust could possibly be hiding. He even uses the hose and all of the attachments I've misplaced for my own vacuum. There is a serene expression on his face as he works.

"How much of the vacuuming is to piss me off?" I ask.

He powers off the machine, and for a second, I think he didn't hear me. Finally, he mumbles, "About twenty percent."

Wow.

"Why?" I don't need to elaborate. We both know what I'm asking.

"I deal with a lot of messed-up shit at work."

"What do you do, anyway? Han Solo impersonator?"

"Yes. Looking for a Chewbacca. You game?" He's squeezed

a laugh out of me, and he smirks in return. "Lawyer. Have my own shingle, but do some pro bono work on the side."

A lawyer donating his time. What the shit? Does. Not. Compute.

"How about you?" he asks.

"I'm in marketing. For a software company. Evadon. You didn't hear that through the wall already?"

He ignores the jab. "Sued them on an employment matter not too long ago."

"So you were made to be my Lex Luthor. I don't follow what about your job makes you vacuum, though."

"Maybe I lied. Maybe it *is* just to piss you off."

I narrow my eyes and glare, wondering if he's really a lawyer at all.

"By the way, nice illegal fire-escape garden you have out there." He smiles like the demon spawn he is and pushes his vacuum through The Hole before dragging my sofa back against the wall behind him and letting the sheet fall into place. "Interesting no one's reported it… Yet."

"I hate you!" I call out, like a normal person would shout "good night!"

"Feeling's mutual!"

I take a half step forward, staring at that curtain. I listen to the soft scrape of his vacuum as he drags it across the room, the steady whir as he starts on the floors in his bedroom. It's a disturbingly long time before I finally walk away.

# 9

I dial into the first of today's endless series of calls on the global campaign structure.

"If I can just interject for a moment—" Anthony says, two minutes into the call. "I do not recall agreeing to that first bullet."

"It's just a preliminary punching bag, Anthony. We proposed a kit model instead of having an execution team at the global level because it gets the campaigns into market quicker. We agreed—" I start.

"We clearly did not agree if I have questions."

I mute myself and sigh gustily, closing my eyes and begging the heavens for patience. And then the memory of Jack smirking down at me after his Chewbacca crack flits through my mind.

I *should* be thinking about how to retaliate for what he did to my garden. Instead I'm imagining what he could be doing to my *other* garden. My lady garden.

No, ew. It's my deep need to be liked. Curiously, I've never felt that need with Jack, but clearly the overgrown path to not giving a shit needs a machete taking to it every now and then.

The rest of my global project calls go the way of the first: two steps forward, one somersault back. Rochelle assures me she'll talk to Sam to sort out the disagreement on methodology Anthony broached today. I give her a weak smile and thank her.

"What's going on with you?" she asks, leaning forward and folding her hands in front of her. "You look out of sorts."

"I'm fine." At Rochelle's skeptical look, a sigh flops out of me. "It's just that the stuff with Anthony is exhausting, and I'm having some issues with my neighbor." I blush profusely. "Annoying and dumb one-upmanship. I'll be fine."

"I'll talk to Sam about Anthony. The neighbor… I don't know what's going on there, but sometimes the only way to win a game is to not play. If you need to talk, I'm here. Okay?"

I nod, eyes misting. I'm a sucker for a sympathetic ear. And she's right. Retaliating for the garden is probably dumb.

Margie is filming somewhere downtown until late tonight, so I won't be seeing her, but Avery is supposed to stop in and help with the wall. I jump in a rideshare after work, too exhausted to walk but too poor to take a taxi. I need my raise.

I regret my decision when my ride pulls up and the door to the black SUV opens. A high school–aged girl with long blond hair and white skin, wearing shorts that look more like denim underwear, hops out and allows me access to the very tight third row of seating. I sigh and wriggle my way in, praying the combo of AC-vent air fresheners and being wedged in the back doesn't give me a yak attack. The teen pushes the seat back until it slams against my knees. I grab at my legs and let out an involuntary whimper.

"Did that hit you? Sorry…" the girl says.

"It's okay."

"I like your top. It's cute," she says with enough vocal fry to crisp a churro.

"Thanks," I say warily.

Her friend, a brunette with shoulder-length hair and olive skin, tears her eyes from her phone to turn and take in my top.

They whisper and giggle, and I shift my legs to the side of my squashed seat, wondering what exactly is wrong with my simple, blue, work-appropriate shirt.

In the front passenger seat, an older white woman in a neon-yellow tank keeps an eye on all of us from the mirror in the sun visor. Her thick-framed glasses match her top, and her veined hands are covered in silver rings. A young Black man in a suit leans against the window in the front row, paging through a newspaper on his iPad. He's seated next to the brunette teen who is currently showing her phone to the blonde who let me in.

Thank God for technology and its ability to provide a social shield for the antisocial. I lean over with difficulty and reach for my tote, pulling out my own phone.

Text from Margie:

I was thinking about ideas for your garden retaliation. Maybe post in some fan forums that Jack's phone number belongs to Lucas. The man will have no peace.

I'm taking Rochelle's advice and refusing to play the game. Even if I was planning to engage, I wouldn't want to screw around with Jack's phone and potentially mess with people's immigration situations.

No! That's too far. And I'm not retaliating.

The car stops. I groan internally, annoyed that we're picking up a sixth passenger.

"What is this, a clown car?" the old lady in the front says. There's always someone who makes that comment. The driver chuckles dutifully.

The blond girl's groan is not internal. She huffs it out in

frustration and opens the door, pulling back the seat. Just the sight of the heavily pregnant woman waiting to board makes it clear there is no way she can squeeze here with me. To her credit, the blond girl climbs in beside me without a word of question or complaint and pulls the seat to close us in.

The pregnant woman thanks her and heaves herself onto the seat vacated by the blonde. "Lovely. Air conditioning," she murmurs gratefully.

My phone vibrates.

Oh, you've discovered a moral line in the sand? That's interesting. I figured when you started dabbling in biological warfare the sky was the limit.

I bristle.

Har. Har. If I'm such a bad person, what does that say about you, then?

That I'm just as bad.

"What did you do? The biological warfare thing?" the blond girl next to me asks. She is unashamedly reading my text messages.

"Um, it's nothing. My neighbor," I answer. High school girls are unpredictable creatures. There is no ignoring or rebuking her. I do, however, pull my phone up and away from her view.

"You did biological warfare on a neighbor?" the brunette asks, turning around with interest.

"No, no. It was just a cat. My neighbor has allergies, so I—" I see the pregnant woman's eyebrows angle up in judgment. "I mean, I wanted to make him itchy so he'd move. But that's because he's forever doing obnoxious things to me." The need to defend my honor to this jury of my peers is as necessary as it is ridiculous.

"What did he do?" the old lady asks, angling her body to look at me from the front seat. All eyes are on me, including the driver's occasional glance through the rearview mirror.

"I mean, he plays his music super loud, the same song over and over on repeat, when I'm hungover. And he cooks the nastiest things, only on days when he knows I was out late."

The teens look invested in this reality show of mine. The brunette shakes her head in disapproval of Jack's antics. "He takes my sopping wet clothes out of the dryer and sticks his in instead, then leaves my stuff on the dusty folding table to get that mildew smell."

That wins over the pregnant woman. She looks furious on my behalf.

"There were, like, three whole days when a dog was barking nonstop in his apartment, and I convinced the super to check inside because I was sure my neighbor had abandoned a helpless animal. But it was a recording playing on his laptop. A recording of a dog barking...for three days."

The old woman looks aghast. I eye the man in the suit. Which story will win him over? "Our super painted the stair banisters black, and my neighbor removed the WET PAINT sign on his way out in the morning. I ended up getting paint all over my favorite top, and I was late getting to work because I had to run back into my apartment and change."

That does it. The suit is in.

"What have you done to him besides the cat thing?" the blond girl asks.

I recite the ways I've retaliated, skipping some—like that time I posted a fake petition from him in the lobby, asking for signatures to support turning the basement into a sex club—since

I don't want to lose my front-seat support. Before I know it, the rest of the story—about the wall, my thinking Jack was a cheater and his attempt to kiss me, him throwing my mom's words in my face, and his plans to buy my apartment—all pours out.

"You should, like, tell everyone in the building he's a sex offender," the blond girl says.

"That's probably illegal," the guy in the suit says. "Maybe have a conversation with your other neighbors and see if they've had similar issues with him?"

"Talk to the super!" the pregnant woman says. "Or the building owner."

"Tried that," I say. "Jack only tortures me. Gence, our super, says he can't do anything. I suspect he thinks I'm to blame. Plus, he's pissed at me because I opened that hole in the wall."

"How about you hide something that reeks in his apartment?" the brunette says, and I clamp my mouth shut before I can tell her what I already did with those cans of tuna fish. It occurs to me that the two high schoolers keep plotting vengeance, while the adults propose diplomacy. Do I have the emotional IQ of a teenager? The thought is sobering.

"No, I think… I think the others are right. I need to figure out how to resolve this in a mature way," I say.

"Glitter! Oh my God, *yes*. Put some in his shampoo," the blonde says.

"What would that even do?" the brunette counters. "He'd just wash it out."

"Um, *trust me*. Glitter is like an avoidant ex-boyfriend. The minute you think he's gone for good, he shows up again to wreck your shit."

"'Seek revenge and you should dig two graves,'" the driver says, piping up suddenly.

“It’s glitter,” the blonde sasses. “Not an axe murder.”

“Is this your stop?” the driver asks me, and I’m surprised to realize it is. The pregnant woman files outside, and I clumsily stumble my way out of the third row behind the blonde. Once I’m on the street, I turn to thank the car’s remaining occupants for the crowdsourced advice.

“Good luck, honey! If all else fails, just kick him in his gonads,” the bloodthirsty, bespectacled grandma calls out from the front seat.

People around me on the sidewalk gawk in confusion. The car pulls away, lively conversation trickling back to me through the open windows.

When I get upstairs, I am desperate for four things: a cup of tea, my reading socks, a new book, and someone to finish taking down the wall for me.

I settle for the cup of tea, reaching for a cabinet door under my kitchen counter to retrieve my kettle. Instead, I retrieve the door. It falls off its hinges, and I recoil, still holding onto the handle for some inexplicable reason as it glances off my big toe.

“Ow, ow, ow. *Ow*.” I hop around, pulling my foot up to hold until the worst of the pain subsides. A sneaking suspicion crawls up my spine.

The cabinet still has its screws, but the thing came out with no resistance, so they must have been loose. The cabinet next to it appears to have loose screws, too, though I don’t try to open them. In fact… All of the bottom cabinets have loosened screws.

Jack.

He didn’t loosen the top cabinets, probably because he didn’t want to kill me, just enrage me. He must have discovered the tuna fish.

I find a multitool in the junk drawer and refasten the cabinets securely. And then I seethe.

I don't hear him on the other side of the wall.

Quickly, before I lose my nerve, I run out of my apartment and down two flights to 3B. The father answers on the second knock.

"Hi!" I say, trying my best to feign cheerfulness instead of hysteria. "That project Olivia put together. Did she use all that glitter?"

3B, to my delight, has buttloads of glitter to spare.

Back in my apartment, I rummage through the cabinet under my bathroom sink until I find a squeeze bottle. I fill it part of the way with water and then try to pour the glitter, as best I can, into the bottle's narrow neck. It gets all over my sink and floor.

"Dig two graves," I mutter.

I rush across the room and flap the sheet out of my way, hurrying over to Jack's bathroom, sure he's going to erupt into the apartment at any moment. My pulse gallops.

His shampoo bottle is sitting on a toiletry organizer hanging from his shower head. I lift it out gingerly, as if the sound of it sliding against the organizer will summon him like a genie. Shampoo and conditioner in one. Good—no separate product to dilute the impact. I unscrew the cap. Almost all gone. Perfect. I squirt the contents of my brew into the bottle and shake it up. Spying his shower gel, I give it the same treatment.

If this goes the way I hope it will, Jack's going to look like he dry-humped Tinkerbell.

I set the shower gel back where I found it, wishing I could see his stupid face when he realizes what I've done.

Mission accomplished, I retreat back to The Hole to start on more demolition, my smile brighter than it's been in ages. The idea that I may be part of this problem tickles the back of my mind, whisper-soft but niggling.

The smile fades as I take in my wall. The drywall on my side has all come down, more or less, but the areas where there was lath and plaster beneath it is riddled with pockmarks. It's proven really tough to take out the plaster and rip out the narrow horizontal slats beyond. It gives me anxiety to see Mary Sue this way, but I reassure myself that it's for a greater good. Soon this wall will be down, then back up again *with soundproofing*, and then my apartment will belong to me.

We haven't started work on Jack's side yet, though stabbing through the lath has opened up little holes here and there on his side. The only sizable spot still fully open to Jack's apartment is the original Hole, although it's now a touch wider and taller. I can still spy undetected as a result—which I do the second I hear Jack's door open.

He's shrugging out of a gray suit, headed for his bedroom, when I peep past the sheet. I'm about to duck when he stops in the middle of the room and turns around, facing his kitchen but not moving other than to toss his jacket on his sofa and tug the tails of his dress shirt from his pants.

I can't see what he's doing, since I can only see the expanse of his back. I frown and shift as quietly as I can to my knees. My workouts do not allow for squatting for that length of time. This vantage point makes it so that his sofa blocks his ability to see me, but I can just see over the top.

Unbuttoning. He was unbuttoning. He wrests the white dress shirt off his shoulders and then pulls his undershirt over his head in one smooth motion. His shoulder muscles ripple as he pulls the shirt off. His smooth olive skin looks warm to the touch.

He reaches for his belt and yanks it out of its loops with a quick snap. And then his hands return to his middle, and his waistband goes slack.

My mouth goes dry.

"Hey, Jason Bourne. Your spy craft needs work," he calls out.

I drop the sheet and lean back against the wall. Shiiiiit.

"I was just wondering what smelled like tuna fish in there," I shout, my face contorted into a permanent cringe.

"Right."

There's a knock on Jack's door, and I send a silent thank-you to whomever has chosen to enter Satan's den. Until I hear a female voice.

"Jay!"

"Anna Banana, how'd you get in here?" Jack asks.

"Someone let me in. Here's your banister hideaway key. I was going to let myself in and wait for you, but I figured knocking first was probably better. This hole is ridiculous!"

I lift the sheet in time to see Jack grabbing "Anna Banana" up in a huge hug, lifting her off the ground and pressing a kiss to her cheek. The look in his eye is undeniably warm, caring. My stomach turns as he beams down at her—tall as she is, he's taller still—and he throws an arm over her shoulders, pulling her close.

"Yeah, it is. I— No! Get away from there!" he calls.

Anna has lifted the sheet and is surveying my apartment. I can't make out her features, but her hair is in a ballerina bun, and her jaw is so defined it should be sold late nights on QVC as a steak knife. She doesn't see me sitting on the floor, and I close my eyes, awaiting exposure. But it doesn't come.

I hear them talking in there, and I stew, a fine head of rage building. Until I hear her ask, "Why's it smell like…like tuna fish in here?"

I stifle a laugh. I thought he'd noticed what I'd done to his radiator, but I guess not.

Anna and Jack chat comfortably, though there's a brief

indication that there's trouble in paradise when Anna recounts an argument with her friend and Jack tries to interject with advice.

"Yeah, I don't need you to fix this, okay? Sometimes people just want you to listen. Not fix. *Listen*." Anna's voice betrays that this is a long-standing bone of contention.

"I'm not trying to fix it. I'm just saying, if I were you—"

I'm pacing and worried about drawing attention to myself by working on the wall when Avery shows up about an hour later. His hair is still damp from his after-work shower, and he's in khakis and a blue button-down. If Margie was here, she'd have told him he looked like a lumberjack accountant here to tax my wall to pieces.

"I brought you food," he says, waving a bag emblazoned with "La Taqueria," the name of my favorite Mexican restaurant.

"You're a good friend for many, many reasons, but your ability to know when my stomach is grumbling and my fridge is empty has got to be one of your best qualities. The girl who wins your heart is lucky."

He smiles and sits next to me on the sofa, handing over my veggie tacos. "Speaking of love, Mom and Dad are looking forward to seeing you on Friday."

"Me, too. They're my faves. I can't even imagine being married for that long. Fifty years!"

"Fifty-plus years with the same person sounds like heaven, if it's the right person."

I grunt, and Avery shakes his head. He knows why. My longest relationship didn't make it past one year. And that was one goddamn contentious year.

Anna Banana laughs on the other side of the wall.

"What's going on in there?" Avery gestures toward The Hole.

I just roll my eyes in answer and make a jerking-off motion.

He laughs, but then his expression goes pensive. "Hey, do you think I'm too set in my ways? Too predictable?"

"No..."

Something in my voice makes him frown.

I hurry to add, "You're just conscientious. You're like Greenwich Mean Time. People can set their clocks off of you. But that's amazing! Think about me and my neurotic people-pleasing. Or Margie and her dangerous, extroverted risk-taking. Stable is *so* much better."

"Boring, you mean."

"No, not boring. Avery Vaughn, what's going on? Where did this come from?"

He shifts uncomfortably and lifts one broad shoulder dismissively. "Had a professional disagreement today at work with a visiting colleague from another lab. It grew heated and got personal. Doctor Cassidy—er, the colleague, I mean—said... Whatever. Doesn't matter. Thanks, Pen."

"Doctor Cassidy is now my mortal enemy. He—"

"She."

"She can choke on a can of tuna."

"Why tuna?"

"Hello?" a woman's voice calls from the other side of The Hole. I tense up, but before I can warn him away, Avery pulls the sheet back.

Anna beams at him, and Avery looks momentarily shell-shocked. I mean, she's pretty, but not stop-you-in-your-tracks—Okay, okay, fine. She's pretty. And she's...Jack's sister, I realize. The girl from the photograph!

"5A, I wanted to introduce you to my sister because she won't stop approaching this hole until I do," Jack says, coming to stand at Anna's shoulder.

"Do you want to come over?" Avery asks, standing to push the sofa *I'm still sitting on* out of the way and helping Anna step through The Hole. I want to smack him with my taco.

I wipe my hands and set down my food, trying with all I've got not to let my annoyance show as I face Jack and his sister. I smile tightly. He's the dildo who once taped down the buzzer for my apartment so it'd ring nonstop. And left a box of trash in the lobby addressed to me. Who just unscrewed my cabinets. Who *wants my apartment*. I don't know why I'm relieved that this woman is his sister—it shouldn't matter. That I had any reaction at all is aggravating as shit.

"Penny," I grit out, introducing myself.

Anna clamps a hand over her mouth, her eyes crinkling with mirth.

"Holy hell. Okay. I've been dying to see The Hole, and it did not disappoint. You are a legend. *Legend*. This is *so* something I would do. And I thought there would never be anyone who got under Jay's skin more than me, but I was so wrong."

Anna pauses and tips her head to the side, quizzically. "I know you."

"Uh, we met," I say.

Jack frowns. "When would you have met? Anna's never been here."

"No, I was here the day you moved in, remember?"

Jack's lips firm, and he crosses his arms. "Oh, yeah. The Seth fight."

Anna's bubbly smile drops, and she narrows her eyes. "Stop. It was early days for us, so I don't blame—"

She stops herself, as if recalling her audience. To Avery and me she says, almost apologetically, "I came by Jack's that day because I was having trouble with my then boyfriend, *now* fiancé." She waggles the sparkler on her finger.

Avery looks crestfallen, but only to those who know him well. He removes his glasses and rubs a napkin over the lenses, his eyes downcast.

"And Jack, being an annoying big brother, had different ideas than I did on how to handle it. We ended up not talking for a while."

She looks uncomfortable with the confession and glances up at her brother.

"Yeah. My ideas involved stringing him up by his balls for cheat—"

I'm close enough that I hear Jack's muttered comments, but Anna must catch enough of them, too, since a cutting look ends them.

She turns to Avery, continuing the conversation, but Jack turns to me. "I changed, by the way."

My brows pinch, confused, but then I take in his sweats. He doesn't know how much he's changed in my mind ever since I found out he wasn't a cheater, especially with the proof of it here in my apartment, chatting up my friend. Thankfully, Jack's apartment-poaching plan helps me maintain at least some of my disdain.

"We can work on the wall if you're done eating," he says.

"Ah, your sister's here, though."

"She'll keep herself entertained." He nods at her and Avery, deep in whatever the hell they're talking about. I catch Anna asking Avery if he lives here with me, and he protests so much that it's borderline insulting.

I shrug and wolf down the last two bites of my taco, then reach for my tool and goggles.

As Jack and I work on the wall, Avery—who was supposed to help make this wall work go faster—drifts off toward the fire-escape window with Anna, the two of them sharing a laugh. Anna is a talker, and she's found the best listener on the planet.

"This sure is hard work!" I call out, mentally willing Avery to stop playing with a long vine branching in from one of my plants outside and ditch the look in his eyes whenever he gazes at Anna. He doesn't acknowledge my comment, but when he notices me watching him, he gestures to his eye, his heart, and Anna with an exaggerated look of longing. I point at the plant and slice a finger across my throat.

Avery wouldn't have appreciated this simple truth after his coworker argument, but his face is truly what you'd see in the dictionary under "reliable." In college, he played the role of mother hen to me and Margie, since the two of us seemed hell-bent on risky behavior back then.

I squirm, thinking of a twenty-one-year-old Margie barefoot on the subway after somehow losing her shoes at a club and Avery stripping off his socks to force at least some barrier between her and the floor.

He's endearingly earnest, gets his hair cut more regularly than any other person I know, and always carries a ready smile in his back pocket. His heart is as pure as they come. I've often lamented that we had a brother-sister vibe right off the bat; he's one of those people whose relationships have all been slipped on and off like comfy old sweaters. He's never a source of drama, which makes him a rare breed on the verge of extinction. And right now I'm worried that he's in a tailspin over unavailable Anna, which would be super out of character for him.

She does seem fun, I have to admit. She's a little too loud, but I've been accused of that myself. And there always seems to be a laugh rippling below her surface, ready to geyser its way out in an explosion of mirth and charm. But every now and then, when she's not talking with her wild hand gestures, when she's just listening to Avery's quiet and reassuring murmurs, a look overtakes her face, one that suggests there's a vein of sadness threaded through her core. She reaches out a hand, gripping Avery's arm as she makes a quip, and they both laugh uproariously.

I tip my head, appraising the situation. She'd be easy to mistake for a manic pixie dream girl. Or at least, that's the facade she's rolling with. Either way, Avery is ensnared.

Jack mops his brow with his forearm, and his own expression is inscrutable as he takes in Anna and Avery giggling by the window, their heads bent like coconspirators. The look on his face is gone as quickly as it appeared, and then he's bent in front of me to retrieve the dustpan at my feet, teasing my nose with the salty scent of sweaty Jack and smoky pine.

"You don't have to—" I start to say, but he ignores me and straightens, peering down at me while clutching the dustpan. I could reach out and rest a hand on his navy-T-shirt-covered chest. I could flick one of those pebbled nipples with a nail. Instead, I look up at him with an undoubtedly dumb expression and snap, "Or clean. Whatever."

He arches an eyebrow and moves away, sweeping and tidying up. I sneak glances at him, unsure what to think of him now that I know my initial prejudice was bogus.

He started out friendly. Did I drag the dickishness out of him? Or is he hiding around everyone else, and I just got to see the real him? I think back. Our exchanges have nearly always been obnoxious. But how many times did I misinterpret something he was doing or saying and lash out when maybe he wasn't planning on being a jerk? How many of our sparring matches were my doing entirely? How many of his actions have just been one-upmanship?

"Let's grab a drink!" Anna shouts, startling me out of my reverie.

Avery is on his feet so fast I'd swear he had a spring attached to his ass.

I glare at him. *We are not grabbing a drink with these people.*

"Let's do it," he says.

"No—" Jack says.

"I can't—" I start. I turn my glare on Jack. He rejected the idea even faster than I did. Rude. *I'm* rejecting *you*.

"Fine. We'll go alone," Anna pouts. She presses a kiss on Jack's forehead and calls for Avery to follow. He does, with ludicrous speed.

"Heel, doggy," I whisper as Avery hugs me goodbye.

He whispers back without a pause, "I'm in love be happy for me call you later love you."

They're out my door a second later.

"Ugh."

"What's your problem?" Jack mutters.

"Besides the pleasure of your company? How about the never-ending saga that is taking down this impossible wall?"

"Well, we could take it down faster, but I'm trying to avoid kicking around lead-paint dust. Or asbestos."

*"What?"*

Jack smirks.

"Why aren't we wearing masks or something?" I cry.

"Relax. There's no lead paint or asbestos. Probably." He ducks the pillow I wing at him and laughs out loud. Then he retrieves his trusty vacuum and begins methodically tackling every inch of my apartment.

"Was the thing you said about vacuuming real? About your job?"

"Yes."

"Why? How does it help?"

"The people I work with just want to make their lives better, want to stay here to do it. Sometimes the system isn't fair to them. The vacuuming... Cleaning soothes me, I guess. I like ticking one item off my to-do list. When I was sixteen, my dad fell ill and a lot rested on me, so I needed an outlet."

The confession feels real. It thaws something inside me, releasing a twinge of contrition and embarrassment along with other things I don't want to examine. I cover it by wiping my end tables with a rag. I'd always assumed his vacuuming was about me. How vain. And here I've been trying to strip him of something that brought order to the chaos of his day. I can understand the impulse.

"I garden for the same reason. It's a de-stressor."

"De-stressor because some dick is vacuuming all the time?"

"Not everything is about you," I say, smiling up at him. "Besides, it's you soundtracking my life that's more annoying than anything."

"So I shouldn't play 'In Dust We Trust' tonight on repeat?" he asks.

"I don't know that song."

"Chemical Brothers. It doesn't really have lyrics, though. Maybe 'Dusty' by Soundgarden—"

"Play whatever crap you want. I bought noise-canceling headphones, baby."

"I play my music for myself, 5A, not to torment you."

I make a sound that expresses my disbelief about his claim and bend to pick up a nonexistent speck on my rug.

He wraps the cord around the vacuum and squints at me, clearly debating something.

I'm shocked by what it is.

"I was thinking of ordering pizza."

My eyes are Jupiter-large. I remain silent.

So does he.

"If you want to join."

I want to say no. This feels dangerous. This is uncharted territory. This is… My stomach rumbles. Two tiny tacos clearly weren't enough for dinner.

# 11

In the end, Jack vacuums in his apartment and then orders the pie—plain cheese and not some weird fruit-and-meat-combo topping, blessedly—and I run off to shower before it arrives. I don't examine too closely why I put on makeup at ten o'clock at night. But when I take the seat Jack indicates, I swear I detect the intoxicating scents of woodsy cologne and mint mouthwash.

We eat. Jack puts on the Mets game and swears at it every once in a while.

"Why do you own a 'Penis Colossus' magnet?"

"Won a contest."

I swallow my laugh and shake my head.

"A gift from one of my cruder friends. Oh, come on," he says, the TV snaring his attention. "Catch the ball."

"You're one of those? A couch coach?" I rip my pizza into bite-size pieces. "Boring."

"I'd be torn up by your disdain if you ate pizza like a normal person," he says. "The hell is that?"

"It's called 'if I had a knife and fork handy, I'd use them instead, but I'm too lazy to get up.'"

He stares at me, absolutely horrified.

"Really? You, Mr. Vacuum-To-Control-The-Chaos himself,

can't understand not trusting a floppy piece of anarchy leaking sauce and cheese and oil everywhere?"

He grabs a slice purposefully, folds it in half, and takes a bite, staring at me all the while. To prove a point.

I've never been so gratified to see a renegade chunk of sauce fall on someone in all my life.

"Ah, shit." He looks adorable, pressed in the far corner of his sofa, grimacing over his shirt. I feel a sudden, appalling wave of affection for him.

There have been times during the game when I was sure he was watching me, when I could almost feel the heat of his gaze moving from my cheeks to my throat, to...other places. And the feeling—that tense, heavy awareness in the air—made me want to crawl into his lap, biting and licking my way up his neck, to tease him into a response. But right now... I honestly just want to give him a hug, to curl myself into his side while he grumbles at the game.

Instead, I say nothing and pick apart my slice with a smile.

"Gloating is not attractive."

"I'm not trying to attract you. I leave that to the poor, unfortunate Yelenas of the world." I'm midway through her name when the pizza tastes sour in my mouth.

"Why do you still remember my appraiser's name?"

"Mind like a steel trap."

"Left to rust in the elements?"

"Hmm."

"More like jealous and too chicken to throw your hat in the ring. I get it."

My next bite of pizza goes down hard. I don't like whatever this is. If he's going to live next door to me, I can't indulge whatever this banter is leading toward. I don't last with guys. I'd be squatting where I eat. A fling next door, *forever*, if he buys his place. It hits me like a blow to the stomach. Which, in turn, annoys me. *You were wrong about him cheating, but that doesn't mean he's not a dickhead.*

*Who you kind of goaded into being a dickhead, but still.*

There's the sound of fumbling in the hall, and then Avery and Anna burst through.

"Goddamn it, the people in this building need to stop letting people without keys in," Jack announces.

"This is cozy," Avery says, smiling broadly at me. His inebriated surprise at my pizza détente with Jack is evident. He's probably proud of me for growing up or something.

"I'm sleeping over," Anna tells Jack.

"Me, too," Avery says to me.

Jack sighs and gathers up the pizza box as Avery and Anna retrieve the last two slices. "I guess I'm sleeping on the sofa."

"Me, too." Avery gives me a silly smile.

I raise an eyebrow at Avery. "You're tipsy on a weeknight."

"I'm not."

"Your ears are red."

His face grows red, too. To glimpse Avery, disheveled and handsome, minus his glasses, one wouldn't be blamed for thinking he'd drop some toxic frat-guy cockiness on them. Instead, he's down-to-earth and capable of blushes in front of a girl he likes. I stand and link arms with him, leading him toward The Hole.

Before I step through, I turn toward Jack. "Thanks for the pizza. Unless it was poisoned."

"Too painless," Jack says from the kitchen, without looking up. But there is humor in his voice.

Meh. This is all *Pirate Duke*'s fault. I can't do anything of an R-rated nature with him—I don't *want* to do anything of an R-rated nature with him. But I do not want to be at war with my neighbor forever, either. How do I make this truce long-standing while maintaining a healthy distance?

As I ready my sofa for Avery, I pin him down with a look. "What is going on with you?" I whisper. "She's engaged. This isn't like you."

"I'm boring," he whispers back. "I've been boring and playing it safe my whole life. I want a fiftieth anniversary someday, too, Penny! Maybe I'm not on my way there because I'm always doing what this thinks is right instead of this." He points to his head and then his heart. And then he pushes the sofa up against the wall right under The Hole and flops onto it before I've had a chance to fully tuck in the sheet.

I frown. If this were literally any other guy, I'd think he was thinking with neither of those things. But this is Avery.

"Besides," he says, yanking the blanket from my hands, "I'm not trying to sleep with her. I just like being around her. Okay?"

"Whatever you say, Drunky McDrunk." Who am I to judge, when my own personal life is such a disaster?

It isn't until I'm back in my bed that a very bad thought surfaces, and I launch myself into an upright position. The glitter. There will be no truce if he uses that shampoo or shower gel.

Avery is snoring on the couch. Though we've still got the sheet up to cover The Hole, there are places along my pockmarked disaster of a wall that have punctured through to Jack's side, so I can tell that his apartment is as shadowed as my own. I tiptoe to the sofa and step up on it, straddling Avery's prone body and gingerly pulling back the sheet.

Jack is sleeping on his side on his own sofa. The moonlight

reveals his hard jaw, sleep-slackened in slumber. He didn't shave, so it's covered in stubble, and his arm is flung over his eyes. He doesn't look like a human disco ball…yet.

I stare at his shadowed bathroom door longingly. There's no way for me to leapfrog over him and get to his shampoo.

He didn't shower earlier, so he's definitely going to in the morning. But maybe he'll reach for a fresh bottle, since there was so little shampoo in there to begin with?

Maybe.

I'm awoken by my own mumbling, and by a strange feeling. I open my eyes and stifle a scream, but it emerges anyway as a choked squeak.

The morning light in my bedroom is faint, trickling in through the open space between my curtains. Jack is leaning over me on the bed, his face looming close, his hands braced on the mattress, bracketing my shoulders. His skin…sparkles.

I draw the covers up over my nose to hide the hysterical, fear-tinged laughter bubbling up within me. *Please be a dream.* "I know what you are," I whisper, visions of an iridescent teen vampire flashing through my mind.

Jack leans closer until his face is just two inches from my own. I can feel his breath on my face, minty with the promise of retribution. And then he opens his mouth.

"Sleep with one eye open."

My eyes widen, and he straightens, walking out of my room without another glance.

I worry my lip and sidestep a woman walking her dog, my sneakers eating up the space between my apartment and my office without me noticing.

That was *stupid*. Glitter allowed for no plausible deniability. I should've gone with something subtle. Like the bird-crap-fire-escape thing he did. *Or you could've bowed out of the game, like Rochelle said.*

Whatever! It's done now.

I'm so wrapped up in my thoughts that I almost miss the big white trucks unloading lighting equipment and a whole lot more in front of my building.

I text Margie, and she responds right away: she's on my floor. With all that's been going on, I'd forgotten the show was filming in my office sometime this week. I rush to the elevator, eager to tell her about the development with the apartment, but when the doors open, I crash into someone.

We both drop our bags, bend to retrieve them, and speak at once.

"Sorry! I—" we say. I look up and freeze.

"Hey! The Femme Fatale. Don't tell me… Penelope?"

Holy shit. Lucas Webb is squatting right across from me in the lobby of my office building, doing super-sexy things like gathering up his stuff and mine, remembering my name, and breathing. He extends a hand to help me up.

I cling to him, staring into his eyes—they're not arrogant or cocky like Jack's. They're calm. Self-assured. I'm faintly conscious of whispers crescendoing around the lobby as people realize who I'm holding hands with. I release my grip on Lucas and brush the wrinkles out of my skirt. "Oh, hi. Yes. That me." *Words. Hard.*

"You visiting us on set? We're up on twelve."

I shake my head. "I'm actually here to work. I work here. In building. On twelve." *Stop. Babbling.*

He smiles. It's a kind smile, but one that lets me know he's used to starstruck idiots. "I've got to run an errand. Nice seeing you again."

We say goodbye, and then he's gone, hefting his bag over his shoulder as he walks across the lobby, his slacks absolutely loving his ass. Necks break as people double-take in his wake, and I float up to the twelfth floor on a cloud pulled by cherubs.

I beeline to the boardroom, where I spy Margie's statuesque frame, but Rochelle heads me off. "Penny, hi! What are you doing Friday night?"

"I—"

"There's a dinner after my staff meeting, and I'd love for you to come. Sam Greenfield is going to be there."

"I'm supposed to be at an anniversary party—"

"Maybe you can go after. Listen, this is very important. You can casually work in how the global project's going, and that'll grease the wheels when we ask for that raise for you."

"Or we could just ask for it and point to all my hard work even before this…"

Rochelle's expression does not change. Not a flicker of an eyelash. Not a twitch of the lip.

"Okay, let me know where to be and when."

Margie is perched on the edge of my desk when I get to my cubicle. She snorts when I tell her about the exchange. "Pushover. You can't miss Mr. and Mrs. Vaughn's anniversary party. Avery rented out the hangar deck of the *Intrepid*."

"I know. His dad served on the ship during Vietnam. Look, I'll be there. Just… Just a little late, maybe? Ugh, I need the money to get my mortgage, Margie."

Margie shrugs and sucks in her lips. "Okay..."

I decide to change the subject. "I saw Lucas downstairs. He remembered my name."

"He asked about you, actually. And I don't know why you're surprised, Pen. You're hot, and you spit a joke about murder at him the first time you met him. Not to mention his thing for redheads. But you're not doing the go-nowhere thing anymore, right? That's why we've had a two-year dry spell?"

"Yes..."

She tugs on a strand of my hair.

"I did a stupid thing," I confess.

"Besides agreeing to go to a dinner on the same night as your best friend's party for his parents?"

"Stop making me feel shitty! No. Not that."

"You slept with Lucas? *How?* You haven't seen him since that day you came to set."

"No, not— No. I did a thing. To Jack."

"You slept with *him*?"

"No! I didn't fucking sleep with anyone."

Heads peep over cubicles.

I lower my voice. "I didn't sleep with anyone. This is worse."

I explain about the glitter, and after I finish, Margie stares at me a bunch. I can't tell if she's questioning our long friendship or if she's delighted. Goddamn poker-faced actor.

"Say something!"

"I'll help you brainstorm. He's going to hit back. You hit back harder." Someone calls her name. "My scene. Got to go."

She stands, and I roll my chair toward her, wrapping my arms around her middle. "This is why we're friends."

She snorts. "This is why we're going to end up in prison."

# 12

Jack sparkles like a Vegas showgirl. His face, his forearms, his hands, even the clothes he changed into after work, are coated in way more metallic glitter than I anticipated would make it to six thirty in the evening. His dark hair is positively diamond-dusted. And that hair is rumpled, as if he's been self-consciously running his fingers through it all day. He looks irked. He looks like a fancy chandelier. He looks…

Kind of fucking hot. I lick my lips and pretend to peruse the three tools laid out on the floor. What the shit was that errant thought? I push it away and debate whether or not to play "Golden" by Harry Styles on repeat for him tonight. The look in his eye suggests that I should maybe save that one for another time.

He rolls up his shirtsleeves and rips down a torso-size strip of what looks like rigid wire mesh. "I had court today." His tone is deceptively mild.

"Cool."

"No. Not cool when you're advocating for someone to stay out of prison and you look like you're about to whisper, 'This is the skin of a killer, Bella.'"

*Excuse me, what now?* He knows *Twilight*?

"Oh. You're not…the world's most dangerous predator." I

feel bad. Did I cross a line? I think I crossed a line. "Why *are* you covered in glitter?" I try.

His steely gaze cuts me off.

I will bluster through this. "You aren't blameless, you know. More broken toes and birdseed in my future?"

"You don't want to know what's in your future."

"Oooh, so scary, M. Night Shyamalan."

My door buzzer's high-pitched whine scares the shit out of me, but it heralds Margie and Avery's arrival, a welcome buffer. I wait for them at the top of the stairs.

I hear Margie giving Avery advice regarding his troublesome colleague before they round the landing and come into view.

"Sexual tension," she says.

"God no," Avery mumbles.

"We both know you don't do casual, so you—"

"Not true. There was Tabitha."

Margie purses lips as red as her tight crimson pants and continues her climb. "Oh my God, Avery Vaughn. A one-night stand you ended up dating for two-and-a-half years is not casual. You don't do casual, so you need to get yourself into a relationship. It'll remove the pressure of your office crush."

"Rivalry. Not crush."

"Sure. Hey, Pen. He retaliate yet?"

"No," I whisper. "He's doing the whole psychological warfare thing right now, making me anticipate it. Why are you dressed like you're gonna sell crêpes along the Seine later?" I take in her black-and-white-striped top, jaunty black cap, and the very-appropriate-for-construction six-inch heels. Avery has, of course, showered after work, but his pullover is wrinkled, and he looks uncharacteristically disheveled.

"Why are you wearing a push-up bra to work on a wall?"

I fold my arms protectively across my tight and tattered purple college tee, a lie on the tip of my tongue that I just can't dislodge.

Margie exchanges a look with Avery. "No comment," he says, holding his hands up as he slips by me into my apartment. But then he quickly adds, "Except to say that those are not usually hanging out so close to your chin."

"Help me take down this wall already."

Avery and Jack exchange pleasantries. Avery spares a single amused glance at Jack's razzle-dazzle but remains mercifully silent about it.

Margie is not so tactful.

"Shine bright like a diamond," she murmurs when she sees him, a laugh in her voice. Jack gives her a withering look.

Following Jack's lead, Avery dives in to help with the wall. Margie carts bags of garbage down to the basement, clomping down the hall in a borrowed pair of my sneakers. I never once look in Jack's direction, which is immensely satisfying. The work is going so well that I have to force myself not to remark on it for fear of jinxing it.

And then it's jinxed.

Jack's buzzer goes off, and a few minutes later, Anna floats into his apartment like a pollen-riddled spring breeze. "Why do you look like you're about to take me to Neverland, Jay?" she asks.

Margie's laugh rings out all the way from the stairwell.

"Anna, hi!" Avery calls out.

She beams when she sees him and scuttles over to my side of The Wall to reach him. She pauses when Margie reenters the apartment, recognizing her immediately. "Oh. My. Lord. You're Linkletter! I watch you! My fiancé Seth loves your show."

Margie arches an eyebrow. "Not you, though?"

"No! I do, too, totally—"

"I'm teasing. I'm Margie. Nice to meet you. You must be Jack's sister." She glances at Avery. "Heard too much about you."

She says it so quickly and casually that only I pick up on the "too." She loves doing that—subverting what people expect to hear. I once heard her tell some difficult restaurant patrons at the place she worked in college, "Fuck you very much," with a tremendous smile and wave as they were leaving. The guests thanked her and smiled back. She said it was a test of her acting.

"Are you going to be at Avery's parents' anniversary party?" Anna asks Margie. I frown. Why is she talking about the party? At Margie's nod, Anna claps a hand over her mouth. "Seth is going to be so upset he can't come."

"He's not coming?" Avery's expression is as far removed from disappointed as it can possibly be. He must realize that because he quickly blanks his face.

I, on the other hand, want to stamp my feet and scream. My worlds are colliding. What the hell is Avery doing inviting the enemy's sister? I mean, Jack feels less like the enemy than before, but he's plotting my downfall! That's enemy-adjacent, at least. I drop down heavily onto the sofa.

"No, he has a thing with his old high school buddies. But Jack agreed to be my plus-one."

All eyes snap to Jack, but he only has eyes for me. The demon is smiling. *Smiling.* He knows I'm irked. I don't want him there. I may throw him off the ship. Launch a cannon or whatever at his head. He doesn't want to be around me and defunct museum weapons.

"Can't wait to come and celebrate true love," Jack says, bending to rest his arms on the back of my couch just behind me.

And then he reaches deep into my cushions and pulls out *Pirate Duke*. Motherfucker. "We're all just looking for a love like this, amirite?" He stands tall and waves the book and its tawdry cover around.

My cheeks are fire hose–worthy, heated to a fever. The woman on the cover has a shredded pirate's flag draped strategically over her privates, one leg wrapped around the Pirate Duke's waist as she arches toward him. The eponymous hero looms over her on a bed, his lips pressed against her cleavage.

Jack opens the book. "'One hand palms the globe of her—' Holy shit, this is explicit."

I leap up, round the sofa, and snatch it from his hands with a glare. Margie's snort barely penetrates my anger. "The only thing you're in love with is yourself," I hiss.

Jack's gaze flits over the room, taking in the fact that everyone else is pretending to be engaged in conversation. He leans forward, perilously close, and pins me with his gaze. "Do you blame me? There's so much to love."

I roll my eyes, and his stupid fucking dimple brackets appear. "This wasn't your punishment, by the way," he says in a purr that slides up my spine.

I stretch up, until there's nothing but a breath between my lips and his. I see his gaze slip, a darting look as I tug my bottom lip in with my teeth. "Will I enjoy this punishment?" I whisper.

His eyes widen and dilate, gray overtaken by black. His chest expands with his surprised breath. "That can be arranged."

My pulse is a battering ram. I've been sucked into a spell of my own making. Almost. I straighten and force out a laugh. "I could die of cringe for you. Guys are so predictable."

He opens his mouth to respond, but I run to a far corner of the wall. And then I slowly release a breath, trying to get *Pirate*

*Duke* and Jack out of my head.

Once again, it ends up being Jack and me doing actual demolition and Avery, Anna, and Margie sitting around my apartment. Avery and Anna laugh and swap stories, while Margie looks up every once in a while from a script she's reading to interject amusing anecdotes of her own. It would be a fun and lively environment if I didn't want this flipping wall to come down and be put up again as soon as humanly possible.

It isn't until the food arrives that I realize those bumps on a log ordered takeout. Jack and I reluctantly halt our work to eat. Jack sits on my sofa with Anna, my coffee table pressed up close to their knees. Avery sits in the armchair closest to where Anna is seated. He offered the chair to me like the gentleman he is, but I declined in favor of sitting cross-legged on the floor. He and Jack talk about work.

Margie is in my other armchair, legs draped over the seat's arm, her back against the other. She's still reading.

I throw a veggie egg roll and a scallion pancake down my gullet and chase it with a bite of chicken and broccoli. "Latest episode?" I ask her, leaning over to look at the script.

"No. It's for a movie. Lucas is in talks to star as the lead, and there's a part for me, he thinks."

"That's awesome!"

"Yeah. It's violent, though. But kind of camp. I'm into it." She hands it to me to review.

The meal feels too cozy. Like a real group of friends hanging on a Thursday night. This is unacceptable. I shake off the trance, force myself to stop watching Jack's mouth move as he speaks, and stand, tossing the script onto my kitchen counter.

"What's that for?" Anna asks, pointing to the jumbo package of Command hooks I'm opening.

In response, I set up a little ladder Gence loaned me and attach a hook to the ceiling, right near our dividing wall. "The wall is filled with lots of holes going straight through now. Temporary fix." I ascend and descend a bunch, attaching a handful of hooks at regular intervals. And then I go to the hall closet and retrieve the discount grommeted curtains I bought.

I attach the first set of curtains to the hooks and survey my work. Though The Hole is still the only place to get through to either apartment, the holes everywhere, even covered with mesh and bits of plaster in some cases, left me feeling too exposed. The black curtains now hang floor to ceiling and do an admirable job of blocking the entire wall.

Avery stands to help me set up the other hooks and curtains, and that seems to be the cue for the others to begin cleaning up for the evening.

When all is swept and vacuumed, I set our plates in the sink. Jack's shirtsleeves are rolled up to his elbows, and he rinses and puts dishes into my dishwasher without a word. The kitchen feels even smaller than its tiny size warrants, the air heavier than it's ever felt. Jack brushes behind me to grab paper towels, and it's the equilibrium-upsetting equivalent of being electrocuted. He shows no sign of having the same reaction.

Anna interrupts our flow, insisting to her brother that the night is young and a bar is in order. Again.

Avery, of course, enthusiastically agrees and insists we go, even though going out on a work night is so unlike him, let alone twice in one week. Margie turns to me and shrugs, grabbing her purse with a raised eyebrow. I pretend to be engrossed in the button panel on my dishwasher, privately hoping they'll have all gone away by the time I look up. That is, until Jack presses the wash cycle button and towels off his hands, leveling me a flat look.

"Complicated, finding that wash button."

"Yeah, I'm not going out, sorry. Work tomorrow, and I'm on point for a big project. And then I have an after-work thing before the party," I announce.

To Avery, I offer an apologetic look. "I just have to put in an appearance at a dinner, and then I'm coming straight to your party. Okay? I tried to say no, but Rochelle wouldn't let me. I couldn't avoid it."

Avery looks momentarily aggrieved, but it's gone in a blink. "All right. Just don't miss my speech? I have to point to you in the crowd for a joke at the beginning."

"Of course!"

Everyone files out of my apartment, and I move to make way for Jack to do the same. But he stops next to me, as if this was a party we hosted jointly and we're seeing our guests out. Alarm streaks through me. He was supposed to leave!

He smiles and then dips down to whisper, his lips brushing the sensitive skin of my earlobe, "Nice try, coward. I'm not going anywhere."

# 13

Despite my curtain barrier and the pots and pans I quietly set up around The Hole as a rudimentary alarm system, I still had a sleepless night. Part of it was a sexy-time dream I can't quite recall the details of, but that definitely had something to do with *The Pirate Duke*. And the remainder of my restlessness was down to dread. How nuclear will Jack's retaliation be? On a scale of nocturnal haircut to something way worse, how bad are we talking? And even more disturbing—like the sloughing of an old skin—my dislike for Jack is being shed with alarming ease.

Work was a long trudge through a Siberian wasteland of competing PowerPoints. Anthony decided to present a framework that proposed a completely divergent path to the one we've been working toward, which necessitated a response pitch deck—the dueling banjos of the corporate world. Exhausting. I ran it to Rochelle, who grabbed Sam Greenfield in a conference room to get his input.

"Sit tight while I talk to him."

"I just have to run and get ready for this thing I have tonight, actually—"

"It'll be five minutes."

It has been forty-five minutes. I linger near the kitchen,

where half-closed blinds obscure my view into the glass-walled conference room. I can only see the back of Sam's head, but Rochelle's tight smile is clear. She's not thrilled. Shit.

I look at my phone for the time. Come *on*. Rochelle and Sam are going straight to the restaurant from work. I can't show up to Avery's in my black work pants and top. I need to take a cab home, and even then I'm not going to have a ton of time to get ready.

Hallelujah! Rochelle is emerging from the conference room. I rush over.

"Oh, Penny! I thought you'd have gone by now," she says.

Only the briefest flicker of eyelashes betrays my irritation at the discovery that I could've left without issue after being told to sit tight. Or anger at myself that I stayed where I was told like a good little doggy.

"Sam and I were talking about other things, too, but all he said about your slides was, 'It'll be interesting to hear both of them present their views.'"

So President Snow wants us to Hunger Games it out. Which means a further delay in getting my raise—and thus my fucking mortgage.

"Oh. Okay."

"I'm sure it'll be fine. Don't worry. Want to ride over to the restaurant together?"

"I have to get ready for my friend's anniversary party for his parents, actually. Going to run home real quick and then meet you at the restaurant, if that's okay? But I can't stay really long…"

"Okay. We'll play it by ear. See you in a bit."

The cab, of course, hits every red light on the way home, and I've practically bitten a hole through my cheek from nerves by the time it pulls up in front of my building. I race inside and rush through a shower, cursing Anthony's name for leaving me with no time to wash my hair.

I set a new record for getting ready, and as I sweep my Ri-Ri Red lipstick over my mouth, I'm pleased to note that my lips look plump and my teeth are sans red stains. I fluff a copper-and-sunset curl. One-day-dirty hair isn't hurting things, either.

A pair of black strappy heels, a little spaghetti-strapped red dress that makes my waist look tiny and my boobs look fantastic, and I'm ready to leave. I grab a shawl for my cleavage, since it's not exactly work appropriate, and step into the hall just as Jack bounds up the final step, back from the gym by his appearance. He looks flummoxed for a moment, his eyes darting over to me.

"What?" I snap. "Thinking of England?"

He raises an eyebrow and inserts his key into his lock. I am *not* still smarting over his comment from a million years ago. But now he definitely thinks I am.

"Thinking of something," I think I hear him mumble.

My cheeks are on fire. I've outed myself—and sounded like a shrew in the process. I notice he's addressed most of his glitter problem, though here and there I catch the twinkle of an errant fleck on his neck or cheek or leg. Pair that with a fresh haircut and he looks… Ugh. He looks good.

"With normal people, I wouldn't have to say this, but with you… Can you not show up to Avery's party wearing *that*?" I gesture to his ripped workout shirt and shorts.

"Stop trying to change me, 5A. I need someone to want me for *me*." He gives me another once-over with a strange smirk, raising the specter of my cursed *Pirate Duke* thoughts, and closes his door with a bang.

"Oh, Penny is just the best there is, Sam!" Rochelle says. "I mean, you give her anything at all, and she gets it done."

"Too bad we can't clone you," Sam Greenfield says with a laugh from across the table.

I'm a corporate hostage. Avery's party has started, and I'm missing cocktail hour. There is no graceful way to exit this table, and Rochelle whispered in my ear earlier that this was laying some track in getting my raise.

My lips stretch over my teeth in what I hope is a smile. "I think I saw that movie once."

Sam Greenfield throws his head back and laughs too hard. The tip of his nose is red. His cheeks are red. He's half in the bag. It's shocking to see someone so corporate get so hammered. There are some folks even higher up than Sam here, and a number of his peers. I wonder if they'd make me a VP if I slurred over my appetizer, too.

"Rochelle, I really need to get going—" I whisper.

"You saw Penny's slides," Rochelle says. "I think we can agree that Anthony's idea was interesting, but Penny's is going to get us to market faster."

"Yes, yes. I think it's the way to go. But why don't you tell me about your thoughts, Penny?" Sam says, taking a long draught from his glass.

Rochelle smiles encouragingly. I want my raise, and I want the project to move along, but I need to get to the party right now.

"So, when we were thinking about the best way to centralize things, gain economies of scale, etcetera, the only hiccup was that it would deprive the regions of applying their individual expertise as far as their audiences and target accounts," I begin.

## VIOLET LUMANI

The *Intrepid* is a giant warship-turned-museum, steel gray and imposing and docked on Manhattan's West Side. It's lit up gorgeously right now, its hull towering above me. I rush into the Welcome Center building on the dock alongside the ship, toss my bag onto the security desk to be inspected, and pass through the metal detector.

The elevator takes too long, so I race up the metal stairs. My panting nearly drowns out the music drifting from the event space as I cross the covered metal gangway to the hangar deck. Under normal circumstances, I'd be more interested in my surroundings, but I've been to more than one event on this ship, and I am late as shit.

The cavernous space is filled with round tables festooned with white tablecloths and beautiful green topiaries punctuated with flowers and strung with fairy lights. Though the room's walls and ceiling are dark, vivid blue and purple spotlights cast cool light throughout the room.

It looks magical and beautiful, and my heart melts a little that Avery handpicked all the details for his parents' special day. There are easily four hundred people here, most seated and laughing. A band plays light jazz at the head of the dance floor in the center of the room.

"Where the hell have you been?" Margie demands, storming over to me looking like an Amazonian princess in her gold, figure-hugging dress. "Why didn't you answer your texts? We're sitting at the table next to the Vaughns." She points. "Go say congrats to them, beg Avery for his forgiveness, and come sit and scarf your salmon. Speeches are coming up."

I release a relieved breath. I was hoping Avery would save the speeches for after the meal.

I shuffle along behind her as fast as my heels will allow, and the Vaughns leap from their seats as I approach, their welcoming smiles bringing tears to my eyes. They're the best sort of people, always proud to know you, no matter what you're doing. Forever radiating kindness. The kind of people who work the soup kitchen on Thanksgiving each year, and they bought me a beautiful locket with pictures of Avery and Margie for my graduation. They're the bar that every other relationship on the planet aspires to reach.

"I'm so sorry I'm late. You look gorgeous, Mrs. V.," I say, bending to kiss her soft cheek. And it's true. With her short-cropped white hair, twinkly green eyes behind gold-wire-framed glasses, and papery skin, she usually looks like she belongs on the wrapper for cookie dough—a Food Network domestic goddess. But right now, in her red sequined gown with its smart little jacket, her hair styled in an elegant swoop, and her green eyes lined, she looks exquisite. It's not just what she's wearing, either—it's the look in her eyes when her husband comes within her field of vision. Mr. Vaughn looks stately, his dark brown skin glowing with good health. He's carrying his black suit on his frame as well as he must have carried the uniform he wore on this very ship when he served. I kiss him on the cheek, too. "Congratulations to you both. You're an inspiration to all us single folk."

"We try our best." Mrs. V. laughs.

"Mr. V., you're going to have to show me how to fire one of those mean guns on deck."

"What do you need a weapon for when you've got that wit of yours? I always tell Avery you're the funny one."

There's a flat look in Avery's eyes that makes me quail inside.

I circle the table to hug him and whisper, "I'm so sorry. I got stuck at that work thing, and I'm the worst, and I'm sorry. I'm here for the speech, though."

His lips firm, and then the flat look fades. He sighs. "It's okay. We figured you wouldn't be able to say no to your boss and leave in time. You're too weirdly scared about getting fired. Just thought you'd break away earlier than this. Margie bet me twenty bucks you wouldn't be here until after dessert. I wrote you out of the speech when you weren't here after the salads were served."

My heart gives a little kick, but I have no one to blame but myself. "Change it back! I'm here now!"

"Maybe. Let me walk you to your table before your food gets cold." He pushes back from his seat and presses a hand against the small of my back to lead me away. I say my goodbyes-for-now and turn to my table.

Where the devil is staring back at me.

"You sat him with me?" I hiss at Avery. Jack's cleaned up nicely in a sleek navy suit, and he looks fucking sexy with his hair styled into his mildly mussed look. It makes me want to run my fingers through those locks, though I'm not sure if I want to smooth it or mess it up some more. A roguish smile plays about his mouth, bringing out a hint of dimples. He knows I'm distressed to see him. He's thrilled I'm distressed. Or maybe this is where he plans to stage his next attack?

Avery levels a patient look at me. "You don't get to complain."

"You like his engaged sister. The Avery I know would never pursue someone who was taken."

"The Avery you know is boring and sexless. And he isn't going to find that," he gestures behind him at his parents, "by being that way."

"I didn't say that!"

"And I'm *not* pursuing, I told you. I'm being a friend. Her fiancé is a loser. He's like an emotionally immature Punxsutawney Phil, showing up every year to play with her emotions and destroy her before disappearing back into his hole. But yes, I like her, I'm not going to deny it. I'd swoop in if the fiancé wasn't there."

"You're walking me to my table just to have an excuse to be near her, aren't you?"

"Yes."

I point a finger close to his face. "You are honest, but also terrible. Honest and terrible."

I march ahead of him and take the seat next to Margie. I'm surprised to see that Lucas is sitting next to her, chatting pleasantly with Anna and graciously ignoring all the surrounding gawkers. I take my seat and greet La on my right with a hug, then nod politely at the others at our table before steeling myself for Jack.

"You look hot. Doesn't she look hot?" Anna says by way of greeting.

"She's all right," Jack says, his voice a low rumble. I feel my cheeks flame, like it's the most elaborate compliment I've ever received. I refuse to make eye contact.

"Breathtaking," Lucas says with a grin. He adjusts a French cuff on his tailored shirt and winks at me.

Avery, who after over a decade of platonic friendship probably thinks seltzer water has more sex appeal than I do, nods his head vigorously, staring at Anna's profile. "Totally."

"Lucas, you have a thing for redheads, don't you?" Margie says. "Especially this redhead."

*Shit stirrer.* By her own account, Webb found me pretty. That's it. But I see her eyes dart toward Jack. She's trying to press a button that doesn't exist. And even if it did, I wouldn't want it pressed. I kick her under the table, and she jerks.

"Why are you kicking me?" she demands, as I slink down in my chair.

Lucas laughs. "Yes and yes. Though I need you all to excuse me for a moment. Gotta take this call." He stands and saunters away, holding his phone to his ear.

"Lucas Webb? Oh. My. God. I would die. *Die*," Anna moans.

Jack tosses his napkin onto the table. "How sweet. Are we going to be talking about 5A's love life all night?"

To my mind, Lucas was being sweet and polite since Margie put him on the spot, but Jack's annoyance is delightful.

"No, actually. I'm about to go give my speech. If you all will excuse me." Avery straightens his slate-checked jacket and matching vest. It's a three-piece suit that fits him like baby oil, and Anna notices.

"Pound this." Margie hands me a glass of red wine.

"I'm not going to pound at the Vaughns' party!"

Margie shrugs. "I tried."

"What does that mean?" I ask, but before she can answer, Avery's speech begins.

"Ladies and gentlemen, if I can have your attention for just a sec. Thanks," Avery says into the microphone the band leader hands him. "I'll be brief, I promise. I just wanted to thank you all for coming here tonight to celebrate two really incredible people: my mom and dad."

The room bursts into applause, and Avery tucks his mic under his arm to join in, clapping as Mr. and Mrs. Vaughn wave.

Mr. Vaughn kisses his wife's hand.

"You know, I'm lucky. I grew up knowing true love existed. I saw it every single day at home. But it's one thing to see it with your own eyes, and it's another to find it for yourself. I figured if

I could *articulate* what love was, I'd be able to find it. So I asked around. My friend Penny once told me that love, *romantic* love anyway, was like three-day-old sushi."

There are chuckles, and I blush to my roots as Avery winds his way to my side. Now I know why Margie wanted me to chug the wine. Jack is watching me with interest from across the table.

"Hey, Pen, why was that again?" Avery holds the mic to my mouth, and I want to yank him by his tie so he hits his face on the table.

I clear my throat. "Because it *looks* pretty good. But you don't go for it because you know you'll end up sick in the end."

The chuckles intensify into laughter, reverberating through the ship's ballroom. I will Avery to feel my wrath as he rests his hand on my shoulder. Jack's expression is inscrutable.

"You told me to put the joke back in, and I did," Avery murmurs. "Thanks, Penny," he says louder. "And then my friend Margie once said—"

"Nope. Don't rope me into this," Margie says loudly, and the laughter seems to shake the rafters.

La reaches across me to clink glasses with Margie. Lucas rejoins the table just in time to catch the exchange.

"Okay, okay. So, like I said, I asked around, searching for the words, but my friends weren't any help. And I made my own observations, but I kept falling short of what I had seen with my folks. Then, one day, I went back home to visit and saw my parents through the window. They were laughing with each other, and my definition of love finally found me: Love is...laughing together. Love is talking, communicating. Love is offering up your whole heart on a platter but getting a replacement from the person you're offering it up to. Love is wanting the best for the other person while still loving yourself. Love is growing together.

Love doesn't mean you'll never hurt each other, but it does mean apologizing if you do, because love is fighting, but never to win. Love is moving through this world and this life in quiet caring, together."

Avery moves closer to where his parents are seated. "Mom, Dad..."

A waitress rushes over with a champagne flute.

Avery accepts it with a grin and lifts it up, his dark hair reflecting the blue stage lights overhead. "May we all be so blessed as to eat the three-day-old sushi you two did." There are cheers and then tinkling glasses.

I wipe at my eyes roughly. This is a unicorn of a relationship. Most people get donkeys.

"You're such a romantic," Jack says.

I glare back. "Sushi."

Mr. Vaughn sweeps Mrs. V. into his arms. The music kicks up, a slow dance, "Lady in Red." The couple dances alone for a spell before pairs trickle onto the floor around them.

"Avery told me his parents almost broke up a few years into their marriage," Anna says. "Seeing them right now, you'd hardly believe it."

I freeze, my water glass suspended en route to my mouth. "No," I say, more to deny it than to disagree.

"No, full-on, they were ready for dee-vorce. But Mr. Vaughn told Avery they started talking it through, made a commitment to work on it together, take it day by day. Said love is a trust fall you take, each and every day. And here they are, how many years later?"

She sighs, a contemplative look on her face. "But... It shouldn't be *too* hard, right? Like, sometimes pulling the plug is the right thing to do. Even if it wasn't for the Vaughns?"

La says something that makes Margie, Jack, and Anna laugh, but I don't hear anything beyond the rushing in my ears. The Vaughn relationship has been…almost tainted in some way, at least to me. Like breaking a porcelain figurine and gluing it back together. I'll always know the cracks were there in their relationship. It's childish, I know. But if the two best and most loving people in the world had a hard time being in a relationship with one another—if the most stable and loving relationship I've ever seen is a daily trust fall—what does that leave for me?

I wolf down my food, though I ate at the dinner that made me late for this one. But second dinner helps me concentrate on something other than the depressing understanding that I'll always be alone. This lady in red is feeling very blah. I feel eyes on me and pause to give Jack a dirty look for watching me eat like a starved kitten. He raises his eyebrows innocently.

Lucas stands suddenly and reaches out a hand to me. "Want to dance?"

My shock is enough to shake me out of my melancholy. I allow him to pull me up, refusing to even glance in Jack's direction as Lucas leads me out onto the dance floor. It's another slow dance. "Lover" by Taylor Swift. With his hand on my waist, we sway, and then Lucas twirls me, surprising a laugh out of me before he pulls me close again.

"Everyone's staring at us," I say.

"You get used to it."

"Like fish in an aquarium?"

He smiles. "Speaking of, while you were eating your salmon, all I could think about was this time I had to eat *so* many bites for this show we were filming. Take after take. And afterward I was unbelievably sick and my agent was terrified I had mercury poisoning."

"So I reminded you of a time you got sick. That tracks."

He tosses his head back and laughs out loud. I grin. And it becomes clear that Lucas isn't only good looks, charisma, and acting ability. He's also kind. The conversation shifts to his membership of the board of a charity that feeds hungry children.

I'm about to ask him something when a deep voice behind me asks, "Can I cut in?"

*Oh for fuck's sake.* Lucas stops moving and releases his hold on me, stepping back with a slight nod at Jack. My heart hammers.

"Sure," I say. "I don't want to hog Lucas if you want a turn with him." Jack ignores me, and I reluctantly accept his outstretched hand with a sigh. The slide of his palm against the thin material of my dress at my waist burns.

Ed Sheeran's "Thinking Out Loud" starts to play. We move together, a slow sway, neither of us saying anything for a long while.

"What are you plotting?" I finally ask, staring up at him. His grip on my hand tightens, and the one at my waist pulls me in closer.

"You don't want to know."

My pulse leaps. "You have a speck of glitter near your left eye."

He snorts. "Pretty sure I've got some on my taint, too. You're diabolical."

"Got the idea from some teenagers in a rideshare. They're evil."

"Teenagers? Surprised it was only glitter, then."

"They came up with worse. I didn't want to maim you. So why'd you cut in?"

"Hard to think of England with you way out here."

"Seriously."

"Seriously? Okay. I—"

A lively song comes on, and the cheer from the crowd cuts off whatever he was about to say. I fight my disappointment as more people crowd the dance floor and Jack leads me back to our table. The atmosphere is becoming more and more festive.

La, to my surprise, tries to pull Margie and myself onto the floor, is rebuffed, and proceeds to go it alone, busting out moves I've not seen since the one-month period, senior year of college, when Margie and I convinced ourselves we were into clubbing.

"Holy shit. Look at her go," I say. "The confidence to dance like no one is watching in front of four hundred people."

"She's something," Margie says. She's watching her in wonder. La has drawn a crowd and generated a kind of small dance-off. But she's taken the time to bring a wallflower of a little boy into the circle. We can hear his laughter from here.

"I want to be the kind of person that sparks spontaneous dance-offs. Why aren't I that kind of person?" I say.

"Because you have no rhythm, and people would think you were choking if you tried. Come to the bar with me?" Margie demands. I wipe my lips with my napkin and shove back from my seat, eager to escape Jack.

"Oh, are you going to the bar? I'm coming, too," Anna cries. "Come on, Jack!"

I swallow my groan. Lucas stands to join us as well. Avery sees us on the move and rushes over as if tethered to Anna's ass.

"One big nerd herd, moving en masse to the bar," I mutter.

# 14

The bar closest to us is mobbed, so we move to the one across the gigantic room. Lucas is waylaid by a group of fans and waves us on. The walk is an awkward one for me and a boisterous one for Margie, Anna, and Avery. Anna and Avery have linked arms and are singing show tunes at the top of their tipsy lungs. Margie is loudly monologuing Shakespeare. But in the Shakespeare in the Park production of *Love's Labour's Lost* last summer, I distinctly remember her playing Rosaline, not Berowne.

"And I, forsooth, in love! I, that have been love's whip..." she shouts, throwing her arms wide.

Jack and I trail them, silent, making me feel like we're chaperones at the world's shittiest high school dance—a commentary on the people we're babysitting, not the quality of the Vaughns' party.

"Your sister is nice," I say. I have no idea how to have a normal conversation with the man next to me.

"Thanks. She likes you...all, too." His voice is strained, as if he also isn't exactly sure how to speak to me without spitting fire. He almost looks perplexed by my cordial tone. He shoves his hands into his pockets and tips his gaze up to the ceiling. "I wanted to apologize for using the stuff I heard through the wall against you when we argued. It was out of character for me. I'm going to do my best not to hear whatever is going on over there at your place until the wall is fixed. Okay?"

I falter a little, an uncertain feeling swirling inside me, and he grabs for my elbow to steady me. "Wh—what made you think of that?" Is he remembering that he almost kissed me right before making that out-of-character-for-him comment?

"It's been weighing on me," he responds. "That's why I cut in."

"Oh. I— I'm sorry about your—" I gesture to his entire body. "The glitter thing. It… It pains me to say it, but you wouldn't have looked terrible as a *Twilight* extra."

He gives a little laugh.

Quickly, before I can change my mind, I say, "I have a proposition for you."

"Does it involve thinking of England? What would Lucas Webb say?"

I suppress a chuckle. If the structural integrity of my hate collapses, the majority will landslide away. I need a new footing with Jack. He isn't a cheating asshole, but that doesn't mean he isn't a good, old-fashioned, regular asshole. One who, admittedly, can be amusing sometimes.

"You'll never know. You promised not to listen through the wall," I purr. He makes a face I can't read, and before he can lob an insult or worse, apologize again, I rush to add, "No. It does not involve thinking of England. I was wondering if maybe we could call a truce and try to be…normal neighbors?"

"We'd have to be normal people first, and I'm thinking that at least half of this equation doesn't qualify."

"Don't talk about yourself like that. Being normal is a stretch goal you might just reach if you try hard enough."

"Okay. So what do normal neighbors do? Want me to come by and ask to borrow a cup of sugar?"

"If you need it, sure."

"Eggs?"

"Okay..."

"Flour?"

"I'm not a damn supermarket."

Jack's laugh gusts out of him, the comet's tail of a loud breath. It's gratifying. "I was going to bake you a neighborly cake. Your loss."

We've reached the second bar, and this one is jammed up as well. Jack takes our orders, and Anna insists we bring our drinks out to the tables set up on the open-air deck a few steps away. Margie excuses herself from our group, still tipsy and looking positively incandescent, saying that La has returned to the table and she doesn't want to leave her there by herself.

"Wait—" I protest.

"I'll be right back with La."

The outdoor terrace off the hangar deck is intimate, and Avery's decorators have softened the severity of the warship with greenery and faux creeping ivy. It's quieter out here, and cheerful, with crisscrossing strings of vintage-style Edison bulbs hanging over our heads. There are a half dozen rectangular bar-height tables and chairs set up, tablecloths and little covered candleholders on top. Manhattan's brilliantly lit buildings are reflected back up at us from the dark, glittering Hudson River beyond the deck.

Jack takes the seat across from me at the table, next to his sister. Avery, of course, grabs the seat to Anna's right. That leaves a seat open for Margie, whenever she reappears, on my left. Avery and Anna huddle together, lost in conversation once more, their backs practically turned to me and Jack.

I tap my fingers on the table and look around, pretending to be utterly engrossed in every detail of a waterfront I've seen more than a few times. Anything to avoid looking up at Jack's candlelit face.

"Three dots, three dashes, three dots. You're tapping out S.O.S.," Jack says.

My fingers freeze mid-tap. "Why do you know that?"

"Boy Scout. Why do you? Dad a scout leader?"

I shrug. "Mr. Vaughn taught me." I take a grateful sip of my wine to pull the rip cord on the current conversational thread. *What the hell is keeping Margie? She dragged me to the bar and abandoned me.*

Jack runs his finger around the rim of his glass of scotch, over and over, in a nearly hypnotic way. He glances up just as I'm looking at him. Our gazes lock. "So what other hidden talents do you have?"

"You tell me. You've heard enough of my conversations to figure me out." I break off our eye contact.

"I told you I'll try not to listen anymore… And like you haven't overhead anything about me through those walls in all these months? Come on. I'm not exactly mouse-pissing-into-cotton-quiet on the other side of that wall. What have you heard?"

I sniff. "Your vacuum?" I say it to be funny, but he looks vaguely uneasy, maybe because it's a violation of our truce. So I hurry to add, "What else? Besides your penchant for sad coffeehouse music… I may have overheard you making snarky remarks at your TV when the Mets are playing. They suck, by the way."

"Sometimes. Hence the snarky remarks. What else?"

"You've got a friend named Mark who is obsessed with WWII."

"Moth. His real name's Luis, but his nickname is Moth

because he's always drawn to the worst, most dramatic situations. He's the reason I have this scar. Tried to jump in and save him during a fight and took on friendly fire." He points to a scar on his chin, and I lean in to see the pale white line. We're nearly nose to nose when he dips his chin down, and for a second we stay there, sharing the same breath. His lashes are longer than I realized. And his eyes are heat and mist and… I scramble back in my seat.

"This is scintillating stuff," he drawls, then rests his elbow on the table, his cheek on his palm.

I mimic his pose, noting that his gaze dips to my cleavage and away, lightning quick. "Okay. Here's something interesting. You're going through a drought."

"How do you figure?"

"Never brought a woman home in all the time we've been neighbors."

"Maybe I stay at their apartments. Or maybe it's because I'm scared my neighbor will chase them away." My eyes stray to Anna and then guiltily move back to Jack. "What is it?"

"About that… I have a confession to make," I say.

"Undying love."

"You're back to deluding yourself again. Am I going to have to duck another failed almost-kiss?"

His lips curve in a roguish way. A *Pirate Duke* smile. A silent songbird in my chest flutters its wings. "Nah. I don't know if you've noticed, but I've got a giant ego." He smiles at my over-the-top scoff. "But it's a giant, *fragile* ego. House of cards. Can't handle any more rejection. Guess you'll have to be the one putting the moves on me."

"You should totally hold your breath for it," I say, and smile in response to his laugh, despite myself.

"So. Your confession...?"

"My confession. I..." I lower my voice so that Anna can't hear and lean forward.

Jack leans forward to meet me, his eyes a galaxy of reflected colors in the candlelight.

"When I met your sister the first time, she ran out of your place crying about a cheating asshole. I thought that asshole was you."

"That's why you thought I cheated on the 'girl in the picture'? Well, you usually think the worst of me, so that's nothing new."

"Yeah, but that was the *first* terrible thought I ever had of you. And it kind of set the tone."

"Oh! So that's our Big Bang, huh? I'd wondered—not that I gave you a ton of thought, of course—but I thought it was very suspect how you went from 'welcome to the neighborhood' to brawling alley cat. Guess that explains it." He takes a sip of his drink, then stares down at the amber liquid. "And now that you know you were wrong?"

"Well, since then, I've compiled a dossier's worth of things I dislike about you, so." I bite back a smile, but Jack's flies free, dimples and all. He has a rakish mouth. A mouth I realize I'm staring at when he clears his throat and sits back.

"Only a dossier? I rented out a warehouse full of filing cabinets for you. Real *Indiana Jones* shit."

"In preparation for everything I'll discover on you? Or have you been compiling things you dislike about yourself for me? I hope it's the latter. Huge time-saver. Your flaws are glaring, but there are just *so* many."

He takes a sip of his drink and dips his head with a grin in recognition of the point I've scored on him. "So normal neighbors," he says.

"Yes. Although I'm not sure if I know how to be normal around you. Antagonizing you is like muscle memory at this point."

"Hypothetically, do normal neighbors"—he waggles his eyebrows, so I know I'm going to hate whatever comes next—"retaliate for being glitter-bombed?"

"No. Hypothetically, if one neighbor were responsible for a glittering, it was probably because the other neighbor had done something to deserve, if not that specific reaction, then definitely *some* reaction. But if, say, the glitter recipient were to retaliate for being glittered, it would just perpetuate a nuclear arms race that couldn't possibly end well. Probably best for the glitteree to graciously admit that they were party to the lead-up to their glittering. Hypothetically."

"You're a loon."

"Never had a complaint before." I've had so many complaints. "Don't expect to have complaints in the future, either."

A smile pulls at the corner of his lips. It's very distracting. "The future? In general? Or did you have someone in mind?"

"Hmmm." I take a sip of my wine and innocently raise my eyebrows with a shrug.

He laughs. "The suspense. All right, truce. And how is this… Even though I'd still love to buy your apartment and my own, I'll help you put up the wall."

"*You?* Fix the wall?"

"That look is insulting. La said she would only be able to set you guys up and then you'd be on the hook for the rest of the work. This way you don't need her. I know what I'm doing. Unlike your 'crew.' And Gence said he can do the finishing work for a small fee. He's got a side business. I'll even split the cost of materials with you."

"Why would you do that for me?"

"Because it's what a normal neighbor would do?"

He holds up his glass, and I clink to cement the agreement. I can't repress my grin at the thought of putting up a wall *with Jack* to replace the one I broke *because of Jack*.

His eyes drop to my lips, then languidly climb to meet mine again. I feel my pulse speed. This corner of the terrace feels private, insulated. Intimate. And Jack's mysterious little half grin feels like a fishing lure. My knee bumps his, slides. I'm not confident it was accidental.

"Wonder where Margie is?" I ask, trying desperately to break this spell, whatever it is. He's always got a certain swagger to him. But right now it feels magnetic. Like he knows what he's got, and I'm lying to myself if I pretend I don't want it. Fucking *Pirate Duke*. He's back to rubbing his finger along the rim of his glass.

"Want help looking?"

He says it softly, the way you'd call a stray over to your car. I swallow hard, nod wordlessly. He turns to Avery and Anna, leaning over to say something in Avery's ear.

Avery looks at me questioningly, but I pretend not to notice.

Jack reaches for my hand.

I slide mine into his firm, callused grip, and we make our way into the party, working through the crowd.

I stare up at his profile, heart beating in my ears, as he scans faces in the blue-tinted light.

I don't know what I'm doing.

We move through the hangar deck, from one end to the other, but Margie is nowhere to be seen. At the very end of the hall, stairs to the right lead up to the flight deck or down to the bathrooms. Jack leads us down, the pulse at my wrist hammering like a tell-tale heart between our palms. The stairwell opens to a small alcove, painted black, with three doors leading to unisex bathrooms. There's a curtained closet to our right that appears to function as storage for additional chairs.

No Margie.

*You weren't looking for Margie. You want Jack Craig.*

Jack turns to me and says, "Maybe she left."

"Hmm."

He sees something in my face that has his eyes darkening and his hand tightening on mine. He tugs me closer.

I lift my chin, our eyes lock. My bottom lip feels heavy. I wet it with my tongue.

His lids twitch; he's registered the invite. He leans in.

*Oh fuck yes, kiss me, you menace.*

"Your move, 5A." His breath is warm against my ear, his cheek a sensuous, rough slide against my soft one. Goose bumps erupt along my arms. His face is so close. I can smell the whiskey on his breath, the fresh sandalwood-and-pine-spiced scent of his skin. Why did I think he smelled like car air freshener? There's an electric current between us, licking and looping. I can't think. I'm pure instinct. Ravenous.

I take his face in my hands and pull him down to me, open-mouthed, tongue seeking.

He moans deep in his throat and yanks me close, his teeth biting my lip gently, his tongue dipping in and out, tangling with mine. We're dueling, vying for dominance. His hand grabs my silk-clad ass, and the other wraps more tightly around my back. He lifts. I feel my red dress ride up, feel his hot hand on the back of my thigh, holding me against him.

He maneuvers us behind the curtain into the storage area and presses me against the wall without once removing his lips from mine. My hands are in his hair, then dig into his shoulders.

He nips at my lobe and eases me down off his thigh until I'm standing, clinging to him.

"You are so fucking hot." His mouth is now on my neck, sucking, biting, kissing. "Sometimes I think you were put in my life to torture me." His head knocks a few errant wooden hangers on a coat rack, and he swears. I laugh, then gasp when he growls, running the hand that isn't on my ass over my throat, skimming slowly, turning my face.

He drops his head to my neck, running the wet underside of his bottom lip up my throat until he reaches my ear. And then he hooks his finger under the crimson spaghetti strap of my dress and leans back, staring at me with heavily lidded eyes, asking permission. I give a barely-there nod, and he tugs the strap down slowly. His breathing is as ragged as mine. The fabric hugging my chest goes slack on one side, held up by my pearled nipple.

*Things never last. Even the Vaughns barely made it work. What's the point of trying? You might be living next door to him for a long time. What are you doing?*

He pulls at the other strap, dragging it down my shoulder. He lowers his mouth to the neckline.

*Milk keeps longer than guys around you.* My mother's words echo in my ear. They're a bucket of ice water. I push off him and turn my back, sorting myself out.

"What's wrong?"

I sip the heated air in the coat check and turn, trying to control the riotous prison break of upset within.

"This isn't right. I don't even *like* you. I'm not interested in you," I say. *I don't mean it*, I want to shout when I see his expression.

Jack, with his hair disheveled from my ministrations and his hard-on unavoidably evident, looks like he's been smacked in the face with a bat. He recovers quickly. "No kidding? I mean, I apologize if I read your tongue down my throat the wrong way."

"I'm sorry. This was a mistake."

He laughs. It's not a kind sound. "This isn't what 'normal neighbors' do in your book? Too bad." He crosses his arms. "For the record, though, I don't like you much, either."

I turn and push through the curtain, needing to get away before I cry.

Jack follows in a rush, his brows drawn together.

At that moment, Margie and La emerge from one of the bathrooms, arms around each other's waists, looking a bit disheveled themselves. Margie and I take in each other's appearance in shock, and the next thing I know I'm on my back, my dignity has fled, and my ankle is on fire.

"Her heel. Oh no," La cries.

"Pen! Are you okay?" Margie rushes over, helping me sit up. I see my strappy shoe, heel wedged in a grate. Fucking warships and heels don't mix. Mortification and pain fight for supremacy within me, but the former is the best medicine.

"I'm fine," I say, shifting. "Just tweaked my ankle."

Margie reaches for my foot.

"Ow, ow, ow, fuck," I hiss.

The next moment, I'm hefted up in Jack's arms as he strides up the stairs.

"I made you tea," Jack says stiffly, setting a mug on my coffee table. I silently curse the fates who thought it'd be *hilarious* to have the guy who was kissing my cleavage twelve hours ago—the guy I sprained my ankle fleeing—also be the guy who insists on taking care of me as I convalesce. "There's a cookie, too. Don't eat lying down. And use the ice pack I gave you."

For a moment, I ignore him, continuing to lie there on my sofa with my foot propped on a pillow, my head resting on several others Jack fluffed for me, and the ice pack in question on the coffee table. Then, like a recalcitrant teen, I pick up the cookie and purposefully take a bite while lying down. I regret it instantly when the crumbs fall down my throat and spark a coughing fit. I sit up. A sip of scalding hot tea to sort out my choking proves an equally bad idea.

The taste of the cookie barely registers as I take another, safer bite, and it's not because I've burned my tongue. I can't get the taste of Jack out of my mouth or comprehend the colossal lapse in judgment that led to us pawing each other in the storage closet at Avery's party.

Still, there is a stirring of something as I relive bits of last night. I curse Jack again. *I don't like you much, either.* Ugh. I can't even dissect the situation properly without getting hot and bothered. Where is my self-respect?

Wait a second.

"Are these… Are these my hi-hat cookies?" I shout around a mouthful. "Where did you get them?" I glare over my sofa back into Jack's apartment. He's in the kitchen, drying a glass.

"Gence gave them to me."

Oh. My. God.

My phone rings, saving Jack's life. I answer via my earbuds, reluctantly tugging the ice pack onto my ankle.

"How are you feeling?" Margie asks.

"Better than before. Rest, ice, compress, elevate for the weekend. ER doc said it should be good after two to three days." I gingerly rotate my ankle and wince. "I hope I don't need to take Monday off."

"You need to stay off it or it could get worse. Work can wait."

I grunt.

"I'm serious. Pen, I know your dad's shit left you and your mom in a rough place financially, but you're not in that place anymore. You've got savings, you've got us, your job isn't going to fire you if you take a beat to just recup—"

"Yeah, can we just change the subject?"

"Fine. Here's a subject change. I can't believe you chose to go to the ER with him over me."

"I did no such thing." I scowl. Jack isn't visible in his apartment, which means he's in his bathroom or bedroom. "He's the last person I wanted to go with. But the party wasn't over, Avery couldn't leave, and I couldn't have you abandon Avery just because I don't know how to walk."

"How is Florence Nightingale?" she asks. "No more sucking face?"

"How's La doing?" I ask in return. She chuckles. In a whisper, I add, "We barely said a word to each other the entire time we were at the ER. And this morning it's been the same, but he won't leave me alone. He keeps trying to take care of me."

"What a monster. Avery is driving his parents back to Massachusetts, and I have this photo shoot right now, but after—"

"Don't stress it. I'll survive." I glare at the remains of *my* cookie. "Florence may need you to take care of him when I'm done with him, though."

Yesterday was awkward, but at least I had ankle pain to distract me from Jack's cool and reserved, albeit aggressive, caretaking. Today, though I still can't flee properly, my ankle is feeling loads better. I've been robbed of my shield.

This morning he showed up with an obscenely large first aid kit, one no single male should own, and insisted on rewrapping my ankle with an elastic compression bandage. The memory of his hand gently cradling my foot has me scowling.

"Are you hungry?" Jack asks from his side of The Hole, his face an aloof mask. I want to pinch him, just to see something other than that blank stare when I'm still so unsettled.

"No." I am a ravenous liar. "But I do want you to tell me why you're being nice to me," I snap.

"Masochist, clearly." At my look, he runs a hand across the back of his neck. "I feel responsible. If we hadn't been—"

My face overheats.

"If we hadn't made that *mistake*," he says, and there's a bite to that word, "then you never would've gotten hurt. So it's the least I can do. And taking care of people has always been my thing, so— What are you doing? Why are you standing?" He hurries over.

"I need to use the restroom. I have a crutch over there, you don't need to—" Before I can finish, I'm scooped up and carried to the bathroom. I am wearing shorts and a tank top, and the feel of his skin on mine is disorienting.

Because I know he'll be waiting for me when I'm done, I have to run the faucet to overcome my stage fright. I set aside the novelty of knowing that someone, a male who isn't Avery, will most definitely be there to lend his assistance.

I reemerge, hopping out like a wounded little flamingo, and Jack again hefts me up like nothing. He carries me back to the sofa, and I rest my hand against his chest, resisting the urge to let it roam over his firm pecs. He deposits me gently on the sofa in front of the lunch tray he evidently prepared while I was in the bathroom.

"Eat. It's spaghetti Bolognese."

"You made— Why aren't you eating?"

"I already ate," he answers simply.

These short, clipped exchanges are torture. "Listen, I don't dislike you. Not entirely," I say. I grab at his hand.

He stares down at me.

I release him.

"You should write for Hallmark." Jack moves through The Hole to his apartment. I take a bite of his surprisingly good cooking and mentally note that his moving casually through both our places feels somehow intimate. He returns with a tablet and drops down into one of my chairs.

"What are you doing?"

He glances at me. "Reading."

I shift and swallow my bite. "Here?"

"Would you rather I leave?"

"No, no. I just— What are you reading?" I ask. Something flickers in his eyes, and it's a break from the impassive reactions I've gotten from him the past two days. He looks alert, amused, something else. I double down, eager to draw him out, though I'm not sure why. "Is it good?"

"It's...very good," he drawls, the words sliding against me and caressing places they shouldn't. "Educational."

I lick my lips, eyes wide. The energy in the room has shifted. What the hell is he reading?

"I can read you a little," he offers.

"You want to read to me?" I repeat blankly.

"Mm-hmmm. Do you want me to read to you, Penelope?"

I find myself nodding.

"This part I liked a lot: *The air between them crackled like an angry sky. Ronan's hand slid up her leg to her damp core. His teeth captured one perfect pebbled nipple. Bethany arched with a cry.*

*'I thought you didn't want me anymore,' she panted.*

*He lifted his head from her breast. 'Shall I show you how much I don't want you?' He slid a finger into the heat of her—*"

My mouth has gone dry, because all the moisture my body contains has pooled somewhere else. What. The. Fuck.

"That's— Why are you reading *The Pirate Duke's Pleasure*?"

He shrugs, his smoky eyes piercing. "I was curious after reading that bit the other day. Wanted to see what you...like."

Oh my God.

His gaze drops back to his device and he continues, "*She fisted her hand in his thick hair. 'Charles!' she whimpered. She pushed his head down, slowly, past her taut belly. 'I need your mouth...here.'*"

Am I pregnant? I'm pretty sure I'm pregnant. I'm pretty sure every person capable of childbearing in a three-block radius is pregnant.

"Are you okay?" he asks.

I stand suddenly.

He stands with me, setting his tablet down. "What do you need?"

"I need…" *To break a headboard with you.* "I need to take a shower," I gasp. A cold one.

He reaches for me, about to hoist me up to shepherd me to the bathroom.

I still his attempt and bring my mouth a whisper's breadth away from his.

He freezes for a moment, and then his lips move over mine, and we kiss in earnest as his arms come around me. He eases me down to the sofa, his delicious weight settling against me.

I arch, rubbing against him, and he groans into my mouth. His tongue tangles with mine, and then he's kissing my neck, sucking, biting.

"Wreck me. You fucking wreck me," he says.

He pivots so that now he's on his back and I'm on top. I straddle him and lean forward. He pulls my tank top down, exposing me, and his tongue is on me, licking, flicking. His mouth moves to my other breast, and his hands are on my ass. I reach between us to run my hand over the hard ridge of him, leaning back.

"Ow!" I cry. "My ankle!"

Jack freezes. "Shit, let me—"

He sets me down gently next to him on the sofa. "I'm sorry. We shouldn't be doing this when you're injured."

Sanity washes back over me in a wave of cold clarity. He breathes heavily, then stands abruptly and walks away.

# 16

Margie's apartment, a rent-controlled gift from the grandmother who helped raise her, overlooks the American Museum of Natural History. We often like to walk through the museum together, especially when one of us is in crisis. There's something about strolling through a building that's been around since 1877 that screams, "Your problems are not permanent."

But right now, the museum is long closed. It's dark out.

And I have a hickey. I pull out my phone to look at my reflection again and rub the unsightly thing like it'll scrub off. It looks ridiculous. *Ridiculous. And hot? No.*

My nipples tighten. Disgusted with myself, I leap up from Margie's sofa and throw my apartment keys and some essentials into my purse. I reach for my crutch.

"Where are you going?" Margie asks, looking up from her magazine.

"Back to my apartment. I'm not going to hide."

"It's late!"

"It's not even eleven."

Margie purses her lips thoughtfully but doesn't say anything for a bit. She's already made her feelings about Jack known, in addition to all the things she'd like to do to him for "hurting" me.

"And don't do anything stupid to Jack. Okay?" I say.

She looks mildly guilty. "I may have signed him up for a shit ton of MLM websites. Oh, and about a dozen used car dealership listservs. If he isn't already being spammed by skin care and dietary supplement offers, he will be."

"Margie! I *told* you I was the one who kissed him and then lobbed an insult at his head when I made him stop. And where did you even get his email address?"

"Internet search? His work email was public... Okay, okay! I screwed up. It's just that I don't like seeing you upset. It'll probably all go to spam anyway. Bright side? Maybe he's in the market for a gently used Camry."

When I'm just about ready to go, Margie follows me to the door to lock up. She holds me by the shoulders, peering seriously into my eyes. "If you need me—doesn't matter what time—you call me, and I'll come to your place. Okay?"

I smile and hug her impulsively. "Love you. Won't come to that. And I wouldn't dream of tearing you away from La tonight."

Margie's blush is the first I've ever seen on her. "Take the day off of work tomorrow and rest, fool."

A little while later, I climb the stairs to my place, moving slowly with my crutch. Jack's muffled voice drifts into the hall.

*You should knock*, I think. And say...what, exactly? *Sorry I made out with you—twice—and then bailed, but you gave me a hickey bigger than the one I got from Johnny Song at Melissa Ortega's quinceañera in ninth grade, so we're even?*

I try to let myself into my apartment quietly, tiptoeing through the dark as best I can with a crutch to my room. My phone vibrates. My stomach clenches at the sound, though Jack's TV is loud enough to drown out the vibration. I hear a second voice in there with Jack. It sounds like Moth is over. I look at my phone. Mom.

Honey, I haven't heard from you.
Are you okay?

A thought takes hold. I switch apps, confirming that I don't have much time, and then rush to dress by the light of my cell phone. It isn't even five minutes later that I'm back out the door, on my way to the Port Authority.

The sea is inescapable in Stone Harbor, New Jersey, surrounded as it is by the Atlantic's brackish waters. But it's also in the air, clinging to your skin and leaving you looking exceptionally dewy if you're in town longer than a heartbeat. The salt clings to your hair, making for some killer body, but the wind renders it impossible to run a brush through. The town has a special smell, especially at night when the sunbaked buildings cool.

I breathe it in—all that briny evening air—and am flooded with memories as I walk from the bus depot to Mom's place. Walks to school. Prom. Waitressing at Gretchen's Diner and making fun of the shoobies—our nickname for tourists—with the other locals. Walking with Mom on the beach after Dad left us. Holding her as she cried.

I was eternally grateful for our home's proximity to the bus depot when I discovered the wonders of...anyplace other than here. Mom's house is up ahead, faintly lit by a streetlight and the single bulb at the top of her steps that she always leaves on at night. The house is a small, nondescript beige box set atop pilings to elevate it against flooding. The white lattice skirting the entire perimeter obscures those pilings. It's a handful of blocks from the beachfront McMansions owned by summer vacationers, but, except for that shared sea air, it might as well be on a different planet.

I pause in front of the house with a sigh and look around me. A cricket sings in the distance. Mom's door opens. She was watching for me.

"Hi." I climb the stairs with my crutch. I notice with a spasm of sadness that my mom's face is more lined than the last time I saw her, her cheeks drooping into jowls I don't remember being there before. Her hair has a bunch more white. Or maybe I'm just imagining it since I'm long overdue for a visit. "It's three thirty in the morning. I told you to just leave the key under the mat."

Mom accepts my hug and presses her cheek to mine. "I couldn't sleep knowing you were on the road. No good comes of being out this late. You should've waited until morning to come. You could have just taken the early bus out and—"

"Lemme hop in my DeLorean real quick and right that wrong. See you in the a.m."

"Smart mouth. Come in." She chuckles and bustles me toward my childhood living room, forever festooned in the Christmas colors and holiday decor she loves. A crystal vase of plum calla lilies, the exact size of the hole in my bank account this month, rests on an end table. I take a seat. The room feels smaller to me, like walking the halls of your old elementary school. I shift on the sofa. It shouldn't feel that way. Sure, I've seen Mom sporadically, but mainly in neutral territory—restaurants, a cousin's house. It's been a good year since I've been back in this house.

"It *is* nice to have you here. I just wish you'd waited until morning is all. Here's some tea. No caffeine, so you can sleep. I just made a pot." Mom hands me a cup and sits across from me with her own cup.

"Thanks." I play with the sugar cube on the pink-and-white saucer.

"What's wrong?"

"Nothing. Just tired."

"You took the day off of work. And you came all the way out here in the middle of the night for nothing? Are you here to stay? It's about time, honestly."

"No, I'm not."

"Tomorrow we can go look at that house—"

"Mom, I really don't want to move back."

"But why?" She sets her cup down, the browbeating to come evidently requiring all her faculties.

"Because..." I don't want to have this conversation, and especially not in the middle of the night, but I know her. She won't leave it be.

"This place has always felt like one of those flowers that blooms once a year for a few hours before its petals clamp up tight until the next time. And I always felt trapped inside."

There's a melancholy to seasonal towns like this, full of life and activity during the summer and then a shuttered ghost town of eight hundred residents the rest of the year.

"I don't want to feel that way ever again. Maybe that's why I love New York so much. All that activity, all the time."

"Oh my God, you got a therapist, didn't you? Why? You want to pay someone to listen to you talk about how I've ruined your life? Someone to tell you how awful your mother was, even though I'm the one who stayed? Who struggled to provide a life for you after your father left us?"

"I'm not seeing a therapist, Mom. I— God, this place. It's

time to get to bed. It's really late."

"You say you hate this place, but you don't. If you did, why did you come?"

"Because I love *you*, and wanted to see you." I set my cup down with a clatter and run my hands over my face. "And because I kissed a guy. And then I hurt his feelings. It's a long story... And I'm kind of terrified of what happens next."

I peep up at her through my fingers. "Do I apologize to him? Tell him what I really think of him? Why can't I just let things happen like a normal person?"

"Did you ever stop to think you're feeling that way because you're subconsciously avoiding settling down and putting down roots in New York? You wanted to come home. You came home." She stands, gathers up my cup, and then pauses, a sympathetic and knowing expression on her face. "We can talk more in the morning. Your bed is made up. I freshened the sheets."

By the time I pad into the kitchen, my crutch barely needed, it's clear my mom has been up for hours. She's curled the ends of her short hair so that it dusts the underside of her chin, and she's wearing a pair of khaki shorts and a tee from Joe Canal's Discount Liquor.

It took me way too long to fall asleep, my mind busy replaying my last interaction with Jack over and over. But at least I'm dressed for the day. The digital clock atop the stove still calls me a lazy bitch, though: quarter past noon.

Mom turns and hands me a plate. "I made you some eggs. I only had wheat bread."

"Wheat is good, thanks. Do you have coffee?" I pull a fork out of a drawer and lean against the counter, picking at my plate.

"Tea is better for you. Hot water in the kettle." Without coffee, I will literally die, but it feels churlish to demand it when she's made me breakfast. "Hurry and eat. We need to go."

"Go where?" I ask around my mouthful of eggs, but she's already grabbing her handbag.

"We're going to be late. Come on."

I chase after her with a makeshift breakfast sandwich. Minutes later, we turn onto Greenly Street. Disbelief dawns. She would not. But sure enough, she did. We roll to a stop in front of the home that once belonged to the late, great Cathy Santini, she of full-size-Halloween-candy-bar fame.

A realtor—tall, fair-haired, and relatively fit—waves from the porch. His light-blue eyes and white eyebrows give him a washed-out look.

"Brian!" My mom waves back as she exits the car.

Brian. I frown, a memory niggling. *Maryellen's son Brian asked about you the other day, you know? I ran into him at the grocery store. He's a realtor now.*

Being back here, having Mom attempt to manage my life… It brings a crushing but familiar weight to the center of my chest. I'd forgotten the constant state of vigilance living here necessitates.

The Brian my mother kept mentioning to me was a vaguely familiar phantom from the past, hidden somewhere in a corner of my mind, but I couldn't place him entirely. Now that phantom has been pulled into the light. Brian *Backerman*. His last name comes to me suddenly, making me wonder what critical piece of information was bumped from my brain because this info was taking up that space. His pale hair is thinner on top, but otherwise he still looks more or less like his high school self.

As he approaches, I remember he had the longest white-blond eyelashes that forever made me think of twin albino tarantulas.

He reaches our car—still has the tarantulas. "Wow, Penny. I haven't seen you in forever." He pulls me in for a hug before I can react.

I pat his back exactly twice and lean away. "Hi, Brian. Likewise." *To the point I forgot you existed.* I have to force a cordial note into my voice. Brian didn't do anything. My mother is the one to blame.

Brian's eyes light on me with undisguised interest. God knows what my mom has said about me or how much she's pushed for a match on his end. "Well, come on in and see the place. It's such a great property. Cathy was a neat freak, and she kept up with the maintenance."

My mother beams at me. I wonder if she senses the murder behind my benign look and is ignoring it or if she's truly oblivious.

"Mrs. Santini died in this house, right?" I ask, pausing before the threshold.

"Well, yes, but—" Brian stammers.

"I don't think I really want to live in a place where someone died."

"We're just looking, Penelope." My mom's voice carries a warning. "But if you truly want to skip this, maybe you can go grab that coffee you wanted with Brian."

Rage. Rage. Raaaaage.

Brian bats his tarantulas at me, a hopeful expression on his face. "I'd love to treat you to a coffee."

I want coffee. The prospect of finally obtaining some is the only thing keeping Cathy Santini's home from being the site of an additional death. "Okay. Coffee."

Mom fairly skips back to her car, mission-accomplished vibes oozing from her every pore.

Brian's car is not a car at all. It's a bright-orange contraption that looks like a golf cart and a military Jeep had a baby. The top is striped navy and white.

I pause. "What is this thing?"

"You've never seen a Moke? No, I guess you wouldn't in the city. Fully electric. Charges in just eight hours." He raps his knuckles against the orange roll bar.

"Only eight?" I quip.

Brian chuckles. I slide into one of the white racing seats before fumbling with the seat belt. I bet Jack's retort would've been epic.

Coffee is at Beach Brain, a few blocks away, but it takes an age for us to get there since the Moke only gets up to twenty-five miles per hour. Brian waves to other locals, relishing the attention. When we get to the shop, Brian takes my order, and I slide into a booth decorated to look like a beach ball.

Brian slips into the seat across from me, one with a closed beach umbrella poking out the top. "Can I confess something?" he says, leaning forward and glancing around for curious ears. "I had the biggest crush on you in high school. The *biggest.* I can't believe I'm here with Penelope Huff. I owe your mom a bottle of pinot grigio."

"Ha. Thanks." I owe my mom something, but it isn't wine. Though it does feel nice to be wanted—to be liked—even though it's not by the one I like. For a second I imagine letting go. It's so exhausting fighting Mom and her potent forever-pressure. Especially when I owe her everything. I could forget about my apartment angst, move back, let this guy across from me, eager as a puppy, take me out. Buy Cathy Santini's house and do marketing for a local hotel. Let the petals slam shut each year.

I'd be trapped inside, sure, but at the moment that doesn't sound like the most terrible fate.

Brian's not unattractive, though I feel nothing when I look at him. He doesn't have slate-gray eyes that warm with humor when they look at me. He doesn't have a smirk that makes me want to claw his clothes off. He isn't Jack. And nothing about the life waiting for me in Stone Harbor is what I want.

"I'm so sorry, Brian, but can you bring me back to my mom's, actually? I only had enough time to slip out and grab a cup of joe before I run for the bus back home."

"Your mom said you were going to take the rest of the day off…" His disappointment is palpable, and while I'm not the one who set him up with false expectations, I still feel guilty about letting him down. When he drops me off, I run inside, grab my small bag of belongings, leave a note for Mom, and hustle to catch my bus back to civilization.

And Jack.

# 17

Despite the lack of sea air, I breathe easier in New York. My life is here. In this building. In apartment 5A. Which means it's time to face my problems head-on. I heave in a breath, pull the strap of my tote bag up my shoulder, and confirm with my phone's camera function that my hickey is still concealed beneath a thick layer of cover-up. And then I knock on Jack's door.

It's a few agonizing seconds before he answers. My heart pogos around my chest at the sight of him. When he sees me, his eyes narrow, and he crosses his arms.

"Can I help you?" His voice, even at the worst of our exchanges, always had a warmth to it. Humor. Care. I realize that now because it's gone—and what's left is glacial. I feel a little bereft.

"Hi. Listen. I wanted to talk about the elephant in the room."

"Not nice to call people names."

My eyebrows pinch together, and I hesitate a beat. This isn't going well. "Ah... What I mean is, let's try... I want to try this again—"

He snorts.

"I— I didn't mean it when I said I don't like you. I shouldn't have said that." Especially shouldn't have said that right after I had his hands all over my ass. I wince. "And I left the other night because I— I mean, I'll get to that. But I'd like to—"

"Hey, Jack." There's a purr behind him. Yelena, the appraiser, her bounty of cleavage spilling from the sweetheart neckline of her blue top, pouts prettily. "Can I ask you about—"

Her eyes flare with recognition when she notices me, and she hesitates. "Oh, the neighbor from the hole."

She makes me sound like a hobbit. I clench my fists.

"Yelena, meet 5A. Formally meet, I mean. 5A, this is Yelena," he says.

I take a halting step backward, unsure if I want to flee or take a swing at him. Everything I planned on telling him dies on my tongue. He's watching me with a shuttered look I can't read. I give them both a tight smile, and he turns to Yelena.

"Give me a second while I deal with this. Almost done." He says "this" like he's about to salt a slug on his porch.

I squeeze the strap of my bag until my palm aches. "Anyway, I'll make it quick since you have company. The main reason I'm here is that—"

"You want to try this again." He sneers. "You said."

The speech I prepared on the bus fails me, along with my courage. "*This*, being neighbors. Normal neighbors." I am reversing course faster than Sergeant Al Powell's squad car from Nakatomi Plaza in *Die Hard*. It makes me dizzy. My unspoken words are razor-sharp. They claw at my chest. I want my sofa, my blanket, my apartment, and I don't want to leave it for a month. "If we're going to buy our places, and maybe be neighbors for a while, we're going to need to be cordial. We got off on the wrong foot."

"That what you call the closet? Or the sofa?" Jack says.

His sarcasm cuts through my second-hand guilt. My nostrils

flare. “That was a *mistake*, like I said.” The angry words trip from my lips, pitchforks in hand, while the rest of me cries out, *It wasn’t a mistake! I wanted to come here and tell you I want to work on me. Maybe work on us. I’m the mistake! I ruin everything.*

“All three of those things were your fault, incidentally. Getting off on the wrong foot, the closet, the sofa.” He tips his head, and I hear a little bit of the old fire in his voice. I’d rather have a hot war than a cold one with him, I realize.

“Yes to the first, debatable about the second, though you didn’t help things with your idiocy, and the third… I blame *The Pirate Duke*. So let’s just bygones it out and—”

“Is ‘bygones-ing it out’ similar to your idea of ‘normal neighbors’? Because not interested.”

I open my mouth to respond, and he cuts me off. “I already told you once, messing with me is fine. Messing with my job isn’t. I’m getting nonstop emails to my work inbox for juice cleanses, vitamins, and essential oils. And cars! Every POS from here to the river is available for no money down, did you know? The nudist colony interest form was a nice touch—points for creativity there. I had to spend an hour clearing that shit out and unsubscribing instead of working on my client case files. You know, the people at risk of rather time-sensitive legal matters? I’m sure that has nothing to do with you?”

*Fucking Margie! Loyal, angry Margie.*

“I said not to! The second I found out about it, I…” My explanation dies on my tongue in the face of his judgment. Shit. I need out of this conversation. Immediately.

“We’ve got another few days of demo, and then we can get started on the repairs. I want to forget you exist.” *LIAR.* “And I can’t do that until all open space between our apartments is sealed up. Will you be getting the materials, or should I?" I demand.

He peers down at me like I'm an alien species. His jaw has a dark dusting of stubble. He's usually relatively clean-cut, so right now he looks like Harrison Ford's evil twin. I glower at him, unblinking, wanting to kick him in the nuts and run like hell so that he's forced to share some of the hurt I'm feeling.

"You said you would help build the wall when we were on the ship. Are you backing out of that offer?" I press.

His lips firm, and I remember the feel of them on mine. Is he thinking of what followed him offering to fix our wall, too? I blink away the burning sensation in my eyes, willing myself not to cry.

"I don't remember a ton about that night, you know. Lots of alcohol. Only thing that really sticks out at all as important is agreeing to fix the wall," he says with a smile, a hard glint in his eye. "I'll buy the stuff."

Snapping a snide remark back in response comes as second nature to me now. I have to force myself to smile sweetly and press forward instead.

Jack inhales sharply, his ego probably expecting a kiss instead of the *Street Fighter* three-hit combo I want to deliver. We'd be nose to nose if he wasn't so tall. I hear Yelena in the apartment behind him, shuffling around. Is she there to appraise the place? Hang out? Get motorboated? *Why is she here?*

"Good. Buy the stuff. Oh, and I'm going to want to get it done sooner rather than later. Planning on bringing someone by." *LIAR*. "I think you've heard enough moaning from my room, so the soundproofing is very—"

He closes the door in my face. And I realize that I desperately need professional help.

My knee bounces as I take in the reception room. It's all things Zen and bright in here, with whitewashed furniture, light-gray walls, and greenery everywhere. I admire the lacy plant in a macramé holder dangling from the corner of the room and make a mental note to ask the therapist where she got it. The six-foot potted palm plant next to my umber vegan-leather chair, though… I examine the fronds, noting the yellowing tips of the leaves. The two windows next to the plant are giving it a sunburn. I'm edging it out of the direct path of the light when the therapist calls my name.

"Ah, I was just… Your plant is—"

"Thank you. I'm Wendy Halloran. You must be Penelope. It's nice to meet you. Do you want to come in?" She has long, straight dark hair, luminous dark brown skin, and the long, lean build of a yoga instructor.

"Penny. I'm Penny. Penelope is what people call me when they're mad, mostly."

She smiles and gestures that I should follow her into her office, and I scurry behind, taking a seat on the soft beige sofa opposite her chair. I take a white throw pillow with a needlepoint canary on the front and hug it to my middle.

"Your office is very calming. The waiting room, too. By design, though, right? Using psychology stuff to get people to relax… I'm a sucker for calming environments. I researched the crap out of everything before I decorated my apartment. Is this Benjamin Moore Edgecomb Gray? It looks like it, but lighter. Maybe cut with some white? I—" I force myself to stop. There is an indulgent look on her face, one that isn't quite neutral, but not judgmental, either. "I'm going to shut up now."

"No, not if you don't want to. Do you want to talk about your apartment?"

"I mean, maybe… I'm here because I just… I had a crappy thing happen with my neighbor."

"Tell me about it. Or maybe start with a little about you?"

When I started my hunt for a therapist last night, I didn't expect to find one so fast, let alone one who'd respond to my query the next morning. And when she asked when I'd like to start, and I jokingly responded with, "How about fourteen years ago?" I didn't expect her to say, "Well, all my yesterdays are booked, but today I had a cancellation if you really want to get started immediately."

I shift on the sofa and realize I'm violently hugging the pillow to my chest. I deliberately set it on my lap, bird side up.

"I— You know my mom would freak if I ever told her I was in therapy."

"Why's that?"

I trace my finger over the little thread bird. "She doesn't believe in it. Got to tough it out, whatever life throws at you. Therapists only make you hate your parents," I mimic.

"And what do you think?"

"I don't think *that*. But I used to think I didn't need it because I had my friends Margie and Avery to talk to, and because I turned out fine no matter what life threw at me… But I think I overestimated how fine I am. All this nuttiness with my neighbor Jack really hit that home."

"Are you comfortable sharing more?" Wendy tilts her head, her expression open and earnest. Her degrees are hanging across the room, denoting her PhD and master's and all the other proof that I'm here with a professional. "Tell me about Mom. Or Jack.

Whatever you'd like."

I nod, quickly before I lose my nerve, and start talking. Not about Mom, though. I tell her about Jack. About what he looks like, his snark and humor, about our fighting and the games we played and how my bias formed on false pretenses started it all. It is a stilted and meandering telling, an uncomfortable stream of consciousness that picks up momentum as I go. And suddenly, there's an avalanche of mental baggage falling out of me, and my eyes are stinging, and I'm accepting my second tissue.

"I'm an idiot, because I have been nothing but awful to Jack, and I like him, I do, and yes, he was awful back to me, but that was *before* the party, and it just feels like things changed there, and he even took care of me, and then I broke everything. And now he's with that appraiser."

"Do you know for sure that he's with her?"

"No. But..." My shoulders slump. "It doesn't matter. Even if he's not, look at the Vaughns, like I told you! A daily trust fall? How the hell do *I* make something work when *they* barely did? I'd just ruin it all with Jack anyway and end up living next door to an ex forever. I have *never* made a relationship last, so there's no reason to think it'd be different with him."

"I'd say one difference is...you're here. Committed to working on yourself."

I make a face, reluctantly accepting her words as true.

"Let me ask you, Penny: you briefly mentioned your work on our call. There, if a project is difficult, does that mean doing it doesn't have value?"

"No, of course not."

"So why, when it comes to relationships—yours, the Vaughns you so admire—why does difficulty in that sphere mean that the endeavor doesn't have value?"

I open my mouth. Close it. I hug the pillow again, her words and the confusion they churn up somersaulting through my mind. I take a bracing breath.

"That was good. That was a good and cleaning deep breath. Maybe do that again."

I do. But I've got nothing to say in response to her thought grenade.

Wendy's voice has been melodic and soothing this entire session, but it gentles even more when she says, "Maybe another way of thinking about difficulties in relationships is… Isn't there perhaps beauty in choosing one another each day? Over and over?"

I make a noncommittal sound. Even if a relationship being hard is part of it… Even if it's worth it despite the difficulty… Jack is angry with me and may have moved on. And, regardless, I'm still very much the mess that is me.

When I do speak, it's to say: "Can we maybe do this twice a week?"

# 18

My bathroom is hot in the mornings, the sun beaming directly through the window. My hair dryer makes it even more so.

The clatter is so loud that I hear it even with my hair dryer going. I turn it off and listen for another sound. The seconds tick by.

When I hear the sound again, it squeezes a shriek out of me. I rush to The Hole and stick my head under the sheet.

"Stuff is here. I'm taking off work today to try and finish bringing down thc wall and get started building. You've got an hour before you leave for work if you want to help," Jack says, taking in my wet poof of hair with a dispassionate expression. He's sweating, sporting a Mets cap, jeans, and a blue T-shirt. *Lick him. Run your hands up his chest.*

*No, brain.* Must. Keep. Away. From. This. Man. That is the only way to survive now.

His sofa has been pulled back from the wall, and a pile of two-by-fours and tools have taken their place. It's only seven a.m.

"You're not serious."

"You said you wanted it done sooner rather than later."

"I need to get ready for work. I'm still a mess."

"You look like you always do." His tone makes me want to leap through The Hole and wrap my hands around his throat. I realize I haven't covered up my hickey yet when his gaze snags on my neck, but if anything, the reminder of our stupidity makes his expression grow frostier.

"You can't take down this wall just yet. What if I bring a guy home?" I have no plans to bring any guys back to my place. It's a taunt. I want it to sting, like Yelena stung me.

"By the time that happens, this thing will probably be fixed. And if not, I can make myself scarce."

Absolutely zero fucks detected.

I start to pull my head back when he calls out, "Wait."

My pulse skips, and he pulls something from his pocket, holding it out to me. I reach for it: the receipt for the supplies.

"I'm going to need to make a drywall run at some point. And then the molding and whatnot, too, so that's not everything you'll owe me, but I figured you'd want to start tallying it up."

I wish there was a way to slam a flap of fabric in your wake. He starts up his vacuum as I stomp away.

My phone rings before I can reach my bathroom. Margie. She never calls. And never reaches out this early.

"Um. Hello?"

"You back?"

"Yeah, I didn't stay long. Came back Monday afternoon." I rub at my temple. "Need to fill you in on the stupidity."

"I'll need details later, but first, did I leave a script at your place? The one I was reading the other night? I can't find it anywhere." She of the forever-deadpan delivery sounds borderline frantic over the phone. "It's Lucas's copy, and I need to return it."

"I'm not sure." I look around. "Wait, yes. It's on my counter."

"Oh, thank God. Okay, I'm going to swing by and pick it up after you get out of work."

"I can bring—"

"No, it's fine. I don't want it traveling after the heart attack I had trying to figure out where I left it. We'll meet at La's, grab a bite, you can fill me in on mom drama, and I'll walk over with you."

My call waiting beeps and my pulse spikes. Mom. My ribs draw together, bracing. One wrong word and I won't be able to defuse this bomb.

"Talk about timing. All right, see you later," I tell Margie. I inhale deeply, steel myself for the conversation, and click over. "Hi, Mom." I set her on speaker and head into my bathroom, fiddling with my foundation.

"Oh, you answered finally! I still can't believe you left without saying goodbye."

"I texted you when I left. It's not like we didn't communicate. And you texted back. I would've said bye if you were home, but when I got back from that setup with Brian you foisted on me, you were out."

"I called you. When you were on the bus, after you got home, all day yesterday."

I pivot away from my bathroom and head instead to the kitchen. More coffee is required for this conversation.

Mom makes a disapproving noise when I remain silent and then changes the subject. "You're going to need to come down the night before the baby shower. I convinced Katie and her mom to have it in my backyard. You know how nice it is for entertaining back there. You're going to help me decorate."

My eyes sting. A party I never agreed to attend, for people

I barely know, is one I need to show up for the night before to decorate because I'm now somehow co-hosting? After being manipulated into almost-viewing a home I didn't want to buy and maneuvered into a coffee date with a guy I didn't want to spend time with.

"I can't, Mom. I told you I'd check if I can even make it that weekend..." My finger hovers over the end button.

"Of course you can come! Brian will be there. He said you two had a blast. Don't be—"

"The guy, Mom." I have to raise my voice to be heard. It startles her quiet. "I'm back with the guy I told you about." I want to throat-punch my psyche and its sick sense of humor when Jack immediately springs to mind.

There's a pause and then, "Oh?"

I pinch the bridge of my nose. The less she knows, the less I'll have to remember when I tell her my fake relationship is over. "I think you'd like him. He's real honest." What other adjectives describe Dad on Opposite Day? Or describe Jack on any normal day? I think of his work, his caring. "Nice. Just a really kind and honorable guy." I close my eyes. "I'm kind of crazy about him." The last bit comes out as a lament.

"When did you make up? You just got back—"

"We met up when I got back." The image of Jack with Yelena hanging on his shoulder makes me want to break my mug on my counter. "And things just kind of fell back into place. I'm supposed to meet him after work for dinner." I wrinkle my nose, shame pooling in my belly. *Liar, liar.*

"Is it really all that serious? Because Brian—"

"We've been seeing each other for a few months. It's getting to be serious, yeah, but... We'll see!" I sound as upbeat and chipper as a ray of sunshine shoved into a rainbow shoved into a puppy's ass. A joy turducken.

"Okay... Brian will be devastated, but... Don't let me keep you." She sounds strangely subdued. I have to force myself not to dwell on it. I've spent far too many nights dissecting her moods or words like they were science-class frogs.

"I hope you're not wearing anything black. It doesn't suit your coloring. No man will find you attractive if you remind him of a struck match, Penelope."

"Nope, I'm good. Talk to you later," I say, watching with a frown as the sheet covering The Hole billows slightly.

I hang up and slump on my kitchen stool. Now to decide how long to keep a fake significant other around before telling Mom it's over. Maybe I draw it out for an age and then on the way to introduce him to her, I show up in tattered clothes, mascara running, screaming about how the love of my life was nabbed in the middle of the street by an unknown enemy and pressed into service in Her Majesty's navy. He's doomed to pursue pirates on the high seas, but one day he seizes an opportunity to *join* the pirates, trying with all his might to find his way back to me—only to discover me at the altar about to exchange vows with his biggest rival.

I gust out a sigh. *Pirate Duke* is so hot.

The memory of a hand skimming my silk-covered breast and a mouth on my neck in a closet on a different waterborne vessel blazes through my mind. I slowly release a breath, fighting the wildfire that streaks up my spine. *Do you really like Jack, though? Maybe it was just proximity to a decent-looking male. Forget about the fact that you reacted to Brian like you would a bowl of oatmeal. Jack sucks. He doesn't deserve sexy gymnastics with you. He deserves a kick to the head.* And this violent sentiment has absolutely nothing to do with his little tête-à-tête with his appraiser.

*Maybe he was just having her finish the appraisal?*

I snort and pick up my coffee mug. *With all that cleavage?*

I hear Jack's vacuum going, and then, as quickly as it flared, the wellspring of denial and annoyance runs dry. I like that menace more than I can say.

# 19

La Smith is packed, but when Avery and I show up, La greets us with a welcoming smile and gets us a table immediately. She also fusses at me for my ankle, though I assure her I am fine.

"I'm happy for Margie," I tell Avery once our dinners have been served and La is back behind the bar, "but squatting where you eat—where *we* eat... She's as bad as me with guys."

"La's not a guy," Avery offers unhelpfully.

"I know, but I mean, if she and La don't work out, we'll need a new restaurant."

Avery swipes a fry but then cuts me a piece of his fish. Boy Scout can't even steal properly. "This thing with La seems different somehow."

I shove a bite of fish into my mouth and mutter, "Or maybe you're in love and wearing rose-colored glasses." Though I begrudgingly admit to myself he's right.

Instead of acknowledging my comment, he asks, "Was Anna over at Jack's?"

"No, I haven't seen her. What's going on with you two, anyway?"

Avery shrugs a broad shoulder, and a flash of naked vulnerability washes over his face. I've never seen him put himself out there with someone he wasn't sure of. It's so foreign to see him this way.

"Haven't heard from her since the party. She mentioned some issues she was having with her fiancé and…um… She tried to kiss me up on the flight deck, but I didn't want her to do something she'd regret. I mean, I wanted to kiss her, obviously, but not like that. I think she got offended. Anyway, I'm just worried."

"Wow. Okay… You know what I think?"

"Jägermeister was invented by the devil?"

"Yes, it was, but also, you need to take the advice you've always given me: take a breath, let things happen how they will. Don't force it. Don't sabotage. Just be."

He grunts in acknowledgment and gives me a wry look. "I'm very wise. Should we order Margie something to eat?"

I pull out my phone to ask Margie exactly that when I realize she texted me about a half hour earlier.

Can't make it. Retakes. Incoming, though—Lucas needs that script. Told him to meet you at La's.

"Margie isn't coming here. Lucas is!" I immediately drain my wine and fuss with my hair.

"Her costar?"

"Shit, he's here."

La's at the entrance, taking over for a very flustered hostess. She points in our direction, and Lucas Webb strides through the crowded restaurant. The music never stops, but it's a record-scratch moment for the patrons here.

Lucas smiles. "Penny, my femme fatale! How are you?" He's wearing a white cotton Henley shirt and dark slacks, and there's a rope of gold around his neck. His teeth are white and even, his blond buzz cut immaculate. "Avery, great party. Thanks again."

I offer a half hug. The guys shake hands. "Join us for a drink?" Avery asks.

Lucas glances at his watch and nods. "I've got time for one. What are you drinking?"

Avery pulls over a chair, and Lucas hails the waitress. And just like that, I become the envy of every woman in this place, sitting here with two incredibly handsome men.

One drink becomes a handful on top of the two I had before Lucas arrived. But the time flies as Avery shares details about his work—which Lucas soaks up like a sponge, explaining that he never knows when information like that might come in handy for an acting job—and Lucas talks about his quest to break into movies. With the exception of two feature films, he's been relegated to TV, stuck in his long-term contract on the show.

I laugh when appropriate, exclaim, show outrage, but I largely stay quiet, my mind drifting to the demon on the other side of The Hole. But then Lucas's eyes are roaming my face, and I'm not sure if I imagine his gaze lingering on the part of my neck still shadowed by the hickey Jack left there. My hand goes straight to the spot I applied cover-up to so meticulously this morning. I palm the area and rest an elbow on the table, hoping the effect is more interested head-tilt than confused puppy. *Ha, ha, I'm a super-normal human female who wasn't necking like a teen with a man I thought I hated. I'm totally not the type to put a hole in a wall or chase away someone's appraiser. Normal!*

"So, tell me more about you, Penny," Lucas says.

"Me?" I'm so startled he wants to know about my plebe life that I nearly reveal the hickey. To cover, I kind of bobble my head, hand still firmly pressed to my neck. "Oh no, I'm boring."

Avery snorts.

"You're not boring to me. Killer slow dancer. Plotting

murders and all." Lucas winks, and it is pure sex on a cracker. I am unmoved, damn it. My pipes seem to work only for Jack. How depressing.

"Okay. Well. Prepare to be amazed. I'm originally from the incredibly exotic state of New Jersey. South Jersey, actually. I went to NYU for undergrad with Margie and this dunce." I gesture toward Avery. "Go Violets..." I mime a cheerleader and slap my hand back over my neck, remembering. "I, ah, studied communications. And I once did a bit of acting myself, actually."

"Oh, really?" Lucas sits back in his chair. His expression is pleasant, but there's something there, hovering on his face. Apprehension? He's not as good an actor as he thinks. "A budding actor. What have you done? Let me guess... I'm thinking... community theater? Commercials?" He thinks I want a job.

"Very close. Pluck Cluck Chicken, actually—the fast food place down on Fourteenth. I dressed up as their mascot for one miserable month in college and held a sign down by the park to try and get people to come in. The smell of that costume haunts my dreams. Like body odor and chicken grease." I am seductive as shit, talking about smelly chicken costumes. Jesus.

Avery laughs. "Pluck Cluck Chicken! I haven't thought of that in forever!"

Lucas laughs, too, harder than I expected. It draws the attention of a local newscaster and her husband seated nearby. They're regulars, and until Lucas showed up, she was the hyper-local celebrity people gawked at. "I'm sure you were a convincing chicken, though."

I pick at my food daintily, wishing I could rip into my burger the way I was doing before Lucas got here. But I never eat much in front of men I don't know well.

Maybe all those breakups were just because I was hangry.

Gotta call Wendy and tell her I've had a therapy breakthrough.

Avery's eyes slip to my neck, and I see him frown. I, well lubricated at this point, have no idea what he's looking at. I vaguely remember I'm supposed to be covering my neck. Oh, right…hickey. Crap. I haven't told Avery about what happened with Jack because I didn't want him discussing it with Anna, but I can see the question in his eyes. How visible is this thing? I need to see how bad it looks. And I desperately need to pee.

"Will you excuse me for a second? Just need to use the ladies' room," I say, sliding out of my seat with my purse.

It isn't until I'm standing in front of the bathroom mirror that I realize all those drinks have produced one fairly tipsy Penny. I decide to give the woman in the mirror a much-deserved pep talk.

"You're so fucking hot, with your little black work dress and your…" I lean forward to investigate a spot of something in my teeth.

*No. Stop. That's the old you. You're not trying to be hot. You're not trying to attract Lucas. You're not going to contort yourself into his dream girl only to let it be another flash in the pan, not even to prove you don't need Jack. You're not interested in repeating the same old patterns anymore. With anyone, including Jack. And besides…*

"Jack is *maybe* sexy, but he's… He's a pig! Yes! Made out with me and then whatever that was with Yelena the next night? He's not nice. And beauty fades. Pig is forever." My voice quavers. I can't even convince drunk Penny of any of this. I'm doomed.

On my way back to the table, I toss my hair over my shoulder and try to remember how humans walk. Pretty sure I nailed it, until I see Avery watching my legs in concern. It also occurs to me that I forgot to check out my hickey in the mirror.

"I think it's time to call it," Avery says, standing and handing me a water. "I'll walk you home, Penny."

"I don't mind walking her home," Lucas says. "You have your morning meeting, and I need to pick up my script anyway."

Avery says nothing, but I see the question in his eyes. I pat his cheek. "I'm okay walking with Lucas. Let's get out of here."

There's an end-of-summer breeze in the night air, refreshing and just sobering enough to steady my gait. Lucas throws his jacket on my shoulders, and I smile up at him in appreciation before hugging Avery goodbye. Lucas waves away his car service but probably regrets it when a handful of paparazzi start snapping pictures of me leaning heavily on his arm. The flashes are blinding.

"Who the hell called them?" Lucas mutters.

"Who is she, Lucas?" one photographer calls out.

"Did you give her that hickey?" another shouts. My face is lava red.

Lucas waves the questions away. "Gonna have to dig your dirt up elsewhere, fellas. Nothing to see, but if you want to take the walk with us, be my guest. Just give us some space, okay?"

That seems to deflate the paps, and two of the three disperse. One trails us at a distance for a bit, though I lose sight of him as we approach my building. We probably bored him into submission, our conversation pleasantly superficial.

We climb the steps to my apartment, and instead of feeling the tension of Jack's eyes on my ass, I mainly just want to get to my place and take off these shoes. For a few seconds, there's just silence punctuated by squeaking stair treads. And then Lucas says, "Margie mentioned she left the script here because you're her go-to for running lines."

"Yeah, I do them in stupid voices to see if she can remain in character with an over-actor."

Lucas chuckles. "I've got to hear that."

We reach my landing, and I let us into my place. "No way."

There's a noise beyond the sheets hanging across the wall: Jack. I wonder if Yelena is there, too. The image of her hanging onto Jack's shoulder floats past my mind's eye like Casper the Busty Ghost.

"Come on. You can't tell me something like that and then not do it," Lucas insists.

"Fine. You want a drink?" I make sure to ask that question nice and loud. Though a part of me worries Lucas may get the wrong idea, a bigger part of me hopes Jack gets the wrong idea. To make him jealous, like he did to me with Yelena.

"Wine would be great," he says.

I twist the cap on the wine, stashing the top in a drawer and smiling as I think of Margie. Lucas joins me in the kitchen, and I hand him his script and a glass.

"You pick the scene," he says, casually sipping.

I fill my own glass and set the script down, flipping over to a tabbed page. My eyebrows shoot up: the sex scene is a hot one. Filthy. Restraints and blindfolds and—

"Yeah, not this one," I say.

Lucas's expression doesn't change from the completely innocent one he's sporting. But then again, he's an actor. "Oh? What's wrong with it?"

"Nice try," I say. He laughs and gives me a playful "caught me" look.

I flip purposefully through the pages and chuckle when I land on the scene I want. The violence between the two hitman brothers on the page makes *The Godfather* look like *Mary Poppins*. And there's definitely no kissing or ravishing happening here. I arch a questioning brow.

"You were plotting a murder the first time I met you, so it makes sense you'd find the most bloodthirsty scene now," Lucas says with a laugh.

I wander into the living room, reading aloud. "Please! Please! Just let me..."

Lucas leans over my shoulder and peers at the script. "Get over here." He playfully grabs my arm, and I press my wrist across my forehead like a damsel in distress. "Get on your knees. Now!"

I sip my wine. "You don't have to do this. I'm sorry!" The scene calls for a whimper as Lucas's character brandishes a gun.

He nods, his lips scrunched in surprised approval.

I mouth, "Pluck Cluck Chicken."

He growls, "I don't want to hear your fucking sorrys. You had time for sorrys. Open your mouth and suck on this."

The script calls for a gun to be placed in the kneeling brother's mouth.

Lucas grins, and suddenly the sheet on my wall bursts forward, a ghostly figure waving its arms and launching itself at him.

"What the—" Lucas shouts.

"You put your hands on her?" the ghost yells in Jack's voice, full of muffled fury. I scramble away and stare, my hand pressed against my mouth. Jack stumbles off the sofa and flails, kicking over my coffee table in his efforts to wrench himself free of the sheet. Lucas bats at Jack's blind reach and leaps onto the sofa behind him. Their shouts merge into a confusing word soup.

"Jack, stop! We were reading his script for a movie. A movie!" I shout, finally finding my voice. And suddenly Lucas cries out. His eyes latch onto mine, shock and alarm flashing across his face as he tumbles backward off the back of my sofa through The Hole, his feet tangled up in the sheet, wrenching it off Jack as he goes. He lands with a ridiculously loud clatter-crash.

Jack stares at me, breathing heavily, his hair disheveled. I blink and rush to the sofa, looking through The Hole. Lucas is lying on his side amid a stack of two-by-fours and debris, moaning softly and holding his cheek.

"Reading a script?" Jack asks me, his voice cracking slightly. I ignore him and climb through The Hole.

"Oh God, Lucas, are you okay?"

"My phone," he mumbles. I help him sit up and reach for his phone in his back pocket. He takes it and places a call, touching a hand to his jaw and wincing. "Dan," he barks. He winces again and holds his hand against the side of his face. "You need to come get me. I sent the driver home. Address?" He looks at me and holds out the phone. I recite my address into the receiver.

Jack peers down at us through The Hole, his expression almost comically horrified. I push him back and scramble through The Hole into my apartment to grab Lucas some ice for his face.

"I'm fine." Lucas waves away my fussing when I return, but he accepts the ice pack. His agent, Dan, who calls to mind a refined grizzly bear, rushes over in record time and insists on getting Lucas checked out at the hospital, despite his objections. I ask to ride along, but Dan rejects my request. Lucas doesn't contradict him.

Evidently, one of our neighbors called the cops during the melee, and two police officers arrive just as Dan and Lucas are about to leave, forcing them to halt their retreat and share what occurred. One of the officers starts laughing so hard at the misunderstanding—and at the fact that a goth ghost essentially scared a prominent TV celebrity into falling backward through The Hole—that his partner has to tap him none-too-gently to stifle his giggles.

Gence, on the other hand, does not see any humor in the situation. He is glowering at me, though it wasn't my fault. Not directly, anyway. I push away the feeling of encroaching remorse. How was I supposed to know this would happen?

Lucas limps away without a goodbye to me, radiating offended fury, after the chuckling officer asks if he'd like to press charges against the sheet. Dan quickly follows behind him.

# 20

Jack is sitting on my sofa, his hands steepled between his knees in front of him. He's wearing jeans and a faded blue T-shirt, stained from his wall-demo efforts. I sit beside him as the police and everyone else clear out.

We're quiet for a long while.

"Wow," I say. I clamp my mouth shut, fighting the urge to babble nervously. God only knows what I'd say after everything that happened tonight.

Jack makes a choked sound in the back of his throat that sounds like agreement.

I can't do silence anymore. If he's not going to say something, I have to. "I'm going to have to bake Gence some cookies. He's really angry," I say, latching onto the one thing I can maybe fix right now.

"He's diabetic. Type two." Jack doesn't look up at me as he says it.

I absorb that and swallow a horrified gasp. Of course Gence is diabetic. He probably thinks I've been trying to kill him this whole time. I cover my face with my hands. The image of Jack in that sheet, my spooky savior, flashes through my mind, and that laugh bubbles up again, this time spilling out past my fingers.

"What?"

I drop my hands and look up. "You're literally the worst white knight ever."

"I wasn't trying to be your fucking white knight, Penny," Jack snaps, and there's real bitterness to his voice. "I was trying to save the guy. From you."

The bubble of laughter inside me deflates, and it's punctuated by a painful lurch in my chest. "What?"

He shakes his head, casting his eyes heavenward. "Okay, I guess I'll spell it out for you. I heard you and that guy in your apartment, and I decided to warn him against making the mistake of getting mixed up with you."

Something's off. I don't know Jack that well, but all of our hallway sparring has made me surprisingly adept at figuring out when there's another layer to his words—something he's trying to bury beneath the facade. He's trying to project frustration, anger, contempt. But underneath that? I hear shame, pain… maybe jealousy? I don't know. His eyes lack the spark that lights them up every time we fight; instead, they're darting and shifty, trying their hardest not to look at me.

I don't think Jack was trying to sabotage a date. His words when he was fumbling with the sheet come back to me. He genuinely thought I was in trouble, and he was genuinely trying to save me. My heart squeezes. I want to climb onto his lap and pull his stupid lips down to meet mine. I want to push him down, straddle him, and—

He notices me staring at him and snaps, "Stop looking at me."

Okay, so he's still a dick.

As I contemplate what to do with all of this, my stomach breaks the silence by rumbling something fierce. Of course, now that the apartment is finally the quietest it's been in months.

"Hungry?" Jack asks, snarky as shit.

I want to respond with something tart ("No, my stomach's learning a new language"), but since Lucas joined me and Avery while I was still nibbling, I never ate a proper dinner. My fridge is empty, and I'm fucking famished. After everything that happened tonight, what more does a girl have to lose?

"Actually, yeah. I could eat," I say.

Jack is quiet for a moment, but then he says, almost sheepish, almost a question, "There's a diner down the block."

I squint one eye at him. I'm well aware of the places to eat in my neighborhood. Does he think this is news to me? Or is he thinking of coming with? I stand cautiously, and he stands, too. That answers that.

As we make our way down the creaking wood stairs, I find myself staring at his back, at the ridges and bulges of his shoulders, at his solid form. An uncomfortable warmth spreads through me at the thought he was trying—*so* clumsily—to defend me. *I was warning him off* be damned. A voice in the back of my mind reminds me that he'd have to be a total villain to hear what he heard and *not* try to stop it. I shush it.

Let me have this. Just for a bit.

The diner is swathed in silver and shades of red and reeks, in the best, most delicious way possible, of grease. We grab a booth, and a waitress approaches to hand us menus. I notice her eyes taking us in—me still in my work dress with wild hair in tangles down my back, and Jack in his construction clothes, patches of white dust all over. To her credit, or maybe because she's seen plenty of weird crap on her late-night shifts, not even an eyelash flutter betrays her thoughts.

"Pancakes," Jack says, without cracking the menu open. "And a vanilla shake. No whipped cream." I raise a brow, and he shrugs. "Comfort food."

"Pastrami Reuben. Dressing on the side. With french fries," I say to the waitress, raising my voice to be heard over the outburst of raucous laughter from some college kids at a nearby table. I hand her both menus. "Comfort food," I agree.

"For an O-lineman." Jack's knee bounces under the table, the subtle vibration of the table and his shifting giving it away. He has a pensive look to him, too.

"What is it?"

"Do you think your actor broke his jaw?" Jack asks.

"Oh, are you afraid you went too far trying to ruin my date? You sure saved him from me. Only took breaking his face to do it."

His jaw tightens, and I sigh.

"He isn't my actor, and it wasn't a date. Poor guy was just picking up a script. And I don't know if he broke his… God, I hope not." Culpability stings its way through me. I pluck a sugar packet from the container on the table and toy with it. The babble wins a hard-fought battle. "If he did, I can always just break your girlfriend Yelena's arm or something. Then we'd be even."

Jack's knee goes still. His expression is almost entirely blank, except for a slight shake of his head. And then, "I'm not with Yelena."

"She was at your place. Late."

"Finishing the appraisal. I had to beg her to come and do it outside of work hours because I had a financing thing to contend with."

It's as if a boulder guarding the entrance to my heart has been shoved aside, allowing radiant heat to seep in. I have to stop myself from beaming with joy. Instead, I force a casual tone. "You shouldn't feel bad. Just like me scaring Yelena through The Hole was partially on you, this… This was on me. I didn't know you'd be there. Or, if you were, that you'd still be up." *But I'd hoped because I'm immature and wanted you to be jealous.* "And even then, I didn't think about the stuff we were saying, really, or what it might sound like to someone overhearing."

"You didn't think I'd still be up? When you told your mom—" Jack stops talking abruptly and wipes a hand over his mouth. "I was demoing the wall and…lost track of time. And you can't absolve me of blame. That fight—"

"First of all, the only fights I saw were between you and a sheet, and between Lucas and The Hole."

"Hilarious," he says flatly.

"And second of all…I'm not trying to absolve you of guilt. I'm just owning up to my part. I chose the scene we read. At random, but still. I…" I grimace and trail off. I look down at my phone on my lap, noting that Margie has called. I make a mental note to call her back and type out a quick text to Lucas, who will probably regret putting his number in my phone back at La's:

> I hope you're okay. Let me know what they say at the hospital. It's Penny, by the way.

When I raise my eyes, Jack is watching me intently. I sigh. "So, yeah. Not all on you. *Although* this wouldn't have happened if you'd kept your promise not to listen through the wall anymore."

He grunts.

I bite back a smile. "I'm not just talking about you listening when Lucas was there. You heard me talking to my mom?"

"I wasn't trying to. I told you I'd make an effort not to listen. Kind of hard, though, when you're constantly blasting your phone on speaker and you've got the vocal subtlety of a bullhorn. Why did you tell her you've been with the actor for months if you're not dating?"

"I didn't. I never said Lucas's name. I made up a relationship so she'd stop trying to set me up. It was just a coincidence that Lucas came back with me to pick up his script."

Our food arrives, and I throw myself at my sandwich with orgasmic enthusiasm, eating my feelings with abandon. Jack pauses in the process of cutting up his pancakes and stares. My mouth is full, so I give him a defensive look. He suppresses a smile.

I chew, slowly, and narrow my eyes at him.

"Even though it wasn't technically a fight, I still feel bad," he finally says, around a bite of pancake. "Brawling, *even with a sheet*"—he stops my taunting in its tracks—"is not something I'm used to. I think the last time I hit anyone at all was in a college bar fight I didn't start. That's the Moth thing I mentioned. The scar on my chin." He chews and looks contemplative. "Anyway, I don't like the feeling."

"I would've thought you brawled constantly with that mouth of yours." I take another bite of Reuben.

"I'm big enough it doesn't encourage a ton of that." He dips his pancake into a little pool of syrup. "And I've always been more of a champion-the-underdog sort anyway. Bullies tend to back down pretty quickly." He smirks. "Except you."

I snort and swallow my food, wiping a strand of hair out of my face. "*I've* bullied *you*? Because of you, I've had to redo at least twenty loads of laundry."

"You put a gigantic purple dildo in the dryer with my whites. Do you know how awkward that conversation was with Gence? His wife was scandalized. Thing kept slamming up against the glass like a fucking sledgehammer."

I snort-laugh. That trip to Velvet Whisper set me back ten bucks, and I never knew if that investment paid off.

"Laugh it up."

"Whatever. At least I didn't steal your underwear, pervert."

Jack draws on his shake straw and stops. "That wasn't me."

"Right. Then who?"

"I have absolutely no clue, but I haven't stolen any underwear."

I absorb that, unsure of whether or not to believe him.

He sets down his shake, and the devil in Ms. Huff decides to dip one of my fries in it and scarf it down. The sweet-and-salty combo of French fry and milkshake is one of my childhood faves. At his look, I blush.

"Sorry. I should've asked before—"

He snatches a fry from my plate. "Didn't know we were sharing is all." He gamely dunks the fry in the shake, but his face shows he isn't a fan.

I smile, about to tuck into my sandwich again when he lifts his milkshake and tips it in my direction, the straw not far from my mouth. The mood shifts, slowing until the drunken disorderliness around us becomes white noise. I open my mouth, lean forward, and wrap my lips around his straw. I watch him as I take a pull, sucking hard, feeling the milkshake cool and coat my tongue. There is a strange intimacy to this shared straw that sets my heart skittering around my chest for purchase. I sit back, running my tongue over my lips, watching him watching me.

I clear my throat. "Thank you," I say, simply. His attention is fixed on me, his eyes unreadable, and I feel something shift inside me, creaky from disuse.

We grab the check and then walk back, the quiet and the dark reminding me a bit of our time on the hangar deck at the Vaughn party. But this silence is a lot more companionable.

"So, was this the worst date you've ever been on?" he asks suddenly.

"Didn't realize we were on a date." Jack doesn't look at me, but I see his smile in the dim light. It fills me with a warm glow. "No. This wasn't the worst."

Jack gives a little laugh. "What was the worst?"

I blush, even in the dark. "It's bad... Okay, so this was after college. Don't judge me. I was wearing a booze bra...where you can smuggle booze into places, and it makes your boobs look bigger? I was broke! I didn't want to assume he'd pay for me. And...I don't know why, but I decided to get the biggest honking cup size they made. I was a little less secure in those days. To this day, I still don't know how, but I sprang a leak in one of the cups. I was wearing white. The guy pretended not to notice, bless him, but between the cup differential and the— Stop laughing! Fine. What's yours, then?"

"Worst date...besides this one?"

"Hmm."

"Okay...worst date... None, actually. I'm pretty amazing."

I push at him, but he doesn't budge. He does chuckle, though.

"Fine. I went to dinner with this girl, and halfway through her entrée I mentioned something about it being tax day, and she freaked out because she hadn't filed her taxes or an extension, insisted she had to go... I ended up going back to her place and doing them for her in QuickBooks." He shrugs.

"Oof. You're a fixer, huh?"

"Yeah... Force of habit, maybe."

"Who fixes things for you?" I say it in a funny way, but a strange look comes over Jack's face.

We reach our building, and he pulls his keys out, letting us in. When we've reached our landing, I find my stomach knotting up, unsure where we go from here.

"I need sleep. But... You're going to be okay alone? I mean, joking aside, this was all kind of intense," Jack says.

Okay alone? I've always been okay alone.

His concern warms me. It makes me want to rest my head on his shoulder, dip my tongue in the shell of his ear, bite his lobe. The whole tableau, with the swashbuckling move through The Hole, and the non-fight… It was all a little too *Pirate Duke* on crack for me.

And yet. I only *just* started therapy. Wendy may have had a point about hard times not being a deal-breaker, but that doesn't mean I've magically healed and stopped being a roadblock to healthy relationships.

I shake my head at the thought, then nod vigorously when I realize his frown has grown. He mistook my headshake. "I'm fine, Jack. Thanks."

We unlock our respective doors. I look up at him, pausing before heading in.

"Night," he says. I give him a small smile.

And then I take in the mess of my living room. My sanctuary is a fucking disaster. I kick at a broken coffee-table leg as I lumber through the destruction. There is a giant red splotch on my rug—Lucas's wine spill—which I didn't register earlier. My sofa is covered in plaster.

I sigh and glimpse Jack through The Hole as he disappears into his bedroom. My inner romance-novel aficionado tells me to stuff my worry over my perfect little apartment and my emotional damage for a bit; there are more pressing items to unpack at the moment. I rush to my bedroom in a daze, replaying things in my mind as I get undressed.

My last thought as I drift off is that Prince Charming on a white horse has nothing on Jack Craig charging through a hole in the wall.

# 21

The world feels different the next morning.

For starters, my living room is immaculate except for the wine stains on my sofa slipcover and the rug. Even my broken coffee table has been cleared out. How did I not hear a vacuum going in here? Maybe I've built up an immunity to Jack's noise.

There's a note stuck to my fridge with a magnet, too. The magnet is of a white piña colada–like cocktail with a wedge of pineapple on the rim. Below are the words "Penis Colossus—Cancun."

*I'll have the couch and rug cleaned.*
*Pick out a coffee table so I can replace it.*

*-J.*

*P.S. Iced coffee in your fridge.*
*And why don't you own any magnets?*

I take the note off my fridge and press it to my chest. It feels like… Honestly, it feels like lying in bed this morning, preparing to come out to face my destroyed living room: warm and cozy, but simultaneously aware that there's been a seismic and somewhat destructive shift. One you know you can stay under the covers to avoid dealing with for just a few more minutes.

I pull open my fridge to grab the iced coffee Jack bought me, and my thoughts about poor Lucas have me cringing to myself. I send him another text and then get ready for work, slowly, scrolling through my phone as I brush my teeth. Dozens of emails from the overseas folks working on the global project. And—yikes—five missed calls from Margie and three from my mother. Mom's were from about an hour ago, but Margie's spanned the entire night.

I tuck Jack's note in my shoulder bag for some unknown reason and pull out my phone to dial Margie. The sight of Mrs. Russo taping something to Jack's door brings me up short. I approach her, spying the handwritten invitation to her prayer circle.

"Oh hello, Penny."

Bursting with goodwill for Jack, I commit to clearing the name of the wrongly accused. "Hey, Mrs. Russo… I've been meaning to tell you, it turns out I was wrong about Jack and the whole killing chickens thing. He was just—" I think fast, searching for something believable. "Singing. In the shower. He's a *terrible* singer. Sorry for getting it so wrong."

More assurances follow before Mrs. Russo is confident she doesn't need to save Jack's soul. And then I'm off to work, calling Margie as I walk to the office. She picks up before I even register a ring on my end.

"What. The. Fuck. Happened?" Her tone is no more excitable than her usual monotone, except that it's a bit more clipped.

"God, Margie. Mess. Jack heard me reading from the script and—"

"Why are you talking about Jack? What does he have to do with Lucas ending up in the ER?"

"He's the reason Lucas is in the ER."

A pause, then: "Start at the beginning."

I fill Margie in on everything, from my taunting Jack about needing the wall fixed so I could bring someone home (and him not caring) to Jack cleaning my apartment at some point between the time he climbed back through The Hole and me waking up this morning.

"He thought Lucas was attacking you and forcing you to—" Margie repeats it slowly, as if not quite believing what she's hearing. "And then he decided to just…fucking Kool-Aid Man his way through the wall?"

"Margie. No joke. Exactly that."

"Well, they've cancelled today's shoot because of Lucas. No one—besides me, now—knows exactly what happened to him, except that he spent the better part of the night in the ER. I hope he's not out of commission. The show can't really keep going without the titular character."

"Oh God. Margie, I'm so sorry…" The horror in my tone does nothing to capture what I feel. If I killed Margie's big break through my own stupidity, I'll never forgive myself.

"Let me call you back. I need to call… I need to call a shit ton of people. Bye."

The sunshine and the brilliant sky somehow make me feel worse about everything. Yesterday's rain would've suited today's mood perfectly. I'm almost grateful when I get past my work building's bright lobby and up to the mahogany confines of the Evadon offices.

I make myself some terrible coffee, needing the additional caffeine, and wind my way past the cubicle maze, throwing my headset on and resigning myself to hours of conference calls and sedentary blah-ness.

We make some progress on the global project, mainly because Anthony is on "holiday" for three weeks. But even that isn't enough to lift my spirits.

I text Margie and ask if she has an address for Lucas.

She texts back:

Why? Want to finish the job? Make sure to hold the pillow down over his face way past the point when he stops moving. He might be faking. He's a good actor.

Funny. Can you help or not?

She texts back an address, and I order some flowers and a get-well balloon. At the last moment, I splurge and add a corny teddy bear holding a sign that reads "I feel crappy when you ain't happy."

I sit back, gnawing at my lip, and then pick up my cell, dialing Lucas's number.

"Hello?" His voice sounds garbled through the phone.

"Lucas, it's Penelope. I am so sorry. I can't believe this happened. How are you? What have the doctors said?"

"Who— Oh. Penny."

"Yes, I— I wanted to see how you're feeling."

"Broken jaw. Wired shut. Sprained wrist." He says it through gritted teeth, and it comes out mumbled and stunted and barely intelligible. "That. Fucking. Asshole."

"He thought he was protecting me, and…" I trail off, thinking that maybe reminding Lucas that he fell through The Hole himself isn't the best thing to do when apologizing.

"Why was there a hole in your wall?"

"It's a long and wild story…" And then I amplify my crazy by wobbling my head like I'm in an old talkie film and affecting a Bette Davis kind of voice. "Maybe I can…tell it to you over a smoothie, handsome?" I smile weakly, cursing my babble. "A smoothie… Because the jaw…"

I clear my throat. "Anyway, he jumped through and… I just feel awful about this, Lucas. Truly. I know Margie's upset, too. What can I do? Is there anything I can do to help?"

"Stay. Away."

I swallow, blinking back tears.

"Ah. Okay, then. I— I'm sorry."

"Wait," he grits out, but I end the call. He doesn't try me back.

I'm sweating, and my breathing is rough. I'm having a hard time keeping the waterworks at bay.

This reaction, the tears, all of it, is not only because I hurt another person with my thoughtlessness. And it isn't because the guy I am going to be living next door to—if I can find a way to afford my place in time—maybe deep down did want to warn another man away from me, because milk really does keep longer than my relationships.

No. I've had a visceral reaction to rocking the boat since I was a kid. In fact, I have an almost pathological need to do the opposite. It's the reason I don't demand the raise I deserve or tell Anthony what a roadblock douche he is. It's only ever *not* been that way with Margie and Avery…

And Jack.

With my friends, I've developed a level of trust over a long period of time. With Jack… Well, I didn't give a shit what he thought of me, and trying to capsize his boat has always been top priority over keeping mine on an even keel.

But now I'm clinging to a dinghy, smack in the middle of a hurricane, all because I wanted to make Jack jealous despite knowing I'm not emotionally healthy enough to be involved with him romantically. I feel exposed and embarrassed in a way I can't quite understand.

I don't feel like walking home, so I hail a cab. Mom calls as

I'm sitting in the dark confines of the car, listening to the loud advertisements on the screen in front of me. Throat tight, chest heavy, I send her to voicemail, preferring the ads to whatever demands she's been marinating.

Back at my apartment, I spend a good hour with my plants on the fire escape, the clipping and pruning restoring some of my sanity. Enough that when Jack gets home, I can face him.

I'm dressed like someone from a workout video from the eighties—some of Jack's music must've inspired me—but he returns before I can fully rethink my wall-demo ensemble. I lean through The Hole as he closes his front door. "Hi…"

He looks like he's sucked down buckets of coffee today, to no avail, but even an exhausted Jack in a suit is sinful. He gives me a strange look as he sets his bag down before tossing his mail on the counter. I check my expression, hoping my *Pirate Duke* thoughts weren't that transparent.

"Um. Are we still working on the wall?" I ask.

"Sure. Let me get changed."

I climb through The Hole, and Jack is changed in less than a minute. He waves me over to his kitchen and wordlessly hands me a beer from his fridge. I accept with a nod and then await his command, pretending I don't want to squeeze his biceps. Him playing the swashbuckling hero is the worst thing that could've ever happened to me. I'm not ready for a relationship, no matter what I feel about him.

"How's the actor?" he asks finally.

"Not great." I list Lucas's ailments and then mention that Margie's show has been put on hold until the showrunner can decide what to do.

"That why you were crying? Your eyes are all red."

I don't answer. Instead, I grab a mask and some gloves from

the counter and put them on.

Jack sighs. "All right, I got the plaster down on this side and bagged it. We'll finish with the plaster on your side and then take down the beams."

"Aye, aye, Captain," I say. Which just brings *Pirate Duke* back to the forefront of my mind with a vengeance.

Later, after we've cleaned up, I spy Jack on his sofa through The Hole, surrounded by folders and documents, laptop open on the coffee table in front of him.

"What are you doing?" I angle over my sofa to peer over his shoulder.

"Work. Summary judgment response due tomorrow." He taps away at his laptop. "Need to fight to avoid having the case dismissed."

"What's the case about?"

"Woman suing her ex for emotional distress and adverse possession. That last one is like theft."

His piney scent must be his soap or aftershave, since it's been amplified by his shower. I spy a fleck of glitter on the back of his ear and bite back a smile. "Theft of what?"

"Her 'best years'—"

I am over his sofa, sitting cross-legged next to him with one of his files open on my lap before he can finish his sentence. I read, "'Client says ex strung her along for years with 'just-the-tip' emotional connection, enough to keep her hanging and hoping. He thought her decision to leave was sudden. But he lost her in pieces, every time he played his push-pull game.' Wait, she left him and then sued him?"

"Yes. He ghosted her, blocked her on everything, then came back to try and reestablish the relationship. She allowed it but got angry and resentful over the next few months. She dumped him, then sued."

"Holy shit, she said she wants to sue for lost hotness?" I read. "I am dead. Why do you look so stressed?"

He sets down his laptop and runs both hands through his hair. "There are lots of cases of women suing for wasted or lost time in other states—and here we have intentional infliction of emotional distress..."

"Yes, we do." My face clearly says he's the source of my emotional distress.

He ignores me. "We have IIED cases in this state. But none where the woman broke up with the fiancé first. I need to figure out an angle to help her claim."

I flip through some of his other papers, reading snippets here and there. "I thought you did employment law. Or wait, you said something about trying to keep someone out of prison too?"

"I do it all. Criminal law, I mainly do for free. Other cases like this and the Evadon one pay the bills."

"Ahhh, so that's why you took this lady's case."

"No." Jack's voice is surprisingly firm.

"Oh. I can help you. If you want?" I have so much of my own work, but this feels a bit like peeking through the keyhole of who someone is—who Jack is. I can't help myself.

He hands me a file. "Flip through her statements and texts and emails, look for anything we can use to suggest her ex was cruel, manipulative, that sort of thing."

I page through the file, taking in all the printouts, adding sticky notes to items I think might make sense for Jack's filing. An hour into my hunt, a scrap of paper wedged in between two documents becomes visible.

*Thank you, Jack. You're the only one who didn't laugh.*
*-Sophie*

I hold up the note, a question in my eyes.

"She went to tons of lawyers and got laughed out of offices across the city. She deserved to have her pain treated with dignity." He shrugs.

"You think you can win?"

"No. This case is virtually unwinnable. IIED is hard to prove. It's a four-prong test. Even if we can meet the criteria for all four prongs—the severity of the treatment, the intent or reckless disregard for her feelings that caused the distress, the direct link between that conduct and her harm, and all the verifiable harm including physical symptoms—New York's threshold of evidence for this stuff is super high."

"Why would you file if you can't win?" I cross my legs more fully and pull his blanket over my shoulders.

"Just because you can't win doesn't mean the case shouldn't be filed. Sometimes people sue just to be heard. I want to get past summary judgment so that the case isn't tossed and she can force people to listen."

He wants her to feel heard. I stare at him, slack-jawed, warmth I can't explain spreading through me.

"What?" he asks, staring back at me. It feels like a strange spell has been cast.

"You have glitter on your ear."

His lip twitches, and he shakes his head.

We work through the night, side by side in a strange little apartment cocoon. And in some small way, helping him with his work—helping Sophie be heard—feels like a balm for the guilt I've been carrying today.

# 22

Wendy has a notepad on her lap. I find my eyes drifting toward it, wondering what she's written about me so far. Neurotic? Fixated on a dude? Boring? Winning smile and killer balayage?

"So, what's going on, Penny?" Wendy asks with a smile.

My mind is a blank. "Ah, nothing much. I'm feeling pretty good."

"Okay, great. Anything you want to talk about today?"

"Um, sure… You know the actor Lucas Webb? Well, he fell through the hole in my wall and broke his jaw."

Her eyebrows fly into her hairline, and her mouth hangs slack for just a moment before she collects herself. Part of me feels like I'm winning at therapy. If I can shock a professional…

I tell her all about the mishap with Lucas and Jack, which leads to the disclosure that Jack is *not*, in fact, with Yelena. Which leads to talking about the warmth that has infused every look Jack and I have shared in the days since Jack fought the sheet. Which leads to talk about the work on his case.

"Will you tell him you've developed feelings for him?"

"I mean… I don't know that I'd say *feelings*? I like him. He makes me laugh. I feel comfortable around him. Except for the sexy-time tension."

"Sexy-time—"

"So, yes, I like him. A lot. And I'm attracted to him. He's got these, like, deep dimple things when he smiles that make me want to…um. Yeah. But 'feelings' is a strong word."

"Okay—"

"I could tell him, but what if he just wants a hookup? What if he's not interested in a relationship? That would *hurt*. Or, worse, what if he's interested in a relationship, and I have to tell him I'm not ready for anything because I'm trying to fix my damage with you?"

"I wouldn't say fixing—"

"Defusing a super-sad bomb?"

"N-no. I wouldn't phrase it that way, either. But I will say it's admirable that you want to work on your mental health."

My lip twists. "Tell that to my mom."

Wendy pauses and then writes something on her notepad. "You've mentioned her twice in the context of not approving of therapy. Her approval is important to you."

Apprehension tingles along my scalp. It wasn't a question, but I answer. "Yeah. Doesn't everyone want their parents' approval?"

"What happens when she disapproves?" Wendy asks, pen poised over her pad.

I bite at the inside of my cheek, and my gaze locks on that pen. "Nothing. She just wouldn't be happy. I feel bad when she's unhappy."

"You feel responsible for her feelings?"

"She's my mom." She writes and I hurry to add, "But this is all not a big deal, truly. Usually it's…" I shrug, the words not coming, my ribs feeling too small for my frame. "It's *fine*. She's got strong opinions."

"What happens if you don't go along with those opinions?"

"Nothing. I mean occasionally, she'll take matters in her own hands."

"Do you have an example of that?"

"Like with my visit recently, she kind of tricked me into going to look at a haunted house and then pressured me into a coffee date with a realtor ghost, so I can move back home..." I clock Wendy's confusion and explain in more detail, watching the groove between her eyes get deeper and deeper.

"Are you aware that you can love someone and still make choices that disappoint them?"

I open my mouth to defend Mom...and close it. My throat is tight. I understand Wendy doesn't approve of Mom's antics. I don't approve either! But she's my mom. I remain silent, bracing for her next question, sure I've just unlocked a new facial expression. But Wendy surprises me by changing the subject.

"Can I ask: you've mentioned your mother, friends, coworkers, your neighbor... You haven't mentioned a father. Was one in the picture?"

I snort. "Yeah, not long. My dad left Mom and me when I was fourteen years old. I haven't seen or spoken to him since." My voice cracks halfway through the statement, to my great surprise. "He– He left."

"I'm so sorry, Penny. That is a painful thing to go through."

I shrug, laughing self-consciously. "It's okay. It's ancient history. I'm over it. It's—" My voice fails me again. "Sorry, I don't know where this is coming from. I've always just been angry about it instead of whatever this is." I brush at my eye.

"Anger is a foot soldier for sadness," Wendy says.

"Your next pillow, have them needlepoint that instead of a bird," I joke.

Wendy remains quiet.

"I– I mean, yeah, I was sad. It wasn't fun to go through. I remember thinking, 'How can you abandon someone you love like that?' And then I realized… I guess he didn't. Love us, that is." Another tear. Fuck. And another. I bow my head, resigned to full-on waterworks.

I knew there was damage there. I knew it was a sore spot in my psyche. But this? There's a geyser of hurt that's built too much pressure to remain below the surface anymore.

I accept a tissue, knowing I'm going to have a headache after this visit. And then I explain why my dad left: "Mom finally called him out on his cheating, though she'd known for a while. And that was it for him."

"How did you feel about that? Your mother calling him out."

I blow my nose noisily, then wave my tissue-clutching fist in a faintly frustrated gesture. "I– He wasn't the greatest father, but I loved him. That's what you do when you're a kid, right? You love your parents. And he… He taught me some stuff, I guess. How to throw a ball. How to plant things without killing them. I helped him with his landscaping business for a few summers before he bailed."

I snatch another tissue, my voice growing thicker. "But for every kiss I got on a feverish forehead, there were twenty angry freak-outs over nothing. Tension whenever he came home in a bad mood, Mom crying after finding out about another woman. I could tell Mom was unhappy with him, but–" I shake my head. "She was worse after he left. Miserable. We struggled a ton with bills. She kept saying she should've just kept her mouth shut." I slam my rolled-up ball of tissues into the little trash can to the left of my leg.

"Why do you–?"

"Even a broken pot holds some water, I guess. Better than no pot at all. I don't know." I fold in on myself. My tone is clipped. This raw nerve needs a respite. I pull my hair over my shoulder and thread the strands through my index and middle fingers aggressively, like a monkey trying to self-soothe.

"We talked about the Vaughns last time, and you were alarmed by the idea that in a healthy relationship, the parties *choose* one another each day. Do you think that, maybe, some of your fears related to relationships and commitments are grounded in this trauma? That one of the most foundational relationships you can have—the one you have with a parent—resulted in you *not* being chosen? That a parent-child relationship should be exempt from the 'choose each other each day' idea, but when things became difficult, your father didn't choose you?"

I drop my hair and sit back, feeling as if I've been smacked with a two-by-four.

The day is a hazy one, like the entire week preceding it. The clash between summer and fall has led to a streak of weather that is by equal turns unbearably warm and extraordinarily damp. It's a match for the discomfort I feel inside following my therapy session a few days ago.

I adjust my hair clip to pull more hair off the back of my sticky neck and lean against the copier, listening to the loud whining of the beige beast. All the rooms on this side of the building face the onslaught of the glass-amplified sun each morning. Doesn't matter how little light peeks out from the clouds, the air-conditioning is no match for the mini-greenhouses the conference rooms and copier room become.

My stomach calls my name, and I ruthlessly ignore it, promising myself a wrap from the cafeteria in—I glance at my cell—half an hour. Instead of counting down the half hour till noon, I turn my attention to the framed minimalist motivational posters on the wall and sigh. Less than five weeks left to finish the global project, earn myself a raise, and get myself approved for a mortgage so that I can formally offer for my place before my lease is up.

No pressure.

**DON'T DECREASE THE GOAL.**
**INCREASE THE EFFORT.**

The poster shouts at me in white block letters on a black background.

*Fuck you, poster.*

The global project has legs, but Monday—when The Professor is back from his vacation—is looming large. I feel like a woman possessed, working all hours to get the framework built out, thinking through every angle I possibly can. Rochelle nods approvingly whenever I share status updates with her, but the downside to all of this, besides killing myself with work, is that work on the wall has slowed. Jack seems to be similarly wrapped up with a case, so we agreed to table the remaining wall demo until the coming weekend.

"I told them," my coworker Donna says, just outside the copy room. "I said if I don't get that title, and the payday to go with it, I'm walking. And they gave it to me, like that."

"What's your title going to be? Finally a director?" Donna's favorite lunch buddy, Judith, asks as they pass. I barely hear Donna answer in the affirmative.

Fucking *Donna* got a promotion and a raise? She spends more time gossiping than doing work, her voice is nails-on-a-chalkboard unpleasant, and she takes every opportunity she can to henpeck everyone around her. The Vanna White of the company also loves showcasing other people's efforts as her own. And I know for a fact she refuses to work evenings and weekends. What the hell kind of ladder am I trying to climb if Donna is beating me up it?

I grab my printouts and walk to my desk, flopping the stack of copies down with a *thwack*. Three years and no increase. Rochelle said she's tried. And yet *Donna* gets a raise? I sit heavily, slumped in my chair.

I need to rage to someone, but Margie's filming a commercial her agent booked for her. Avery's always lab-coated and covered in the cooties he studies, so he can't pick up until way later. Mom… I laugh. She hates this job. I'd get a more sympathetic ear out of my dry cleaner.

I pick up my phone and scroll, pausing on a name in the Ds. It belongs to the only person I kinda, sorta, really feel like talking to at the moment, which worries me.

*Demon*. It's how Jack is listed in my phone. Gence made us exchange numbers when he was trying to head off our little war at the pass. The picture I added to his entry was the first horned, red-faced, evil creature Google served up.

*Do I…?* I click to start a text.

Hey. It's Penny. From next door.

I delete it. Too formal.

I try again, enjoying the fantasy of *maybe* texting Jack.

Jackoff Penny here

I snort. Friggin' autocorrect. I've just deleted the "here" when Rochelle peers over my cubicle wall, startling me. "Hey, Penny, the pivots you sent are great." She gives me a bright smile and disappears back over my wall.

I look down at the text. No, no, no. To my utter horror, I

accidentally hit send when I was startled by Rochelle. What's worse, he's already responded.

I can't tell if you're calling me a jackoff or if you're making a demand of me. Punctuation matters.

I drop my phone. And then I drop my head in my hands. My face flames.

And then…I laugh. I laugh until the Donna promotion angst is a distant second to the exhilaration of sparring with Jack.

I sit back in my chair and pick up my phone, rereading my text and his response. The same mischief-maker that led me to dip a french fry in his shake has me typing out: Meet me for lunch and I'll tell you which way I meant it.

I delete that immediately and write out the much more respectable:

I think we both know which I meant.

His response is gratifyingly instantaneous, as if he was waiting for my message.

Yeah, the latter. Got it. What's up?

I grin and debate for a second before harnessing my chi and texting:

I'm starving, and everyone I like is busy.

The dots representing his impending response linger for far too long, and my anxiety spikes. I try on ways of backing out of that invite before he can decline, ways of backing away from how I just put myself out there.

Pick the place.

At his response, all the breath in my lungs whooshes out at once. I type out the name of a lunch spot not far from my office and, pretending not to have stalked him and googled his office, ask if it's too far.

That works. Meet in twenty.

I log out of my computer and grab my purse, racing to the bathroom to touch up my makeup. "You would fix your face before meeting anyone," I announce as I apply fresh lipstick and a touch of cream blush. My hair is a rat's nest from the weather. I comb my fingers through it, wincing when I tug out a strand.

*Relax. You live next door to him. This is not a big deal.*

I want to run to the restaurant and post up, like a mobster scoping out a joint before a sit-down with a rival family. Instead, I force myself to go back to my desk and hammer out a few more emails. The walk to the restaurant feels like an eternity because I slow my walk to a leisurely tourist speed. I even pop into a boutique and try to look at shoes. I'm five minutes late.

He's not here. The restaurant isn't big, and I can tell immediately he isn't in it. I look at my phone, but there are no missed texts or calls. My ego—I refuse to call it anything else—plummets to somewhere in the vicinity of my ankles. Was he kidding about meeting me? Is this another prank?

"Someone ordered a jackoff?" a voice murmurs behind me, and I whirl around. Jack is smirking down at me, and the sheer roguish charm of him, of the humor in those gray eyes, makes me want to leap on him, smooth my hand over his stubbled cheek, and run my tongue over his lower lip. Instead, I take in a steadying breath and give him a roll of the eyes. Turning my back on him, I lead us to an open table.

The place is über-modern, the walls covered in outsize

paintings of lunch items. A giant grilled cheese here, an enormous tuna melt there. A waiter hands us menus as we take our seats, and I smile when Jack orders a salad. No comfort food for the health nut today.

"I'll have a grilled chicken sandwich, please. No mayo? And a seltzer water." I hand the waiter back the menu.

"No mayo," the waiter repeats, his expression blank. He brushes his pale hair from his eyes and gapes at me.

"Yeah… Just the chicken and everything that comes with it, only no mayo?"

He nods slowly, and I'm not encouraged to see he's written none of our order down. He gestures to a guy nearby to fill our glasses with water.

"So," Jack says, a dangerous spark in his eyes. He's in black suit pants and a pale-lavender shirt sans tie, his dark hair styled into a respectable-looking 'do. "Didn't expect to get a text from you, like…ever."

"Unpredictability. Keeps the enemy on his toes." I waggle my eyebrows.

"Very Sun Tzu of you. 'The whole secret lies in confusing the enemy, so that he cannot fathom our real intent.'"

"Something like that, nerd."

"Nerd, I can take. But enemy? Still?"

"Okay, frenemies. Since we're breaking bread and whatever."

Jack grins. "I didn't realize it was you texting at first. I…don't have you in my phone under your name."

"Oooh, what am I listed as?"

He fiddles with his phone and holds it out: "Grinch" is written in the First Name field. I laugh out loud. There's a picture of the green monster in the contact file as well.

I pull up his contact in my phone, taking a sip of water and holding the phone up for his review.

"Demon? Could've been worse."

Our food arrives, and I look down with dismay. It's some minced beige meat on top of a bed of greens. It looks like someone dropped cat food on a plate. There's a small roll to the side of the mess.

"Sorry, can you tell me what this is?" I ask the waiter.

"It's the chicken you ordered."

When it becomes apparent that I'm not going to say anything further, Jack says, "She ordered a chicken sandwich."

The waiter blinks. He's young, looks stoned, and I'm supremely uncomfortable about the whole situation.

"No, no, this is fine. It's okay. I can have this," I say, desperate for the topic to be over.

Jack eyes my plate dubiously.

"Seriously, it's fine."

"No. It's not. You ordered a chicken sandwich. That's what you're getting." To the waiter, he says, "Can you get her a grilled chicken sandwich, please? No mayo. I'm going to need you to write that down." The waiter scrambles to pull out a pad and jots it down, forgetting the chicken mess in his haste to get back to the kitchen.

I'm simultaneously envious of Jack's ability to calmly demand what he wants and also mortified by the whole thing.

"Can't wait for my spit sandwich," I say, because I feel like I have to say something.

"It'll pair nicely with the spit Bolognese I made for you."

Jack pushes his plate into the center of the table and gestures for me to eat. He takes a bite of salad. "So, what made you ask me out? I've been waiting for this day for ages and ages, just glued to my phone."

"Dumb." I huff out a chuckle, pushing some salad around. "I didn't ask you out. You're a distant third in my affections behind Margie and Avery, but they're all tied up. I needed an ear to bend."

"Bend away. I'll just be here licking my wounds."

I sigh. "A lady I can't stand just got promoted, and I've been waiting for even a tiny raise for ages, and…nothing. It just *sucks*. I've been killing myself, nights, weekends—"

"Fuck 'em. If someone doesn't recognize your worth, you either force them to recognize it or you walk."

"Wouldn't it be easier to take up vacuuming and pancakes?"

"No. Vacuuming and pancakes are for closers."

I let out a wholly attractive grunt-laugh and tear apart the tiny roll the waiter left behind. I can't bring myself to eat Jack's salad. My stomach hates me right now.

"Speaking of work, is your schedule going to let us get cracking on the wall again tomorrow?" he asks.

I nod, my mouth full of stale bread.

My chicken sandwich arrives, and I give the waiter a weak smile, overly effusive with my thank-yous.

We finish up, Jack insisting on paying and leaving a respectable tip despite Chicken SlopGate, and we walk outside. I thank him, blushing for God knows what reason as I stare up at him.

The edges of his lips curl upward into just the tiniest of smiles, and for a moment, this foggy day is blindingly bright.

"All right, I'd better get back—"

"Yeah, me too. Thanks again for lunch." I clear my throat and turn, forcing myself not to look back.

I've taken no more than ten steps when I give in to the urge and glance back over my shoulder. And I can't be sure, but something about his too-casual posture tells me that I just missed him looking at me, too.

# 23

That night, after once again whining about my lack of raise to Margie and Avery on a group text, I crawl into bed with my copy of *Pirate Duke*, rereading my favorite parts, my own favorite parts reacting to the memory of Jack reading *that* passage. I don't see Jack that evening, and my resistance to leaving my bedroom—to possibly seeing him after asking him to lunch—makes me feel a little like a coward.

The next morning, true to his word, Jack is ready to tackle the wall extra early. "Hey! 5A. Come to The Hole!"

Despite entering my bed at a very reasonable hour last night, I had a hard time sleeping, and it shows: dark circles under my eyes, a crabby disposition, and an exhaustion coffee hasn't put a dent in. I am in no mood for Jack's cheer right now. And he's definitely cheery. I can hear it in his voice. I long to dive back under the covers.

I step up to The Hole, and he grins at me. "Come on over, please?"

I sigh aggressively and walk through to his side of the wall. "What? I'm not done with breakfast."

His face is serious, and his hands are behind his back. I narrow my eyes as I watch him.

"Penny, we've known each other a while now." His voice is a warm rumble. It does things to the hairs on the back of my neck, like the thunder before a summer storm. "And I know it hasn't always been exactly friendly between us. But…"

Where is this going?

Jack gets down on one knee. I draw in a breath.

What. The. Fuck.

He pulls a small circular saw from behind his back, the cord hanging from it as he holds it up as an offering to me. "I rented a circular saw to help this project along."

"You're such a dick," I say, releasing my breath in a wheeze. I feel like crying, and I don't know why. Maybe because with my track record, the closest to a proposal I'll ever get is this circular-saw bullshit. God, I really didn't sleep at all last night, did I?

Jack chuckles. "You didn't think—" He feigns horror. I plant my palm on his face and push with all my might. He loses his balance and tips over, laughing.

His laughter is aggravating as shit. Which makes me think of another irritation, and the source of my restless sleep.

After having a series of decidedly dirty dreams all week where Jack featured pretty prominently, I decided to download an app to see if I really do moan in my sleep. I listened to the recording after I got tired of reading last night, and the answer is yes. Yes, I do.

Jack hasn't said anything further about hearing me moan, and I'm not about to ask. Plus, I'm not entirely sure the moans are *all* from sexy dreams. I also have the occasional nightmare. Lately, the two have been one and the same.

My phone rings: Mom. I send it to voicemail. She texts.

I ran into Brian again, and he said he'd love to hear from you. I got his number for you since I haven't heard anything further about that guy you said you were seeing. I told him you'd give him a call. Such a nice boy.

My hands shake. Jesus. To be able to pry, insult, manipulate, and control all in three lines. Talent. I pocket my phone.

"My mom. She's trying to set me up with a guy. Forced me into grabbing coffee with him last time I was down to visit," I share.

"Forced you? How does that work?"

"If you'd ever met my mom, you wouldn't have to ask."

Jack scratches his eyebrow, and it's clear there's something sticking in his craw. His eyes drop to my lips, and I unconsciously dart my tongue out to lick them. Maybe it's not his craw something is sticking to.

"And I don't know why I shared any of this," I snap, desperate to break the spell he's casting.

"Maybe it's because you wanted me to know."

"Riiiight."

"Attempt to make me jealous? Let me know you're in demand?" he says, weirdly upbeat.

I blow a raspberry.

"Scoff all you like. We both know you lied when you said you didn't like me." He smiles, and his sidelong glance makes me blush. But there's an earnestness to the cockiness. A speck of vulnerability?

"I—" I clear my throat, debating, gathering my courage to me like a tattered blanket. "I like you. Okay?"

"Oof. Took a lot out of you to admit that, didn't it?" Jack's grin is face-splitting. "Here's a secret, you incredibly infuriating woman: I like you, too."

My heart jolts, invisible electric paddles sending awareness rampaging through me. My pulse rockets to what has to be an unsafe level. *He likes me. He's standing close. He's taking my hand, tangling his fingers with mine. Oh God. He's tipping my face up to look at him.*

I know, as sure as I know anything, that Jack wants to kiss me. I see the question in his eyes. I swallow hard.

"I like you," I stammer. "A lot. And I find myself… sometimes…wanting to maybe do things with you that are of an R rating. Or NC-17. Or maybe—"

"I got it," he says, his voice low and extra gravelly. Oh fuck is it sexy when it gets like that.

I shift from leg to leg, looking down at our entwined fingers. "But. I am bad with guys. Like, *really* bad. You heard my mom. And I'm pretty sure I would fuck it up, and things would be ten times worse than they were before we…*liked*…each other. No, don't argue, it's true. But! I started therapy!"

I wrinkle my nose, aware that I announced my therapy the way someone would announce a silver bullet during a werewolf hunt. "And I know it's not, like, a magical cure, but I'm working through some stuff. And… And when I'm done with that, if we still like each other, I'd maybe, sorta, not vomit in my mouth if you were to try and do whatever you were thinking about doing a second ago." *Have to throw a joke in there, you freak show.*

Jack doesn't laugh at my joke. He doesn't react at all at first. But then he lifts his gray gaze and tractor-beams me in with it. "Okay."

"Okay?"

"Okay. I understand. I hope therapy goes well." He lifts my hand, turning it palm-up, and drops a slow kiss on the sensitive skin of my wrist. And holy shit does it ring my bell. "Back to work, slacker." He releases me, and I have to force myself to move.

The work to take down the rest of the wooden slats does go way faster with Jack using the circular saw, and our breaks are few and far between. The echo of our earlier conversation hangs over both of us like a hot fog. Jack orders us sandwiches for lunch, grinning when I inspect my chicken sandwich and find it perfectly sans mayo. I order us Indian food for dinner, refusing his money, since he refused mine. We're just about to get back to our work when we're derailed by the sound of a knock at his door. A feminine voice sounds on the other side.

Anna appears with a tearstained face, a red nose, and jerking shoulders from weeping-induced hiccups. She looks beautiful and tragic, a willow branch bent by a windstorm.

A brunette tendril has escaped her severe bun. She brushes it back, draws in a deep breath, and cries out, "I broke up with him," before launching herself at her brother.

I melt back into my apartment to give them privacy, but with most of our wall gone, I can't help catching snippets of their conversation—nonsensical outbursts of love and hurt and hate and regret from her, and murmured comforting words from him. Jack hugs Anna close, letting her cry it out. And then he wipes her tears and sits her on his barstool while he makes her tea.

He says all the right things and then chases them with ice cream. He is sweet and tender, and it causes an ache to blossom in my chest.

I am hiding in my bedroom with the door open because I am *not at all nosy*. For the moment, things seem to have quieted. I text Avery:

Anna broke up with her fiancé.

Avery responds with a gif of a man who goes from sobbing into a napkin to dancing in jubilation.

I shake my head.

Avery Vaughn, I thought you were a gentleman. Give the girl a proper mourning period.

No. I am but a gentleboy. Not yet a gentleman. Teach me, Dime Store Yoda.

Avery...

Relax. I'll be her shoulder to cry on... Do you want to be my best man?

I can tell even through the phone that Avery is ecstatic.

Who are you? Avery Vaughn would never chase someone who was taken.

I haven't pursued her. I pushed her away when she was taken. And I was mainly kidding just now, but even if I wasn't, she isn't taken now, so maybe stop with the judgment? When have I judged you? I can't try a different path when the one I've been on has gotten me nowhere?

Okay, okay. Good lord.

Woof. That's the closest thing to a fight Avery and I have ever had. I hold my breath, waiting for his response.

There is a long pause. And then:

Is she okay?

There's the Avery I know. Though he told me her fiancé sounded like a colossal ham sandwich—boring, boorish, undeserving of her—he is still worried about her feelings.

I hear Jack offering up his bedroom to Anna. After tucking her in, I hear him puttering around in the destruction that is our living rooms, although it's clear he's trying to keep the sound to a minimum.

I exit my bedroom and look around. I tried to clean a bit as unobtrusively as I could, but this place is still a mega-disaster. Jack looks around wearily and sighs.

"You so want to vacuum, don't you?"

"More than I want oxygen, yes. But she passed out right away, and she's a light sleeper. And she wanted to be alone, so I won't be bunking with her. I'm going to be huffing this dust in all night." He removes the sheet he threw over his sofa and eyes it dubiously.

"You can sleep with me. My bed, I mean. Not *with* me," I hear myself say, like the babbling monster I am.

He stops, goes very still. "First lunch, now bed?"

"You're the worst. Offer retracted."

"No, it's not." Beneath his weariness, there is amusement in his expression, and something else I can't put my finger on. He crosses his arms and appraises me. "You sure that's a good idea?"

The way he says it, in an almost-growl, hits me south of the equator. Hard. "Why? You— If you can't behave yourself, I can always go crash at Margie's and you take my bed. Just don't go through my underwear drawer."

"No, I can behave. Was worried about you keeping your hands to yourself, actually. Even with the therapy."

I make a scoffing noise, halfway between a laugh and a snort.

"Your friend's probably got Lara over, anyway." He says it

without any kind of inflection, albeit in a slightly rushed way. He saw Margie and La exiting the bathroom at the party. He knows they're getting hot and heavy. "So... Okay, then. Thanks."

I am very conscious of my breathing when I say, "Right. Okay, then. I'm going to go shower..."

We regard each other until I force myself to pad to my bathroom. Where I take a very cold shower.

What the hell have I just done?

*You were trying to be nice.*

Was I?

I close my eyes and let the water run over my face. This is a very bad idea. *Bad, bad Penny.*

When I come out of the bathroom, Jack is emerging from his. His hair is damp; he's wearing shorts and a shirt. I find myself wondering if that's his normal bedtime attire or if he's being modest for me.

Even though it's just sleep, I'm nervous as a virgin. I give him a half smile and call out, "Right this way, m'lord." *Control yourself, you moron.*

He gives me a wry glance and follows me to my room. Once in, he looks around at all my little knickknacks and photos. It's cozy and tranquil, everything designed to suck you in and hug you close and make you feel safe.

"Stop being nosy."

"Only fair since you snooped in my room." At my affronted look, he says, "Picture on my wall? Oh, and you missed a ton of coins under the bed."

"I don't know what you're talking about."

"Right."

I lick my lips, my mouth suddenly Sahara-dry. "You— You can have that side."

He gets in on the left side of the bed, and I flick off the lights, then slide in on the other side, the sheets cool against my legs and arms. Why did I choose shorts and a tank top? I push my bedroom-fashion regrets aside as we face away from one another. Jack's bed is a full, maybe to accommodate the weights and crap in his room, so he wouldn't have had much room if he'd bunked with Anna. Mine is a queen. Bigger than his, but still. There isn't much space separating us. His body heat is a burning brand at my back.

"You have a lot of plants in here," he says.

"Your eyes work. Congrats." I grab for my cell and scroll through, the faint light illuminating the room somewhat. I'm poking blindly around my apps, looking for anything to avoid thinking about him in my bed.

"Thank you. For this. I wasn't looking forward to that dust all night."

"Of course. Sleeping with me is always a better choice than lung damage."

I feel the bed move, hear him laugh. His rear slides against mine. I tense. He shifts slightly, angling his body away. "Dancing cheek to cheek," he says, humor lurking in his voice.

It's a long time before I fall asleep.

# 24

I reach for the Pirate Duke, running my hands up under his shirt, pressing my palms against his hot chest. He groans deeply in my ear. He jerks when my fingers brush his nipple. I do it again, pinching. He gasps and runs his hand up over my breast, pulling the top of my bodice down, drawing me free of the cloth and testing the weight of me in his hand. He returns the favor, pinching my nipple, wresting a breathless gasp of aching ecstasy from me. I reach down and grab him firmly, loving the way he instinctively rubs against my hand. He lifts his head, staring down at me with a fierce expression. "Fuck."

I frown. I was expecting flowery prose. Something about me being a rose ripe for plucking, or some crap about wanting my nectar.

*No, no, stop questioning. Stay in the dream.*

He toys with my nipple again, wrenching a moan from me, and I'm pulled back into the moment, losing the thread of my thoughts. He lowers his lips to my breast, watching me from the eye not covered by that black patch. As he smiles, his face changes slightly. His hair color becomes a touch darker, his uncovered eye shifting from green to a pewter-gray.

His lips are a breath away from mine, and then his mouth is on me, his wicked, wicked tongue drawing, pulling. I buck, opening my eyes and staring up at him as he grins at me.

*Wait. Jack?*

*No, damn it. Stay in the moment. Stay in the dream.* I reach for him again, rubbing—

A sound wakes me up.

I've moaned so loud and long that it penetrated the veil between my very raunchy dream and wakefulness. My eyes pop open as I remember who is in bed with me.

The sound awakens Jack, enough that he groggily opens his eyes. He smiles a slow, sexy, piratical grin. "Good morning. Told you you're a moaner."

He reaches for me, and I press a hand against his chest, my eyes as wide as my lids allow. I see the split second when it dawns on him what is happening. His lips draw closer. Another moan sounds, this time decidedly *not* from me. Jack moves against my hand. Which is in his pants. Wrapped around him. I register the velvet feel of him, the impressive shape, the damp tip, in the eye-blink before I jerk my hand away.

Oh my God.

We both roll onto our backs. He throws his arm over his eyes. I am a marble statue, barely breathing.

When a few minutes have passed, and I'm not even sure he's still awake, I say, thickly, "Ah. So… About that. I thought I was dreaming…"

He hauls in a bucketful of air and releases it through the pursed *O* of his lips. I try not to look at the blanket bunched around his hips. When he finally speaks, his voice is sleep-deepened.

"I knew you wouldn't be able to keep your hands to yourself."

I cringe, my eyes locked on my shadowed ceiling.

"I know I'm irresistible, but—"

"Oh my God, don't joke!" I shove at his arm, pushing it off his eyes. He rolls over, pinning me partially under him. He is dazzling in the pre-sunrise light. The weight of him is delicious. His stomach is pressed to mine, skin to skin where my shirt has ridden up. His leg rubs against mine, between mine.

*Do we let this happen?* I see my question reflected in his eyes. The world has narrowed to Jack. Every muscle is strained to the breaking point with *want.* I shift my leg, the one trapped between his, letting my thigh rub up, just a bit, against his erection. He hisses out a breath.

Jack drops his head. "You're wiped out."

"You're exhausted," I answer, and it feels like a pressure valve in my chest has been released.

"We've been burning the candle at both ends."

"I read once that sleep deprivation mimics drunkenness. Bad decisions, you know?" My lips are dry. I can't muster enough energy to take in as much air as I need. "What I said last night. It still applies."

Jack tenses. "Yeah, don't sweat it," he says, his tone mild. He rolls away from me and sits on the side of the bed for a few seconds before launching himself up and out of the room, his impressive erection leading the way through his tented shorts like a phallic dousing rod.

I grab for his pillow and press it atop my face, breathing his scent in, shouting silently. *What fresh hell…?*

The faucet in Jack's bathroom runs for a long while. He never comes back to bed.

And I never get back to sleep.

The guy in the cubicle next to mine drops something, and I recoil. It's been that way all morning. My brain and my body are treating all sudden sounds like pouncing rooftop assassins, temporarily yanking me from my shock-induced stupor.

My phone vibrates: Mom.

You didn't call Brian. I texted him to ask.

Heat floods my body. She won't stop. She doesn't listen. I throw my phone on my desk, returning to the report I was running.

My phone rings. I barely glance at it, expecting it to be one of my mother's famed technological double-taps. It is not.

*Lucas Webb.*

Butt-dial? Diatribe? Wondering why I, a peon who is friends with one of his costars, keeps reaching out as if we're bosom buddies? Why is he calling me? I worry at my lip and sit back in my chair, debating whether or not to let him go to voicemail.

The ringing stops.

Another incoming call. Lucas Webb.

Mom isn't the only one who won't take no for an answer.

"Hello?" I half stand, looking around my cubicle to make sure there's no one nearby to eavesdrop.

"Penelope," Lucas says. My name comes out in three hard-fought syllables. His voice sounds like he's talking through a mouthful of cotton balls.

"Lucas… H-how are you? How are you feeling?"

"Better. Listen, my agent didn't grab the goddamn script when I was carted out of there. I think it's still at your place. Can I come by?"

All of that, and he didn't even get his script? Oof. "Oh. Wow… I haven't seen it, but… Of course. Is after work okay?"

He agrees.

I rush out to meet Margie in the park for lunch, grateful she was free for a couple of hours, since she's been so occupied with the commercial grind. And she's prompt for once, carrying two gigantic iced coffees in her hands. I notice the people she passes noticing her. People always give her an extra glance or two because she's so incredibly stunning, but now I detect recognition in their gazes. This show, *Glass and Carter*, is putting her on the map.

And I've ruined it.

I stand and hug her tightly. She squeezes me back, at first with one arm and then with both, her hands still clutching our coffees.

"I've said it before, but it's been a minute since the last time: I'm so so so so so sorry about the show."

I say all of this pressed into Margie's bosom because she's taller than me and practically on stilts. I don't try to hide the tears lodged in my throat.

She laughs. "Shut up. Let's sit." I give her another squeeze, refusing to let go, and she waddle-walks me to a bench, standing there until I drop down. She hands me my coffee and then sits next to me, murmuring, "We've got an audience now, wackjob."

I stare at her with wide puppy-dog eyes and take a long pull on my straw.

She sits back with a sigh. "Stop giving me that look. I don't blame you for the thing with Lucas. Actually, I find that whole story fucking hilarious, except that...you know...my job's in limbo. But it has never once crossed my mind to put that on you, so stop feeling bad."

"I love you."

Margie waves her free hand dismissively. "I love you, too. Now shut up about it, please? The cast's meeting soon to discuss. Waiting on the showrunner to call us. Lucas has to have his jaw wired shut for at least six weeks. I don't know. Whatever. It'll be fine."

"He called me. Lucas."

Margie's eyebrows shoot up, and I fill her in on his request.

"What else is going on with you?" she asks.

"Oh. You know." Red hair equals no ability to repress blushes. God's own lie detector. Or anxiety detector. Or heightened emotion detector. I'm a tomato.

"Christ, you're extra today. What is it? What did you do?"

"I kind of, sort of, touched Jack's wiener."

Margie knows me. My silly antics kept her amused in college. My babbling gives her life. Right now, she looks like the cackle she wants to release is warring with her shock that I've managed to surprise her. She shakes her head, her face *so* blank I fucking know there's a smile under the mask. She studies the passing pedestrians, the sun-dappled green space around us, and then deadpans, "Start at the beginning."

My tale of woe takes five minutes, and it's another five until Margie stops laughing. When she finally does, I wish she hadn't.

"You like him."

"Yes."

"You're attracted to him."

"He's… Well… I mean… Yes."

"You're going to get with him."

"Absolutely not."

"You're so annoying. You light up when you talk about him, Penny. Even when you despised him, he challenged you, and you enjoyed it. I could tell. Shhhh." She holds up a hand. "Let me finish. There is no way my friend Penelope would've been in a closet with a guy if she didn't want him. You've admitted you like him. That you're attracted to him. I don't understand what the problem is. Explore it."

I set my drink down on the ground and press my thumbs into my eyes. "I want to, damn it." The image of Jack hovering over me in bed makes me shiver. "But he's buying his apartment. We'll be neighbors for ages, possibly. You know things never last with me!"

"Could be something else for ages if you open yourself up."

I pick up my coffee and nudge a rock with my shoe. "This is all because of La. You're like those converts who start preaching the gospel to everyone. It's the fucking worst."

Margie swallows a smile, a blush high on her cheekbones. She dated women in college, so this whole thing isn't out of left field. But her history, with both men and women, was always casual. Margie isn't a head-over-heels sort. Catching feelings was what other people did. Not Margie. Margie had fun.

"Never felt this way. Never will again. She's a pisser, and a boss, and I want to carry her around in my pocket everywhere. So. Yeah. I'm screwed."

Margie shrugs and sips her coffee. "Let me preach to you the word, Penelope. And the word is love." She looks contemplative, puzzled even, for a second, as if even she can't believe what she just said. And then she gives a buoyant and beautifully ginormous smile in response to my expression. "Holy shit, can you believe it? I'm in love."

# 25

I mull over Margie's little monologue for the rest of the day. It takes up so much real estate in my mind that I autopilot my way home after work. I'm so preoccupied that I almost forget about Lucas coming by to pick up his script. His text reminds me.

I'm outside your building.

I chew my lip and text back.

Rounding the corner now.

I'm casually texting with a TV star like we're pen pals after I indirectly broke his jaw with my shenanigans. Life is absurd.

I don't see him until he emerges from the back of a car parked in front of my building. He's still handsome, but his face shows signs of losing the battle with The Hole, even with his sunglasses on. And he looks like he's lost weight. Probably on account of his jaw being wired shut. He pulls off the shades with the hand that isn't bandaged to his mid-forearm.

"Hi," I say awkwardly.

"Hi," he replies.

"Alrighty… Let's go check for your script." I turn to lead the way into my building and up to my apartment.

"I'm sorry," he says to my back, "about my behavior on the

phone. That wasn't nice of me. This wasn't your fault."

I turn. "I *feel* responsible. I chose that scene. I didn't tell you about the hole in the wall. I didn't know my neighbor would jump through it, but when he heard what he did… Funny thing, he actually thought you and I were on a date and– Anyway, I'm sorry, too. I don't blame you for verbally flipping me the bird."

"Forget about it. My agent had the police report buried. I don't want any of this getting to the press. You can make it up to me by never speaking of it again. Okay?"

I give him a small smile, and he bares his metal-filled mouth slightly. Beggars can hardly be choosers. I'll take what acts of grace I can get.

"You look good with braces," I babble. He shakes his head, but his expression lives somewhere between chagrined and amused.

When we reach my apartment, I warn him about the state of things inside. *Please don't let Jack be home.* I can't handle an awkward confrontation after last night, or an awkward confrontation between him and Lucas. I especially can't handle both.

Jack is, of course, home.

He's cleaned up both his place and mine, finally wielding that vacuum he was pining after while his sister slept. There is no wall left between our apartments. My heart is in my throat as he exits his bedroom and sees Lucas standing behind me. I couldn't read his expression before he noticed Lucas, but now it's completely shuttered.

"Uh. Hi, Jack," I say. His gaze is penetrating and aloof. He approaches us, and I clear my throat. "You remember Lucas…"

Jack surprises me, holding out his hand to Lucas. "I'm sorry about what happened. I misunderstood the situation and thought you were—"

I feel Lucas stiffen next to me as Jack approaches. He raises his strapped-up right wrist to show Jack why he won't shake hands. But then he does something surprising and alarming: he throws his heavy arm over my shoulder and pulls me to his side.

"It's all right. Apology accepted. You were trying to protect this one." He gives me an admiring glance as I fix an owl-eyed stare on him. "Just don't mention it to the media and we're good." He gives my shoulder a squeeze. There's a lusty, banked heat in his eyes.

I'm being used to recoup Lucas's lost machismo or something. I don't like it. But I remain silent because the guy has to drink his meals for another month because of me, and because I think I see something coiled and ready to strike behind Jack's blank expression. Jealousy? Or maybe it's residual dislike. When you form an opinion of someone that includes "forcibly makes women fellate him," there's not much room for growth. Jack makes himself scarce shortly thereafter.

We find Lucas's script in the pile of magazines and mail on my kitchen counter, probably all swept up when Jack cleaned my apartment. Lucas rolls it up, clutching it in his fist and shifting awkwardly.

"About before… I should explain," he says.

"Yeah."

"Look, that guy may have cost me this part." He holds up the script. "Filming for my show is on ice right now—and he looked like he wanted to launch himself at me all over again when he spotted me with you. You're not going to give me grief over a little revenge, are you?"

"He didn't hurt you, Lucas." I sigh. I want to have sympathy for the man, but right now it feels like I have nothing left to give.

Like my tank is running on fumes. "You fought The Hole, and The Hole won." I pause. "But your little stunt was for no good reason anyhow, because he wasn't even jealous."

Lucas snorts. "Sweetheart, you don't know what you're working with if you believe that." He glances down at his watch. "Well, maybe I'll see you on set sometime. If the show doesn't get cancelled." He throws on his sunglasses and gives me one last tight metal smile before heading out.

After Lucas leaves, I hug the idea of me and Jack like a teddy bear, breathing it in and squeezing it to me with all my might. Playing out the fantasy of giving in after that absurd wakeup. Of us together. Of me becoming enough of a normal human via therapy to let it happen. Or maybe the point of therapy is to realize that being sort of not-normal…might be okay, too? Ugh.

Right now, our apartments have merged into one mega-apartment, and I find myself wondering what it looked like back in the day, as one unit. Of what it could become. A bigger kitchen, for sure. Maybe keep the two bathrooms, but move the bedrooms to one side…

I drag my cleaning supplies over to his side of the apartment and scrub at the remnants of tuna fish behind his radiator, gagging a little as I do. I'm done and thankfully on the floor of my living room, chiseling out little bits of plaster and wood around the edges of the wall we didn't get with the circular saw, when the door to Jack's apartment opens. My heart goes back to its regularly scheduled beating when I realize it's just Anna letting herself in, her phone to her ear.

"Hey, Penny," she says and then pauses. "Avery says hi."

I blanch and recover quickly, smiling a hello, reminding myself to give Avery a talking-to about rebound etiquette, regardless of whether he wants to hear it from me. She wanders to the kitchen, pulling a soda from the fridge, and then goes into Jack's bedroom, the phone still pressed to her ear. I hear her throaty laugh as she closes the door.

Keys jangle again: this has to be Jack. I drop the Avery-and-Anna speculation and get back to scraping like mad. I see Jack enter from the corner of my eye. He tosses his keys on his counter and knocks on his bedroom door before heading in, emerging with some wall-work clothes. After a quick change in the bathroom, he grabs his tools, and I watch with undisguised interest as he carries a stool to the very opposite end of our former wall and climbs on top. I force my eyes off his ass as he tackles the remnants of wood and plaster dangling from the ceiling.

We work like that, in silence, for what feels like forever. It's actually less than half an hour.

"How's it going?" I say, the quiet finally breaking me.

"Great."

"Seems great. You look overjoyed." I don't like me when I'm nervous. I wish I could trade places with Lucas right now. A wired jaw might help me out.

I scrape at a stubborn piece of lath caught in the wall.

Jack moves his stool a foot to the left.

"Have you ever done therapy? Is that the phrase? Done therapy? It sounds wrong. Therapized? Huh. Anyway. My therapy is going well. It's like cleaning out an attic. Gotta move the stuff closest to the entrance before you get to the things moldering in the back. Mouse droppings and whatever. Getting there, though! Some days it feels really heavy, but others, it's like I'm lighter? I'm starting to notice things I didn't before, too. Working on tools to shore up boundaries or whatever. Sense of self. Blah blah blah, you're not listening."

"I'm listening. Good for you." His tone isn't at all sarcastic. He's sincere. Curt but sincere.

"Lucas was trying to make you jealous before. Isn't that nuts? He was mad about the jaw thing and decided to use me as a prop. D-bag move. Don't worry, though, I told him you weren't jealous."

Jack grunts. The quiet stretches. We don't talk again until I'm sweeping dust into the dustpan and Jack is unwinding his vacuum cord.

"So, I touched your dong, huh?"

I blurt it out just as Jack is switching the vacuum on. When it starts up, I pray that maybe he didn't hear me and curse my stupid mouth. The vacuum switches off.

He stares at me and then up at the ceiling. In a superhero flick, this would be the moment he calls forth lightning to smite me.

"'Dong.'"

"You know, your—"

"I know what you're talking about. I'm questioning your frat-boy choice of noun."

Every capillary on my face and neck fills with all the blood it can hold. I feel overheated. A surreptitious glance in the wall mirror confirms that I am, in fact, a lobster.

"Well, whatever. Your winky. That's what Mom used to call them. 'That boy just likes you 'cause he hopes you'll touch his winky, Penny.'" I mimic my mother and close my eyes.

Jack flicks the vacuum back on.

I disintegrate into a pool of mortification and fiddle with the garbage bags of dust, hauling them to the basement despite Jack's insistence on multiple occasions that he run them down. I need the escape to clear my head, even if it does come with an eau-du-basement-mildew-and-trash olfactory assault.

When I return, Jack is winding up his vacuum cord.

"Well, g'night," I say quickly, heading to my bathroom. I am *so* ready to put this day to bed.

"There are worse ways to wake up, by the way," he calls out.

I suspect he was saving that particular grenade for my retreat.

# 26

The office is quieter than usual. More than one person decided to squeeze in an end-of-summer vacation this week. Meanwhile, I had to come in early for this global call, since not everyone could meet at our regular time. I've resorted to creative coping mechanisms.

"If I can interject here…" the Professor says.

I take my highlighter and press it firmly to the square reading "If I can interject" on my handmade Global Call Bingo card. I'm one square away from victory. And from having my soul crushed. All before nine thirty in the morning.

"Before we get this to our localization teams, we really need to talk about the cover for this asset…" he continues.

I peer down. *Wants to revisit something already decided on ages ago.*

Bingo.

"Anthony," I interrupt gently, "we already worked through that while you were on vacation, and branding has already reviewed. We really can't delay things because—"

"I insist that we should. The imagery is not evocative enough. The woman is looking down instead of up. She's holding a pencil. Does it not convey—"

I need my raise. He is not doing this to me. Not with the

finish line fast approaching.

"No, I'm sorry, but I really insist that we move on. We circulated this for comment three weeks ago. The regions have weighed in. You were on vacation, but we received approval from Carla, who you had filling in for you. We're on a tight deadline, and nice-to-haves like revisiting settled to-do list items after one person returns from vacation are unfortunately not something we can accommodate. Now, moving to the next agenda item, unless there's any objection?"

I don't give anyone time to object, because I'm positive Anthony would. I railroad my way to the next topic, feeling like I could karate chop my desk in half from the adrenaline rush.

Rochelle comes by my desk, eyes super round with disbelief, after the call ends. "You. Were. Amazing. I was multitasking, but I caught that verbal ass-beating. Good for you!"

I sit back in my chair and feel like I'm showing every tooth in my mouth. "Thank you! Now get me that raise. Ha."

Rochelle's expression flickers, probably from shock at my direct demand—even if it *is* softened by a laugh. "Yep, we're on our way to trying for it!"

What started as a shit day actually ends up being pretty productive and great. I shut down Anthony's nonsense, got as close to demanding a raise as my people-pleasing heart could without combusting, and secured budget approvals to run our first global campaign through the framework we've been developing. And my idea to build the framework in tandem with a real test campaign means that we'll be ready to roll on a launch way sooner than management was expecting. I'm feeling myself as I open my front door.

Jack is already home when I get there, arranging two-by-fours along the dividing line between our two apartments. The wall is gone, and the area has been demoed, sanded, and cleaned to the point where The Hole feels like a memory—albeit one that still has my muscles aching.

He glances up at me, then sits back on his haunches, surveying me. I look my fill right back. He looks rakish. Handsome, in a rumpled, five-o'clock-shadow kind of way. He is *totally* a dark-haired young Harrison Ford right now. This version of Jack bears an uncanny similarity to the way I first imagined the Pirate Duke, a connection I choose not to examine too closely.

"What's different?" he says. "You look…excited?"

I have to purse my lips to keep the force of my "fuck yeah!" feelings in check, but they cannot be contained. With Jack, they don't have to be. He knows I'm extra. Plus, it's not every day I put Anthony in his place. I'm not doing the usual second-guessing thing, where I agonize after trying to assert myself. I'm forcing myself to ignore the peacemaking harpy in my brain. "What's different is that I demanded the damn chicken sandwich, no mayo. Figuratively."

His expression is a tangle of confusion and amusement as he stands and towels the dust off his hands. "Amazing. What exactly is a figurative chicken sandwich?"

"I stood up for myself! At work!" I explain about Anthony. Jack laughs at my homemade bingo card and frowns as I recount Anthony's interruptions.

"Oh, you'll appreciate this one: 'Penny, we know you have the best of intentions. It's just that your intentions are not a match for your knowledge in this arena.'"

"Dick," Jack murmurs as he approaches.

I stare up at him and nod. "And he says it in a soft voice. He's like a nasty *T. rex* dressed up as a friendly brontosaurus. But I finally shut. Him. Down. BOOM!" I laugh out loud, and seized with a sudden urge, I throw my arms around Jack's neck and give him a joyful hug.

I hear him chuckle in my ear as he hugs me back before swinging me around. "Proud of you. How's that chicken sandwich taste?"

"Incredible." I smile up at him, and he sets me down, our bodies sliding against each other as he slowly releases me. His gray eyes darken. The vibe in the room shifts immediately. Dongward.

I clear my throat and brush an awkward hand on his shoulder, removing dust that doesn't exist. "Back to work!" I crow, turning on my heels with eyes as big as Carmine's famous meatballs. "I'm gonna change. Be out in a second."

I take way too long to change, taking the time to do important things, such as lying on my bed and staring at the ceiling, and mouthing *He's so fucking hot. UGH* to myself in my mirror.

When I emerge, Jack is seated on one of my kitchen stools, looking up different types of trim on his iPad. I hum as I walk around the apartment, checking out my mail and nibbling at my leftover ravioli from the night before.

"Do you mind?"

"That you're here? Yes. But I figured I don't have a choice," I say around a mouthful of pasta.

"Ha. Seriously, though, humming is my biggest pet peeve."

"Hmm. You the same guy who plays music on repeat to bother your neighbor?"

"Nope. You've got the wrong guy."

"Humming. I could've driven you mental by humming the past few months?"

He nods.

"Well, you've revealed your kryptonite now. Foolish." I waggle my eyebrows. *"Dangerous."*

"Maybe I'm learning to trust you."

I hum out the theme to Disney's *Beauty and the Beast* and wave my hands like I'm conducting an orchestra. His mouth flattens into an unappreciative line.

"We're like *Highlander*," I say with a grin. "There can only be one happy person in this apartment at a time."

"Okay… Watching *Goodfellas*. Referencing *Highlander*. I've heard you throw around a few other references… You were a tomboy, weren't you?"

"I was a girl who watched what my dad watched. And your whole gender-norms thing is gross."

"Yeah, yeah. But your dad liked those movies so you like those movies?"

"He *watched* those movies, I said. Most of them he couldn't be bothered with. *Highlander* pissed him off. I adored it. *Bloodsport*? I practiced Van Damme splits all over the house. He couldn't stand it." At Jack's questioning look, I reluctantly add, "He'd never rent a movie more than once. He craved novelty. Guess it wasn't only movies, seeing as how he left his wife for someone else."

"Oh." There is softness in Jack's eyes. Compassion. For me.

I force a smile. "You'd think he would've loved the ones with *happy endings*, but nope, thrill was gone after that first watch."

"Stop telling Jack your problems," Anna says from the doorway of Jack's bedroom. She's been in and out of the apartment every day since her breakup. Right now she's in one of his shirts and a pair of shorts. I freeze, mortified that I inadvertently shared something so personal in front of someone who is pretty much a stranger to me. I don't want to examine why I didn't feel the same about sharing with Jack.

Anna heads to the kitchen and opens the fridge, where she

glugs white wine into a regular water glass before slamming the refrigerator closed. “He feeds on that shit. Don’t be surprised if he tries to rescue you, too.”

Jack stands and runs a hand through his hair. “Anna, please go to bed.”

I frown at Anna, questioning. She shakes her head at me pityingly. “That’s his thing. Haven’t picked up on that yet? White knight!” I notice for the first time that she’s slurring a little. “Good old Jack. Pride of the Craig family. Perfect Jack! Lawyer. And he’s always right… He was right about Seth each and every one of the fifty fucking times he played me. Loved being right about that, huh? But you’re wrong about Avery, Jack. You don’t know how wrong—”

“Anna—”

“Jack even saved our mom’s life once, from choking. He was *sixteen*! Who knows the fucking Heimlich at sixteen? Isn’t that amazing?”

“Okay, Anna.”

“Full ride to college, but he worked two jobs anyway to help pay the mortgage. He was working to pay our bills long before that, though, back when he was a teenager and Dad got sick.” She gestures with her glass, wine sloshing over the rim onto the floor. “Family fixer! When I broke my leg and couldn’t dance anymore, you remember what Mom would tell me? No, you don’t, because you weren’t there. It was, ‘Be more like your brother.’ You’re not even human. You don’t have feelings like normal people. No time for a girlfriend when you’re a fucking cyborg, racing around saving the day to keep yourself from *feeling* anything except satisfied at how completely perfect you are.”

An angry look crosses Jack’s face for a nanosecond. He ushers Anna back into his room, trying to claim her wine cup.

I wipe up the spilled wine and try not to listen to their raised voices. Opening his under-sink cabinet to toss the soiled paper towels, I view the fire extinguisher with new eyes. The giant poison control card on the fridge, too. He isn't a hyper-guarded, overprepared weirdo—he just had to grow up faster than he should've, had to take care of the people around him. He still does—still *is*. Jack emerges a few minutes later. He looks harried.

I feel a pang of sympathy for him. Difficult family members are kind of my thing.

"What was that about Avery?"

"She's just… She's wasted right now. Argued with her ex. Ignore her."

"Is she okay?" I ask.

He nods and rubs at the back of his neck. He looks exhausted. "She's not doing well with the breakup. And when she's like this, she's a little like a leaf in a rainstorm, sticking to whatever solid object crosses her path. Until the go-round."

He picks up a piece of wood, and I wonder if Anna's nasty remarks stung. There are worse things than being called a hero, but he looks as upset as I've ever seen him. And tired. He's been on the sofa since the other night when I molested him.

I move to him and still his hand. The touch is like a zap, loading the air around us with crackling energy Nikola Tesla would've been impressed by. I don't know if I imagine his thumb rubbing my palm, but my breath seizes just the same. I force myself to speak. "Maybe we avoid kicking up more dust tonight. How about I order Chinese and we watch *Bloodsport*?"

His skin and mine are touching. I can barely think of anything else. I wonder if he's thinking of that, too—thinking about the fact that he had his Jake Gyllenhaal in my hand as a result of a different dusty night.

He gives me a wry and resigned smirk before agreeing to my offer.

Not long after, we're sitting side by side in my living room, polishing off the remains of some damn good General Tso's and watching the cultiest of cult classics.

"The fact you can quote this movie by heart..." Jack says, shaking his head and tucking back into his bowl.

"What? I'm a cinephile. I'd say that's one of my better qualities."

"You've got better qualities?"

I hold up my chopsticks. "I have a weapon."

"Tough talk. What are you going to do? Wait until I fall asleep and handle my... What was that again?" He deploys the dimples. Oh, he has to know what he's doing. Those are military-grade, surface-to-lady-bits missiles.

I nearly choke.

I fold my napkin demurely on my lap. "I have no idea what you're talking about."

Jack laughs.

We settle into a cozy kind of silence while we watch the movie, interrupted only by the occasional verbal jab, and later by Anna's departure. About halfway through, when he's returning from a snack break, I murmur, "You know, you're a lot like Frank here." I gesture toward the frozen Van Damme on the screen. "Protector. At least from what I know of your work and what Anna said."

Jack's smile fades, and he flops down onto the sofa. I instantly regret saying anything, and I'm about to press play on the remote when he says, "That make you my Ray Jackson?" The levity in his voice sounds forced as he compares me to the main character's friend.

"More like your Chong Li," I say, referencing the primary antagonist. "This apartment is our Kumite."

Jack's lip quirks as he surveys me. Then his gaze drops to the bowl of chips in his hands, and he sets it down on my end table. "Maybe life is a Kumite. And when you've had to be strong for a really long time—to fight for the people around you—it's hard to stop."

He clears his throat. "Give that to me." He playfully grabs at the remote and presses play before shifting so that he's lying down. His head rests on a pillow pressed against my thigh, and I fight an animal urge to push his hair off his forehead.

He's revealed something profound. I can feel it, but I don't know the right way to react. So I say nothing. We watch the movie, the companionable silence tinged with a little something extra, an edge of disquiet radiating off him. At least for a little while.

When I realize that he's fallen asleep, I only just resist combing my fingers through his thick locks. Even an innocent touch without consent feels like a huge no-no—especially after the debacle in my bedroom. So I content myself with just watching him.

When he's asleep, he really doesn't look much like a gremlin after all.

# 27

"Your analogy with the chicken sandwich, how you stood up for yourself and didn't beat yourself up for it afterward," Wendy says, adjusting her long skirt over her legs as she shifts position. "That was really wonderful, Penny."

"I'm not going to lie, it felt *good*. Like there was a Penny I didn't know about, hiding out inside this shell, and when she comes out, she will fuck your shit *up*. Sorry about the cursing."

"Not at all. You should say what you feel. Your awareness of yourself is growing, which is exactly what we want to see. But let's pivot for a second, because I think this is related. Let's talk about your mom. Last time, we touched on your father leaving because she confronted him about his affair..."

I shift uncomfortably. I just got an A+ in therapy, basically, and here Wendy is, about to give me a pop quiz I haven't studied for. "Yeah."

"Do you see any correlation between that discussion and this one?"

"I—" I pause, frowning. Mom demanded her chicken sandwich, didn't she, when she told Dad she wasn't going to take his cheating anymore? When she told him she was embarrassed to show her face in town because of him. And that chicken sandwich upended our lives. Mom, bedridden. Me, fourteen, food shopping, cleaning the house, keeping Dad's plants alive, telling the school they needed a substitute again because Mom wouldn't be in. Why was the chicken sandwich so awful for her but so good for me? Unless…

"For *years* now, I've heard from my mother about how terrible it was that she confronted my dad. About her regrets." I brush a tear from my eye, roughly. "And maybe hearing it so much, hearing how it ruined her life, as shitty as that life was… Maybe that made it so that I never wanted to stick up for myself, either."

Wendy's close-lipped smile and slight nod tell me I've gotten a hole-in-one.

I set the plant I just bought—my new emotional support plant—on my end table, plumping the orange and gold leaves. It perfectly complements the new throw pillows I ordered and the anticipation-of-autumn decorations I've busted out for the mantel of my faux fireplace. Just because I'm living in a construction zone doesn't mean I can't be festive. And basic. Festively basic!

Jack looks up from the counter, where he's eating a bowl of cereal. "Won summary judgment, by the way. Case goes forward. Sophie is ecstatic."

"That's amazing! I'm so happy!" A warmth spreads through me. There's something strangely intimate about the way he casually shared something about his day as if we were mid-conversation.

His brow furrows. "Are you okay? You look like you've been crying."

"Nothing. I'm fine. It's…" Might as well say it since I already told him I'm working on myself. "Had a rough go of it in therapy. That's all."

Jack nods but thankfully does not pry. He's already started to tackle the wood framework for the wall, I note. The sight leaves me feeling a bit sorry for myself, but I'm not sure why. Maybe I'm still feeling fragile after that power session.

Jack waves a paper to get my attention and drops it on the granite countertop. "Gence slipped this under my door. Three weeks left to tell him if you're going to buy your place if you haven't already."

I inspect the floor of my entryway. "He didn't slip anything under mine."

"Well, you've been trying to put him into a diabetic coma for the last several years, so..."

I harrumph and set about watering my new plant.

"I was, you know. Jealous."

I tip my head to the side, feeling like I've wandered into a conversation I'm not a party to. "Come again?"

"Didn't the first time."

"Ba dum tish." I roll my eyes and make a drum sound.

"I said I was jealous. The little actor was right." He stares right at me when he says it, no shame in his molten silver gaze as he lazes back against his counter.

My mouth becomes a perfect *O* of wonder. That tiny confession sends my pulse galloping. My apartment grows ten degrees warmer from one moment to the next. "Why are you telling me this?"

He shrugs. "Because I wanted you to know. You're doing therapy, that's great. I'm waiting patiently for you to figure things out. Doesn't mean I don't think of–"

"Jake Gyllenhaal."

"What?"

"Nothing, continue."

He frowns a little, looking a touch more hesitant than before. "I got jealous, was the moral of the story there."

I want to squeal. I want to run to him, plop myself in his lap, and bring his lips to mine. I want to rest my head against his chest and cry. I want a whole lot of things. But today's session with Wendy proved I'm far from okay as an individual, let alone ready to tackle being a pair. So I squelch the feelings down, deep down into a lockbox I'll paw through at night for fantasy fodder. And I resort to what I know: humor.

"He's not little…" I cast a dreamy glance at the ceiling and sigh. "He's divine. And *very* muscly."

Jack chuckles. "I said I *was* jealous. But then again, he's a better actor than you. He sold the attraction thing."

"And I didn't? Let me bust out some sonnets I've composed."

"About me? I'm flattered. But I'd rather finish the wall. Grab that board." Jack shakes his head, standing to set his dish in the sink.

I rush to change, and when I emerge, I have to resist the urge to dive back into my bedroom.

Jack. Is. Shirtless. Positioning a board vertically in his living room and marking something with a pencil on a post. My mouth feels like I've been sucking down saltines for days.

I stare. And stare some more. He's fit, and he clearly works out, but he's not a vanity-muscle kind of guy. Lucas is that type, I realize—his as-seen-on-TV abs seem manufactured specifically to make you want to wash all your laundry against his chest like an old-timey country maid. Jack, on the other hand, is just strong, but not in a showy way. His body is lived-in. He has pizza and pancakes and laughs. And honestly? It makes him feel more real, more substantive, more alive, somehow.

As a result of Jack's dishabille, I spend a good chunk of time holding two-by-fours level for him to secure to other two-by-fours, while staring down at his head, or at his profile, or not-at-his-crotch when he's up on a stepladder. Anywhere but at all that bare skin.

My buzzer sounds, and I gratefully abandon Jack, despite his complaints about crooked boards, to answer it.

"Hello?"

"It's me," Margie says. I buzz her in. A few minutes later she rushes inside, waving a magazine over her head before she notices the state of my apartment and shirtless Jack. "Oh. I forgot that construction-worker cosplay is your kink. Hi, Jack."

Jack steps off his stepladder and reaches for his shirt. "Hey, Margie."

She holds the magazine out to him, and he frowns, accepting it after pulling his T-shirt over his head. I mourn the loss of that bare chest. It occurs to me that he's never felt compelled to remove his shirt before. Did he just strip for me? He totally did. Maybe. I think.

"I'm glad you two are here. Since that involves you both," she says, tipping her chin toward the magazine.

Jack swears. I step over to him to see what he's looking at.

I'm on the cover of the magazine, leaning on Lucas as we exit La's. In a small inset photo, Lucas's face sports extensive bruising. The lurid headline promises love triangles and violence.

"It's all over the internet, too," Margie says. She picks up the drill and gives it a whir, stopping when Jack glares at her.

I grab my phone off the counter and search with shaking hands. Some articles make me out to be a Jessica Rabbit seductress, red in the head, fire in the bed. I tremble. There are no photos of Jack, although one article shows the legal aid society he works for. One outlet has printed the police report and leaked information from the hospital detailing Lucas's injuries. Another paints Jack as violent, citing a bar brawl on his record—the same fight he told me his friend Moth embroiled him in.

I sit down on my sofa. *Oh, boy.*

"Lucas is famous, but not like...DiCaprio famous. But I guess having your jaw wired shut and closing down a television production is big news. Plus, nothing else remotely interesting is happening, so..." Margie shakes her head, sitting next to me.

My phone rings. Mom. A faint tremble vibrates my fingers. I just want some space. I've had six missed calls from her. I decline the call and fall sideways so that my head is in Margie's lap. "How do I fix this?" I moan.

She pats my head. "Ignore it. Some new scandal will hit, and it'll be old news soon."

I brush stray strands out of my eyes. "Are you okay?" I ask Jack.

He tosses the magazine down and runs both hands through his hair, rumpling it to holy hell. "I don't love that they have a picture of the office. It'll have a chilling effect on people coming by to ask for help, especially with immigration issues, if they think there are photogs hanging around. And I don't love that this is now the second time other people might be hurt by our association. The glitter was whatever, but I had to set aside a court brief to deal with my inbox after the gag you pulled with all that spam."

Margie lifts her hand like a first grader tentatively volunteering to read aloud. "I should mention, that was my fault. I told Penny I wanted to post your number on the Lucas fan forum, but she told me not to. I was drunk and irked enough to opt for an alternative." She squints up at Jack, looking very contrite. "That's my bad. I'm sorry."

"She told me—" Jack's lips tighten almost imperceptibly, except to someone who has been observing his facial expressions for the last few hours like Michelangelo about to carve a bust. "But that does nothing to help this situation—" He gestures toward the tabloid. "At least you two look cute, though," he spits out at me.

I glance down. There's a shot of Lucas and me on the street the day he came over to get his script. Our interaction was completely innocuous, but the cropping of the photo makes it look so intimate, and Lucas almost appears to be looking down at me with a soft expression.

I feel Margie shift and glance at her. Her eyebrows are straining for her hairline. Her lips twitch, and as I sit up again, she gives me a loaded look that tells me she has information to share. I make a questioning face, and she gives her head one tiny shake in the negative, tipping her head almost imperceptibly in Jack's direction.

I pick up my phone and text her.

What?

Her phone erupts into the loudest goddamn chime on the planet. Jack narrows his eyes at us.

Margie picks up her phone and looks up at Jack as she opens it. She types out a response to my question.

My phone vibrates audibly.

He is so, so, so jealous.

No he isn't! He's pissed right now. BUT. I have to tell you what he told me earlier.

*Chime.*

*Vibrate.*

I'm telling you. Trust your much smarter, much more worldly friend. He is jelly.

"All right, I'll give you two some privacy to handle the clearly unrelated texts you're receiving." Jack steps through the wooden framing to his apartment.

My phone vibrates again.

I think he knows we were texting each other.

"O*bre*, Penny, no offer on apartment from you?" Gence says as Jack and I descend into the lobby in the morning. "Maybe you moving out?"

I chalk up what I think is a hopeful tone to the fact I've been feeding a diabetic man blood sugar spikes for the better part of the year. Besides, he's talking to Jack, too. I think.

"Not moving, Gence. I'll be by to formally offer as soon as I sort some stuff with the bank," I say.

Jack stops to say something to Gence and then follows me outside. I awkwardly throw a "bye" his way and turn to bolt down the sidewalk.

He hesitates. "Listen, I'm sorry. The tabloid wasn't your fault. I was just angry at the situation." He looks like he needs a spoonful of sugar to make that medicine go down.

"I feel like I've been a source of drama for you lately. Between the phone prank, the glitter, this. And then there's the *Intrepid* closet and our sleepover."

He shifts, looking pained. His voice drops an octave. "Wouldn't say I minded those last two."

I chew at my bottom lip and lock eyes with a photographer across the street. "Oh my God." The photog snaps a few more pics and then rushes off. "I've got to go."

Shockingly, I breathe a sigh of relief when I get to my office. Here, things can be chaotic, but at least it's chaos I'm used to. Donna is standing by one of the conference rooms, staring at me as I make my way down the aisle to my cube. She's seen the articles. I know it.

The global project launches today, with all paid, earned, and organic media—in all languages—going live like a rolling wave across every region. And I'm the one the group tapped to present on the global rollout call to hundreds of sales and marketing pros. I'm equal parts flattered and nervous as shit, but more than anything I'm still pinching myself that we actually got to this point. I push away thoughts of tabloids or sexy neighbors or TV stars, or any of the other nonsense cluttering up my mind.

I practice my presentation script and polish my PowerPoint slides. My phone alarm goes off: fifteen minutes until preso time. I run to the bathroom and reapply my nude lipstick. I regret fiddling with my eyeliner after I inadvertently—and absent-mindedly—give myself a very evening-friendly cat's eye. Shit. No time to fix. And I look pale. Wan. I pinch my cheeks.

Showtime.

I'm third on the agenda. I try to remind myself that everyone can see my face as I fidget nervously through the first two presenters.

"And with that I'd like to introduce to the call Penelope Huff, Senior Marketer from North America, who will walk us through truly exciting news," Sam Greenfield says.

*Thanks for the intro, President Snow.* I pin a smile to my mouth and un-mute myself. The butterflies in my stomach have become attack dogs. I thank him and try to sound like I'm not reading from my script as I talk about the way the project came together and what the new global campaign infrastructure will allow us to do as a cross-functional global team. I'm talking about our goals when my throat and mouth go dry. I swallow, clear my throat a bit.

"Next slide," I croak, sneaking a sip of water during the transition.

The slide housing the imagery of the ads, of the assets we created as a team, flashes up on the screen. The different languages, the beautiful key art… My eyes well up. I helped build this. It's because of me. We're not curing cancer here, but… I set aside my papers.

"And what you see on the screen here is what's in market as of today. We're extremely proud that in such a short amount of time we not only pulled together a framework—which we'll refine and improve upon with each campaign—but that we've also launched the very first global motion this company has ever attempted. The same look, feel, and message in stereo across the globe, across multiple channels." I beam into my camera.

I crush the rest of my presentation, and I barely register the rest of the presenters, instead looking to see if my webcam-projected self is visibly blotchy from nerves. Thousands of people on a Zoom call staring at your face and slides would rattle almost anyone. But no… I look pretty darn close to the way I did that day in Jack's bathroom mirror, the day Margie decided to snoop. Glowing. Vivid. Like myself in high def.

I rush to Rochelle's office as soon as the call closes.

She sits back in her seat, the picture of satisfaction. "You did incredible."

I smile from ear to ear and adjust my black shift dress before sitting across from her at her desk. "It was a huge effort from everyone. I'm just the mouthpiece."

"Your brainchild. You helped keep it moving. Delivered the framework on time and launched a campaign using that framework. I'm blown away."

"Yeah..." I smile, feeling super shy. "I guess I did. Think Sam Greenfield is happy?"

Rochelle smiles. "I know he is. He sent me a note."

I lean forward, forcing myself to say the words. "Think I can get that raise? I've got two weeks to get approved for a mortgage, so I really need it."

Rochelle's smile never wavers. "Let me see where we are with that."

I skip out of work a little early, eager to celebrate the global launch with a glass of pinot noir and the new gloriously trashy installment of the Pirate Duke saga, *The Pirate Duke's Revenge*. Or at least as much of both as I can consume before Jack gets home and we have to work on the wall.

I'm shocked to find that Jack is already home. And that the wall is now nearly entirely covered in drywall. In fact, the only opening between my apartment and Jack's is where The Hole originally existed, smack in the center of our line of divide. The drill stops, and I see Jack poke his head through the narrow opening between our places.

"Hey. I took a half day today. Inspector came by to take a look, so I figured I'd bang this out. The wall, not you. Don't get your hopes up."

He has white dust in his dark hair, and the dimples that peep out when he smiles are almost perceptible as he greets me. He is silly and hot, and visions of his smooth, bare skin dance through my mind as I gawk at him. I look at the drywall.

"Good progress," I say.

"No comeback? Really? Things that dire?" He steps fully through, into my apartment. The place looks so small now. And darker. And there's this feeling that, although Jack's crowding the remaining space with his height right now, the second that last panel goes up, he'll disappear behind it forever. Ridiculous, but… I try and swallow past a throat that feels coated in sawdust.

Jack frowns. "Is it the tabloid stuff?" He sounds caring. He sounds like he'd hug me if I let him. It's too much.

The air between us grows tense and heavy. A fairly recent version of me would have thrown herself at Jack right now, letting the dam break over us both.

But the Penny of today knows better. I am not ready for this. Wendy may have said I can work on myself while in a relationship, but I know it's a recipe for disaster. I need to leave things alone until I'm ready.

I take three giant steps backward, putting much-needed space between us.

"I'm a mess. I told you how my dad left me and my mom, and it's fucked me up worse than I thought. I sabotage relationships. I'm no good at them. The wall's almost done, so just whatever you spent so far and whatever it costs with Gence, I'll pay you my share and we can just go our separate ways."

This confession is like lancing an infected wound: painful, but bringing relief at the same time. I snatch up a long strip of paper. It's from the drywall and still has gravelly bits of the gypsum plaster stuck to it. I twist it around my index finger, letting the rocky fragments bite into my skin.

"Separate ways? You said you were in therapy. Working on things."

"Yes," I say miserably. "But I don't know how long that'll take. Okay?" I spit out the last word. "Maybe I'll never be normal."

He closes the space I just put between us. "Do you or do you not want—"

The paper I'm winding around my finger rips, snaps really, sending a once-in-a-lifetime shot of shrapnel directly at Jack's face. He slaps his hand over his eye and half turns, half bends.

"What the fuck!"

"I'm so sorry! It was the drywall! Oh no, did it get in your eye? I'm sorry!"

Jack walks over to my mirror and blinks rapidly, pulling at his bottom lid. His eye is a vicious red.

"Maybe wash it out with water?"

He looks at me in the mirror. "I'm going to wash my eye and then we're going to *talk* about all of this. Understand?"

He storms through the narrow space that remains to be drywalled, and I spring into action, grabbing my purse and keys and running out the door.

Because I'm a coward.

# 28

Avery found me sitting on his stoop when he got home from work, and he didn't press me for details as to why I was there. He just fed me snacks and waited with a sympathetic ear if I needed one. But after a few hours of him looking down at his phone uneasily, he finally confessed I was making him late for a date.

Anna was a mess at last check, so I'm assuming she wasn't who he was going out with, but I didn't ask. I didn't want to bring her to mind just before he dined with someone else. Still, the prospect of being at his place if he decided to bring any date back after dinner was bleh, so off to Margie's I went.

I found La there, though I shouldn't have been surprised. Margie and La fed me properly, La making an osso buco so delicious, with a sauce so flavorful and complex, it had me wondering if that's not what won Margie over. But gracious as they were, letting me loiter there for hours and even offering to let me sleep over, the loaded looks they were sending one another forced me to accept that I was interfering with amorous plans left and right today.

It's obscenely late when I get home. I open the door as quietly as I can and curse my decision not to sleep at Margie's when the hinges squeak. Why have I never WD-40'd these things?

There are no lights on in my apartment. I shine my cell light on the room and slip off my shoes. My heart dive-bombs to my heels when I see that the last open space between our apartments has been covered with drywall, the last sliver of a connection between our places severed. I set my bag down and suddenly feel like crying.

I run my hand along the wall, feeling like Fortunato from "The Cask of Amontillado." That single panel of drywall has sucked all the air out of my lungs, out of the room. I want to expire from loneliness.

I let myself into my bedroom and scream.

Jack is lounging in my bed. His feet are crossed, his back propped against my headboard and all the pillows I own. He's reading. He looks up. I gasp.

Not only is Jack Craig in my bed, flipping through my new copy of *The Pirate Duke's Revenge*, but he's also wearing an eye patch.

"Your eye," I say.

"Scratched cornea," he says. "Went to the clinic after you ran away."

"Oh." I swallow. "I'm so sorry, Jack."

It's not a real eye patch. It's gauze taped to his head. But with his dark shock of hair, his broad shoulders cradled by my pillows, and my saucy reading material resting on that belly I have daydreams about… He's the fucking Pirate Duke incarnate.

Goddamn it.

I lick my lips. "Why— Why are you here?"

"We didn't get to finish our conversation." He sounds almost polite. Deceptively so.

"It's late. We're both tired. I told you. I'm sorry about before. I'm a mess." I'm loitering at the threshold of my bedroom like

I'm a visitor, which I hate, so I step fully into the room. "You sure you hurt your eye and not your head? Seems like you're lost. Your bedroom is ten feet to the west."

"My apartment is east of you. Come here."

"But—"

He swings his legs over the edge of the bed and stands. "Can you come here?"

"Why?"

"What are you going to do? Stand there all night?"

I cross my arms. "We'll cross that bridge while you live under it."

He huffs out a laugh and approaches slowly. Prowling.

Then he's standing in front of me, and I'm tipping my head to look up at him.

"What do you want?" I don't mean it to, but it comes out in a whisper.

He picks up a lock of my hair, running it through his fingers, feeling the texture of it. He smells like crisp soap, a hint of pine, and the promise of something very bad. He's looking down at the strands of hair he's playing with. And then he runs that lock gently up my neck. Goose bumps erupt up and down my arms.

"I have a theory," he says.

My heart is beating like a tin-pan symphony inside my chest. "What are you talking about?"

"I think you're using therapy as an excuse. A wedge to avoid getting involved with me."

I can't catch my breath. His voice is soft, weaving its way around me, tugging me closer.

"No," I murmur, my heart contracting with the knowledge he's right.

He leans forward…and brushes my nose with his. "Yes."

I blink. He's looking at me with that inscrutable mix of detached observation and amusement. My lips feel heavy. I need his mouth on mine. "What—" My tone almost sounds desperate. "What is happening right now?"

"Whatever you let happen. You want me. I want you. We like each other. God knows why, but we do. I've already seen the worst of you, and I want more. You've seen the worst of me. We'll take it slow. And every time you get the urge to bail, I need you to remember that I live next door. You can't run far."

I'm going to hyperventilate. I want him to get the hell out of my place so I can sort this all out in my head. I want to push him back on that bed and mount him like a racing jockey.

"'You can't run far.' That is so romantic," I say.

"Breaking balls is better than breaking hearts. I'll take it."

I choke out a laugh, still trying to regulate my breathing, still resisting the urge to rub up on him like a cat in heat. The pull to touch him, to be near him, is more intense than anything I've ever experienced. It's terrifying.

While I'm wrestling with myself, he crushes my reserve with a few firm words. "I'm going to kiss you now."

I tilt my chin up ever so slightly, and he catches my lips in a slow, sweet kiss that seems to seep into every cell of my being, puffing them up, filling me until I could float away at the pure sensation of it all. The kiss from the closet was a frantic thing, the hunger of two clawing people desperate to get at each other. This, though… At first, it's a whisper of his lips against my full bottom one, and then it deepens, languid and careful, the kiss of someone who has all night.

Something in me snaps. I try to take more, demand more. I clutch his back, his firm ass, trying to pull him to me. But still he sips, small kisses, small slides, small grazes. I take his hand, urging him to run it up under my shirt, growing frustrated when he keeps it on my hip. He smiles against my mouth, knowing what he's doing to me. In response, I press the palm of my hand hard against the heat of him, rubbing him through his pants, relishing the firm feeling of him. He groans, some of his willpower draining away. I fumble with his fly, moaning into his mouth.

My phone begins vibrating. He lifts his head, amused, while I cling to him and pant. He runs his hand from my throat down my torso and then around to my back, slowly pulling the phone from the back pocket of my jeans. He places it in my hand and then slides his hand back to my rear, cupping and squeezing before taking a shuddering breath. "Okay. We take it slow starting *now*." He presses his lips to mine again in a quick peck.

I don't know what else to do now that my brain has been irrevocably broken, so I look at my phone. Text. From Lucas.

Can you talk?

It's a second before I register any of it. Jack glances down and sees who the message is from.

"He— He probably just wants to talk about the tabloids."

"Hmm." He returns to my bedside, grabs his keys from the table, and slips on his shoes. "We'll talk tomorrow." Jack boxes me in until I feel my back touch the wall. He plants his hands on either side of my head, then bends to plunder my mouth with his tongue until I'm on the verge of overheating and my toes feel like curling.

"What—" I gasp, when he lifts his head. "What if we do this and then I refuse to talk to you again?"

"I might give some thought to punishment."

My breath stutters. "Being subjected to your personality ought to do the trick."

He straightens and smiles. "Clever way of making sure you keep me near. You're fooling no one, 5A. Come lock up behind me."

At the door, he gives me another lingering kiss, his hands running along my back, my ass, pressing me up against him. My hands are in his hair, and I'm weak when he gives me a loaded look. It sends a rush of heat through me. I catch sight of the mess I've made of his hair, and I vaguely wonder what I look like to him. In the mirror, I see copper hair disheveled, lips swollen… I glance down. My bra is askew and partially peeking out from the neck of my now dangerously low top.

"How did you unhook my bra?"

He shrugs. "The hooks fell apart on their own. Sword in the stone–like."

I push at him, and he laughs. I close the door in his face for a change.

And I'm left not knowing what the hell just happened.

# 29

"Am I using therapy to keep Jack away?" I moan to Wendy. I snap a thread on the poor pillow-bird's beak with my nail and quickly set it down before I can inflict more damage.

"Do you think you are?"

"Maybe? Yes? I think."

"And why do you think that is?"

"Have you met me?" I ask archly.

Wendy spreads her hands out, conceding the point. "Okay. But there's no rule that says you have to remain single or chaste while doing this work. You can give yourself permission to explore it."

"I guess you can't write me a doctor's note to get me out of it?"

"Do you want to get out of it?"

I wrinkle my nose, annoyed with this Socratic questions-answered-with-questions thing. "No, I don't."

Wendy nods.

I flop back against the sofa cushion. "Can't you just…tell me what to do?"

Wendy smiles, but slightly, as if in response to a joke she's heard told many, many times before. She probably has. "No. And you don't want to be told what to do, either."

*"Ugh."*

"Penny, from what you've said, Jack sounds supportive of

your therapy and is willing to take it slow."

"I know. He's sweet. And understanding. Add that to the fact he's hot and funny, and he's the *worst*."

"The worst," Wendy agrees.

"He is!" I insist. "Because he's different from any other guy I've ever been involved with. And he makes *me* want to be different. And I'm trying to be different! Not just for him, but… But I'm also scared out of my mind by all of this. This whole thing is like walking through a terrifying haunted house." I pause. "A sexy one."

"You know, Penny." Wendy's lips twist. "It's not a bad thing to have somebody to hold your hand as you walk through a haunted house."

Gence comes over the next evening and muds both sides of the drywall, caking spackle all over the seams and giving firm instructions not to touch. I try not to take offense that his instructions are mainly directed at me, as if I'm a child who can't resist poking the thick white wall goo.

Jack stands at my elbow as Gence muds down my apartment, still sporting his eye patch. At one point, I think I feel a finger run down my back, but maybe it's wishful thinking.

I want to tell Jack that I hate the thought of not hearing him vacuum. I hate not glancing over and seeing him whenever I want. I want to Kool-Aid Man through the wall myself when I think about it. I want a lot of things.

Instead, I say nothing, and Jack makes zero moves to repeat the kissing from yesterday. There is no reference to his theory or taking it slow, nor to anything else. I don't seek him out that night, and he doesn't come to me, either. I have to remind myself it wasn't just another dream.

The next day, Gence is back to sand and mud some more, and after he's done, Jack brings his vacuum over and takes care of the dust in my apartment. He maneuvers around my living room, his dark head bending every now and again to inspect a renegade speck. I watch him out of the corner of my eye with a mix of thirst and confusion. What the hell was the other night? Has he had a change of heart? I reflexively return his friendly smile when he gathers up his vacuum cord and offer a quick, impersonal "thanks" when I trail him to the door.

I tell myself it's fine, even though it's as if Jack pulled all the warmth and color from the room after him, leaving my apartment cold and quiet. And then I realize that he's already tackling the dust on his side and I can barely make out the sound. I want to lie down and pull my throw blanket over my head. Instead, I bang my hand on the wall for old time's sake—and pull my hand away covered in spackle.

Shit. Gence is going to kill me.

I grab a spoon, try to smooth out the area, and somehow make it worse. Nothing left for it, I skip into the hall, practically running to seek out Jack's help. And not because I want to see him, spar with him, be near him. No. It's just because my apartment is so quiet it might as well be on the moon, and because Gence is really going to kick my ass.

Time to test Anna's white-knight hypothesis.

He opens his door a second after my insistent knock and immediately takes my breath away. I want to dig my nails into his shoulders like grappling hooks and scale him like Everest. I want to tuck my head onto his shoulder and watch action flicks. I lied.

I just want to be near him.

"Missed me already?"

"Never. I need your help. I smooshed the spackle when I hit the wall."

"I thought I heard knocking. You could hear the vacuuming?"

I shift, uncomfortable, and tuck a strand of hair behind my ear. "Not really. I banged on the wall because I figured… It's like breaking champagne to christen a new boat. New wall and all."

Jack sucks his teeth. "Shit. Good luck with Gence." He starts to close the door and laughs when I push to keep it open. "Let me get my stuff."

I watch him work, spreading a thick coat of spackle against the area I messed up and then smoothing and skimming away the excess.

"What did Lucas want?" he asks casually.

I grin, remembering his admission that he was jealous. "To whisk me away to Paris?" I say. He turns to slant me a one-eyed glance. "It was what I thought. Don't say anything to the tabloids. Call his PR folks if anyone approaches, et cetera."

He nods, continuing his work on the wall. He's wearing a short-sleeve shirt, and I follow the line of his arms up to his shoulders and down to his back, remembering the look of it without a shirt.

He must catch the heat in my eye because his own darkens, and he stands.

"Want to order in? I—" My phone vibrates.

"Maybe. You going to answer that?"

I duck my head with a smile and pull out my phone, pleased to hear the hint of *something* in his voice just then. "It's probably my mom. I told you she's been all over me, trying to set me up with some guy I went to high school with… And maybe she saw the tabloid stuff… Oh no."

"What?"

My eyes water. I tremble. "It's my mom's friend…" I struggle to get it out, my throat closing against my words.

Jack takes my phone and reads.

Penelope, it's Monica. Your mom is on her way to the hospital.

"I— I need to go." I snatch my phone back and race around my apartment, grabbing things to throw into my handbag. I check my phone. Lyft and Uber will cost hundreds, but I don't have time for the bus.

"What are you doing? How are you getting to— Where is it you're going?"

"Stone Harbor. About three hours from here. God, I—"

He covers my shaking hand. "I have a car. I'll take you."

I look up at him, his face distorted by the wash of tears I'm trying not to let fall.

He runs to his apartment to load up an overnight bag as I lock up. I don't even recall rushing down to the lobby or getting into the taxi Jack hails. But as we pull away from the curb, for the first time in many minutes I think of something other than my nagging worry.

"I thought you had a car?"

He gives the driver an address and sits back. "Parking lot is near the river. Too expensive to keep the car here."

I type furiously on my phone, texting Monica back in the hope that she can provide some more details.

A short time later, we're in Jack's car and speeding over the George Washington Bridge. I watch as the bridge lights blur into a river of white, and I tell myself it'll be okay. But I feel like crawling out of my skin.

Jack breaks the silence. “You okay?”

I settle back against the leather seat and look over at his profile, at the lights sliding along the hard angles of his face. “I’m…okay. Thank you. For taking me. I— She’s always complaining about how often she sees me.” My voice hitches a little. The regret is an anchor tied to my neck, weighing my head down.

“I think all moms do that.”

I turn to stare out the window some more.

“My mom talked a good game about looking forward to peace and quiet when we left for college, but she definitely shed more than a few tears when it finally happened,” he says, shifting gears.

My chest hollows. “Mom never wanted me to leave at all. She got married and knocked up young, spent her life pandering to my dad, and then decided she’d get a second chance at life by living vicariously through me.” My therapy-sourced realizations are out before I can control my mouth.

His voice is quiet, even in the hushed, dark confines of his car. “Why wouldn’t she want you to leave if she’s living vicariously through you?”

There’s a faint hum in my ears—an echo of guilt and freedom ringing in my chest. “Because she didn’t regret all of her life decisions. Just some. Staying in Stone Harbor from cradle to grave is cool with her, so it has to be for me. It’s why I love my apartment so much. Going away for college was something she tolerated. Moving to my place… It was like cutting the cord. She… She loves me, but she’s a control freak.” Speaking the words aloud is like crossing a bridge that crumbles behind me. I sigh and shift to face him more fully.

Jack glances at me, and I analyze him as objectively as I can.

I don't know how I pegged him for a villain. That seems so far away now. He may look like a sexy pirate, with his rumpled dark hair and sharply intelligent light eyes—well, *eye*, thanks to the patch—but he doesn't have the requisite uncaring and selfish streak to pull it off. He's a sleeper hero. He was all along.

"See anything you like?" he says, his voice a warm rumble in my stomach. "What are you thinking?"

"I'm thinking I'm sorry. About your eye, I mean. You look like a pirate."

"If I were a pirate, I would've already claimed that booty." He scowls. "What? Why are you laughing?"

I groan, but he's managed to break up a little of the oppressive cloud hanging over my head. "Come on, man. You're better than that."

"Let the record reflect, your honor, that that terrible joke was intentionally offered up to get a smile out of you. A sacrifice pop fly to advance my base runner to second."

"Well, you play ball like the Mets."

"You shut your pretty mouth," he says. His lips curve, the dimples popping in and out of view with the passing streetlights.

"So you've heard tons about me. About my family," I say. "Distract me. Tell me about yours." I *need* the distraction. Not only from this clawing worry… I need to break this spell he's cast over me. I don't trust it.

"My family. Okay. Well, you met Anna—and heard her whole opinion of me." He grimaces. "My parents are like a Norman Rockwell painting. High school sweethearts. Went to college together. Married right out of school and settled into suburban bliss. Had kids. Boy and a girl. Got a dog—a few over the years. And my parents are still totally in love with each other, kind of like Avery's. Never heard them raise their voices to one another.

Or to us, for that matter."

A pang of envy strikes. "Sounds pretty perfect."

"Perfect." Jack's mouth twists into a self-deprecating angle. "Yeah, that comes with its own stresses, you know."

"Living up to it?"

"Anna… I don't know if she even tried. I guess she did, for a while, but… There was an accident, and it messed her up for a bit. It seemed like she was feeling better about things, but then… I don't know what happened with her. After a while, if she thought it would piss off me and my parents, she'd do it.

"I did the opposite. Dad got sick? Instead of chasing girls, I got a job to help with the bills. I had to drop Anna off at her dance class every week. I cleaned the house after school. Eventually, if you do a thing for someone long enough, they come to expect it of you. Did my best to live up to everyone's expectations, but *man*, those things were sky-high. A prison of expectations, I guess."

"Mr. White Knight," I murmur. "Driving damsels in distress to the Jersey Shore."

He opens his mouth, then hesitates.

"What?"

He shifts gears and then glances at me. "With you, I've always been able to be a little bit of the bad guy, too. Which is… liberating, I guess."

I crack out a laugh. "I knew it! You enjoyed being an asshole!"

"You enjoyed it, too."

"I admit nothing." My admission is evident in my voice. "I was always justified in my actions."

"Justified, huh? So what was that brown stuff on my mailbox?"

I shift. "Chocolate."

"Thank God. And the erectile-dysfunction mailing list you put me on? Justified?"

"I mean, I don't know for sure, but probably."

"Well, I didn't find it funny. My granddad died of ED."

"Oh no, I—" It takes me a beat to realize that what he's said makes no sense. I notice his grin, and I smack his shoulder.

He shifts away, laughing, and then his voice becomes a low growl, the bass of which I feel everywhere. "Always wanted to try one of those pills. For recreational purposes, of course."

We drive along, the banter helping the highway mile markers melt away. But stress has a muscle memory, and I find my teeth clenching harder, my shoulders growing just a little more taut, when we get about twenty minutes out. I call the hospital, but they have no record of Mom being admitted. That's promising, right? Unless she had to be airlifted to Camden? I look up the number and quickly dial. No record.

We exit off the highway, and Jack looks around as we pass the quiet marina and then head over the shadowed drawbridge into Stone Harbor proper. Without any leads to go on, I give him directions to my mother's place, and the silence stretches as my fears and worries eat up the scenery in my mind.

We pull into her driveway of white crushed shells, the tires making crunching sounds that feel especially loud, given it's just after midnight. The house is dark.

We get out of the car. The scent of the ocean hangs heavy in the air, the way it always does. There's a cold bite to the nighttime breeze. Her house, her block even, feels especially desolate.

I run up the steps and ring the bell, hearing its chime echo through the house. That gets no response, so I start pounding on the locked storm door and peering through windows.

Jack shuffles up the steps behind me.

I pull my phone out and call Monica. The call goes straight to voicemail. I try calling my mother's number again, and the upstairs lights go on in the house. They're followed by hallway lights on the first floor. The curtains part.

Mom.

I see her startled face in the window. A mix of relief and an awful, creeping suspicion washes over me.

She unlocks and opens the door, then she's standing in front of me in her nightgown.

"Penny?" she says. "What are you—"

"Monica sent me a text saying you were on your way to the hospital." My voice claps like thunder in the inky, dark quiet of the street.

My mom must think the same because she pokes her head outside, noticing Jack for the first time and pausing momentarily before ushering us in. She settles us in the Christmas-colored living room. Jack folds his tall frame onto a green-and-red-plaid armchair. I sit near him, on the hunter-green slipcovered love seat, as my mom bustles out of the room before I can interrogate her.

"Are you okay?" Jack asks.

I bite at my lip and turn my eyes upward, staring at Mom's ceiling fan. I shake my head. "I don't know what's worse: being maybe-manipulated into coming down here, or the prospect of her really being sick. I know it's the latter, but…"

"Maybe she isn't well."

"We'll see," I say flatly.

My mom comes back with tea and a plate of Stella D'oro Swiss fudge cookies. She fusses with our napkins and cups until I can't take it anymore.

"Mom. Why did Monica text me?"

"Honey, maybe we can talk about this when the company isn't in the room." She looks at Jack pointedly.

"Jack isn't company."

She sits upright. "Jack? As in the Jack Craig from the articles about you?" She says it with a horror in her voice, like I've invited Stalin over for biscuits.

"That's me, ma'am. Fighter of TV stars. Wrecker of homes," Jack says. He isn't disrespectful in his delivery, but there's almost a relish in the way he's painting himself the villain. He's enjoying being the bad guy of the story here, too. Or maybe it's for my amusement.

I shake my head. "Yes, that's the same Jack, and no, he isn't what the stories made him out to be. Lucas fell through a hole in my— Never mind."

"Are you…together?" my mom asks.

My "uh" perfectly intersects with Jack's definitive "yes." I glare at him, and he gives me a small smile, just a tiny flex of the lips. I swing my eyes back to my mother.

"Is this the one you said you were with? The—"

"Why are we talking about him when we're supposed to be talking about you? Did you put Monica up to it? Texting me? You look fine."

She smooths her hand over her napkin. "Of course not. I— Well, I went to the supermarket and saw all those tabloids about you, and I turned them all around to face the wall. And I hadn't heard from you since you ran out of here, really, and you didn't respond to my texts, and after seeing those articles I was just so worried about you. Anyway, I started feeling *awfully* dizzy and faint, so I called Monica over and she said she'd take me to the hospital. And I was on my way there, but then… Well, Monica asked me when I'd last eaten anything, and I realized I hadn't eaten a thing all day, because the supermarket thing happened really very early, and after that, like I said, I was just so worried about you. So instead of going to the hospital, we stopped over at the diner. I'm feeling much better now, actually."

"You're fine," I say. I choke down the maelstrom of relief, outrage, and about a dozen other feelings I can't even pinpoint in this moment. I press my hands to my temples, rubbing. "You had, what? A rumbly tummy? So because of your machinations—"

"Machinations? I just told you I was on my way to the hospital."

"Because of you, I am down here at midnight, and I've dragged poor Jack along for the ride. Unbelievable."

"Well, I thought you might come, but I honestly didn't expect you until maybe tomorrow. You can't blame me for that part. I always tell you nothing good happens after midnight. You shouldn't have been driving at night in the first place."

I stand, abruptly, and Jack follows suit. "I'm going to find a hotel—"

"No! You'll sleep here! You can sleep with me and… And Jack can have your room."

I grit my teeth and persevere, keeping my voice calm, not wanting to spark an argument. "I'm going to find a hotel room and then come back tomorrow."

I turn on my heel and flee, ignoring my mom's protests.

Only when I'm back in the warm leather embrace of Jack's car and we're backing out of the driveway do I feel like I can breathe.

Jack drives for a bit before finally asking, "You good?"

"Super."

"Where are we going?"

"Turn down this street. There's a stretch of hotels on this strip." We drive for a while, circling, the NO VACANCY signs mocking me at every turn. I pull out my phone and finally find one that lists a last-minute deal for tonight.

The Sunset Cove Resort is one of the nicer places on the island. We pull into the parking lot, and I trudge into the lobby, barely registering our chic beach surroundings. At the front desk, I try and haggle a bit over price, but the tired night clerk won't budge. It's more money than I'm used to spending on much of anything, but I pull out my credit card. Jack approaches and throws down his before I can hand mine over. I protest.

"I insist," he says, signing the receipt and taking my hand to pull me along. I'm too tired to argue.

The room has two queen beds. It's pretty, a space full of blues and whites, with a balcony facing the ocean. I pull open the sliding glass doors and lean into that surf smell, trying not to let it drag me back into the quicksand of memory.

I can sense Jack behind me. And I feel like I need to say something.

"I'm sorry I dragged you—"

"I volunteered. Nothing to be sorry about."

"She's just… I should've known. She's like that." I hug myself and peer into the dark. "She wasn't a bad mother. She just… Life disappointed her. Everything disappointed her. So she wanted control.

"And that control was over everything. She practically had me wearing a chastity belt for years. Even little things could end up being a landmine. The outfit you decide to wear to church. The cookies you want to bring to a bake sale. The way you want to do your hair for prom. That could be a war. Every day, normal things could blow up into conflict, and she was relentless. So you learn to avoid them as best you can. To look for triggers. It's hard to make yourself smaller than you are. To be the stillest version of yourself. It takes effort. Practice. But it's easier than fighting everything all the time."

Not "you." *I.* I learned to be the stillest version of myself. I wonder if Wendy would be proud of me for noticing, even if correcting myself out loud is a bridge too far.

Jack pulls me back against his chest and gently brushes my hair out of the way, pressing a kiss against the sensitive skin where my neck meets my shoulder. I shiver. We don't say anything after that, but the mood has shifted. I'm not comfortable in the circle of his arms any longer. I'm a tangle of nerve endings and awareness. Every brush of fabric, every minor shift, sets alarm bells sounding all along my skin. My breathing has picked up.

"You still sporting that chastity belt? Good thing we got two beds in here—"

I turn in Jack's arms and pull his head down to mine, crushing our lips together, hard. I didn't know how much I craved this, how much I wanted this, the singing in my veins, until I'm finally feeling it all again. I grab his thick hair in my hand and pull him more firmly to me.

His arms go around me. The ever-combustible air around us has erupted into a conflagration, burning away every rational thought. He spins us, pressing my back up against the glass behind me, and his large hand skims its way up my torso. His tongue tangles with mine.

I run my free hand under his shirt, raking my nails gently down his stomach—God, I've been dying to touch that stomach. I run a thumb over his nipples, and real-Jack enjoys it as much as dream-Jack. They wander, my hands, until finally they're playing with his waistband. I look up at him and dip my fingertips inside. He groans.

I release his hand and waistband, pulling at his shirt, desperate to have it off, and he leans back to let me, snatching it from me and tossing it into the room. He pulls me in, closing the sliding door and locking out the humid sea air.

We stare at each other, breaths chainsawing in and out of both of us. And then I grab him by the waistband of his jeans again, pulling, until his single visible eye, meltingly intense, is inches away. He gathers the material of my tank top into his fist and pulls it down, stretching it until the tops of my breasts are on display. He runs an open mouth from the skin revealed above my bra to my neck. I hear myself moan.

I rip my tank over my head and feel my bra go slack: the magic bra-unhooking maneuver again. I'm impressed, but there's a shot of green threaded through that feeling. I push away thoughts about how exactly the talent was developed and resolve to enjoy it. But then he's pulling my bra off, and I'm topless in front of him.

He sucks in air like someone about to be submerged, and I feel my nipples tighten. The way he's gazing at me. I want to tilt my face to that sun and let it warm me all day, every day. He pulls his eyes from my chest, and I hear his words in my head: *You want me. I want you. We like each other. God knows why, but we do.*

"You're the most beautiful—" His voice is strangled.

I feel like a goddess. I am barefoot, bare-chested, clad only in my shorts while Jack Craig worships me with his one good eye. He holds out a hand, and the second I place mine in his, he's got me pressed up against his chest, skin to skin. The friction of his chest against mine is a pleasure-pain I've never felt this intensely before. He stares down at us, at my breasts crushed up against his golden chest, and he bends his head until his forehead touches mine.

"You had an intense day." He sounds pained. "We're supposed to be taking this slow. We need to stop…"

"You don't want to—?"

"Holy shit, Penny." His laugh is a shuddery thing. "Are you kidding me? You have no idea how many nights I've thought of nothing but this. Since way before you and I made nice."

"You know all that moaning you hear through the wall? It's because I've been dreaming about you."

I run my hand down the hard angle of him and hear his indrawn breath. He closes his eye and grabs my hand, holding it tight, stilling it.

"Do you still want to be a little bad with me?" I whisper, going up on tiptoe to brush my lips against his cheek, my mind dizzy from the feel of my nipples dragging against his chest.

He picks me up and carries me to the bed after that, and somehow in a tangle of tongues and hands, we both lose our pants along the way. He stands and sheds his boxer briefs, and… Good lord.

My eyes shoot up to his. "I'm— I'm glad I signed you up for that ED literature."

He laughs, his smile utterly gorgeous and private and all for me. My eyes slip, taking in broad shoulders, hard chest, narrow waist… I want to sink my teeth into him, to brand him. Wrap my arms and legs around him and stay until I'm barnacled to his side.

He reaches for something in his bag, then pulls a condom on.

*This is happening. This is happening.*

He settles over me, the smile still on his face. I feel his hand on my hips, pulling my lacy nothings down as he leans back. I briefly thank the heavens that, for all that Mom was overbearing and controlling, her advice about always sporting fresh and matching underthings was sound. His mouth works my neck, and then lower…and lower… It's glorious and so fucking frustrating.

I've had months of foreplay. I need him *now*.

"Oh, okay, ohhh. That's amazing, and we're going to circle back to exactly what you're doing there, but I want you *now*," I say, the demand in my voice startling even me.

Jack lifts his head, and his lips quirk.

"I want my chicken sandwich," I say.

Jack's smile widens.

And then all thought is crowded out by an angel's choir because Jack is touching me, shifting me, moving me, rubbing. My knees are pulled up. And finally, finally, he settles where I need him. My breath hitches, and Jack looks like he isn't breathing at all. He's watching me, his one good eye gone black.

"Good?"

My response is to dig my nails into his shoulders and try to pull him down. He doesn't budge. Instead, he begins an achingly slow slide. *Yes. Yes. Yes.*

"Are you okay?"

My answer is a tortured whimper. He asks me that too fucking often. I ignore his question and grab his hips, tilting my own up. And Jack's gratifying groan finds an answer in me.

He shifts, hitting something I'd been unaware existed until now. I think I scream, but I can't tell. It's an out-of-body experience. Otherworldly. And then Jack is working me, sweating over me. Levering an arm under me and pulling me up at an angle that is as close to heaven on earth as I've ever discovered.

Jack. Fucking. Craig.

I pull his head down to try and kiss him, but then the sky breaks, and I arch, shuddering uncontrollably, a wrung-out wreck of a person.

That does it for Jack, and he follows me over the edge.

We stay like that for a bit, his weight feeling wonderful, pinning me to the bed. I run my nails up his back, enjoying the feel of his smooth skin. Of being able to do this to him. Do *that* with him.

"Five-fucking-A," he murmurs into my shoulder, kissing it gently. He shifts his hips slightly and reaches down, standing to dispose of the condom in the bathroom.

I lie back, enjoying the view of his departure almost as much as I enjoy watching his return. He is shameless and glorious.

"You were confident, to bring that with you."

His grin is wicked, pure Han. "I brought more than one." He leans down, half covering me, his arms bracketing me. "They're left over from my single days."

I can tell he's lying from his voice and his smile. But the rush of jealousy I feel makes me want to roar. I narrow my eyes, and his grin widens.

"You have something in your teeth," I say sweetly.

"Oh. You're right. I do." He leans over and takes my nipple in his mouth, grazing it with his teeth. And then it's as if the first time never happened.

Jack. Fucking. Craig.

# 30

Jack takes my hand and presses it to his lips as the car crunches its way up Mom's shell-paved driveway late the next morning—after a very scenic tour around the hotel room. There is a child shouting and adult laughter emanating from the backyard.

I walk to the gate and shake my head.

Classic Mom. I should've anticipated the buffer. She's invited her friend Monica and Monica's daughter Sarah, my old high school acquaintance. And Sarah brought her very loud toddler. I remove my hand from Jack's arm, forcing myself to stop touching him, and lift the gate latch.

No way.

It's not just Monica and Sarah. There are tables with tablecloths. A spread of food big enough to feed, if not an army, then a modest battalion. A fucking balloon arch. It's a baby shower. Katie Singer's baby shower.

And there are a shit ton of other people here.

My fury builds. I told her I didn't want to come, and she forced me anyway. I tamp down my rage as I greet Katie, congratulating her, introducing Jack, and moving on to nod absently at other familiar faces.

Mom doesn't look especially thrilled to see Jack. Although

between his eye patch and the tabloid stories…

"Oh. My. Stars. Penny!" Sarah rushes over. She was always petite, but time and childbearing have given her luscious curves. Her dark-brown hair is pulled back into a neat braid, and all I can think of when I look at her is Mom calling her husband "homely." I return her hug. Unlike her mother—or mine, actually—Sarah was always sweet.

"Our little Penny! You're famous these days!" Monica's nasal voice rings out. She's holding her squirming grandson on her knee. He pushes off her and screams about sitting on the chair by himself, pulling one of her graying corkscrew curls. "Daniel, let go! Fine. Go sit," she admonishes as the child scrambles into one of the deck chairs at the umbrella-ed table.

"Hi, Monica." I resist the urge to confront her about the text that scared me half to death. There's nothing to gain from that quarter. She, like my mom, is never wrong. "Sarah, Monica, this is Jack."

"Oh! The magazines didn't have a picture of you, but I had Sarah get on the Google and do a little searching. We weren't sure it was you, though, in the picture."

"Well, I hope I stack up well against the picture from *the Google*." Jack smiles and nods at them both.

Sarah flushes and gives me a miserable look, whispering, "They wouldn't stop until I did it. Your mom accidentally posted Jack's name four times as her Facebook status."

Sarah's son Daniel refuses to budge from his seat, scribbling on paper after paper with the assortment of crayons on the table. Both Monica and Sarah are oblivious to my need for space, so I gesture for Jack to sit in the only available chair and drag the box that usually houses my mom's outdoor cushions over to the table.

"Are you a pirate?" Daniel asks Jack.

Jack grins and leans close to him. "Yep. A pirate duke." He waggles his eyebrows at me.

I roll my eyes but feel a thrill entirely incompatible with a backyard gathering blaze through me.

Mom looks hale and hearty, fully recovered from yesterday's health drama and pleased as punch with herself. I sigh inwardly, quailing at the thought of telling her that luring me down here was not okay. Maybe it's just better if Jack and I get going—

"This is you." Daniel shoves a drawing at me. There's a gigantic circle for a head, random splotches inside it that are clearly meant to be eyes, and assorted sticks poking out from the circle that I suppose are…limbs?

"The head is…to scale, I think," Jack murmurs.

"Dick," I mutter. "Mom, Jack and I can't really stay—"

"Oh, good! Brian!" my mother shouts, waving to someone by the gate.

I can't believe her.

"Brian, so glad you could come by. You're too sweet," my mom coos.

"Yeah, no worries, Mrs. H. My mom said you needed this for the party…" Brian holds out a foil-covered tray. He notices me, his eyes widening with delight.

"Perfect. You should stay! You and Penelope had to cut your coffee date short."

So fucking disrespectful. She knows Jack is right here. I give Brian a tight smile in greeting and say, "Nice to see you, Brian. This is *Jack*." My tone, an almost-purr when I say Jack's name, practically shouts, *I've been touching his winky all morning.*

Jack stands and shakes Brian's hand, and Brian's quick darting glance between Jack and me tells me the message has been received.

I feel crappy. I don't like causing people—especially nice-enough semi-strangers from the past—discomfort or disappointment. A possessive hand lands on my shoulders, tempering the shitty feeling. There is something more than a little hot about Jack looking at me with the word "mine" shining through his eyes.

"Penny, where's your restroom?" Jack's voice rumbles in my ear.

"I'm going in—I can show you," my mom says.

"No, no." I have no idea what Mom might say to him if she gets him alone. I don't trust her not to manipulate him. "I'll show him."

I lead Jack into the house. "Would've thought there'd be more plants in here, given your place looks like the party room at a Rainforest Café," he says.

"Dad had the green thumb, not Mom. I—" I hesitate, unsure I want to add more weight to this moment. It's only a second before I settle into the truth, wanting to give Jack another piece of me no one else has ever held. "After he left, it felt good to grow things in a house where we'd been so"—I shrug helplessly—"cut back to the roots." I point out the bathroom door. "There's one upstairs, too, if you want more privacy."

He crowds me against the wall. "I want more privacy." His gives me a sweet kiss, and then his hot mouth is on my neck.

I angle my head back, giving him better access. "Oh. Don't give me another hickey, though."

He pulls away, his eyes gleaming. "That hickey was from me?"

"Of course it was. Who else would it have been from?"

He smiles, and my blood feels carbonated. I take his hand, leading him to the second-floor bathroom, and he pulls me in after him, immediately unbuttoning my shorts and tugging them down.

“I need you. I’m obsessed with the taste of you.”

“Oh God.” I close my eyes as he runs a finger over my most sensitive spot. Breathless, I gasp out, “You’re just jealous because you met my boyfriend Bri— Ohhh.” His mouth is on me, licking, sucking, before he pulls one of my thighs over his shoulder. I lean back against the sink, grasping for the porcelain or his shoulders or any purchase at all as utter ecstasy washes over me again and again.

When it’s over, I look down at him, stunned. He licks his lips, his eyes warm and triumphant, and I pull him up, kissing him deeply and reaching for his pants. I pull my mouth away from his with an effort. “Your turn,” I whisper, relishing his shiver.

When we rejoin the party a bit later, my mom is in the kitchen with a few other women.

“Yes, Penny’s moving back eventually. Getting New York out of her system,” she says.

Jack understands the look in my eye, and the sated look in his own is replaced with concern. But, to his credit, he doesn’t try to white-knight things. He nods, heading outside with only a small backward glance.

“Mom, can I speak to you in private, please?” If looks could kill, her health crisis from yesterday would be very real right now.

“Oh, sure. Give me a bit, I’m just—” She catches my expression. “Sure. Excuse me, everyone. Let me know if there’s anything I can bring outside for you.”

I tap my nails against the counter while I wait for my mother to stop playing waitress. I stop myself when I realize I’m tapping out S-O-S. What I’m about to do goes against the grain. The opposite of keeping the peace.

“Penny, couldn’t it wait until after—” Mom closes the door

behind the departing crowd.

"No. It couldn't. You lured me here under false pretenses."

"I told you I wasn't feeling well!"

"And you were cured by a cheeseburger deluxe. Yes, you mentioned that."

"And 'lured.' 'Lured' to visit your own mother. Sad state of affairs, that is."

I don't push back on Mom like this. Never have. This hurts, but I need to say it. "I told you I couldn't come to this party." My voice cracks. "And you brought Brian here to set me up, despite knowing that I'm not interested. Knowing I have Jack with me. Knowing that he and I are…together." I blush at that, still unable to believe it, even when my sore muscles are screaming that it's oh so true.

"That won't last. He isn't for you."

"You don't know him. You don't even know me."

She opens her mouth to counter, and I raise a hand. My chest is tight, and my vision blurs. I have boundaries now, but they're easier to keep up when the battering ram isn't standing a foot away. "No. No more of that. I need you to listen to me."

I take a deep breath, trying to keep the anger out of my tone. She immediately dismisses anything I say the second I sound at all emotional. *Say it before you lose your nerve.* "I know it's hard for you to understand, but I'm a separate person from you. With different things I want out of life. I don't need you lying to manipulate me into doing the things you want me to do. You have to stop trying to control me."

"Well, if you stopped making a hash of your life, maybe I would. Moving to New York by yourself. Living in a shoebox. Whatever it is you're doing for a living…"

"You make it sound like I deal in black-market babies,

Mom. I'm in marketing."

"Well, I don't know what to tell people when they ask. Brian is a realtor. That Jack you brought with you is a lawyer. That's easy."

"You tell them—" I hear my voice go up in volume and immediately hit the brakes. *Don't escalate.* She has the ability to burrow her way into my nerves like no other. I know that, and I can fight against that. "You tell them I'm a marketer. Or don't. I really don't care. All of that is beside the point. My life is my life, Mom."

"That tabloid thing...men fighting—*an actor* and that one out there... At least the actor has money."

"The stereotype about lawyers is literally that they sell their souls for money, Mom. It's, like, a thing."

"What are you going to do when this fling ends? Or, worse, if it goes on for a while? When he breaks you, and I'm not there to help you?"

"Oh my God."

"Your father was the most handsome guy in our high school, you know. What did that get me? They leave you the second you get older." She turns and fills a kettle with water.

I rub at my eyes, at the burning behind them. I want to cry. Her baggage, her issues, have been mine for so damn long.

"You don't know Jack. He's good. He's kind. He helps people. He's the best guy I've ever known, and I'm fucking thrilled to be...with him."

"Giving the milk away..." She pulls down mugs.

"Okay. You're not going to change. That's clear. So that means the only way off this runaway train is if I do. And I'm trying to, I really am, Mom. I'm sorry your life didn't turn out how you wanted. I'm sorry Dad was an asshole. He bailed on both of us. I understand it hurt. But you don't get a redo in me. It's my life. My mistakes to make, my happiness. My decisions. You think I'm a hot mess, I get it. But I'm not. I have an apartment I love. I have a job I'm really fucking good at. And I have a guy..."

I swallow, not ready to confront the swirl of feelings thinking of Jack conjures up. "You always force your unsolicited 'advice' down my throat and then play the victim. It must feel amazing to have never been wrong once in your life, because anyone who knows you knows you always *think* you're right. But you don't know what's best for me. You don't get a say. Not anymore." My palms go clammy, and a sharp pain rolls through my gut. "And if you can't accept that—if you can't stop yourself from doing it—Mom, I *love* you, but we won't have a relationship."

The kettle starts whistling, an exclamation point on my monologue. My mom calmly removes it from the stovetop and begins pouring. "That's something to say to your mother: 'We won't have a relationship.' After all I sacrificed. You want to make me feel—" she starts.

I turn to leave, to gather Jack and never come back.

"Wait!"

I turn, staring at her dully. Numbness spreads through me. She looks older than ever. I force myself not to cave. Fail.

"Penny... I—ah... I don't mean to make it so that you feel you don't have choices. I just... I worry. It's fear." She shrugs and pulls a Tupperware container of sugar toward her. "I'm not always right. That's the point. I was wrong about your dad. I should have never said anything about his affair."

"It wasn't your fault or mine or your age or anything other than he—*the individual*, not the whole species—was a lowlife."

"Regardless... He hurt me, you know. A lot. Loving someone and having them do that to you is— I thought I wouldn't make it through, but I had you to take care of, so I had to pull myself together and… I guess I…" She swallows, the thin skin of her neck moving. "I thought maybe I could spare you that."

I picture her kissing my skinned elbow and reading me books. I love my mom. I do. It's a complicated love, a suffocated love that isn't sure how to adapt to more oxygen. I force myself to regard her without expression. To stay quiet.

"But… You're an adult now. I can try to keep my opinions to myself." She tucks her white-and-coppery strands behind her ear, in an identical gesture to the one I make when I'm nervous.

"And… Well, I did the best I could with what I knew. Now that I know better, I'll do better. Because I love you."

She swims in front of me, and I blink the tears back until I see an answering sheen in her eyes. I can love her and be my own person. I hug her, feeling how frail she is in my arms.

"Thank you," I say simply, wishing I'd had the strength to do this a long time ago. Wondering if she would've been ready to receive the message then. Hoping that her actions going forward will match her words today. "And… You know unattractive guys can cheat, too, right?"

She laughs and pulls away, swiping at her cheek. "Oh, I know. Kathleen's husband—you remember Kathleen? She owns the laundromat down on Ocean Ave. Well, how her husband got *her*, let alone the mistress he was running around with, too, I'll never know."

She sniffs. "That Jack seems like a bit of a rascal, and I know girls love a bad boy, but I'm sure you're smart enough to pick one you can reform. That's all I'll say about that."

She grabs for her tray of teacups. "Maybe when you find a therapist, you can give me their contact info. I can come up and see—"

"We are not sharing a therapist, Mom, oh my God," I say, exasperated. "And...I'm already seeing a therapist. She's wonderful, and it's been helping me a lot."

"I knew it! I could tell. A mother can always tell when something is different with their child."

"But if you're serious, I can help you find someone of your own to talk to."

"I'm willing if you come visit me more."

"That! That's manipulative, Mom."

Mom nods, uncomfortable with emotion but dealing with it admirably. "Sorry. This is all new to me." She bustles outside, and I follow, swallowing a smile at the thought of how pleased Jack would be to be called a "bad boy" just now.

We return to the table, and Jack raises an eyebrow. I give him a wide grin in return, pairing it with a light shake of my head.

The next hour is a pleasant one. Despite being on our best behavior when we arrived, after the interlude in the bathroom, Jack and I can't seem to stop touching each other. Little brushes, grazes. He laces his fingers and mine and rests our joined hands on his thigh, staring at me with a look I hope I'm correctly reading as a promise. I find myself half listening whenever Sarah or Monica talks, instead replaying the most sinful bits from last night and today in my mind. Jack Craig's greatest hits album.

My mom says something, a joke that swirls over my head. I'm too busy watching Jack. He smiles at me, his eyes crinkled in the corners, his dark hair a rich chocolate spiked with light brown in the sun, those bracketing dimples… There is affection in his eyes, and a wanting that spreads warmth through me, thawing a dark place within me I wasn't really aware was frozen. He's the opposite of my dad. Kind. He stays. He fights for people. Helps. He's seen me at my nuttiest, and he still wants me. And there can't be deal-breakers worse than the ones I've already seen out of him. He brushes a strand of my hair over my shoulder and leans down to plant a gentle kiss on my cheek.

It's a beautiful day.

My phone vibrates. I reach for it, glancing to read the text. My jaw drops.

Jack lifts his hand off the nape of my neck. "Everything okay?"

I gnaw at the corner of my lip, debating telling him. "It's Avery. He's wondering what I'm doing this afternoon. Because he's…um… He and Anna are eloping."

Jack pushes back from the table. "It was nice meeting you all. We need to go." He stalks in the direction of the car, and I leap to my feet, weakly explaining why we're leaving so abruptly.

I hug my mom with a promise to come down again and talk some more, then wave bye to Brian, Sarah, and Monica.

"Wait." I rush to hop into the passenger side, briefly concerned he might leave me behind if I delay him. "What's wrong?"

"What's wrong?" He reverses out of the driveway, sending shells skittering across the street. "There's no way my sister is marrying your fucking friend."

# 31

Silence reigns in the car until we reach the highway and have blasted past a few of the Garden State Parkway's green exit signs. Then my well of self-control runs dry.

"Your sister isn't marrying my 'fucking friend'? Last I checked, they're consenting adults. And they're in love. It's *romantic*." I conveniently leave out my own qualms about the relationship.

"It's not romantic. It's a mistake."

"Yeah, you mentioned that. Care to elaborate why you think Avery isn't good enough for your sister?" I glare at his profile. Just hours earlier, I had my hand on his thigh and was pulling that mouth to mine. Now I want to wrench off the steering wheel and smack him with it.

Jack shakes his head. "This isn't about Avery. It's about Anna. She's done this before. If you knew her goddamn track record… He's a Band-Aid on a bullet wound, but the thing is, her ego never stops bleeding. If you care about your friend, know that he's going to get hurt unless I stop this."

"You don't know that! Her past is the past, Jack. This time might be different." I'm not sure the pleading edge to my voice isn't because I'm trying to convince myself track records aren't crystal balls.

We don't speak again for two and a half hours.

I stare out the window, watching the tree-lined highway give way to town views as we near the bridge to New York. I'm worrying the nail on my thumb. I force myself to stop.

"You don't think Anna's capable of making her own decisions? Just because of her past?"

I hope the long drive will have given him time to cool down, to let his blood pressure drop. Instead, he nods curtly and says, "Yes. That's exactly what I think."

His words initially pinched like a beesting, but the more I roll them over in my mind, examine them, the more the ache grows. Those words, a familiar criticism, echo inside me, taking a wrecking ball to the fledgling hopes I've been nurturing.

We stop at a gas station for a bathroom-and-coffee break, and in the ladies' room, I manage to shoot Avery a warning text that I am en route with a pissed-off Jack.

Jack is waiting for me at the car. I make to pass him by, but he pulls me to him gently and gives me a soft kiss, holding my stiff frame to him. It's the only semblance of affection he's shown me since we left Stone Harbor. My eyes well.

"This has nothing to do with you and me," he says.

"Jack, Avery is the Mother Teresa of my group of friends—the best person I know. He's perfect for your sister. Give her a chance to prove she—"

Jack pulls away woodenly and opens his car door. The warmth in his eyes from a moment ago is gone, his gaze now cold and glazed over. "I'm not rehashing this."

I follow him into the car. My tears are gone. Instead, I find myself trying to relax my clenched jaw. "Well, I am. Your shitty attempt to be an unwanted white knight is possibly jeopardizing my friend's happiness. It's fucked up."

Other than the visible tension in his own jaw, I wouldn't have known he heard me.

Jack keeps pinching the bridge of his nose, his go-to when he's stressed. And at one point, I see him pull out the migraine pills I spied in his apartment once upon a time. I feel a twinge of sympathy, but not enough to forgive his attitude toward his sister…or me.

We cross the bridge, and Jack expertly navigates the darting traffic to get us to our apartment building in good time. He parks us in a garage near our building, telling the attendant he'll be back for the car in an hour. As we walk to the building, Jack finally speaks again.

"I need to know where they're going. What time?"

"I'm not going to tell you."

"Penny. Stop."

"No, *you* stop."

I run up the front steps and plug my key into the lock, then rush into the lobby. Jack follows.

"Anna is rebounding, and—"

"And what? Avery is a dick to swoop in?" I ignore that I warned Avery against doing exactly this, and I look over at him as he pulls alongside me, keeping pace with me on the stairs.

"I didn't say that, but if the shoe fits."

A vein is bouncing in my temple. We reach our landing. The door to my apartment is a few feet away. Home base. I need to get away from him. I fumble with my keys.

"Penny."

I take a deep breath and turn to face him, looking up at his handsome face. My heart lurches. I just want him to say the right thing. To see it. To prove that he's not someone who'll wade into my issues and decide the water's too hot. "I am Anna, Jack. A damaged, no-good-at-relationships adult who has had a well-meaning yet controlling relation try and run my life for me. Can't you see that? If Anna and Avery are doomed, what about you and me? What's the difference here?"

"The difference is me," he says, as if it's the most obvious answer in the world. I wait for more, but he just stands there and blinks at me, as if I shouldn't need to hear any more than that to be satisfied.

"Oh. Wow. So I'm a fuckup, but you'll… What? Step in for my mom? Fix me? White-knight the—"

His expression hardens. "My relationship with my sister is nothing like yours with your mom."

"You're not a control freak? Didn't you tell me that you vacuum every fucking day as a form of control?"

"Jesus Christ, half the time I was doing it to interrupt your conversations with your mother. And the other half… My vacuuming is a coping mechanism. That's completely different. I vacuum so that when I put the vacuum away, I don't need to control anything."

"And yet right now you're trying to stop someone from doing what they want because it doesn't jibe with how you think their life should go. Sounds pretty familiar. Sounds like my mother."

He runs a hand through his hair, and his ability to hang on to his temper is enraging. God knows I'm letting go of mine. "Look, Penny. Avery seems like he has his shit together. Mature. Anna is— She's not. It can't last. You don't know my sister—"

"Actually," I say, my upset making my voice wobble, "it sounds like I know her real well. Can't keep a relationship going for long. Unhealthy with guys. Too damaged to make her own choices, so she needs to have her life micromanaged. About to enter into an *unbalanced relationship that can't last.*" My voice goes up alarmingly at the end.

"Penny—"

I've found my deal-breaker. I need to let him go. The decision to end a fledgling relationship has never stung this much, but it's better now than later.

"Penny, I don't need to *control* anything here. But when things go south with Anna, I'm the one who has to pick up the pieces."

It's a testament to how much I am clinging to this that I find myself saying, "Technically, you don't have to pick up the pieces at all! She's an adult. And so are you. You don't have to prove your worth by being useful to your family, Jack. Maybe it felt that way when you were younger, but you don't have to fix things for others anymore. My mother—"

"I don't have time to parse through your mommy baggage right now, but you're not Anna, and I'm not your mother." I make a scoffing sound, and he snaps, "For a start, I'm not a manipulative fucking mess."

I rear back, eyes wide. I ignore the instant regret on his face.

"I'm sorr—"

"No, I'm sorry, Jack. This is over," I say, the sharp stab in my chest nipping at my anger's heels. I want to double over and howl. I want to demand he tell me over and over that I'm not Anna until I believe it myself. I want him to trust Anna to live her life so I can trust that he trusts me to do the same. I want him to take back everything, the past three hours, rewind until we're back in that hotel room.

My mom's words, about this relationship ending, mock me.

He looks like I've struck him, and then his jaw firms. "I shouldn't have said— No, you know what? This is your thing, right? Can't get hurt if you never try and go the distance. Never give someone a chance. Run when it's hard."

"I gave *you* a chance!"

"It's your decision what happens with us, so..." He runs his hand through his hair again and turns away before swinging his gaze back to me. "So, yeah. Fuck it. *Your decision*." His gray eyes are wintry. "I'll try not to make things awkward, seeing as how we're going to be neighbors for a very long time."

I laugh. It's a tense, ugly, unhappy sound. "You're lucking out there. I haven't gotten my raise yet, so I can't afford to buy my place." I'm a wounded thing, lashing out, trying to inflict some of the pain I'm feeling on him. "Maybe your next neighbor won't be a relationship fuckup, so you can get with someone you actually respect."

Jack opens his mouth and closes it. I don't slam the door on him this time. Instead, I close it slowly, still hoping he'll pour the right words—the ones that will suck the venom out of this wound—through the opening before it shuts on us for good.

# 32

I pick at the scarred wooden armrest of my chair and glance over at Margie. There are, surprisingly, tears in her light-brown eyes as she watches the heart-eyed couple at the front of the room. I guess being in love does wild things to you.

"By the power vested in me by the State of New York…"

I flinch when the duo standing in front of the Justice of the Peace, a mature couple flanked by what appears to be their children from other marriages, launch themselves at each other, kissing with a jubilance so potent I could roast marshmallows on it. I rub at my chest, at the bite of a smoldering ember hidden somewhere in the blackened crater that was my heart.

Margie leans forward in her chair, clapping along with the rest of the people waiting their turn in the yellow-walled City Clerk's Office. Avery's handsome profile comes into view in the seat next to Margie's. He pushes his glasses up his nose, an ear-splitting grin perma-etched across his face as he releases Anna's hand to clap for the couple.

I've had to watch two of these depressing unions so far.

"Avery Vaughn and Anna Craig," someone intones. We all stand and move to the front of the room, with Anna leading the charge. She races to the Justice's dais and turns to us, beaming. Her mahogany hair is pulled back in her trademark tight bun, perfectly setting off her delicate features. Avery joins her, taking her hands in his. Watching them, something inside me pitches.

Margie cracked a joke when we got here, saying that Avery got his hair cut twice for today. He looks as neat as always—not a hair out of place, not ever—but he's lost the hot-librarian look we always tease him about. At least, he has to me. I tilt my head, analyzing him. I've seen Avery with girlfriends in the past, but I've never seen this look in his forest-green eyes before. That's what it is. There's a fierceness, an intensity there, that would've had me sighing if I hadn't just had my heart broken.

They look perfect together. Tall as Anna is, she still just comes to Avery's shoulders. He bends his head to whisper something in her ear, and her cheeks color.

Margie and I stand as their witnesses. Since there aren't a ton of couples waiting behind them, the officiant lets Avery and Anna say a few words to one another.

"Anna, I'm not impulsive. I'm not." Avery shakes his head emphatically. "I research everything. I deliberate. But for the first time in my life, I'm going with my gut because I *know* something… I just know it."

My eyes well, watching him, one of my dearest friends in the world.

"Avery, I love that you love me so much," Anna says, lifting his hand and lacing her fingers through his.

A fleeting frown, a match of my own, passes over Margie's face.

Anna looks to their joined hands and says, "I don't have to fight for your time, or chase you, or twist myself into a pretzel to make myself fit into your life. You're…a grown-up, and kind, and I'm so happy you're mine."

Then they speak the words that bind them together, and

the waterworks begin in earnest for me. Margie is crying, too, so I don't have to explain why I'm a sniveling mess. Anna hugs me, shoving her makeshift bouquet at me. I gaze down at those flowers before handing them off to Margie.

We head to La's for a celebratory drink, and Anna squeals, delighted by my story about refusing to give away the time or place they were getting married to Jack. I leave out the part where I spent hours in her brother's arms, convinced I'd maybe found something my mother always insisted didn't exist.

"He's the family's keeper. He got a job at a gas station near our house when he was sixteen after my dad started his chemo, and he would give my parents his paycheck every week. He ratted me out for throwing a party in high school, even though his friends were invited! Rule-follower was doing the *laundry* when everyone showed up. He kicked them out. It was like he felt guilty having fun or whatever, and so he'd lecture me when I just wanted to *live*. And I already told you he worked two jobs in college, even though he had a full ride, and he gave every dime to my parents, right? Which was nice and all, but… He just has to fix everything for everyone. Martyr complex. It's so fucking basic," she says.

"It's not good to try and control—" I start to say.

"It's not even about control. He's like a jigsaw junkie. Thinks he's got to pick up everyone's pieces and help put them back together, whether they want him there or not."

A spark of loyalty flares. That sounds like caring to me. Love. And I don't know all of their history, but Anna definitely came to Jack with her pieces in hand, begging for his help to put them together again. "But I mean, you went to him when you broke up…" I trail off. It occurs to me too late that I probably shouldn't mention her breakup on her wedding day.

A queer look—a cross between anger and anguish—flits across her face, but it's there and gone again in a blink. I rush to change the subject, drawing Margie over to shoulder the burden of conversation.

Not long after, Avery and Anna say their goodbyes and rush off to do very newlywed things. I find myself fighting off rising panic as I watch them leave. Jack called me once, when I was in my Lyft, causing the air to squeeze from my lungs when "Demon" showed up on my screen. I promptly blocked him, his remembered words bringing a rush of anger. I think of that call now. The thought of going back to my apartment, of maybe seeing him, or not seeing him, has me freaking out.

La and Margie are whispering to each other. I turn to them, standing silently until they stop canoodling and notice me. Then, with minimal prompting: "I slept with Jack, and I thought it was going to work out, but how could it when he thinks I'm an Anna? So I broke up with him." A surprise sob catches me off guard. La wraps her arms around me.

"Hey. You're going to be okay. I'm going to feed you," she says in a reassuringly firm way. Margie offers me her guest room. She and La bustle me back to the apartment.

I pour my heart out, with La running her hand up and down my back in comfort—she's surprisingly like a pack of Mentos, her hard shell shielding a super-soft and sympathetic minty-fresh heart. They flank me on the sofa, sentinels against heartbreak, letting me cry it all out for ages.

Later, Margie pets my hair and feeds me popcorn. La prepares a dinner that looks incredible and that I don't remember tasting.

A commercial comes on for a legal show, and it snaps me out of my misery enough to remember that I haven't asked poor Margie about work.

"The show's still in limbo," she says, waving away my concern, "but a meeting with the showrunner is coming any day now."

I nod wearily and shuffle to the guest room, sniffling and clutching a fistful of tissues.

The next morning, a rainy, miserable Monday, I find myself sitting in my cubicle, wearing Margie's borrowed clothes, staring at my swollen eyes on a Zoom video call. The call ends, and I pull off my headset, glancing up at Rochelle when she stops at my desk with a smile.

"Penny, did you see the request that came in on Friday? Did you send me your feedback on the lead scoring model—"

"Sorry. No. I'll get that to you. What's happening with my raise, by the way?" I drop the last bit with all the subtlety of an Acme anvil crushing a cartoon coyote.

Rochelle's smile is the same one she gives me every time I ask, and I think I read in it everything I missed all the other times. It's uncomfortable, pacifying… It suddenly occurs to me that I'm not sure she ever asked for a raise for me at all.

"I'm going to keep trying—"

I start packing up my stuff, throwing odds and ends into my handbag.

"Penny…" Rochelle laughs nervously. "What are you doing?"

"Oh, I quit." I smile at her, feeling liberated. That light-in-the-heart feeling I only really get when I'm around Jack. At the thought of him, the light dims, but I grit my teeth and press on. I don't have an apartment anymore anyway, without the raise. I can crash at Margie's in that tiny extra room for a while until I find a new apartment and a new gig. I'm just…over this. All of this. I don't want chicken slop. I want my damn chicken sandwich.

Rochelle's shock is gratifying. As is the desperation on her face. "No. Wait. Right there. I'm going to talk to HR right now and..."

"How about I leave, and you talk to HR after I'm gone, and instead of me waiting around for you to *see what you can do*, you find out what you can do and just tell me? It's been three years and a lot of promises, Roch. I've always really admired you and enjoyed working with you, but I'm done. I know my worth, and I deserve a raise. If you can't give it to me, I need to find somebody who will."

I stand, and Rochelle stares after me. In the elevator, I shake off the fear and the inner doubting voice that sounds an awful lot like my mom's. And for once? I just do what makes me fucking happy.

I walk out into the rain and look around, exulting in my newfound freedom but not at all sure where I want to go. The rain plasters my shirt to me as I wander a few blocks, peering into storefronts. A thought occurs, and I hail a cab.

"Hi. Short trip," I tell the cabbie, shivering in the air-conditioned space. "Can you take me to Rizzoli? It's the bookstore on Broadway. Between Twenty-fifth and Twenty-sixth."

That night, I feel less fragile about everything. Turns out that demanding your worth for the first time in your life will do that to you. And spending the afternoon wandering a bookshop, eating your feelings, and getting a pedicure helps, too. There isn't a repeat of yesterday's outpouring of misery, but seeing Margie and La so deeply in love, on the heels of Avery and Anna's wedding, has me feeling like I'm cradling a glass heart in my chest. One that's taken way too many hits over the years, too many of them self-inflicted.

I miss Jack's crisp, piney smell, his dumb humor, his sharp retorts. I miss ripping down a wall with him, building one back up, getting him over to my side of it. I miss feeling him holding me. I miss *him*. Everything about him. The thought of rebuilding the hole he's left inside me leaves me exhausted.

That night, when I'm tucked up in Margie's guest room, reading my newly purchased replacement copy of *The Pirate Duke's Revenge*—my first copy forgotten in my dash out of the apartment—and fighting the urge to check my phone every few seconds, a text finally comes through. But it's from Avery.

"Ugh… Margie?" I yell.

Margie appears at the threshold, her hair frazzled, her eyes wider than I've ever seen them. For once, she's not trying to be the actor and is allowing pure concern and desperation to wash over her face. "Get dressed. We need to get over there."

# 33

Avery is in bad shape when we get to his place. His hair is disheveled, his emerald eyes bloodshot.

"Oh, Avery." I enfold him in a hug.

"She broke up with me in a text, Penny. A fucking text! After being married a day?"

"What did she say?" I ask.

Margie ushers us to Avery's living room and heads to the kitchen.

"Her parents are traveling. She said she's going to stay with them, wherever the hell they are right now, to 'think things through.'" He spits out the words and shakes his head, bewildered. "We didn't even argue. I don't understand."

I hear clanking, and Margie returns holding three bottles. "Maybe she left you because you drink wine coolers."

"Margie!"

Avery hiccups out a half laugh. "You're such a bitch."

Margie smiles and takes a swig, looking at the glass appreciatively. "These are pretty good. I take it back."

"What am I going to do?" Avery groans suddenly, hanging his head in his hands.

"Well," Margie says. "I know your past relationships were all civilized and disciplined and ended on good terms, but… Avery,

I'm shocked you don't know how sudden heartbreak works. How many times have you mopped up after Penny or me? We've had dozens of breakups under our belts, between the two of us." Margie's voice is soft, though her tone has a teasing note. She's always dealt with everything through humor, but her concern for Avery is clear as day underneath it all.

"Never seen either of you heartbroken," Avery says.

I clear my throat. "You're going to cry, Vaughn," I say. "And feel like someone's set your heart on fire and then stomped it out with cleats. And it's going to be a chore to get out of bed. And I don't know when it'll end because I'm only on day two of feeling it myself."

Avery lifts bleary eyes to me, and I hug him to me.

"You and her brother?" he asks.

I nod, and he shakes his head.

"That family has emotionally kidney-punched two-thirds of our group. Unacceptable," Margie says.

Avery's phone buzzes, and he grabs for it, his face falling when he sees it's not Anna. "Speaking of the brother, he just texted. He's on his way to pick up Anna's stuff."

My throat closes up. "No! I can't– I'm not ready to see him. I–"

"You'll hide in Avery's bedroom. It's *okay*," Margie says. The only thing that calms me down is the look on Avery's face. My misery has had time to marinate. His is fresh.

I follow Avery into his bedroom and pace as he neatly folds Anna's clothes–which aren't many–and piles them into the suitcase. Margie's expression says he should chuck that shit in there and be done with it, but she remains silent. The slow and steady way he works at it nearly drives me mental, but then again I'm debating whether or not to leapfrog over the bed and out the door before Jack arrives. Avery closes the suitcase. He sighs.

Whatever he's about to say is interrupted by the buzzer signaling Jack's arrival.

I wrap my arms around myself, a protective hug to ward against the anxious fireworks going off inside me. Avery and Margie rush out of the room to let him up, and I leave the door open a crack so I can peer through if I need to. My heart beats against my ribs like a kick drum. My breath comes in puffs so loud—or at least, it feels that way to me—that I find myself holding my breath when Margie answers the door. Jack's deep voice causes it to whoosh out in a gush.

"I'll go grab her things," I hear Avery say. Panicked, I fixate on the suitcase. Avery didn't take it with him. I back away and turn wide eyes on Avery when he enters the bedroom. He lifts his weary gaze to me and murmurs, "He looks like shit, if it makes you feel better." A scorpion's tail of pain snaps up and stings me somewhere in the vicinity of my chest. It doesn't make me feel better.

Avery gives me a kiss on the cheek and carries the bag out. I hear Jack accept it with thanks.

"Listen… I'm sorry. Anna is my baby sister, and I love her, and she really is a sweetheart, but… She's complicated. We've all got our issues—"

"Yeah. Mommy issues, relationship issues… Lots of people with lots of issues," Margie interjects.

There is a pause and then, "What I was saying is, we all have our issues, our screwups, but the difference is that *some people* try and work on them. I've said things I regret in the past. Really regret. And, given the chance, I'd take them back. But I'm just determined to do better next time."

*Next time.* With the next girl.

"But not everyone recognizes that they've done wrong. That there's something to fix. That's Anna."

I hear a rustle, and I risk a glance through the crack in the door again. He's turned back to Avery. "I'm sorry, man. This wasn't about you. It's about that asshole she was engaged to. She confuses drama and turbulence for love. She always goes back—" He stops. Shakes his head. "He reaches out, and it's like a hit of dopamine. She always goes back to him eventually, and I'm always there to take care of her when he inevitably breaks her heart again. Until now. That cycle ends today. She wanted to come back to my place after she left here, but I told her she could go stay with our parents or with her friends, but my apartment wasn't where she was going to hide out and lick her wounds. It's time for her to grow up and figure things out for herself, and I've got to own my part in the whole twisted saga and stop contributing. I'm only here to pick up her stuff so you don't have to look at it longer than you need to. Anyway… I'm sorry."

The living room grows quiet in the wake of his statement.

Margie taps her chin. "So if Anna was prepared to work out her stuff, you wouldn't have had a problem with her and Avery?"

"I would've questioned the quickie wedding, but no. I would've been thrilled."

There's another stretch of silence, and then: "You see Penny? She okay?" Jack asks Margie, and my heart turns over in my chest. So our argument was exactly what he was referring to. *I'm just determined to do better next time.*

"She's great. Why wouldn't she be? She'll be here soon if you want to stick around." The consummate actor, pretending I wasn't bawling on her sofa the other night. I flinch. I love

Margie and her protectiveness, but I don't want him thinking he didn't matter.

Jack nods, an abrupt, jerking motion. "Great. You're right. Why wouldn't she be okay?" He stands there for a moment in silence, as if he wants to say something more, before clapping his hands on his thighs. "I've got to get going."

I bite at my nail, listening to him make his goodbyes, wishing I could pop out of the bedroom. To tell him that I'm willing to work on me, that I *have* been working on me, and that that really does make me different from Anna. That maybe I'm willing to forgive the things he said if he really is sorry. If he can convince me he didn't mean it. But that's not true, so I don't.

Because he gave me a real deal-breaker.

Because he hurt me, and I'm scared.

Because he hasn't indicated he even wants me back, anyway.

The door closing behind him does nothing to quell the tornado he's whipped up inside me.

Margie's apartment reminds me of a pocket gallery in the MoMA: big, modern, abstract art on the walls, a brass-and-glass coffee table, and bookcases. It's nice, but I've never missed the cozy warmth of my apartment more.

I unblocked Jack on my phone a few days ago, but even still, there are no more calls and no messages from Demon. And that sucks. Because in spite of the shitty things he said, I miss him. I miss everything about him.

Margie looks up from her book. She's pointed out that I do a lot of sighing lately. "What's going on?" she asks. "Lay it on me."

"Nothing." I sigh. "Just psychoanalyzing myself. Continuation of therapy."

"Always fun. What'd you come up with? Hope it's Freudian. What a perv."

I lean back in the armchair and play with my phone. "I'm realizing I looked for deal-breakers with guys because my mom has drummed it into my head that being left by a man is the worst thing that can ever happen."

Margie laughs. "Of course that's not true. There's tons of worse things in the world. But really, I think your problem just boils down to a fear of…love."

"You fucking convert. Everything is *love* with you now. You said Avery's problem was that he was in love with the idea of being in love."

Margie sets her book down. "I'm serious."

"He didn't agree."

"I'm talking about you."

I swallow and pointedly go back to scrolling on my phone. But the thought nags.

Fear of love? I haven't put myself out there, really…ever. Every relationship was like something I put up on the mantel of my life, to be replaced whenever my fancies changed. An ornament, like the seasonal decorations in my apartment. I never had to invest too much of me—my feelings, my real personality, my boat-rocking potential—so, as a result, letting go or breaking up early were easy enough ways to protect myself. I never felt the urge to empty a drawer for someone, to make space for another person in my refuge. The fallout of a breakup has never been more complex than tossing his toothbrush in the trash. If you don't love, you can't get betrayed. You never have to experience things getting difficult and watching someone choose to leave instead of working through things with you.

Jack is not like the others. I know that now. For one, that Pirate Duke–looking douche scares me and thrills me more than anyone I've ever met. And my deal-breaker with him was based on a phantom equivalence, my own fears, and some thoughtless words from him spoken in anger. He's seen the real me now and likes me anyway. He challenges me, makes me laugh… But love?

"You're the worst," I say.

Margie just snorts and continues reading.

I draft half a dozen texts to Jack but can't make myself send a single one. They all feel so…weak. What the hell do you say? *What I'm feeling for you was sorta on track to enter L-word territory, and I was worried you'd turn out to be like my dad, and you saying all that mean shit felt like a deal-breaker, but if you're sorry, maybe…*

I rub at the ache in my chest and look at my incoming call. "Hello?" I answer.

"Hi, Penny. Hope you've enjoyed your well-deserved vacation." Rochelle sounds like she's on speaker, and the tone of her voice tells me she has an audience.

Vacation. Huh. "Uh, yeah. Good times. What's up, Rochelle?"

"What's up is some fun Friday news! I'm thrilled to advise that HR has approved a promotion! We're getting you up to a director level. And it comes with a twenty-five percent bump in salary—retroactive to last month!"

I sit back in my chair, absorbing the words with no little shock.

Margie mouths, *What?*

I shake my head at her. When the silence stretches uncomfortably, I finally say, "Ah… Wow. I don't know what to say. Thank you."

"No, thank *you*. This is long overdue. We'll see you Monday. Okay?" There's a tense pause, as if Rochelle isn't sure if the promotion and raise are enough.

I swallow. "Thirty percent and I'll definitely see you Monday."

I let the silence linger until I'm so uncomfortable, I want to crawl out of my skin.

But then Rochelle's voice comes through, too bright but also tinged with relief. "You got it. Have a great weekend and we'll see you Monday."

I disconnect the call and sit there, stunned.

"What happened? Tell me," Margie demands.

An email comes through. Rochelle.

> Figured you'd need the attached proof of salary for that mortgage. Sorry this took me so long to get you. Your courage sparked mine. See you Monday.

Home. I'm going home.

I run up to my apartment and knock on Jack's door. There's no answer. I chew at my lip. He isn't home. Okay. This will just have to wait a bit…

I open my apartment. There's a slip of paper on the floor.

*I'm sorry. More than you know.*

*J.*

I run out into the hall and fumble with the banister cap, relieved when I see the hidden key Anna mentioned still there. I'm not going to risk him coming and going before I can talk to him. I'm going to wait inside his place and—

Boxes. Jack's furniture is already gone. My heart shrivels in my chest, the death of hope collapsing in on itself, a tiny, sucking black hole.

I stumble out of the apartment and back into my own, and I look across the room through defeated, tired eyes. I can see the browning leaves of my plants through the glass. I dash to my fire escape and throw open the tall window, then race to my sink to grab water. I murmur soothing, nonsensical things and prune the plants for the better part of an hour. I want to cry. I neglected them the same way I neglected my…*thing* with Jack.

Love? For the first time in my life, I think so. We weren't just approaching L-word territory. We had maybe already arrived while we were busy pounding on the wall and eating pizza and fixing The Hole. And now it's too late.

My head dips. I wander the apartment. Somehow, like when *The Wizard of Oz* turns from Technicolor back to gray at the end, it's lost its power for me. It was a hiding place, a refuge I could retreat to so I didn't have to deal with things I didn't want to. But now I know I don't need these four walls to accomplish what my voice can do for me. It took taking down a wall to give me the emotional tools to put them up wherever I need to. Now this apartment is just a place where Jack isn't. I lie there on my sofa for what feels like ages, staring blankly up at the ceiling.

An ache blooms inside me. God, I miss him. He hurt me with his words, but I started the argument. And then I left. Didn't give him a chance to backtrack, even after he started to apologize. He's sorry. And I bailed on him.

I want him back. But any words—even better ones than my brain is currently cooking up—will ring too hollow if I can get him to talk to me. There's no danger in saying the thing, because I can always just say some more words later and leave again. What kind of wobbly foundation would that be?

It's a while before I force myself to shuffle down to Gence's apartment. I still need to lock in my apartment purchase. I almost don't want to now.

When I knock, Gence's wife, Zoya, answers. She's a handsome woman with gray-streaked black hair pulled back in a ponytail.

"Um. Is Gence here? I need to talk to him." My eyes well, and Zoya ushers me to a low couch in the living room. I've never been inside his place, but it's clean and cozy. His wife brings over coffee and sets it down on the table. I give her a small smile, grateful as she goes to fetch her husband.

The table is covered in delicate, crocheted white doilies protected under a thick sheet of transparent plastic. It makes for a wonky surface for my coffee. Gence enters and sits across from me, frowning when I set my cup down and end up spilling a bit. I sigh. I can't win with him.

I pull out my mortgage pre-approval docs, then set them down on my lap. I swallow hard. "Jack didn't buy his apartment?"

Gence sits back, folding his hands on his belly. "You come here to ask me that? No. He didn't buy."

A thought sparks. I lick my lips. This is either the best idea I've ever had, or the worst.

Gence purses his lips. "You come here to drink my coffee? Maybe give me more sugary treats, *katastrofë me dy këmbë*?"

"No," I say, before handing over my documents.

# 34

The next day, Sunday, is a gorgeous one: cloudless blue skies and just a taste of early autumn in the air. I peer out of my apartment windows. It's my favorite kind of day. And it's supremely unfair that I should have one of these when everything is in shambles.

I march to my coffee machine, slippers shuffling along through the boxes in my living room, and go through the motions, making myself some liquid fortitude.

I sip from my mug and take in my apartment. The symbol of my first chapter away from my mom. Breaking free… Maybe not as cleanly as I thought. But I loved it. It loved me back. Right now, though? I don't feel anything for this place other than a twinge of nostalgia. This apartment was once home. That's all.

I check my phone. Jack hasn't responded to a single text. I toss it down and settle on the sofa, half-heartedly committed to reading the rest of *The Pirate Duke's Revenge* and then doing what I need to do.

I'm rereading the same page for the tenth time when my buzzer sounds. I set my mug down and unfold myself from my couch cocoon, frowning as I pad to the intercom.

"Who is it?"

There's no response, so I don't buzz whoever it is into the

building. Last time someone did that, we had a fun package thief make off with tons of stuff.

I'm about to settle back onto the sofa when there's a knock on my door. I open it, and my heart goes supernova.

Jack.

I open my mouth but can't seem to get any words out. Instead, my eyes dart everywhere, frantically taking in every feature, from his furrowed brow to his fingers flexing at his side. The eye patch is gone, which causes me a moment of sadness, as do the shadows under his eyes.

"Before you say anything, I need to tell you something," he begins.

"You didn't answer my texts."

"Damn it, Penny, I said before you say anything. You're throwing me off my— No, I didn't answer your texts, although I didn't know you *sent* any until you just said so. I fucking packed my personal cell in one of my moving boxes and didn't realize it until everything was ready to go and then it was too late. And the thing died, so of course I couldn't even hear it ring. I didn't have your number in my work phone. Or Margie's."

"Who doesn't have iMessage set up on their laptop?"

"I—*damn it*, Penny—I needed to tell you... Well, what I'm trying to tell you. So I went to La's, but she called me a dickhead and kicked me out."

"I need to tell you something very important," I interject, growing uneasy. I want to delay whatever it is he wants to say to me. "About the whole argument about your sister, and...and more."

He rubs at the back of his neck and looks so aggravated it'd be comical if I hadn't spent the past week aching for him, if I wasn't so scared that I've cured him of his affection for me. I want to pull him to me and kiss that expression off his face. I want to hear him tell me he wants me back. I want to hear him tell me he cares.

"Wait your turn. You're making me go all out of order." He heaves a frustrated sigh. "My sister is back with that asshole. I didn't want her to hurt your friend, because I've had to go collect Anna's stuff from more than one rebound's place. I never once considered you and her to be the same. That isn't you. And I wasn't trying to control things… I mean, in this case I was, but it was because Avery matters to you, and he seems like a good guy, and honestly I was just tired of… But I should've let two consenting adults make their own mistakes. It's not my job to fix Anna or always act as clean-up crew."

"So you were white-knighting the situation," I cut in. But he was doing it for me. For my friend. And, I guess, for himself, too.

"Y— Wait. Okay, please, just, like…shut up for *two seconds*? So I can say my piece?" He pauses. "I can't remember what the hell I was saying."

"You have something to tell me."

"Right." He rubs at his temple and then pushes past me, turning to face me from the center of my living room. "So, I took a page out of *The Pirate Duke's Revenge* and… Well, I've commandeered your vessel."

I stare at him, blinking slowly. "I don't have any clue what you're saying."

"I bought your apartment."

"You bought—"

"You love this place. I couldn't let you lose it just because your raise hasn't come through yet. So I signed the papers for it. You can unpack your boxes. But I'm not being heroic. This is piracy. I'm claiming this space for me, too. I'm going to live here.

With you. I mean… I mean, of course you have a choice, but I was kind of hoping I could move in with you. I'm currently on the couch of a WWII shrine, and Moth doesn't smell as nice as you."

Jack rushes back out to the hall and bends to pick something up.

A plant.

"So I was going to get you a golden pothos because I read they mean something about longing and perseverance, but it didn't have a flower, so I passed. And I came across this one plant that had the perfect meaning, but every florist in New York City laughed when I asked for it. Fuck if I remember what it was called now. Then I was thinking tansy, because it means 'I declare war on you' in flower language, and I was preparing this whole *Pirate Duke* vessel analogy, but that's not the most romantic thing. So I got you this. It's a sunflower."

I have been struck dumb. At my silence, Jack blanches—and for once, I let him do the babbling. "It means adoration. Going the distance. Loyalty. Penny, I swear, the Anna stuff… And I shouldn't have said that about you. About your mom. It's eaten me up inside not being able to tell you—"

"I believe you."

That brings him up straight. "Okay."

I move past him to close the door, slowly. And I turn to face him, my hands twisting in front of me. I'm quaking inside, a full cast of feelings jostling for center stage.

He still wants me.

Still cares.

Never stopped.

Bought my apartment.

He's right there, holding a sunflower, and he's perfectly imperfect—my villain and my white knight all wrapped up in one. I just have to reach out and tell him.

But the things I want to say, they're jammed up. I watch the concern growing in his gray eyes. He sets the plant down and shoves a hand through his hair, anxiety threaded through his every movement. "Just spit it out. You're killing me here."

"Don't rush me," I snap.

He holds up his hands, his expression immediately conciliatory. I almost laugh. It's enough to loosen my tongue. "I— You're right. I love this apartment. I think you know what it means…what it meant to me. But…I've moved on."

I've never seen Jack—supremely cool, confident, amused and detached Jack—ever look so crushed. He quickly blanks his face after a glance at the boxes behind me, and I panic, kicking myself. I can never find the words when I need them.

"No! I mean…that place. Home. Is… I've started to think that home is wherever you are." I wave away his words when he starts to talk. "And I don't want you walking on eggshells, worried that if you say the wrong thing I might bolt. So… I did a thing. I got my raise, I fucking demanded it, and I… Well, I kind of hoped you'd move in with me in *your* apartment. Which I signed the papers for. Yesterday."

Jack pinches the bridge of his nose. "You gave up your place for me."

"Yeah."

"And you bought my place?"

"Yeah."

"The one I just moved all my stuff out of?"

"Yeah."

"You couldn't have grand-gestured me *before* I schlepped all my crap across town?" he says. I gasp, affronted, and he barks out a laugh. It's a happy, joyous sound, and he pulls me to him.

He smiles down at me with an expression so euphoric, so heart-melting, that I need to remind myself this isn't some *Pirate Duke* fantasy. Jack captures my face between his hands. "I can't believe you were going to give up your apartment for me."

My gaze drops, suddenly shy, then climbs back up to meet his beautiful steel-colored stare. My mouth goes dry, and my palms are damp. I did the thing. Now it's time for the words. "I love you, you menace."

His mouth is on mine, and I could weep at the pure joy, the relief that courses through me. He's not gone. He's here. With me. And…

I tear my mouth from his. "Well?" I say.

He moves to kiss me again. "Well, what?"

I hold up my hand, pressing it against his face and smooshing it back. "I just used the L-word, and that's a huge deal for me, and I'm feeling vulnerable right now." I glare up at him.

"And?"

"Ew!"

He laughs. "What's not to love about this package?" He waves a hand at my indignant form, then chuckles again when I push him away. "You need to hear it? Fine. You crashed into my life like a literal wrecking ball, made a mess of me, and I wouldn't have it any other way. I love you. Of course I love you."

He nearly falls over my sofa when I launch myself at him, legs wrapped around his waist. He slides his hand under me, hefting me up, and slants his mouth over mine again and again. And then he takes me to the bedroom and reaffirms, with his hands, and his lips, and his clever, clever tongue—along with his Jake Gyllenhaal—that the hotel-room sparks were so, so, so not a fluke.

The apartment is growing dark. I flop a damp arm over my eyes. "You've killed me. You better have nice things to say at my funeral."

"She died doing what she loved."

I laugh, a little puff of air, because I don't have energy for more than that. "She died doing who she loves."

"I like your version better," he says, running a hand down my torso. "That's why you're in marketing."

"You're not ready to go again. We've already gone—"

"That erectile dysfunction literature really was helpful," he muses, brushing his hand against the underside of my breast. "I may have mentioned this in passing, but… Did you know that if you *don't* suffer from erectile dysfunction, you can still take the pills and… Well, let's just say you don't have to get ready if you stay ready."

"Is this one of those 'go to the hospital if you remain erect for more than four hours' things?"

"Guess we'll have to spend the next four hours figuring that out."

"I don't think so." I sigh and then yelp as he nips at my throat. Conflict isn't scary. It's fun, and hot, and we can both be bad with each other.

And that's when the buzzer to my apartment sounds for the second time today.

"Ignore it," Jack says, kissing me deeply. My phone starts vibrating, and I pull away reluctantly. I roll over and grab for it.

"Crap. Margie's here." I stand and stretch, tipping a flirtatious glance at Jack. And then I pull on my long Rolling Stones shirt and shorts.

"I loved you in those, by the way."

"My sloppy seduction worked?"

"Just barely."

I shake my head and move to the living room to let Margie in.

"You were sleeping?" she asks, when she sweeps into the apartment.

"Ah—"

Arms wrap around me from behind, and Jack presses a kiss to my temple. I peek down at him. He's decent.

"So, not a lot of sleeping. Got it," Margie says. A smile hovers around her lips. She's happy for me. So happy, I nearly have to remind her she stopped by to tell me something.

"Oh. Yes. Well, I met with the showrunner today. Lunch. And…"

"Please tell me you still have a show," I say.

"Yes… I have a show. Lucas has been dying to get out of his contract to get into movies more, and he's been obsessed with that script about the hitmen brothers."

Jack looks at me as I cover my face. "Is that the one that… Never mind."

"Anyway, since he can't film our show for a while, but the insurance policy the studio had on him paid out, they let him out of his contract. He's free to flap his little movie-star wings and fly away from the nest. Plus, the movie needed him banged up for a few scenes, so they're actually speeding up their shoot schedule to take advantage of his mouth jewelry. Method acting on steroids. As if there's any other kind."

"That's amazing, Margie!" I exclaim.

She holds up a hand. "Best for last. Best. For. Last. *And*, my little chaos babies… Your shenanigans got me a bigger part on the show. My series-regular role has turned into a starring one."

I jump at her, rapturous that I haven't done her career irreparable harm. Happy for Lucas. Happy for her.

Jack goes to the kitchen to whip up sustenance, and I fill Margie in on everything that's happened in the last hour or so.

"Are you keeping both places?" Margie asks.

Jack calls out a "yes" from the kitchen, and Margie cracks out a laugh. "You know what this means, right?"

I look at her, puzzled, and then smile up at Jack as he joins me on the sofa. I lean against him, unable to stop touching him.

"What?"

"You're going to have to bring down this wall again, Mr. Gorbachev!" She crows it and then covers her face, her shoulders moving soundlessly. "You two just put it up, too." She's laughing. Hard.

I stare at her, dumbfounded, and then I snort. Her giggles, even silent, are contagious. All those weeks and work and money…

"Motherfucker," Jack mutters behind me.

But I notice he's smiling, too, as he pulls me into the circle of his arms.

# EPILOGUE

A lot of emotion can be conveyed in a knock. Sharp and pissy. Cordial and businesslike. Great big pounding angry knocks. A *rap-tap-tap* of happy knuckles across a wood panel. Just now, I heard my first ever long-suffering knock.

I roll out of bed and twist out of the way of Jack's attempt to give my rear a slap. My eyes promise retribution as I throw on a robe and rush to the door.

Gence is standing on the landing. He is shaking his head. "Penny. Come on."

I blush. There's only one thing that could've brought him up here. It's been a glorious six months of coupledom—for everyone but our neighbors downstairs. They never used to hear a thing down there. Guess we just hadn't been making the right kind of noise.

"Quiet hours. Your neighbor in 4A… They think earthquake happening, they say."

I sense Jack behind me before I feel him.

"Sorry, Gence… We…ah…got a little carried away."

Gence takes in our state of undress. The fact Jack is in my apartment. He hasn't seen us together yet. His bushy brows hike their way up his face like lethargic caterpillars. "Oh, ho ho! Look at that. I thought you two would kill each other. Instead, you… do this. *Hajt pra.*"

"I've got him for a month-to-month lease with option for renewal." I shrug, the smile I've been carrying around the past few months literally hurting my cheeks.

"You should buy. No renting," Gence says sternly, looking at the two of us. "When you need officiant, you let me know, okay? I have side business."

I stifle my laugh, mortified that the topic of marriage has arisen so early in our relationship, but I'm nearly pitched into hysterics at the thought of Mom's reaction to Gence conducting our ceremony. She's mellowed significantly, and she's even seeing a therapist she really likes. We're still working on boundaries.

I clear my throat, not wanting the subject of marriage to dangle out there too long. "We swear. We won't make any more noise," I say, giving Gence my most reassuring look. The kind I usually reserve for my team at work when I know an exciting new project will require long hours. It's half promise, half apology for future angst.

Gence harrumphs and rolls his eyes, but there's a fondness in his expression, too, I think? Ever since I switched to making him sugar-free baked goods, he's been way friendlier. And I bake a mean diabetic-friendly snickerdoodle.

The tickling Jack gives me the second the door closes belies that promise, of course.

I turn to face Jack and wind my arms around his neck, feeling like I'm glowing from within. He smirks down at me, his warm gaze full of mischief. He brushes back a strand of my hair, tenderly, and I have to give myself a mental shake. I still can't quite believe this is my life now. I've got my very own white knight with a pirate smile, and I've brought down all my walls and then some. Jack leans down to murmur in my ear, and I shiver.

"Let's go be bad."

# NOT GOOD NEIGHBORS

Gence looks heavenward as he moves down the stairs. He's mumbling when he enters his apartment to find Zoya, straightening as she closes the oven.

"The burek smells good," he says.

"You already ate. This is for tomorrow."

Gence grunts. Their children are coming to visit tomorrow, with their own spouses and children. Which means that the only way to get a piece of burek is to wake up after she goes to sleep.

"Don't make me hide it from you," Zoya says, reading his mind correctly. "So what are the *gomarë* on five up to now?" she asks him, wiping her hand on the dishrag at her hip.

"The donkeys? They are living together, I think," Gence responds.

"Of course they are! I already knew that, *o burrë*. I asked *çka dreqin po bajnë* up there?"

"Too much up and down," Gence mutters.

"The man is a pervert. What I found in the dryer that day… *bo bo…* And someone said he worships the devil. I like the girl better. She tried to kill you, so she's okay in my book." His wife's smile sets Gence's belly to jiggling with his silent laugh.

After the purple monstrosity was found in the dryer, he'd had the idea to drive the fifth-floor occupants out. One of them. Both of them. Didn't matter. He needed peace. So that broken toilet? Two days without fixing. And maybe a dishwasher mysteriously breaks just after Gence was in the apartment to fix something else. He'd even taken all the girl's underwear out of the wash once and thrown them in the dumpster out back before his wife could find him with them and get the wrong idea.

Who stays in a building where one of your neighbors has the disgusting habit of stealing underwear? No one normal.

But they stayed. And they fought. And they gave Gence more gray hairs. And now…together?

He inspects his own wife of forty years, each line on her face reflecting a shared laugh or cry. Are they really so different from the *gomarë* upstairs?

Gence shuffles along to the kitchen and presses a soft kiss to his wife's forehead. "Love is very stupid," he grumbles. And a profound gratitude flows through him as his wife turns to give him a proper kiss.

Zoya presses something against his chest. Her copy of *The Pirate Duke's Revenge*. Gence eagerly opens it. "Finally! You read like a *breshkë*, too slow."

"I take my time." She waggles her eyebrows. "And you'll want to take your time with page one hundred forty-one."

Gence opens to the page and then slowly looks up, his cheeks red. Love is stupid. But it is also very, very good.

# Excerpt from

# *The Pirate Duke's Bliss*

"Perhaps your ears are painted on?" Bethany's smile was arch.

"If they were painted on, what exactly was this incredibly"—Ronan looked down at the naked goddess next to him and shifted uncomfortably as she stretched—"gorgeous creature nibbling at just a moment ago?" His hand trailed a path up her belly.

Bethany's pulse quickened. The ship rocked gently from side to side, but the sensation was as noticeable as air passing through her lungs. "But this is now the third time you've asked me to repeat myself. What other explanation could there be?"

Ronan pinned her with a solemn stare. "That he can hardly believe it? That every time the words 'I love you' fall from your lips, he struggles to accept it?"

Bethany tipped his chin up so that his lips were but a whisper from hers. She smiled softly. "I love you, Charles, Ronan…whatever you are calling yourself these days. I have loved you from the very first day I met you, the entire time you were my enemy, and I love you still. My love for you has weathered every storm." She kissed him deeply, her tongue stoking a fire within him. He groaned into her mouth as her strong hand wrapped around his manhood and grabbed her wrist, stilling her play. "There's time for that. Right now I just want to hold you, my love."

Bethany reluctantly settled back and accepted Ronan into the crook of her arms, his head nestled on the pillow of her bosom.

"There is holding in what I was proposing, too," she grumbled, though he heard the humor lurking in her voice.

Ronan smiled. Some time passed as she idly played with his hair.

"What are you thinking about, Captain Belle?" he asked her finally.

"I am thinking that I am happy. 'Tis a foreign feeling I'm still coming to terms with, my joy. And you?"

"I am thinking how every night for two years I thought of you: the lack of you, or the longing for you, or the having you, the hating you, the loving you… You, you, there was only you. There is no ocean I wouldn't cross nor place I would fear to tread if it meant being with you."

Bethany felt her heart squeeze in response and the moisture gather in the corner of her eyes. "Lucky for us a certain pirate duke bungled everything but still ended up with the treasure?"

"Lucky for us a certain lady pirate saved the day."

"That lady pirate sounds very wise and brave." Bethany pushed up suddenly until Ronan was pinned beneath her. Her expression was serious. "Ronan, I swore no man would ever take my ship, name, or freedom. And yet…I feel free, despite tying myself to you."

"I will never be your anchor. You are the sea, the brine in the wind, the cracks of lightning on the horizon. How could I ever think to contain a force of nature?"

Bethany smiled and arched a brow as she pulled out a lash of rope. "You're welcome to try. I've rather liked your other attempts."

# GENCE'S GLOSSARY OF TERMS

*Though some literal translations may sound harsh, these phrases are often used as a kind of punctuation during conversations in Albanian households. Think of them as the glitter on a vampire—not totally necessary, but adds a certain something...unforgettable.*

A din? – "You know?" (i.e., "You know what I mean?")

A morre veshë? – "You understand me?" or "You get it?"

Boll tash – "Enough now"

Breshkë – turtle (common insult for someone doing something slowly)

Burrë – "husband" or "man"

Çka dreqin po bajnë – "What the hell are they doing?"

Dreq o dreq – "Devil, oh devil" (Zero religious connotation. It's like an annoyed exclamation akin to a "bloody hell")

Gomarë – donkeys

Hajde bre – "Come on"

Hajt pra – "Okay then"

Hajvan – "animal" or "beast" (idiomatically, a goof)

Kastravec – cucumber

Katastrofë me dy këmbë – "Catastrophe with two legs"

Kosova – Kosovo may be the internationally recognized name for the country, but Albanians largely call it Kosova unless speaking to non-Albanians.

Lopë kosit – "yogurt cow" (Basically, a low-grade dairy cow whose milk is only good for making yogurt. Nearly every Albanian I know has been called this very rural insult at least once in their lives.)

Mos e qi mizën në byth – "Don't fuck a fly in the ass" (Loosely equivalent to "don't split hairs." And yeah, this one is something else!)

Mos ma çaj bythën – "Don't chop [or split] my ass" (Akin to "Don't bust my chops," though a bit more vulgar.)

Mos pjek pordhë në tepsi – Literally, "don't bake [or cook] a fart in a pan" (i.e., don't do something pointless or absurd)

Natën e mirë – "good night" (Penny probably mangled the pronunciation. Forgive her—she's trying.)

O bre – "Hey you"

S'ka marre hiç – "has no shame at all"

Shtazë t'egra – "wild animals"

T'hangert dreqi – "May the devil eat you"

T'kap kolera – "May you catch cholera"

T'raftë pika – "May you be struck by lightning" (Another fan favorite in Albanian households. Not meant to be mean or aggressive, more an utterance of annoyance in this context. Similar to "T'raftë Perëndia," which translates to "May the celestial one smite you.")

# Acknowledgments

This book started as a block of marble. Pretty marble, sure (delicate veining, nice color, a match for the cabinets), but still a block. It only became *NGN* when I handed it over to a team of master sculptors wielding their chisels. To be clear, I'm not comparing this to Michelangelo's *David* (this book contains the word "dongward" FFS), but without some insanely talented people, it would still be a lump of stone.

*The Sculptors*

First and foremost: Rebecca Heyman, my amazing editor and friend. You were the first person to clap eyes on this story, and it feels like cosmic wish fulfillment that this is all happening with you! Having you as my editor is like having a secret weapon: sinfully good at your job, hilariously funny, and somehow making me look better than I am. I'm truly the luckiest.

Everlasting gratitude to the entire team at Entangled Publishing: Liz Pelletier, Justine Bylo and Stacy Abrams, thank you for believing in this book and in me; I am humbled and still have bruises from pinching myself! To the editorial, marketing, social media, production, and design gurus: Victoria Chew, Melanie Smith, Meredith Johnson, Heather Riccio, Curtis

Svehlak, Bree Archer, Hilary Davies Shelby, Hannah Lindsey, Britt Marczak, and everyone else who brought this book to life, you are truly masters of your craft. Special thanks to Elizabeth Turner Stokes for creating a cover so gorgeous I nearly cried when I first saw it. To Sherryl Clark, Carla Tyne, and the entire Premeditated team, I am in awe of all you do and cannot thank you enough for going to bat for this book and me.

To my awesome agent, Jon Michael Darga, and the whole team at Aevitas. It's hard not to write a funny book when you've got the world's funniest (and best) agent in your corner. Thank you for shaping both this book and me.

*The Rom & the Com in My Life*

To my husband, Emirson: thank you for providing both the rom and the com in my world (and the tea/honey), and for weathering the highest highs and lowest lows with me. I love you. To my babies, Evalina and Brendon: I'll never stop saying that I am so lucky I get to be your mom. Watching you grow into the funny, curious, creative, and kind souls you are is the greatest blessing of my life.

To my parents, who instilled my love of reading and taught me to shoot for the stars: thank you for every opportunity you worked so hard to give me, and for believing in me until I learned to believe it, too. To my sister Valerie: for pushing me to write, encouraging me, introducing me to Becca, and basically starting this whole crazy ride! To my sister Ariana, thanks for nothing (jk jk. I had to trot out that ol' gag again); you've always been my first baby, xoxo. To my extended family, in-laws, grandma, aunts, uncles, cousins—thank you for the love. And to Nicky, forever in my heart…you would've been proud (while also teasing me mercilessly).

*Readers & Cheerleaders*

To my buddy readers (Brittany Zimmerman, Hannah Li-Paz, Lydia Sharp, Justine Bylo, Lindsey Staub, Jaden Clapsadl, and Rae Swain) and my early readers (Brita Frederickson and Adriana "Beba" Biberaj), thank you so much for making my work sharper and funnier; your feedback gave me life, and your generosity leveled this book up in every way.

To my friends, the "Kalis"—thank you for cheerleading me every step of the way. Special shout-out to Nick for the help with all the Albanian goodness – I'm still laughing at "mos e qi mizën në byth." Truly a poetic language. And thank you to Nell and Leah for your friendship, laughs, and my surprise twenty-second birthday party, complete with drink specials ("some with fire!").

To my work besties and teammates from today and yesteryear, you've kept me sane and laughing.

To Carol Leonetti Dannhauser and the Story Lab in Fairfield, CT, thank you for the dream writing space, and the snacks. To Pamela Einarsen, thank you for somehow capturing a decent headshot (a true miracle). To Charlotte Heyman, for coming up with a killer title—the tiny genius apple didn't fall far from the glorious genius tree. To Betsi Mufson, and all the rest of the behind-the-scenes support crew I am undoubtedly forgetting, I appreciate you. And of course, Kiwi and Coconut, my chihuahuas…I'd thank you properly, but you can't read, so I'll sneak you a few extra treats instead.

*And Finally…*

To the rom-com readers and fellow authors who lit the way: thank you for laughing, angsting, and swooning with me. You're the reason I picked up a chisel, and the reason this marble turned into a story.

*P.S.*

My apologies to Jake Gyllenhaal. You were actually lovely the few times we interacted in the student center computer lab at Columbia University. I just needed a name with a certain number of syllables, and yours was the first to pop into my head. I really hope the catachresis doesn't catch on (though, that'd be friggin' hilarious).

***Home is where the heartbreak happened...***
***...and where she might finally heal.***

Ten years ago, Mila Ferguson left behind a devastating fire, a stolen kiss, and a shattered circle of friends in her hometown of Hart's Landing. But when a crisis brings her back, Mila just wants to get in and get out, unscathed by her mother's constant criticism and unseen by her former crush, Everett McKean.

Only...Everett is everywhere. The town's attractive, beloved mayor has resisted settling down, but he's never stopped wondering about Mila. Having her back in Hart's Landing is the second chance he didn't know he was waiting for—and he's not about to waste it.

As Mila slowly opens her heart to Everett and begins to rebuild her fractured friendships, she wonders if coming home was exactly what she needed. But old wounds threaten to open again when questions emerge about what really happened the night Mila left. Who's really responsible for the fire that destroyed the bakery? And will knowing the truth free Mila from the past, or ignite a blaze that burns down the future she's trying to build?

People say you can never truly come home again, but sometimes coming home isn't about where you've been. It's about who you're brave enough to become.

**Doubling the Trees Behind Every Book You Buy.**

Because books should leave the world better than they found it—not just in hearts and minds, but in forests and futures.

Through our Read More, Breathe Easier initiative, we're helping reforest the planet, restore ecosystems, and rethink what sustainable publishing can be.

Track the impact of your read at:

## Connect with us online!

@Entangled_Publishing

@EntangledPublishing

@ EntangledPub

Join the Entangled Insiders for early access to ARCs, exclusive content, and insider news!

Scan the QR code to become part of the ultimate reader community.